RETR ROAD

———⚭———

By

John Coughlan

Copyright © John Coughlan 2021
John Coughlan has asserted his rights under the Copyright, Designs and Patents Act to be identified as the author of this work
This book is sold subject to the condition that it shall not, by way of trade or otherwise, be lent, resold, hired out, or otherwise circulated without the publisher's prior consent in any form of binding or cover other than that in which it is published and without a similar condition including this condition being imposed on the subsequent publisher.
All intellectual rights have been assigned to the author.
ISBN-13: 9798488509986

This is a work of fiction. Names, characters, businesses, organisations, places, events and incidents either are the product of the author's imagination or are used fictitiously. Any resemblance to actual persons, living or dead, events, or locales is entirely coincidental.

CONTENTS

ACKNOWLEDGEMENTS i
CHAPTER 1 1
CHAPTER 2 15
CHAPTER 3 36
CHAPTER 4 56
CHAPTER 5 78
CHAPTER 6 101
CHAPTER 7 117
CHAPTER 8 126
CHAPTER 9 131
CHAPTER 10 149
CHAPTER 11 178
CHAPTER 12 193
CHAPTER 13 210
CHAPTER 14 236
CHAPTER 15 264
CHAPTER 16 290
CHAPTER 17 335
CHAPTER 18 342
ABOUT THE AUTHOR 347

ACKNOWLEDGEMENTS

Retribution Road is due to the efforts of many people. Firstly to my wife Linda who became a word widow when I took over the utility room and began to pound the keyboard. On the upside she got the TV remote. To my kids who listened to my ravings about the house and in the car, unbelieving of my explanation I was writing dialogue. Apologies to all my friends and relatives whom I bored to death about progress. Thanks to Douglas Skelton for a fine edit, To Sharon Bairden for reading an early draft and being kind in her comments. To Ajay Close for her encouragement and guidance. To Brian Hannan for his work in editing and guiding me through the Amazon minefield.

An especial thank you to all members of the Mighty Johnstone Writers Group without whose feedback and commentary I could have not succeeded.

It's all their fault.

And last but not least, many thanks to that pillar of the JWG, Caro Ramsay. Her stiletto wit and scorn improved my writing no end and I am indebted to her in a massive way for telling me when I was good and calling me, 'numpty baws.' when I was rubbish.

I'm proud to call her my friend.

CHAPTER 1

Paisley 1974

The black mouth of the tenement close yawned like an open grave, reeking of urine and death. Detective Sergeant Frank McDowall locked the car and stared up at the semi-derelict building, the top floors fading into the drizzling darkness beyond the orange flicker of the last struggling streetlamp. The pulsing bass music throbbing the night like Apache war drums was suddenly cut off. He hoped somebody had shot the disc jockey. McDowall started up the steps and wondered why nobody got murdered on the ground floor anymore. He sunk his hands deep in his pockets, gathering his coat clear of the slimy walls. Both flats on the ground floor had corrugated steel sheets over the doorways. Not where he'd chose to be in the early hours of a Saturday morning when he should be tucked up in bed. On the upside he'd escaped the cold shoulders of a bitter wife.

The common stairway was in darkness, reeking of vomit and rancid urine. He gingerly picked his way through a carpet of debris, kicking empty beer bottles and cans through the banisters to clatter into the abyss of the stairwell. McDowall stopped in the flat doorway listening as Detective Constable Brown's questioning of a purple-haired hippy came to an abrupt halt when the girl threw up. The hallway was candlelit, casting moving shadows over bodies draped across each other on the linoleum.

McDowall gasped, covering his mouth with his sleeve.

'This place is reeking. Are you sure there's only the one fatality, Jim boy?'

Brown sighed and wiped a fine spray of vomit from his shoes with a discarded anorak. 'I've counted twenty-two living, but there might well be more.'

'Smells like they all died a week ago.' McDowall stared in disgust at his feet. 'Tell me that's not shite on my shoes.'

Brown shone his torch down, smiled. 'You'd be better off with wellies.'

'It'll take a gallon of Domestos to get that off,' McDowall said, squelching puddles of beer and bodily fluids underfoot.

'Where are forensics? Never saw their van.'

'McVicar says the meat wagon will be another thirty minutes. He's a right spectacle by the by, straight from a Burns Supper.' Brown pointed down the hall. 'Fatality is last room on the left, beside the bog.'

'Did I smell a fire in the close?' McDowall asked.

'Well spotted, Holmes. It's one of Hammond's properties. The tenants refused his buyout offer so their flats were torched.' Brown offered a jar of Vick and sniggered. 'Have you got your jimjams on under that coat?'

McDowall gave him two digits, dipped one into the jar and bunged some ointment up his nose and along his top lip, his eyes smarting at the menthol. Across the hallway a uniformed WPC was vomiting in the toilet, theoretically contaminating the crime scene. He paused in the bedroom doorway, taking in all the old sin and evil. Thick enough to chew. The girl lay on her back, splayed across the soiled quilt on a single bed, her feet on the floor at one side her head flung over the other.

She was in her teens.

She was naked.

She was dead.

McDowall tried to focus on her face. Her matted hair strayed like seaweed across her features but her eyes remained dull, staring, full of surprise. Between her legs squatted Professor Hamish McVicar, passing swabs to his assistant who placed them in labelled containers before making notes on her clipboard. The pathologist was a sight to behold indeed; kilt and sporran topped by a Prince Charles tunic and frilly cravat under his sparse ginger beard. Over that his loose white coat seemed incongruous.

McVicar waved a gloved hand.

'Not seen you for ages, Frank. Keeping well?'

'Torapeachy. You just keep doing your voodoo thing. You know what I need; cause of death, name of the culprit, his address, where he is at this moment, did he have pie and chips for his tea?'

McVicar was not to be drawn. 'You've been watching too much television, Frank. This isn't *Z Cars*. When I know, you'll know. Let me get on.'

'Aye, could you close your legs? You're putting me off linked sausage for life.'

The photographer arrived and McDowall stood back against the wall watching the girl's face bloom into stark relief with every searing flash. Her eyes seemed to follow him as he moved, gazing at him accusingly from behind the ropes of her hair, seeming to ask, 'why were you not here?'

He felt the blood pounding in his ears, skittering like a drumbeat.

He knew this girl.

McVicar stood up, kilt falling to conceal his assets. 'This girl is drugs death number three so far for 1974 and it's only the end of January. Do we have a name even?'

McDowall couldn't have formed a word to save his life and just shook his head and shuddered when McVicar asked if he was all right. McDowall eyes remained locked with those of the dead girl, staring into infinity.

Brown poked his head around the door. 'Want the final tally?'

McDowell recovered. 'Aye, right! What do you have?'

Brown leaned on the doorpost, flicked open his notebook.

'One fatality, the other zombies are out of their heads with drink, drugs or both. Nobody knows, saw or did anything, don't know who they are, never mind where. We'll be getting no sense from this clatty lot.'

McDowall's eyes had drifted back to the girl, mentally colouring her in with life, animating her features. Her accusing eyes stared straight back. Then he steadied himself and moved off the wall, needing to get away. As he passed her took an involuntary step towards the bed, his hand reaching out to touch her face, move her hair. He had to be certain.

McVicar cautioned him. 'You know better than that, Frank.'

He quickly strode out of the room, his face a mask. Brown followed him into the hallway.

'Boss? Are we good?'

McDowall shook his head. 'Look, forensics can't work in this bedlam. Get the plods to herd all the zombies back to the station.' He took hold of Brown's arm, pulling him onto the landing where they leaned over the banister staring down into the pit. The damp on the walls was silver in the dark, glistening like a Hadean water feature. The young WPC who'd been throwing up in the toilet interrupted them.

'Mr McDowall? I've found a handbag under the bed and it's got a driving license in it, so we have a name.'

She made to speak but McDowall held up a palm to stop her. 'I know damn fine well who she is. Angela Stewart. My goddaughter. We have to go tell her parents.'

Brown parked the car outside a row of terraced houses and switched off the engine. A thin band of crimson sliced the horizon like a bleeding artery.

'I'm not driving around the block again, Frank. If you can't do this then get Welfare do it, or a minister, a priest, a rabbi even. Anybody but us. We've left the crime scene, and God help us if Inspector Tannock finds out. I get why you're here, but you should be in charge back down the road at

Castle Crescent finding who did this. If we circle again somebody will call the Polis.' He rested a hand on McDowall's arm. 'So, let's do it, or get back to work.'

McDowall was locked in silence, his memory filled with images of Angela growing up. Her first bike ride, ice cream cones at Saltcoats. Her childhood triumphs photographed for posterity. Getting her name on the Dux Board at Paisley Grammar. Now she was a victim of something that happened to other people, other families. He wiped away the heavy condensation from the passenger window and watched it trundle down the inside of the door, like tears.

'I was her godfather,' he whispered, 'known the family all my life. Robert was godfather to my daughter, Moira and Angela were like sisters.'

McDowall sank his head onto the dashboard. He'd gone to school with Angela's dad. Now he was about to knock Robert's door at six in the morning and tell him and Ethel their last surviving child was dead. Stripped of any shred of dignity. How could someone so bright and beautiful wind up in dead in that place? Robert would be bad enough, but God alone knew how his brother Alec would react.

Brown waited till McDowall looked at him then spoke softly. 'Okay, we're the Polis. This is what we do Frank, so go in there and tell them. Now button up that shirt I lent you and move. Would you rather it was a stranger? It's times like this your friends need you most.'

McDowall nodded and wiped his wet face, eyes burning. Brown walked round to open the passenger door for him. McDowall slid out and buttoned his coat against the cold dread inside him, forcing his feet up the path to the door where he stood frozen on the step, unable to take his hands from his pockets. This never got any better.

Brown reached over McDowall's shoulder and rang the doorbell.

The house awoke in stages. A light came on in the upstairs front bedroom, then the stair light and eventually locks and chains undone, Robert peered around the door, fumbling his glasses onto his nose and struggling an arm into his dressing gown.

'Frank? This is some time to be chapping my door.'

'Listen pal, we need to come in. This is DC Jim Brown.' Robert paled and stepped back, knowing no good thing had brought Frank McDowall to his door with a face like a gravedigger. Behind him Ethel paused halfway down the stair, fastening her robe and asking who it was. McDowall stepped inside and closed the door then gently ushered Robert and Ethel into the front room where they sat mute on the settee.

From the way their hands interlocked they already knew. They always knew. McDowall nodded at Brown to put the kettle on, then stared at the carpet and told them.

Polite disbelief at first, just not possible. Robert gripped his wife's arm tightly, assuring them Angela was with a girlfriend from the Church, they had gone to a party in Milngavie, on the other side of Glasgow with friends they knew. Ferguslie Park was just two miles up the road? Angela had never been there in her life. A mistake surely, the wrong girl.

Ethel began to babble all sorts of theories to deflect the awful truth, which left McDowall to gently demolish each evasion till at last the full horror began to penetrate, trapping them in a hellish acceptance. Ethel insisted she call the friend in Milngavie and all this would be cleared up. Before she could dial Robert gently took the handset from her and rested it back in its cradle. Ethel collapsed to her knees in mute horror. Robert assisted his wife to the settee, placed a cushion behind her, his hands lingering on her shoulder.

McDowall gave them a moment, then continued.

'I've just come from the crime scene.' He paused and began again. 'From Angela, that is. I was as close to her as I am to you. I'm so sorry.'

He murmured the usual platitudes which seemed false and inadequate, realised they sounded robotic and fell silent. He could not erase Angela's face from his mind's eye. Choked, he moved away giving their grief space, staring at the framed family pictures on the sideboard. His own daughter Moira was in some of them. He picked up the one of both families on Largs beach playing rounders, all those wee carefree faces sticky with candy floss and split by cheesy grins. Angela's short life was on every wall and surface. Who could have thought all that promise would end like this?

Robert controlled himself with an effort and whispered. 'Where is Angela now?'

'Still at the crime scene till the medical and primary forensic examination has been completed.'

'You left Angela lying there, alone?'

'She's not alone. There are people with her who care.'

'I need to be with her. Take me there.'

'Can't do that mate. No.'

Robert sank beside his wife, head in his hands. 'How did she die; did she suffer at all?'

McDowall was not going there, not this side of Hell. He clasped his hands and stared at the carpet trying to control the emotion churning in him. 'The investigations only just begun. We'll know more after the post-mortem.'

Robert stared at him in horror. 'A post-mortem?'

McDowall recoiled from the mental strobing images of Angela's face. 'Angela is a suspicious death for now, Robert, but all the circumstances will be fully investigated. It's normal in these circumstances for there to be a post-mortem. It's a lot to take in but there will also have to be a formal identification by you or Ethel.'

Robert shook his head, a soft moan escaping him. 'God! I don't know if I can.'

Ethel began shouting at McDowall, suddenly focused. 'You're telling me my wee girl is dead and now you'll have her cut up, my baby sliced and butchered. I won't let you, it's horrible.'

She sank onto the couch fending off her husband's efforts to comfort her. Robert wept at the opposite end of the couch, so pale now he was blue. Ethel dug her fingers into a cushion and then fell silent. McDowall cleared his throat and shuffled.

'If neither of you feel unable to identify Angela maybe her uncle Alec would step in?'

Ethel shook off Robert's arm and stepped up to McDowall, 'How dare you? You know the reason Alec Stewart will never enter my house. Ever.'

Brown defused the situation by appearing with the tea tray. China cups no less, with sugar lumps and wee tongs. He poured in silence. McDowall took the cup on its wobbly saucer, managing to drop the teaspoon, and sat back down balancing it like a trainee acrobat.

'We need to ask about Angela's movements last night?' Brown opened his notebook at the previous entry, a stolen motorbike, unimportant now.

Robert tore his eyes away from his wife, fumbled a pill bottle from his dressing gown pocket and took two tablets and a gulp of tea. 'Yes, of course. Angela works at Conatal Insurance in Glasgow. Regent Street, she came home as normal, got changed. There was a party in Milngavie, you know how they are at that age. She was to pick up a friend in Johnstone.'

'This friend she gave a lift to, boy or girl?' Brown's voice was gentle, nudging the information out slowly.

'A girl, they were all girls, a pyjama party, overnight. We weren't expecting her back. She's a kind heart, she befriends young people from deprived areas through our Christian Fellowship. Like Ethel and me, she's active in the church.'

'What's this girl's name?'

'Elizabeth Sharkey. We met her three or four times at the church, once when Angela brought her here. Our minister knows her.'

McDowall exchanged a glance with Brown. They knew all about Beth Sharkey.

Robert continued. 'Angela has been sponsoring her for about a year now. Our minister Reverend Goodwillie will give you all the information about her you need. St Andrew's Episcopal Church, Brechin Drive. His number is in our phone book.' Robert hunched forward and stared into his hands. 'She left in the car about six thirty to pick up Elizabeth.'

'What make of car is it?'

'Morris Minor. Black. The registration is UOM 315.'

'What was she was wearing?'

'Surely you know that. You said you saw her.' The two policemen squirmed. Brown became engrossed in stirring his tea, McDowall closed his eyes and saw Angela's body stark in the camera flash. 'When she left the house I mean, what was she wearing? Just procedure.'

Robert read their expressions and slumped back in the couch as he took that in, saw the lie, the evasion in their eyes. His teacup slid unheeded to the carpet. Ethel sprang up and stood over her husband shrieking at him.

'This is your fault. You sent her out to die. You always have your way and now she's dead. Angela involved herself with that disgraceful slut and now our wee girl's gone.' She slapped his face. 'You've killed her. I'll never forgive you.' She sank back down. 'I'll never forgive myself.'

McDowall eased himself between them. 'This won't do. Gently with each other. I understand, but this won't help.'

Ethel turned on him. 'Is your child dead? I've lost two

children now. Two! You have no idea.'

McDowall guided Robert across to the dining room table and sat him down while Brown poured Ethel more tea. She was quiet now, rocking back and forth cradling the cup. McDowall knew Ethel's mental state was fragile since her son had been killed in Ulster. Melancholy, his Gran had termed it.

Robert took a tight hold of McDowall's forearm as he recovered and continued talking.

'Ethel wasn't keen on Angela going out last night with Beth, especially not overnight. But I said she could go. I can't understand how they ended up in Ferguslie Park.'

'Where was she to meet Beth Sharkey exactly?'

'In the square outside Woolworth, about seven.' Robert brushed the tears from his face. 'God in heaven. Can we stop this now?'

McDowall closed his notebook. 'Sure Robert, sure. He wobbled the cup and saucer to the floor. 'Can I use your phone; I need to call in?

Robert nodded from behind the cage of his fingers. McDowall went through to the hall and dialled. He got a cheeky conversation from the desk sergeant about leaving his new handheld radio in his office where the whole corridor could hear an exasperated Control officer trying to contact him. McDowall asked him to update the Inspector and hung up. The phone book on the hall table gave him the numbers of the minister who said he'd be there in ten minutes. Robert's brother Alec heard him out in stony silence then said he would identify Angela if her parents couldn't face that. On his way he said, also ten minutes. McDowall hoped to be gone by then. He also called Ethel's sister and soon family began to arrive in dribs and drabs as people responded to the tragedy. Alec Stewart arrived within ten minutes, nodding to Brown in the hallway, shook McDowall's hand, asked for an update.

'Early stages, Alec. Slowly does it,' McDowall gave him the bare facts.

Alec slipped out his coat and cap. 'You'll be keeping me up to speed on this.' A demand.

McDowall and Alec had history. Schoolboys together, teen-buddies, same football teams until McDowall went to the Police while Alec enlisted for the full twenty-five years in the Royal Marines. A man forged from steel. Alec slid past them and closed the living room door behind him. Alec hugged his big brother who broke down in tears.

'I'm so sorry,' he whispered. 'I can't believe she's gone.' Alec moved towards Ethel but she froze him out, grim-faced with a voice like razor wire. 'You've blood on your hands. The blood of my son. Get out!'

Alec stepped away, his face stoic, and retreated. Ethel was comforted by her sister Lorraine, who'd arrived first and now took her upstairs. Alec didn't leave. He remained, watching over his big brother.

Back in the car McDowall slammed the dashboard hard with the palm of his hand, twice. The finely balanced collection of juice cans and old chip wrappers avalanched into the footwell to land on the mouldering pies and doughnuts. As a boy McDowall hoped life would be full of cake, but reality was full of broken biscuits. All the way back to the station neither spoke, the street lights strobing the road orange as they passed them by. Only the sound of the dross rattling in the footwell and the squeaking wipers.

*

CHAPTER 2

Golspie Road Police Station was a new build much lauded in architect circles but to most of its incumbents it was a collection of random sized shoe boxes put together by a manic child. The inclusion of civilian staff and senior officers moved from Paisley and lodged on the upper two floors were a closer scrutiny than McDowall preferred. He and Brown entered by the rear custody door to evade the bedlam in the lobby where the twenty-odd suspects from the crime scene at Ferguslie were being processed. He couldn't look at them without imagining which had molested Angela. Couldn't trust himself to keep a grip. Nodding to the harassed custody officer in passing they hurried past the spiral metal staircase leading to the basement where the stark cells awaited their unwilling occupants then left into the office corridor past the wedged open fire doors and into their den. These ten offices and canteen was where the detective drones and traffic lived, cheek to jowl with the uniforms, squashed out of the upper two floors now occupied by superior persons who wore the uniform but were politicians and accountants in all but name. Pencilnecks!

They slumped into chairs facing each other across the shared desk. Through the doorway they surveyed the human debris in the lobby while the barebones weekend shift tried to cope. They would have closed the door if it hadn't been propped between the office wall and the filing cabinets, a casualty of overpowering a suspect who'd declined the hospitality of the cells. During that fierce fight the turnkey had his earlobe bitten off and Brown broke his pinkie. Repeated requests to Property had brought no result and now it was a fixture known as the, "Saltcoats Surfboard." McDowall produced two paper cups and a half bottle of Bells and poured a stiff double which they downed in one go.

'I'm shagged,' McDowall groaned.

Brown crumpled the empty cups, threw them in the bin. 'I'm glad that's over. That was torture, more so for you than me. Can we agree never to do that again?'

'My ties to the Stewart family stay between us two for now. I'd be taken off the case in a jiffy if those upstairs found out. Time to find out who's done what. Go see if there's a party-goer list of names yet.' He wondered if Angela's death might be the crowbar he needed to bring down Hammond Enterprises.

Brown paused in the door. 'I'll be back in a minute. Want a brew while I'm at it?'

McDowall nodded and stood in the doorway, scanning the faces of the mob bussed in from the crime scene at Knox Road. One guy looked familiar, holding his coat up over his lower face, enough for McDowall to stride across and lift his chin up for a good look.

'I know you from somewhere, sunshine. Have I lifted you before? What's your name?'

The guy was twitchy, avoiding eye contact, coming down from a drug high. 'It's Cumming. Brian Cumming,' he mumbled.

McDowall snorted, 'Cumming, my bony arse, I mind you now, your name is Michael Brodie and I've nicked you lots. You were growing the weed in a lockup garage and thieving the electric from a lamp post as I remember. Didn't you get eighteen months in the Bar-L for reset?'

'Ah'm oot on parole right now.'

McDowall leant over Brodie, his hands on the chair arms trapping him in place. 'Giving a false name is a crime and you've breached your parole by being in a drug den, drinking, and if we search you what will we find?' Brown returned with two steaming mugs of tea balanced on a clipboard. 'Get this tosser on his feet, bring him with you.' McDowall growled, intercepting WPC Joyce Fairbairn, asked her to go down to records and pull both Beth Sharkey's and Brodie's file. Biscuits to go with the tea would be welcome. McDowall waited in the corridor till the files came, but no biscuits. He scanned its pages as he entered the office and slapped Brodie on the back of the head with it. 'Liar, liar, pants on fire, young Michael. Stop dripping your body fluids on my desk.'

Brown came in and stood behind Brodie's chair, blocking the doorway as McDowell read. Brodie's file in silence, a thick testament to his stupidity and ability to be caught.

McDowall slammed the folder down.

'I remember fine now. The first time we nicked you was for storing stolen electrical goods in a flat above the Stable Bar. The Fire Brigade had been turned out because a neighbour saw smoke coming out the window. That turned out to be a weed extravaganza. Your single end had more electrical goods than Woolworth. At trial, you kept your mouth shut and got eighteen months.'

Brown grabbed the back of Brodie's chair, menacing him. 'Did you know, Frank, this weasel guarded the flat for Hammond?'

'You little turd.'

The clipboard clipped Brodie on the ear. 'I knew there was a connection between you and Hammonds bloody doings. And that link is you. Did you forget the whole point of day release is that you go back at night?'

Brodie mumbled something that sounded like Urdu. Sweat percolated from his every pore, dripping from his nose. He was shaking hard and clasping his jacket close around him. 'I'm on this new staged release thing, I just got confused. Ma brains wasted.'

'Thing is, you've stayed confused for two whole months during which you were dossing at the squat in Knox Road. You do mind that there's lassie dead in your grotty cave? The girl in the bedroom? Angela? Ringing any bells? Was it you that drugged her?'

'I don't know anything about that, Frank…'

The clipboard slapped off Brodie's head. 'Mr McDowall to you, sunshine.'

'Aye right, sorry.' Brodie went on. 'You know about ma problems and that, so Ah was blitzed most of the time. I was just doing pals a favour, caretaker like.'

'Pals? You're a bottom dweller, Michael, you don't have any pals.' McDowall leant close enough to see the blackheads on Brodie's nose. 'There's a couple of choices here for you, none of them good. First is, tell all you know about last night and find yourself back in your cosy wee cell at the Big Hoose. Second, you stay dumb and I hold you on suspicion of culpable homicide, possession, dealing, causing the Ibrox disaster, sinking the Titanic, then grass you as an informer. It's make up your mind time. What's it to be?'

Brodie folded. 'What friends?'

McDowall patted his shoulder. 'Wasn't that just easy, Japaneasy? Me and Brown here are your only pals now. Start at the beginning. Tell us everything you know about what happened to Angela Stewart at the flat last night. Then all you know about Hammond and his doings.'

McVicar was at the mortuary off the Saltmarket. His two assistants, Hemphill and a fifth-year student called Rice, hung back as he discarded his kilt and draped it across a chair. Their pale hung-over faces shone blue in the harsh fluorescent lights. Both exchanged glances but hesitated to ask about the Highland Dress until Rice took the plunge. 'Just want to check, sir, are we to get kilts as well? My brother's a piper if that would be helpful?' suggested Rice.

'If we ever get a dead haggis Mr Rice, I'll let you know.'

McVicar finished scrubbing up turned off the tap with his elbow and taking a towel from the box on the wall dried his hands. Neither Hemphill nor Rice saw fit to comment further on his gangly legs or the scanty cover to modesty given by his long frilly dress shirt. 'You two look as if you came off one of my tables.' He tossed the towel at Rice and pulled on corduroy trousers and a gown. 'Had a good Burns Night, did you?'

'Students' Union,' Rice croaked.

'Friend's flat,' Hemphill whined.

'More drink than poetry, I'm assuming.' McVicar smiled at student memories of his own, wild times indeed. 'Apart from the girl, who else do we have?'

Hemphill checked a clipboard then gave McVicar a summary. 'Three other subjects. One male, two females. Male subject is William Bain, aged twenty-two. He fell into the River Clyde at the Broomielaw from the walkway while attempting 007 drunken acrobatics. Eyewitness accounts suggest he drowned but he probably bashed his brains in while falling, rendering him unconscious and unable to save himself. No suspicious circumstances, lots of witnesses.' McVicar secured his gown and made for the door into the dissection room.

'Put Mr Bain back till later. Who's next?'

'She's mine,' Hemphill blurted, taking the clipboard and flicking the sheets over. 'Name of Carole Mitchell, female, forty something. Washed up dead on the beach at Craigendoran last night. Well chopped up and nibbled by the fishes. Seems she was coming off the Gourock ferry last Monday and her dog, some pit bull monster, tangled her in the lead and fell in dragging her off the gangway. She was pulled into the propellers and vanished but washed up eventually two days later. The dog, Emily, swam ashore at Gourock, is at the pound. Funny really considering.'

'Funny how, Mr. Hemphill?' McVicar raised his eyebrows, sighed. 'What part of the episode do you consider humorous? Are you concluding Ms Mitchell has been overcome by mirth and fallen from the gangway, rather than tripped by her dog before sustaining blunt force trauma and drowning? I will put your levity down to the dregs of alcohol swirling in your brain. What was the condition of the subject on arrival?'

'Wet,' Hemphill offered. Rice choked back a laugh.

McVicar put on his spectacles and peered over them. 'Gentlemen, I sincerely hope you both have more to offer to me today than dubious music hall jokes. Your humour is only appreciated by our silent guests nestling in their trays. Come.'

McVicar led them past the first two shrouded bodies to where Angela rested on the farthest mortuary table and Hemphill killed the lights except those directly overhead. Rice checked the tag on the toe with his clipboard details. Hemphill lifted the sheet away exposing Angela. McVicar flexed his fingers into his gloves.

'This young lady will be our first subject this morning and the tragic reason you two are here at such a horrendous hour after your Burns bacchanal. Her name is Angela Stewart, twenty years of age. Unlike our other cases she has not been the victim of accident or drunken carelessness but has been in the wrong place at the wrong time and abused by vile beasts. We shall deal with her immediately.'

His minions nodded and retreated to the scrub room.

Frank McDowall came into McVicar's' mind. No doubt very aware what was happening to his god-daughter right now in every grisly detail. McVicar did a visual examination as he prepared himself, noting the bruises and raw lesions on her wrists and ankles, the compression marks on her throat, the stains on her thighs and face. He composed himself and pushed the intercom button.

'Rice, can you hear me?'

'Yes sir. I can.'

'Then hang my up my kilt would you, it was my father's.'

Alec Stewart watched Robert from the kitchen window as he escaped into the back garden, away from the strident cluster of women relatives. His big brother was in Hell, crushed by a nightmare from which none of them could wake anytime soon. How could Angela possibly be gone? He remembered the brightness of her smile, how she'd tried to replace Anne, his own missing daughter. The last time he'd seen her at church the week before. He could never say, but Robert should have stopped this mentoring thing, not allowed Angela to have anything to do with that Beth. Robert still believed in the angels while Alec had recognised from harsh experience who and what Beth was. Robert's charitable belief in the goodness of human nature was a weakness that had put Angela in harm's way. It would haunt Robert but Alec could never have uttered that opinion aloud to anyone.

Alec went to the back door as Robert picked up the secateurs from the garden bench and crouched by the flower bed in the light sleet which soaked his thin cardigan, blindly mutilating his prize roses. He dropped the tool down and tore at the stems with his bare hands. Alec left the kitchen smartly moving down the garden shedding his jacket and throwing it across his brother's shoulders. Robert's palms were a bloodied gashed mess from the thorns, but he seemed not to feel the pain. Alec knelt, holding him for a time then led him inside and sat him at the kitchen table to disinfect and bind his wounds. Two of Ethel's relatives brought in a tray of dirty cups chattering like mournful magpies and set the kettle on the hob. Alec switched the cooker off and guided them out with the observation that the free teas were over, kitchen closed. With that done he made his way through the house.

Anyone not immediate family he turned from the door.

Golspie Road Police station had quietened down to a roar as McDowall and Brown, fuelled by fags and Irn-Bru, settled down to interview Brodie under caution. It turned out Brodie had been dossing at the flat since he absconded, feeding himself and his habit by doing odd jobs for the McGrath brothers and Hammond himself. McDowall needed to establish a connection between the McGraths and Graeme Hammond. The fate of Angela Stewart might just be the key, and those responsible for her death were right at the top of his list. He wondered what Graeme Hammond; the heir apparent was doing right now. Quietly waiting for his father to die so he could inherit Hammond Enterprises and its black trade. Arthur Hammond was an old-time gangster, hard and ruthless but had a certain moral code. The son was something else, paranoid, dangerous, vicious and petty with a cowardly streak that made him unpredictable.

McDowall's priority, his way in, was to find what part the McGrath brothers had played in Angela's death and see how far up the tree that took him. Everyone in custody had identified the McGrath's mug shots and named them as being the instigators of the violence and abuse done to Angela in that zoo pen on Knox Road. He and Brown returned to the interview room and reminded Brodie he was still under caution. They also had him sign a form saying he'd declined legal representation. Then he got stuck in.

'Tell me why the McGrath brothers would put you up in their pigpen?'

Brodie was jangling so bad he spilled the paper cup of water he was holding, 'Ah did stuff for them before I went away intae the Big Hoose, so they owed me a favour.'

'That would be over the electrical goods and the car racket?' Brodie stayed silent. 'We'll come back to that by and by. What happened to the girl in the bedroom?'

'The McGraths were on her right away, like dogs in heat so they were. Ah never saw her before last night, didnae know her name.'

'Who organised this party? Did you send out invites or was it more like a word-of-mouth, drop-in clinic kind of thing, drugs, duffle coat, Vaseline, nae knickers?'

'The McGraths organised it, you know, bring birds, booze and money.'

'So, who brought Angela?'

'She came with some other bird that the McGraths knew who gets her gear from them. Ah knew her by sight. She flogs her mutton up around Anderston Bus Station and Finnieston.

Locally, she does Paisley Cross and the Cartside, hangs around the Knox Road flat for punters that wanted a fix and a ride.

'So, you pushed the drugs from the flat and stood guard?' Brodie nodded.

'What was in the flat worth guarding?' McDowall asked.

Brodie shrugged.

'Tell me about more this bird that brought Angela?'

'Don't know, Mr McDowall, I'm half jaked still, I can't think.'

McDowall leant across and rattled Brodie on the ear. 'Think harder. What time did they arrive and how? You best have something to tell me. Give me a name.'

'I think her name was Beth.'

'A minute ago, you only knew her by sight. Why so sure suddenly?'

'I just remember one time she came to get her stuff and had nae money. She was desperate, shaking and sweating, so Eddie did a trade and we all got a blowjob.'

'Very romantic, isn't that nice? Tender almost. She'd need a fix after that. You can look at our picture album later, but for now, describe Blowjob Beth.'

Brodie's legs were jumping under the table. 'Short. Brown hair. Tight short leather dress. Big zip doon the front. Big tits.'

Brown snorted a laugh. 'Brilliant.'

McDowall nodded towards the door and they stepped out into the corridor. 'Brodie is gagging for a fix, he's falling apart. Did you see the electric legs dance? When he starts talking, we'll need to gag him to shut him up. Here's what we'll do. Our priority is to find, or make, a connection to Hammond. Check with Vice in Glasgow and ask Joyce to get busy finding anybody local with a habit, name of Elizabeth or

Beth Sharkey, might also use the name Clarke. More than likely been arrested for shoplifting or petty thieving to feed her habit. Start checking taxi firms for anyone who picked up a fare anywhere nearby about the time of the emergency call. Don't take any shite from them. Tell them it's me asking and if they try hiding their casual cowboy drivers, I'll have the licensing boys all over them till Christ comes back. Get the uniform patrols to search the area for Angela's car, that would be handy. What else?

Brown checked his notebook. 'The call was made at 04.04 from a call box in Ferguslie Park Rd, Paisley. Surprised they found a working phone. Female, maybe Beth Sharkey, described as distressed and almost incoherent. I've got the tape.'

'Great. Get it typed up for me and file a copy. It might be a long shot but get the phone box sealed and see if they can get prints of any kind off the handset. For now, I'm going to poke this wee snake some more and see what venom we can get out. What else is there?'

'Tannock wants an update, in his office.'

Inspector Tannock continued scribbling when they entered his office, and apart from pointing at the chair with his pen, ignored them both. His degree had attracted accelerated promotion, he was the poster boy of Regionalisation. McDowall plopped into the chair in front of Tannocks desk and folded his hands across his belly, Brown perched on the wide window sill. Tannock closed the folder recapped his fountain pen and sat rolling it between his fingers.

'Well, DS McDowall, it's been an early start for all of us. What's happening with this young girl? Accident, misadventure, or was the girl murdered?'

'You know McVicar, he won't say one way or the other. I think we should presume murder for now. Keeps our options clear and gives us maximum resources.'

'Murder invites great interest from many quarters. The Chief, the Press, and many civil organisations. It also eats up precious resources which we do not have so let's keep it suspicious for now. Do we have any leads at all, clues, suspects, evidence?' Tannock pulled over a notepad and squared it in front of him. 'Please go on.'

'Brodie told us that the McGrath brothers are responsible for what went down in the flat at Knox Road which, on paper, is rented to them by Hammond Homes. He says the drugs come from a source in Paisley and he's been working as a foot soldier for no less than Graeme Hammond Esquire. I believe you know both Mr Hammonds, sir.' McDowall grinned wolfishly. 'Is he not in your golf club?'

Tannock made a sucking sound with his teeth and braced his arms against the desk. 'Membership of a golf club is not yet an indictable offence. I'm aware of the obsession you share with both Hammond senior and junior, and need to remind you neither has a criminal record and we have failed to apprehend him, or his father Arthur.'

'That might say more about our policing than his character,' snapped McDowell.

'Is Hammond linked to the death of the girl?'

'Not directly yet but…'

'Then the answer is no.'

McDowall had another stab at convincing his boss. 'When I squeezed Brodie, he burst like a Kia-Ora carton and spilled everything. Based on that I'd like to raid Hammond's antique auction warehouse and some addresses Brodie told us about. Sooner the better.'

Tannock shook his head. 'Now just let's hold our horses. How do you make the jump from a suspicious death in a dingy flat to raiding Hammonds' warehouse? You're investigating the fatality of the girl at the flat are you not? You can't go galloping off at tangents.'

'I'm not galloping anywhere, but there's a link between the two main suspects and Hammond. Both should be explored. The girl died in one of Hammond's slums. If we nail the McGraths with the death at the flat, they'll spill all they know about Hammond. We should move fast before they vanish in a puff of smoke. Even as we speak, they are off and running. Angela Stewart's death could be our way in.'

'We need evidence not your gut feeling. The McGraths are part of what may or may not be a murder. It might be the tragic drug death of a naive young woman. Hammond is very much part of the drug war initiative which will soon fall firmly within the remit of the Regional Crime Squad, and I hope to be part of that team.' He raised an eyebrow in curiosity. 'I hear a rumour you were her godfather.'

The bloody photographer had clyped. McDowall kept his face blank.

'Not true,' he lied. 'As for the Regional Crime Squad! That crowd of useless wankers can't touch Hammond. They've been investigated for being too cosily undercover with Hammond. It's common knowledge they smoke or resell half the stuff they find. At strategy meetings all you can get out they clowns is, "cool" and "hey man". It's like talking to a fifteen-year-old alien or an interview with The Beatles.'

Tannock was not swayed. 'You can't go charging in with the weak evidence you have. Regionalisation is coming at the turn of the year. Three or four years on from now the new Strathclyde Police will have brought vast changes. We cannot appear to be amateurs bashing around like rampaging yokels. Such things are remembered. The Fiscal needs statements and witnesses able to stand up at trial.'

McDowall realised Tannock was concerned about his status in the new Strathclyde Police Force. Once the county forces merged there would be a game of officer musical chairs. Tannock would be keeping his head down, taking all the credit but none of the blame. McDowall and Brown would be left to sweep up the shite.

'Okay, sir,' McDowall conceded. 'What about giving me a bit of wiggle room. Let me use our informant to run down the McGrath boys and link them to the girl. When I have them, they can be squeezed for a deal if they give up Hammond. We can involve the Regional Crime Squad then. We need to get ahead of the game for we've only one shot at a murder case. Yes?'

'Don't railroad me, Detective Sergeant. Put aside your obsession with the Hammonds and tell me what you have. No fairy tales.'

Brown brought the file over and thumped it on the desk.

'We already know Hammond has antique contacts in Eastern Europe, and from there to Turkey. Goes back a long way to when his dad Arthur first set up this route after the war. Hammond senior is in a care home in a bad way at the present. Palliative care.'

'Dying painfully, and good riddance,' McDowall butted in. 'Brodie's filled in some of the gaps in our knowledge. What happens is antique dealers bid at auction and it is all delivered to a warehouse somewhere on the Black Sea coast. This is owned by the contact man in Turkey, who gets the drugs from the Kurds over the Iran border via Afghanistan. The Bulgarian guy is the main agent, the man we want, but we've got a name from Brodie. He packs the goods away in the antiques and ships them to Italy by way of Brindisi.'

'What has this got to do with the accidental death of Angela Stewart? And what's the significance of Brindisi?'

McDowall continued. 'You could smuggle a howitzer through there, Athens is the same. All this is very legit on paper, proper customs papers stamped across the borders. And the mighty dollar greases the rails.

Tannock's eyes narrowed, 'How does Brodie know?'

'Right now, he's got the mental arc of a windscreen wiper but before the drugs stupefied him, he overheard the name of the contact man in Scotland, Anton Tenescu. Brodie knows how the UK end works, the places the gear is cut and bagged. This batch was cut with Vim.'

Tannock drummed his fingers on the desk, McDowall waited. 'How can you be sure Brodie isn't telling you what you want to hear?'

McDowall raised his eyebrows. 'I'm not sure but he's the best we have for now.'

Tannock was struggling between the glory of cracking the bigger case and letting these two be in charge. 'Not much to go on.'

Brown spoke up. 'We know that they switch the drugs onto couriers near motorway services, then into the major city dealers for distribution. The couriers are legit freelance drivers who may not even know what the packages are.'

There was a knock at the door and Tannock rang the bell on his desk, calling out 'Enter.' McDowall had half expected a butler with a tea tray but in came Joyce, a note in hand.

'Sorry to interrupt, sir,' she said, 'but I've got some information for DS McDowall.'

Brown took the message pad from her. 'Cheers, Joyce.' He closed the door behind her, passing McDowall the note.

'Good news and bad news,' he announced. 'Angela's car is outside a scrapyard off Hawkhead Road, Paisley, so lots of bits missing already, including the steering wheel. We've some smudged prints. The call box has been vandalised, so no joy there.' McDowall crammed the note into his pocket. 'We're really getting all the breaks. So, inspector, you were saying?'

'I was just thinking that if we find drugs at Hammond's warehouse, his brief will plead that he knew nothing about the contents. He'll cite the shipping agent, the buyer, anybody. Even if we unearth drugs on a raid, he'll blame one of the occupiers of his rabbit warren sublets. We've been down this road before. Arthur Hammond just needs to muddy the waters. I'll consider linking both cases for now and leave them with you. I'll see legal on the warrant from the fiscal and if I think it justifiable, we'll proceed. I want to see a plan on my desk by tomorrow.' He spun his chair around, wagged a finger at McDowall. 'I also want it understood Detective Sergeant, that I am aware of your service and extensive street knowledge, both here and with the Royal Ulster Constabulary. I know you come from an earlier policing regime that allowed vast independent action. That has to cease.'

McDowall had to admit he'd been largely unfettered and happy in Ulster to flush the drugs down the toilet, beat the dealers until they produced a gun, then shoot them. But these were different times. McDowall leapt up and made for the door.

'Superb. Come on Brown son, let's get on.'

'Note of caution, Detective Sergeant. I want updated, that does not mean every other Easter. It means daily reports on my desk, every end of shift. And I will attend and observe any raid we carry out. I will also make any decision on when these two cases should diverge. Is that understood?'

McDowall understood very well. What way was the shite going to go when it hit the fan? He grinned wickedly. 'Yes sir, absolutely.'

First stop for McDowall and Brown was the McGrath house, a crumbling end terrace with wrought iron grilles over the windows like houses in Spain. There the comparison ended. The landscaping was by Cleansing Landfill and Clyde Carbreakers had obviously delivered rusted car wrecks.

Reeking bins overflowed across the front step. As the two detectives weaved up the path past a collection of scrap bikes a mongrel dog, under the impression it was a lion, came roaring and snapping around the side of the house. It latched onto Brown's trouser leg who danced around like a dervish trying to fling it off. Without breaking stride McDowall bent down, gripped the mutt's collar, heaved it off its feet and tossed it onto the roof of the sagging carport where it perched in the guttering snarling defiance.

'Welcome to Annaker's midden.' He told Brown, who was reaching for the knocker, but McDowall pushed past him and opened the door. 'We're the Polis, we don't do the fucking knocking thing. This door is wide to the world. There might well have been a housebreaking here, a crime. In we go then, we are detectives after all. Be sure to wipe your feet on the way out.'

The flat was minging, greasy carpet reeking of toilet, chips, stale beer, cabbage, and wet dog. Medusa the Gorgon in huge rollers came out the front room, slightly bigger than the dog and twice as vicious. She recognised McDowall.

'Warrant! Where's your warrant? Get out ma house, ya bastards,' she shrieked.

McDowall grinned and kept moving. 'Hullo Greta, nice to see you as well. Still doing the ten bob knee tremblers back of the Legion club?'

He grabbed her by the cardigan and trailed her into the front room flinging her onto the armchair. She popped right back up and swung at him. McDowall ducked, put his hand on her face and shoved her back down gripping her knees between his legs in case she had a go at the family jewels. She settled for a torrent of abuse.

'Now, now, Greta, calm down. Say hullo to my mucker here. Sergeant Brown, meet Mrs Greta McGrath who whelped the dogs we're hunting for. Supposedly a right looker in her time but has had more paying passengers ride her than the Glasgow Underground. She used to cough out weans like beads on a rosary. Grisly Greta is the barmaid at the British Legion for now, but rumour has it that she only wears knickers to keep her ankles warm. Now dear,' he gripped the woman's wrists, 'answer my questions then you can go back to your beauty treatment with the Polyfilla and the welding kit. Tell me where your boys are. Right fucking now!'

Disturbed by the racket on the ground floor, Inspector Tannock came downstairs into the station lobby and stared aghast at the mob herded over the benches and floor. He summoned the Desk Sergeant.

'What's all this, who are all these people?'

'It's the horde from Knox Road sir. DS McDowall wants them kept till he returns.'

As if on cue, a blonde girl vomited in a waste bin, adding to the smell of piss drifting from behind the cleaning locker.

Tannock recoiled.

'This is a not a dosshouse. Put them in cells.'

'Cells are full, sir, and not enough bodies to process them. I didn't have a count to begin with and some have already sloped off.'

'We can't have this. Note their names and addresses then get rid of them unless we have outstanding warrants.'

'You mean let them go, sir? DS McDowall will not like that.'

Tannock slapped the counter. 'I'm in charge of this station, not D Sgt McDowall. Release them immediately. I will have this chaos dealt with now.'

The sergeant rounded up two more officers and sent them to eject the mob out onto the pavement. The constables discovered Brodie sleeping on top of the desk in McDowall's office. They dumped him onto the floor then flung him out into the street like a puppet with the strings cut.

*

CHAPTER 3

Despite Alec's best efforts the Stewart house was still full of people, most unknown to him. Women in the living room taking tea from the best china, the teaspoons ringing softly on the saucers. In the kitchen the men standing quietly in ritual social segregation clutching cans of lager, a soft murmuring the only noise. Defying Ethel's order to go, Alec stayed at the Stewart home, closely watching his brother.

Robert rocked back and forth, his bandaged hands clasped between his knees, staring at the floor, lost in a nightmare, his mind torn by the realisation he had failed in his first duty to his daughter Angela, keeping her from harm. His tortured mind was flooded with images of *The Scream,* with Angela's face imposed. His soul flayed by imaginings of her last moments alone and frightened, calling out for her dad.

He had not been there.

He'd sent her to her death.

Alec whispered softly to his brother, cradling him like he did when they were wee boys until Lorraine came down and passed Ethel's message to leave. The sedative given by the doctor had taken effect and Robert had at last escaped his waking nightmare in drugged sleep He kissed the top of Robert's head and went, deciding that might be best.

Alec took twenty minutes to walk the distance to his small flat in Collier Street. He kicked off his shoes at the door, found one slipper and padded into the kitchen, turned on the kettle. He made coffee on automatic and sat at the breakfast bar gazing through the hatch into the living room, at the only photograph in the room perched on the mantle in a cheap Woolworth's frame.

It was the only personal thing Alec had kept on him when deployed, an anchor for what remained of his soul. A soft black and white reminder of a time when things had seemed innocent, easier. A time when he still had a wife and child. A postcard-sized photograph of Alec and Sheila in sodden raincoats with baby Anne in her buggy, the rain stoating down. They'd been happy then. He'd just got back from a tour in Aden and Muscat and they'd gone to Scarborough in March. Behind them the sea battered off the seawall leaping ten feet in the air. All of them soaked through, baby Anne in yellow raincoat and sou'wester peering seriously at the camera.

What happened? Too many postings had happened, too close together. The endless lonely nights she'd lain awake in that dreary council flat in Portsmouth, worrying, listening to every car that stopped in the street. Would it bring the welfare officer and the Padre? The news she was a widow, Anne an orphan. Sheila suffered aching loneliness, the erosive grind of the baby turning every day into a survival course. Broken sleep, no money no love.

When he was away, he'd be overcome by guilt, trying to phone from God knows where. Stilted wasted conversations, from some crowded portacabin or queued out satellite phone, limited to five minutes. Unable or forbidden even to say where he was. She couldn't deal with what she didn't know. Was he in Aden or Aldershot, Belfast, or Brighton? Was he alive now, at this very moment?

'Are you coming home soon?' she'd asked over and over. 'Will you ever leave the bloody Marines? You love your lads more than me. I love you, and I need you here. I want us to be together, to be a real family, the baby needs a daddy.' Drained by the long stale days withering her.

And himself, worn numb by endless strain and patrolling, and never knowing when he would be ambushed. When he did come home his head full of images that woke him in the dark, crying out in panic. The barbed wire wrapped nightmares, sweat-soaked sheets, the rages.

It couldn't last.

It didn't last.

Alec had been made up to Sergeant and was sent back for the three-month course at Eastney Barracks. It guaranteed five weeks home leave in total, with office hours. He couldn't wait to get home and tell Sheila. He didn't phone or write as he wanted to surprise them. Bursting into the house calling for them he hadn't even noticed the chill that only an empty house has. It was twenty minutes before he became aware of what was missing. He had the takeaway heating in the oven and the wine in the fridge before he found the letter pinned to the noticeboard behind the kitchen door. It was written on the back of the baby's Winnie the Pooh card. He still had it. A rambling thing full of woman stuff he couldn't ever begin to understand.

She hadn't waited for him.

Not a thing of baby Anne's left. He found one small sock behind the couch and a T-shirt of Sheila's under the bed. That and the photograph he'd had in his locker at Newry was all he had. Not a day went by he didn't think of them but now, with Angela gone? He could only hope Sheila and Anne were out there somewhere safe. Angela and Anne were born the same year. There was a double christening, and how proud he and Robert were. What a head-wetting in The Thorn Bar, the brothers singing drunkenly as they staggered up the road. He remembered a photo of Robert and him both holding the babies and staring down at their new-born. Sheila had taken all the pictures with her but she couldn't take the image from him.

Alec was two years younger than Robert, always in bother. "Born to hang", his Gran used to say. His mind was filled with memory of how Robert was quiet, did well at school while Alec was wild, always dogging it. Away up the Brandy Burn with Frank McDowall, guddling for fish, ripping his breeks on barbed wire gashing his legs. Robert forged Alec's sick notes, even did his homework for him sometimes. Robert made something of himself and became an accountant. Mum showed him off in front of her friends. Alec best not mentioned.

And Dad? Alec's hero ever since he was a wee boy. Shot in the spine in some nameless Norman farmyard a month after D-Day. Shipped home in a wheelchair to Mum in a top floor single end in Govan Road, to waste away in a wheelchair over the next twenty years. He remembered Dad taking them down to Elder Park on the wheelchair. His strong arms birling the big wheels faster and faster till they blurred, the cigarette pack between the spokes whirring like a banshee clacker. Robert would stand on the back with his arms around Dad's neck, Alec sitting on Dad's knees feeling his stubble against his cheek.

'Faster, Daddy! Faster!'

When Alec enlisted in the Royal Marines, Dad had told him how he'd never even fired his rifle in anger. Never shot at anyone, never saw who shot him.

"Some frightened wee Jerry," he used to say, "a boy, crapping his pants, just like me."

Just like you, Dad? No way. Nobody ever came close to being like him, not to Alec. He still missed him. Ah well! All over now, water under the bridge. They'd cancelled Dad's war pension the day of the funeral, a grateful nation at work. Dad would not have shirked from taking direct action if he were here, and neither would Alec. Like Dad, the Hammonds would not see him coming.

After the funeral Mum threw his medals out.

He'd fished them out the bin and kept them.

Alec took himself to the Nip Inn on the square to stare at himself in the blown mirror nursing a whisky and his memories. When Sheila left him taking Anne, it was Angela who had been his lifeboat. She was his daughter surrogate, giving him love and hugs and weirdly drawn cards on his birthday. Always bought him socks and a Toblerone for Christmas. When the ice had melted into the malt, he drank it in one gulp and had two more.

Returning home in the wee hours he fell into a drunk sleep

shattered, what seemed only minutes later, by the strident clatter of the brewery barrels on the pavement outside stirred him, dragging him back to reality. This pity and supressed rage were doing him no good. Fumbling his way to the kitchen sink he flung some water on his face and dowsed his head under the tap. He made coffee then stood staring out his window till he snapped out of his fog. Time to shit, shave, and shampoo. No chance of the fourth 'S' these days. He dumped the untasted coffee down the sink. His hand brushed against the last inches in the whisky bottle.

Naw! Best not.

He showered, he changed his shirt, stood in front of the mirror. The top button flew off. Jesus! Size sixteen collars too small now, where had his body gone? Ach! The tie could stay off for now. Keys watch money, what there was of it. He inspected his reflection, smart in the security uniform. Softly Alec, softly, stay cold, keep a hold of things. He would let Ethel calm down then go up in the morning and hopefully take her down to the Co-op Undertakers before his nightshift. That's if she could see past her black hatred of him. He'd ask to borrow McDowall's wreck of a car.

Angela would go into the grave beside her elder stepbrother Kevin. That deep family wound would be reopened with the grave. For now, he would stay focused until after the funeral. He reached for the whisky, pulled the cork and passed the open bottle under his nose, breathing in the sweet scent of peat and heather. When all this was over, he would try very hard to make peace with Ethel, and himself.

He'd find the bastards who had defiled Angela.

He would kill them.

They would die badly.

Ethel woke in the small hours of Sunday still weeping and went downstairs, where Robert lay snoring on the couch. She made tea quietly and took a cup to him as a gesture of apology for her harsh words. She'd poured out a vitriolic tirade that bled Robert's soul. Had screamed her pain into his face, into his mind, into his heart. All his fault, all his fault. He took her hand for a fleeting second and gave her a wan smile. She could and would forgive, but not forget. Robert had signed the papers allowing underage Kevin to join the Marines. He and that man of blood Alec had killed Kevin, allowed Angela to cultivate that little druggie slapper, Beth. Always had to be the good guy, the moral man. Now their children were both dead. Gone forever because of decisions Robert had made. Lorraine came down and joined her in the kitchen. Her staring at the toast was interrupted by the sound of falling china bringing them both to the kitchen door.

Robert tried to stand, made a gurgling sound, and slid from the couch to lie slumped against the sideboard, blue, breathless, clutching his chest. Ethel only stopped screaming when her sister pushed her away and slapped her. She became aware Robert had fouled himself, his eyes rolled back in his head, face slack, dribbling, ashen. Lorraine understood what was happening.

'Jesus! Ethel! Sit there and be quiet.' Lorraine shoved her into a chair. 'Can you not see he's having a stroke or something? The toasts burning.'

She called an ambulance and then tried to find a phone number for Alec. There was a BT recorded message telling her the number was disconnected since midnight.

Ethel was now moaning to herself, isolated deep in her own hellish realisation of loss.

'My lovely wee girl, my lovely wee girl.' She made wounded animal noises and then cried out, 'Oh God! All my children gone. I need to go to them. Wait for me! Wait for me!'

Lorraine knelt beside Robert, holding his hand, talking nonsense to him till the flickering wash of the blue lights on the curtains roused her and she answered the door. Ethel was quiet by then, standing by the cooker watching through the kitchen door, wringing her hands, face stony. The ambulance men unfolded the stretcher and mummified Robert in blankets. As they hefted the stretcher one of the attendants asked who was coming, there was only room for one.

Ethel caught her sister's eye, shook her head. 'You go, Lorraine. God knows I can't. I'm sorry but I'm done. Let me know how he is. I'll go to Angela's room and look out something for her to wear.'

'Wear what, where?'

'Why, for the funeral of course. She'll want something nice, tasteful. I'll look it out for her. She always liked to look pretty.'

Ethel stood aside, watching impassively as the ambulance crew struggled their burden into the vehicle and left, the rooftop beacon washing the street in faded blue. She locked and chained the door behind them, went to Angela's room and lay on the bed in the dark. This was the third person she'd loved taken from her. How different the life lived to the one she'd wanted. Her first husband and love had been Ernest Simeone, a Fifth Engineer in the Merchant Navy whose father owned the Napoli Ice Cream Parlour in the town. The war changed everything.

His ship had been torpedoed off Greenland ten miles south of Cape Farewell. She'd fallen prey to a U-Boat, taking two torpedoes which broke her back and sinking within minutes. Nobody who went into the North Atlantic in winter lasted long. Ethel's unborn baby never knew his father. After the war, she'd met Robert at Stoddart's carpet factory. He'd seemed a good man and she accepted his proposal because she was lonely, and Kevin needed a father. She found love again as time passed and Angela arrived a few years later and he doted on them both. Kevin followed his Uncle Alec into the Marines and she had wept over that, writing to him every day. She had the sense not to post every letter.

Kevin was killed in '71 at a vehicle check point near Crossmaglen. How was it possible to bury both your children? It was a crime against God. Why had she not been able to prevent it? She couldn't bear it all again. Kevin's funeral had been bad enough. Ethel forbade Alec attending the funeral and never spoke to him again.

After dumping Angela's car, the McGraths hid out at Beth Sharkey's place till late Monday afternoon. Gordon woke first, brushed the cans from the bed and dripped stale lager onto the floor. What a weekend. It had passed in a total drunken blur.

Gordon sat up swaying, the empty cans falling onto the carpet. He looked across at Eddie lying naked on top of Beth on the floor. They'd taken turns with the slut during the night. He chuckled and flung an empty can at them.

'Get up ya lazy bastard, lots to do the day.'

Eddie sniggered, 'Ah'm up already.' began to move on top of the girl, gripping her breasts cruelly.

'Enough of this crap,' Gordon said, 'let's get rolling'.' Beth fled weeping into the living room clutching her clothes.

'Where's my stuff? You promised me a bag.'

'Fuck's sake, give her a bag Eddie and shut her up.' His brother flung the girl a packet from his jacket pocket.

'Here! Go powder yer nose.'

Gordon put his hands behind his head and stretched. That Angela had been delicious right enough, a choice piece of shagging. Always the snooty bitch, treating him like dirt all through secondary school. He closed his eyes and savoured again his hands on her flesh and the vast satisfaction of knowing he'd been the first to have her.

Today was the meeting with Hammond to raise cash for the Liverpool deal. No way was he taking Eddie to the meeting with Hammond, that would be the kiss of death to his hopes. He'd have his brother steal a van for transport they'd been asked to find today for the parts guy in Sneddon Street Motors. Best both of them they stayed low and clear off while that pig, McDowall was after them.

Leaving Beth comatose they made their way to the old Vauxhall Cresta scrapper but the engine under the bonnet would have powered a tank. In a screech of tyres and blue smoke they shot over every junction sign on the way down to the Beith Road. At the paper shop Eddie jumped out and bumped into some wee guy in the shop doorway who tried to bolt. Eddie trailed him out onto the pavement shouting for his brother who wiped the window and saw Eddie had some wee fella by the scruff of the neck, shaking him like a rat. It was Michael Brodie.

Gordon grinned like a bear-trap.

'Michael? Did you have a long gab to the Polis this morning? Why have they not sent you back to the Bar L?' Before Brodie could stammer an excuse, the brothers grabbed an arm each and dragged him down the side of the shop to the bushes above the tennis courts, his feet dragging furrows in the leaves, whining excuses. They weren't listening to him; it was way beyond that now. Eddie slammed Brodie hard up against the roughcast.

'What did you tell McDowall about us and where are our drugs?'

Brodie squirmed. 'Look, I left the drugs in the flat. I don't know if the Polis found it. I'm just needing a day or two to get the money I owe. I've got something in the pipeline.'

Eddie punched him in the kidneys and ground his face against the wall. 'In the pipeline, are you taking the pish? It's a bloody turd that's in the pipeline. You!' Eddie thumped him again, Gordon waved Eddie off, lit a fag and blew the smoke over Brodie while he thought about this. The traffic rumbled by on the Beith Road, another aeroplane ambled across the sky on its way to the airport They squinted up as it sailed low overhead, the engine noise swamping them.

'You see, Brodie,' Gordon explained. 'You went on holiday last month. Where did you get the cash for that? Have you been helping yourself to Mr Hammond's money? The cash stacked between the walls better be all there.' He looked at his brother. 'Do you think we should give Michael here more time?'

Eddie spun Brodie around grabbed him by the throat ramming him back against the wall.

'Naw. I much prefer the "or whit" bit.'

'Michael,' Gordon lamented. 'You know how it goes. You break your agreement and we break your body. You got gear from us and sold it for good money. You don't have the cash and maybe the Polis do. So why are you walking about loose? What did you tell that bastard McDowall about us? Did you mention the girl in the bedroom?'

Gordon raked through Brodie's pockets while Eddie held him in a headlock and came up with nearly forty quid. Eddie let him go and Brodie slithered down the wall. Gordon tutted.

'Have you been holding out on us Michael? Not friendly at all, makes things really difficult to stretch a point.' He hauled Brodie up again, who cowered away.

'That's my buroo money, that's to feed us for the week till my next Giro.'

Eddie shook him. 'This is getting on ma goat so it is. Is he kidding us?'

Gordon stared icily at Brodie. The wee nyaff owed them serious money, had tried to do a runner, lost or stolen last night's profits and possibly spilled everything to McDowall. It was time to remind him what end of the lead he was on. 'Hit him a dull yin.'

Eddie drove his fist hard into Brodie's face, popping his nose in a spray of blood and snot. Brodie collapsed at the base of the wall trying to staunch the blood flowing between his fingers with both hands. Gordon fitted the money into his wallet and made a lifting motion to his brother who trailed Brodie up by the jacket. Gordon examined him, balancing the damage against what Brodie owed. Gordon stepped back.

'Eddie, hit him again.'

'My hand's sore belting him but I tell you what…' Eddie stuck the head on Brodie who made a hooting noise and fell face down in the nettles and rolled onto his knees. 'He's getting good at that falling down thing,' laughed Eddie. 'Practise makes perfect.'

Gordon bent down, patted his head. 'I'll give you two days, Brodie, don't you forget now. Do not even think about doing a runner.' He pulled Brodie's head around and glared into his fast-swelling eyes. 'Get your arse back to that flat as soon as, find our money, find our drugs. Or it's another hiding.'

Eddie kicked Brodie onto his side. 'I like you, Brodie. Well, I like hitting you.'

Leaving Brodie in a heap they returned to the car. Gordon was dropped at Gilmour Street station and gave Eddie his orders.

'When we get to Liverpool keep your mind on the job. Be at the Pilot Wharf at Port Lynas near Mersey Bar. About 4p.m., Uncle Chris will be there.'

'Ah'm no totally stupid ye know.'

The car took off in a cloud of tyre and exhaust fumes. Gordon strolled up towards the auction warehouse of Hammond Enterprises. He was ten minutes early, so he slipped into the bookies to wait. He knew something would have to be done about Eddie, who was sampling the goods in a major way, out his box on cocaine now, always that half-mad look about him. A man with no boundaries who didn't know when to stop or couldn't, loved the violence, the total naked mayhem.

Graeme Hammond had succeeded his failing father by default, an unwelcome and hopefully temporary development for the extended family, none of whom thought he could fill Arthur's shoes. He held court in the big office on the first floor with a picture window leading onto a walkway giving a view of the warehouse. A muted television theorised about the forthcoming general election and the collapse of Callaghan's government. Apart from an exit at his back leading down an external metal stairway, the walkway was the only approach. The Big Office, as it was known, had changed little from the firm's founding apart from the addition of fax machines and telephones. Old Arthur had furnished the place in what might be considered, "Imperial Chaos." A maelstrom of pieces from all corners of the earth sharing only one common thread, everything was exquisite and expensive. From here anyone approaching through the warehouse could be seen easily. Few tried anything on with the young Hammond. His reputation of being petty and vengeful was well known, never forgetting a slight.

The last time anyone had dared to cross him Gillespie's Merc ran them over one dark night in a lane. Three times in fact.

Word had soon got around.

McVicar didn't complete the autopsy on Angela until 5p.m. on the Sunday. He always felt an obligement to tidy up the loose ends personally and stayed behind when the mortuary assistants had left. Ghastly gaping stitches closed Angela's torso. Staples would have been neater. He brushed her hair before winding her in a shroud and slid the tray into the cold store. She seemed asleep, Snow White awaiting the prince. In his chaotic office, McVicar swallowed a generous dram then began his two-finger thumping at the old Remington typewriter. The clattering keys always soothed him. He paused the spools on the tape and refilled his glass. He was getting too old for this, maudlin, no longer dispassionate. It would erode him over time he knew, like Frank McDowall, but for now there was twelve-year-old malt. He resumed his typing.

"Sexual activity with multiple partners prior to death. No signs of restraint."

McVicar could only hope Angela had been unaware. He ended the report and sorted out the three copies, one for records, one for McDowall, and the other for the Deputy Fiscal, Findo Gask. He shoved his glasses onto the top of his head and massaged their footprint on his aching nose. He glanced at tomorrow's diary. There were two more dissections scheduled for Monday morning alone. McVicar reflected that he and McDowall had traded the circle of life for an endless roundabout of death.

McDowall had stayed on late at his desk. For a while he stared at the peeling paint on the partition and the scabby filing cabinets thinking himself alone till Joyce Fairbairn brought them two mugs of tea.

'A rough day for you Frank. I'm sorry.'

'That means a lot, Joyce, thanks.'

She spun the folders round to read the covers. 'What's this?'

'Homework, but I know the contents off pat.' Closing his eyes he leant back. 'Brodie is a total loser. Alcoholic parents, an orphan at four, lodged with a harpie of a foster carer who beat him stupid until one day he returned the beating. Absconded from Borstal. Usual track record after that, drugs, burglary, became a fence and a pimp. Spawned a couple of brats and became a big man, in his own head, His spells in pokey were like a football turnstile on overdrive.'

'And Beth Sharkey?'

'A life from Hell.' He pulled a photograph from the file and passed it to Joyce. 'Nice looking girl once. By thirteen she'd been abused by her own father and every male member of her family. By the time Welfare got involved at sixteen she'd fallen in with Brodie and the McGraths who sold her to anybody. They got her on the drugs and she went feral. Medical records say she's had every STD known to man. Probably back on the game right now. Enough to make the Devil weep so it is.'

They sat quietly sipping their scalding tea for a while until Joyce cleared her throat and spoke.

'Sorry, I should have brought a biscuit.'

Frank sighed, pushed his chair back, opened his desk drawer and handed her the last of his goodie stash. When she left, he couldn't believe he'd given her his last caramel wafer. 'Bugger this,' he told the empty office, 'I'm away for a dram.'

Gordon McGrath was climbing up to Hammond's office when Gillespie blocked his path on the stair.

'Hat!' he growled, whipping it off Gordon's head and bundled him up into the office where Hammond waited impatiently.

'I've not got all bloody day,' Hammond told him.

Gordon began nervously, stammering his rehearsed pitch.

'Speak! For fuck's sake,' Gillespie barked.

'Thanks for seeing me, Mr Hammond. It's just that a wee chance for a good deal has come up in Liverpool. See, my uncle works the Pilot Boat out of the Custom House Quay and we can take gear on and off ships. The money is needed upfront, but we're short of the readies right now. We thought you might see this as an opportunity and lend us the start up cash. It's a sure-fire smuggling route, well tried and…'

Hammond held up a hand. 'What planet are you on? I've decided Gillespie will go down to Scouseland and set up things. I've only dragged your scrawny arse here because you've screwed up yet again. Let me ask you a question. Do you know Frank McDowall?'

'Aye, he's lifted us a few times.' McGrath grew bold. 'It's no fair you're taking Liverpool.'

Hammond laughed. 'You cheeky wee shite. You should be carrying your balls in a wheelbarrow and your brain in a thimble. I take what I want. You're lucky not to be looking at the underside of a car for trying to set up your own deal behind my back. Do you think you're Reo Stakis? Cross me again and you'll both wind up in the River Cart with the shopping trolleys. Never mind that, it's a done deal so park your arse. Neil tells me you have a McDowall problem.'

Gordon glanced over his shoulder. 'No problems Mr Hammond. What problem?'

'You have an informer in your ranks, one Michael Brodie? Lifted at some drug shambles you held in one of my properties? The death of a young girl which has attracted the police? Brodie has been chatting to McDowall. Did you not think that's worth mentioning, that it might be termed, a problem?'

'That's been dealt with, Mr Hammond, Eddie gave him a doing this morning.'

'Not vaguely interested in what you think. Brodie is a loose cannon with knowledge of our business, and you've let him off with a wee hiding? I don't give a toss about dead girls, but rumour has it this lassie is McDowall's goddaughter. Brodie is a risk. If you don't deal with him, we will. Brodie, like Liverpool, is none of your concern anymore. Use the single brain cell you share with your brother to give some thought to this Beth Sharkey. Neil will tell you what I want. I'm off home for my tea now, so bugger off and play with the buses in the street.'

Gillespie grabbed McGrath by the jacket and trailed him out onto the landing. 'Listen up dipshit. This coming Wednesday you take this,' he produced a fat package the size of a brick from his coat. 'And get yourself up to Glasgow Central. This other envelope is travelling money. I want receipts.'

'But we had our Liverpool....'

Gillespie pinched his jaw closed with a shovel hand. 'Shuttit! Liverpool and all its doings are over for you so stop banging on about it. Pay attention to me now. Left Luggage locker is a drop, number G27, here's the key, don't lose it. Any time after three o'clock you open the locker.' Neil rapped Gordon's temple head in time with the instructions. 'That's when the big hand is at twelve and the wee hand is at three. Open the locker and take the holdall, leave the money, secure the locker, bring the holdall back to Paisley.'

'Here?'

'Naw! Bampot! Take it tae the polis, give it straight tae McDowall.' Neil skelped the side of his head. 'Call me at Junction 27 transport cafe when you're back in Paisley. Here's the number of the payphone, I'll tell you more then.' Gordon took out a Biro and began to scribble the number inside his baseball cap. Gillespie grabbed the pen and broke it.

'What the feck are you doing? Memorise it, like a spy! Don't write it on your Glesga Filofax for anybody to find.' He flung the cap over the banister, grabbed Gordon's jacket and poked a finger in his face. 'If you fuck up, I will personally organise your demise. Are you hearing me you gormless twat?'

Gordon gulped. 'Aye, okay I get it. What's in the locker?'

'What's this, University Challenge? Do as you're telt.'

He shoved Gordon away. 'And by the by, when Brodie surfaces, you and your defective brother will be helping us with that. For now, just get on your bike and don't screw this up more than your life's worth.'

*

CHAPTER 4

The smell of cordite and the tinkle of brass tore Alec Stewart awake fighting for his life, muscles taut, his body vibrating, arms flailing at vivid enemies, the sweat drenched sheets shackling his legs.

It was three in the morning.

It always was.

Another day to be endured.

The kick of the rifle had been so real he could still feel its butt hard in his shoulder. Disorientated, he panicked, reaching out desperately for Sheila. The bed was cold and empty.

He groaned and wrenched himself up throwing back the tangled bedding sending the nights empty cans clattering to the floor. He swayed trembling on the edge of the bed and up chucked a mix of cider and dodgy kebab, retching himself dry till it seemed his belly slapped his backbone. When the spasms were over, he stared down at the orange light from the streetlamps glistening on the stinking pool under the window. At least it was only the floorboards. Sheila had always complained when it was the carpet.

He'd sold everything when she'd bolted with their child, even the curtains and carpets, leaving himself a single bed, one pillow, and a chest of drawers with two broken runners. His clothes lay in mixed jumbles across the floor, uninhabited islands on a timber ocean. Smaller versions of the large island of despair he was marooned on now. He swayed to his feet, only managing to stay up with both hands on the wall, lurching toward the bathroom, his bare feet making sucking sticky noises on the hallway linoleum. He stumbled, fell against the bath, and slumped on the throne, head in the washbasin and emptied explosively.

There were no fifty pence coins for the meter, so the shower was icy, its glacier fingers stabbing at his flesh as he lifted his arms to protect his eyes, his head bowed. His body was soon numbed but his soul still called out for his stolen family.

What had happened to him?

He knew the answer.

The drinking.

To forget.

To sleep.

Alec turned off the whipping jets, his tears salt on his face and lips. Broken, he sank down and curled up in the shower tray wrapped in an old scratchy man towel. Drained and quivering he trudged back to his room and sat on the bed, staring at the wallpaper of teddy bears and carousels. The clock told him it was another five hours at least before he must go face Robert and Ethel again. He had no words to comfort them over Angela. He remembered Robert confessing to him he couldn't afford to send Angela to college. Alec had made the decision to finance her with his lump severance from the MoD, and despite the sacrifice never regretted it. His stale world was now a soundtrack of silence, a pulsing harmony of vomit, stale beer, and mouldy curry containers.

The flat bitter taste of failure.

He reached under his pillow and pulled out a T-shirt.

Held it to his face.

Breathed in all that remained, the lingering scent of Sheila.

Frank McDowall became slowly aware of being dunted in the ribs by his wife and something flashing in the dark. His glasses still sat crooked on his face on and he'd dribbled enough to stick his mouth to the pillow.

Irene nagged at him. 'I'd be as well with that pager on my side of the bed, you neither hear it nor answer it. Quarter of a century I've been your unpaid receptionist.' She dunted him again. 'It's past eight, and you haven't set the alarm. What time did you come to bed?'

'Right! Irene. Right, I'm up, I'm up. Jeez, how do I know when I came to bed? Shortly after yourself. What day is it?'

'You're getting worse, you need to see a doctor.' McDowall groped blindly for the phone, missed, knocking over the water glass onto the carpet. A tutting noise from Irene muffled by the eiderdown. He fumbled the light switch on and lifted the phone only to find nobody there. He dialled the station and wondered if there would ever come a day, he would do something right in Irene's book. While the phone rang out, he swung his legs over the side of the bed and slammed both feet into the puddle on the carpet. 'Great. Marvellous,' he muttered. 'Hope that keeps up.'

The phone was answered. 'CID Johnstone, Sergeant Brown speaking.'

'You can stuff the polite voice and tell me why you need me at this ungodly hour. You do know it's Monday?'

Brown chuckled. 'It's yourself, Frank. Hope you weren't in bed; it would have been a pity to wake you. Inspector Tannock wants you in his office at nine, sharp.'

McDowall groaned. 'Any idea what for?'

'Not to give you a medal, my son. Something about not having submitted returns to his office since God wrote on stone to Moses? Also, where is his daily update from yesterday? Just guesses of course. I said you would no doubt bring the proper paperwork with you.'

'You'll make a lovely wife one day. I need a favour, photocopy somebody else's figures for January, will you? He'll never spot the difference. Another Home Office survey screwed.'

'Will do, they'll be on top of your locker. One you owe me.' McDowall hung up. Irene cracked one eye at him from behind the rampart of the duvet. His vision was blurred still, and it looked as if there was one big eye in the middle of her head.

'Well?' she demanded.

'Tannock's office, nine. An interview with God no less.'

'You can't!' Irene barked, both eyes wide open now head up off the pillow. She always managed to look like a disturbed tiger these days. 'I've already told Moira you'd run Grant to nursery. Remember Moira? Your daughter? Your grandson?

She's working, as is her husband. If I could drive I wouldn't be asking you.'

'You're driving me crazy,' thought McDowall. 'Right, right, right.' Dressing quicker than Superman he was already hopping into his shoes and grabbing his jacket from over the chair. 'I'll pick them up, no worries.'

He went downstairs shrugging into his jacket. He would sooner face Tannock than deal with an irate wife and daughter combo. He flung on his coat and slammed the door, reflecting that Moira must get it from her mother for both had tongues like a broken bottle. At the car, he stood rummaging in his pockets. Shite! No keys. They must still be on the dresser or the bedroom floor. He tiptoed into the bedroom. He needn't have bothered, Irene lifted one arm from under the quilt, the car keys dangling from one finger.

'Thanks, dear.' His retreat got as far as the bedroom door.

'Francis?' He stopped. 'Try to dress a little smarter for work, will you? Why don't you take that little battery razor I bought you? If you don't look after your appearance, you'll retire a Detective Sergeant. Try to push yourself more.' He began to close the door. 'Francis! Quietly please, don't slam the door and turn on the gas fire as you go?'

He waited in the car for the windscreen to demist, eyes closed, trying to relax. Monday morning, usual shit. McDowall supposed he was lucky still to be allowed back in the house, never mind in the bed after his, "adventure", as Irene called it. His family and the locker room sniggerers assumed Claire and him had been at it like rabbits. Was Irene making him pay, had she only taken him back till he was destroyed by her venom? Her sniping criticism was eroding his soul like a dripping stalactite. Losing patience, he smeared the screen with his hand and cleared a gap, driving off hunched up like Quasimodo.

His daughter Moira greeted him with a frosty peck on the cheek and that face she got from her mother. He wondered not for the first time where his genes were.

'You're late, Dad.'

'You're right, daughter. Morning to you as well.'

A four-year-old tornado came whirling into the hall, one arm in his duffle coat, 'Papa!'

McDowall lifted his grandson into the air, planted a loud raspberry under his chin which reduced him into a fit of giggles. 'How's my wee superman then?'

Moira swept into her coat, picked up her bag and keys, ushered them into the hall and out the door, all in one move it seemed to McDowall.

'Dad! Put him down, you'll only get him wound up.' His daughter was old before her time. What had happened to his wee girl who had once loved a good raspberry herself? He ignored her and dumped a squirming Grant in the back seat, his wee cherub face shining.

It was after nine when he dropped Moira at the office of *Haggerty & Lomas, Solicitors*. He had met Haggerty once, a dried-up skeletal Meccano man who always wore a suit that looked like his fat brother's cast off. Moira was going the same way. The elusive Lomas was deceased and was on the letterhead for tax purposes, or perhaps like McDowall, to take the blame.

'Can you pick up Grant at three?'

'No.'

'Mum said you could.'

'Your Mum says her prayers, but God rarely answers. I'm not retired yet, you know.'

'Thanks!' She slammed the car door.

McDowall turned to Grant. 'Your Mum is a pain in the arse.'

Grant chortled from behind his hand. 'Bad word, bad word.' As he drove out to the nursery at Spateston, McDowall admitted to himself that he didn't like Moira much at all. He loved her, of course as a sort of mandatory thing, but he didn't like her. As for that prat she'd married, David, the defence lawyer, a humourless clone who could do no wrong in Irene's eyes. Both full of themselves, enough said. McDowall's encyclopaedic repertoire of lawyer jokes and stories had not gone down well at the wedding. He thought there was something flawed with folk incapable of laughing at themselves. They richly deserved each other.

At the nursery, Mrs Carson, the head teacher, met him inside the door with the same greeting every day he brought Grant.

'Good morning, Sergeant McDowall, is it safe to walk the streets today?'

'Not if you knew what I know, Mrs Carson. Want to buy a shotgun or a big dog?'

She beamed at their little joke. 'That's a lovely new scarf, Grant, is Yogi Bear keeping you nice and warm? How is your Mummy today?'

Grant smiled cheerily. 'My Mum's a pain in the arse today.'

McDowall cringed and gave her a sickly smile. 'Kids. Wonder where he got that from.'

He escaped with Grant to the cloakroom and waited while the boy piddled and washed his hands. McDowall tucked the boy's shirt in kissing him on the top of the head. 'I'll see you at Granny's later, be good.'

He asked Mrs Carson could he use her phone and she waved her hand towards the office. No doubt Moira would be informed of Grant's new vocabulary. There was an event to look forward to. Anyway, time his grandson began to realise it wasn't all streamers and finger painting. That the monsters in his nursery books were taken from real life.

He got Brown again who informed him Tannock was, "absolutely raging" and could he get there, right now. McDowall hung up and thought it would have been a good week to make like a bear, crap in the woods and hibernate.

At Robert's house Alec rang the bell again, turned up his coat collar and stepped back from under the front porch. Where were they, not both overslept surely? He checked the time again, it was seven, not too early. The curtains were still drawn, no lights showing. Alec was early so strolled down to the newsagents in Beith Road for a paper and three rolls with Lorne sausage. At seven-thirty on the dot he rang the bell again but no sign of life. He sighed and plodded around the back past the gnomes and the wishing well and the trashed debris of Robert's roses. Buster the collie sat whining at the back door, rain slick and matted on its black coat. They looked at each other with the same expression of dreich misery on their faces. He scratched its ear.

'Hi Buster! Where's your mammy this morning, not let you in yet?'

Robert had bought the dog to scare off burglars. Fat chance, it couldn't catch itself with four legs and had stopped barking at anything except biscuits a long time ago. Fat, spoiled, and overfed by Ethel, the dog might savage a dead sheep if pushed. He unchained the mutt and got the keys from under the plant pot by the hut. Once the back door was open Buster shot past him straight to its basket in the hall. Alec stood listening; unaware he was holding his breath. He called his sister-in-law's name. No answer. The kitchen gleamed with wifely zeal, reminding him of a glossy magazine kitchen, where nobody had ever cooked a meal or made a mess in their lives. He shivered. The silence was ominous, suddenly filling him with dread He shook the feeling off, closed the door and turned on the kettle before crossing the living room and drawing the curtains back. Time to make some racket. He turned on the radio to the Mamas and the Papas, *"Monday morning good to me."* and called out.

'Ethel! Robert! It's me, Alec.' Then again, louder. He turned the radio volume up loudly then off.

Silence.

The dog lifted its head from the basket, whined softly and looked at him with sad watery eyes. In the hallway, Alec peered up the stairs and hesitated, fearful she might kick off if he just blundered up and knocked their bedroom door. 'Robert, it's me Alec. Are you OK?'

He began to climb the stair stopping on the half landing, concerned because he felt his hackles lifting, alert as if he were entering a Belfast Lane. He licked his lips apprehensively and called out again.

'Hullo! Robert. Ethel. I'm coming up.'

The bathroom was empty. He knocked on their bedroom door but got no response so peered around the door. Everything was neat and in its place, the bed tight as a Marine recruits. What was going on? Had they gone out early for milk or papers, rolls maybe? Naw, Robert would have taken the dog with him?

They were still here.

His eyes were dragged to the only other door on the landing. He paused at the slightly open door, uncertain, the name plaque level with his nose. *"Angela's Room. Keep Out!"* He called gently through the gap, his voice a hoarse whisper, tapping the panel lightly. The redolence of scented candles hung on the landing. He felt weak and sick, breathed in, and pushed the door open.

All the tapes and books were squared away and tidy on the shelves, the pop posters on the wall where Angela had left them the night she went out forever. The Bee Gees and The Beatles. Bay City Rollers. He leaned against the door jamb.

He knew.

Just looking at her, he knew.

Ethel lay on the bed dressed in her best nightclothes surrounded by Angela's cuddly creatures that peopled the room. He'd seen dead men before, but they'd had life ripped from them. This was different, softer. She was so very still. Alec slid down the door frame and plumped himself onto the dressing stool. The remains of the pills she'd used lay scattered on the floor. He recalled how Ethel's mother had kept piles of painkillers towards the end of her life. He sank to his knees and moved to the side of the bed. A strand of hair had fallen over her face. He gently lifted it away. She looked young and beautiful, more like she and Angela were sisters. He touched her neck but there was no pulse and her flesh was cold. On the floor was a picture of her first boy, Kevin, a first day at school picture. Her hand gripped another photo frame close to her. Alec loosened her fingers and it was Angela's last school photograph, her smile full of life and the hope of long endless summer days. He put it back into her hand.

McDowall turned into the car park at Johnstone Police Office in Golspie Road almost running up the back of a Hillman Imp parked in his usual spot. Being late on a Monday meant spaces were hard to come by.

'Whit knob left that there?' he barked to himself. He lost even more time reversing out into traffic and eventually parked across the road outside the surgery, where a sign informed him this bay was, "Doctors Only." On pain of enema no doubt.

At the front desk Brown greeted him with, 'Morning shortarse,' pointed up at the clock and made a face.

'Aye. I know, I know I know,' McDowall said. 'Two questions. Where's Captain Chaos, and who's parked in my spot?'

'That wid be me parked in your spot,' grinned Brown, then stage whispered, 'and Captain Chaos is behind you.'

McDowall spun around, a painted smile on his face. 'Good morning, sir!'

Tannock had just come out the office corridor clutching a clipboard and some files. Nothing out of place, spotless uniform, he looked McDowall up and down.

'Detective Sergeant McDowall! At last, good morning.'

'Sorry to keep you waiting, sir, bit of domestic this morning.'

Tannock pursed his lips and favoured him with a dead smile. 'Yes well. I suppose we must make allowances for the older members of the force. We all slow down as we get older. My office please, as soon as.' He turned sharply and took the stairs to the first floor. McDowall gave the flapping doors the finger, slipped out of his coat and asked Brown, now on the phone. 'Where's the stuff?'

'On your locker, you owe me a pint.'

McDowall gave him the finger as well. Brilliant! Well, it would just have to lie there for now. Probably be sent for it like a schoolboy for his homework jotters.' He draped his coat over the radiator and pushed through the doors, relieving Joyce of her tea as he passed.

'Thanks, Joyce love. Never looked better than you do at this moment.'

He walked backward to watch her glaring after him. Nicknamed not unkindly, Juicy Joyce, the collator. Juicy to look at, keeper of juicy crime tit bits. 'God!' McDowall prayed, please make me ten years younger, single, restore my teeth and hair and nothing in Heaven or Hell would save her.' Not a prayer there he knew so best to accept he was a wee short fat grey guy past forty. 'Eat your heart out,' he told himself.

Brown brushed past him. 'Put it away dad, that would give you a heart attack.'

Tannock's door was open so McDowall rattled the frosted glass with his fingertips and sailed in to find his boss facing the window behind his desk, arms tightly folded, peering out.

A canteen joke was; why does he not look out the window in the morning? Answer, there's be nothing for him to do in the afternoon. McDowall plonked himself down in the naughty chair, set the foam cup on the floor, took out his fags and lit up.

Tannock turned, sighed, and gestured behind him. 'Door?'

McDowall blew out the match, 'Oh aye! Right!' heaved himself up and closed it.

Tannock fixed him with a pursed lip disapproving look over the poised steeple of his fingers, lips tight as a shark's arse at a thousand fathoms. McDowall felt like a wee boy again at the Wallace school, pulled to the front of the class over late homework and sent to the office. Would he be asked to produce a note from his Ma?

'I do wish you wouldn't smoke, it's a filthy habit.'

'God!' McDowall thought, this sounded familiar, just like the house. He blew smoke at the ceiling. Tannock broke his steeple reached into his desk and produced a Waterford crystal ashtray. McDowall wondered if he only allowed those who outranked him to smoke in his office, thus the fancy ashtray. Only cigars probably, produced for the Chief no doubt and members of the Police Board while they discussed mighty and impotent matters. Tannock pushed it pointedly across the desk towards him.

'Thank you, sir,' McDowall examined it. 'Very fancy, not what I'm used to, more the overflowing bin in the canteen.'

Tannock didn't mention the latest canteen bin fire, produced a small folding fan which he set up to blow the smoke away then sat erect in his chair.

'I know, Detective Sergeant, that you have been here for a long time and will remind you that you qualify for early retirement should you choose. I believe you have extra years due to National Service and then your time with the Royal Ulster Constabulary would also count? Just another six years and you will be able to go, or is it less?'

'You wish,' McDowall thought, but said nothing, just nodded non-committedly.

Tannock continued. 'Until that happy day arrives, I would be obliged if you would show a little more, shall we say, promptitude, when you are requested to come to my office.' He leant forward both hands busy on the desk brushing at non-existent dust. McDowall thought that dust wouldn't dare settle. 'I have,' Tannock continued, 'a very busy schedule of appointments and meetings ahead of me today and your tardiness has set back my diary by thirty minutes.' McDowall raised his eyebrows.

By Christ! Tardiness! Promptitude! Must ask Brown what they meant. He puffed smoke at the fan and watched it swirl away.

'I'm sorry, sir. As I've already explained, a domestic problem that won't happen again.'

'Yes well. We shan't waste any more time on it.' Someone knocked the door and an annoyed Tannock grasped the arms of his chair. 'Come!'

Brown came in. 'Sorry to interrupt you, sir, but DS McDowall left this at the desk.' He handed over a thick buff folder.

'I've been looking for that, thanks Jim.' McDowall passed the folder over the desk as Brown left. 'These are the crime figures for the last quarter, sir. And, of course, a wee update on the Angela Stewart case.'

'Very good. This progress in your administration is most welcome. Maybe next quarter's figures will be on my desk on time. Not a flash in the pan, Detective Sergeant?' he squinted over his Gepetto spectacles at them both and placed the admin file in his tray, squaring the progress report on Angela in front of him.

McDowall managed to look enthusiastic. 'No, of course, I fully realize the importance of all this and the part it plays in the great scheme of things.' He wondered if his nose was growing.

Tannock cleared his throat and sniffed. 'Yes, very good. What I want to discuss is that we've had something passed to us by City of Glasgow Police which may well have an impact on the ongoing Hammond case. I know you are well informed about the increase in the West of Scotland drugs trade, but how well are you acquainted with the current drugs scenario in Johnstone itself?'

McDowall tapped his fag towards the ashtray just missing and defiling the desk with a generous pile. A pained expression flitted across Tannock's face which tickled McDowall as he leant back crossing his legs and staring at the ceiling with what he hoped was an informed look.

'Not a major problem for us yet. Apart from Hammond there are only a couple of local baddies, but the numbers involved are small. Some local raids on chemists and the like. Price goes up, so does the local crime rate. Small gangs tussle every now and then to remind each other where the boundaries are. Drugs are mostly soft although a growing problem is harder stuff from the East. Most of the gangs are into the usual, car theft and stripping for parts, protection and prostitution. Running people over is favoured this weather. As long as they're only injuring each other we usually just mop up the blood when they're done Overall, not too bad. "Z *Cars* we're not."

Tannock peered at him over his spectacles looking like Pinocchio's dad. 'Z *Cars*?'

'On the television? Local Yorkshire police officers catching the baddies? Everything done and dusted in half an hour.'

'Ah! Yes. I see.' He continued to take notes as he extracted a sheet from the file and passed it over the desk. 'We've received intelligence from City of Glasgow Police concerning a quantity of drugs at present in a Left Luggage locker at Central Station, to be uplifted sometime this Thursday afternoon, about three. Comments?'

'All pretty vague and why involve us unless as patsies when it all goes legless? It's like finding a dirty nappy and making somebody else clean it. Why this share and share alike suddenly?'

Tannock leant forward and dropped his voice. 'What you are unaware of is that the money to finance this shipment would seem to be coming from Paisley.'

'The Hammonds,' McDowall suggested, energised by the possibilities. 'I'd heard they were expanding. I could take a closer interest in them.'

Tannock made a wry face and wagged his finger. 'That would be the well-connected Hammonds. Churchgoers, charity sponsors, youth initiatives. They have very powerful connections.'

'The Krays were well connected. Jack the Ripper was supposedly Old Queen Vic's nephew. I don't remember him doing any hard pokey time. Just because Hammond is in the right golf clubs and lives up Cartside means diddly. He's got disposable foot soldiers.'

Tannock pointed a finger. 'I don't want Hammond's solicitor in here again, lecturing me on everything from the Magna Carta to the civil rights movement. I don't want you even breathing in their direction unless you have enough to hang Hammond, and his bloody lawyer to boot.'

McDowall stared in silence at his scuffed shoes. Tannock got up and began to pace the office wiping more imaginary dust of his golf trophies on the sideboard then perching himself against the sideboard and folding his arms. McDowall dumped ash on the carpet under his chair by way of silent comment.

Tannock returned to his desk.

'Enough said on that. The Chief has decided we will share this operation with Glasgow. First thing Thursday you and your partner.' He clicked his fingers and waved his hand as if to summon the name from thin air.

'Jim Brown, sir.'

'That's the one. The two of you will go through to Glasgow and liaise with...' He ruffled the sheets in the folder. 'Here it is. Inspector Devaney of the Transport Police, he'll be at their office in Glasgow Central to meet you. Take this folder with you.'

McDowall rubbed his face and rested his elbows on the desk shaking his head as he pretended to scan the file. Paul Devaney of all people. Liaison might well turn to murder, nothing but bad blood between them. He tried for some wiggle room.

'Sir, I've got more than enough on my plate to be getting on with. Me and Brown are already wading in treacle, uphill. Can't the new super-duper Regional Crime Squad get a grip?'

'The Chief Constable wants local involvement in this across the Central Belt. Cooperation at national level and be seen to assist neighbouring forces in preparation for Regionalisation. We must be seen getting to grips with all crime in a Scottish context.'

McDowall flopped back in the chair and groaned, screwing up his face. He smelt politics. 'Fucks Sake!' he thought. Tannock was wanting to be on Scottish Television with his serious face, pontificating. What a feed of pish. He and Brown would do all the work, only for Tannock to sign the final report and bask in glory at his Command Course selection at Dorking. The final report would be typed up with Tannock's name inserted at appropriate intervals. Unless it all fell flat on its arse of course, then he and Brown would both disappear in a blaze of bullshit.

'I'm actually snowed under just now. I'm following some good leads in the Stewart case.'

Tannock ignored him, slammed the file shut. 'I'll expect to hear from you by Thursday evening as to how it all went with a full report in writing to follow of course. Most importantly, try not to upset anyone more than usual. Keep me updated on the Angela Stewart case. I want that wound up as soon as, don't be dragging it out. I think that's all for now.'

Dismissed then like an errant schoolboy, McDowall left the cold coffee on the floor under his chair by way of protest, banging the door on his way out.

Brown was waiting in their office smirking, offered him the paper hankies. McDowall gave him the finger and the folder.

He gave McDowall a note.

'Two notes in one morning, what's this?'

'That', Brown tapped the note with his pencil, 'is our next task. It's something you might want to body swerve. Since you've just been given a big-word bollocking and can't read because your eyes are still watering, I'll tell you what it says if you like.'

McDowall squinted at the message pad. Brown offered his glasses.

'I don't need your poxy glasses. It says ... 10 Castle Crescent?'

'Circle, Frank. Castle Circle.'

'It's your writing, nothing wrong with my eyes at all.'

'It's the Stewart house and it's not good. Robert had a massive heart attack and passed away this morning. Ethel's taken her own life.'

Even after all his time in the Police, seeing the depths people sank to, this thing sickened him. He'd fancied himself immune. His heart slowed from its jackhammer beating and he breathed again. Images of Angela lying in that flat flooded back. Her life and dreams ripped away and now her whole family wiped out by those two evil gits. Angela, as much a daughter to him as to her dad, Robert. This couldn't be buried or locked away in his deep dark dungeon place along with his other failures. All his childhood and adult monsters. The images of a thousand other horrors stamped around inside his head out and swamped him, sharp in black and white on his mind's eye. It shocked and drained him, crushing the shreds of his belief in good like a collapsing brick wall.

For a boy raised on *The Lone Ranger* and *The Cisco Kid* it had come as a bonecrusher long ago that in the real world the goodies seldom won. He thought of Robert's brother Alec. Where was Alec Stewart right now? There was a loose cannon, that man sweated gelignite.

A thump on the desk, the mail tower fell over. Joyce back with an armful of files. 'This is everything we have on anyone involved or named in the Angela Stewart case. I wish you well.'

When she was gone, he opened the case file and post mortem report. Angela smiled up at him from her school leaving photograph, the sharp bright colours a stark contrast to the black and white prints peeping out from the envelope. Let them lie hidden for now. Hard to grasp it was the same girl discarded across the bed. Died trying to be a good friend to trash.

Over the next hour he lost himself in the files, soothing his hangover with fags and tea with a wee chaser in it. Then he sought leads from Michael Brodie's pathetic crimes. Where could Brodie go, for he was in a hard place between Hammond and the law? Brodie hadn't many choices and would need to get a fix soon. He would surface in some cesspool soon enough. McDowall's brain was melting so he gave up and locked the folder in the filing cabinet. He'd stalled long enough.

He passed Joyce in the corridor with tea but no biscuits. He grabbed his still damp coat from the radiator struggling his arms into it.

'Joyce, if Tannock is looking for me tell him I've gone up to join DC Brown. I'll maybe pick up some tips.'

'On detecting?'

'On suicide.'

'Okay then,' said Joyce, 'but do you not think you should put your shoes on first?'

He looked down at his feet. Joyce and the typist leant across the bar.

'Nice socks,' said the typist. 'Chrissy present? Odd socks?'

'Not odd at all. There's a pair the same in my drawer.' Joyce flung his shoes over, McDowall struggled them on past the laces, stamping and wriggling his feet as he left. He'd barely got the key into the ignition of his old Triumph Herald when someone with a giant umbrella tapped the door. He started to wind the window down before he remembered it wouldn't go back up. His brain refused to stop his hand and the glass thudded down inside the door. 'Limping Shite!'

'I beg your pardon.' It was the receptionist from the surgery. 'I'm glad I caught you, Mr McDowall. I really must ask you, again, not to park in the doctor spaces, it really is most inconvenient.'

'Yes well, really sorry. I was in a rush this morning you see. Women held me back.'

McDowall drove off, the drizzle soaking him through the window. He could bet his life Alec Stewart was planning and wondered was there perhaps a part in that for him.

*

CHAPTER 5

Brown was waiting at Castle Circle attempting to conceal from Divisional Control that McDowall was not actually on scene yet. Two uniforms were already there. They informed him the fatality was upstairs. They confirmed the name, Ethel Stewart, found by her brother-in-law who was inside. The guy sitting on the stairs, name of Alec Stewart. The duty doctor was on his way so for now it looked to them like a done and dusted suicide. Brown told them to give the undertaker a heads up and let him know the minute McDowall arrived, if ever.

'All done,' growled the Sargent. 'What the hell's that thing you're driving?'

'The new squad car.'

'The paint job and the disco light on the roof gave that away. Did it come with seven dwarfs? It's a cigarette tin.'

'It's a Hillman Imp. Brand new.'

'It's a Dinky toy. I'd like to see you struggle a drunk into the back of that.'

Brown didn't take the bait and went on in. In the hall a man sat on the stairs his head cupped in his hands, late forties or so. Brown pulled his notebook and cleared his throat noisily.

'Excuse me, sir, I'm DC Brown. I need to ask you some

questions. Alec Stewart, is it? We met yesterday at your brother's house. Can I take some details from you?'

The man slowly lifted his head and their eyes met. Till then he had seemed ordinary but Brown saw something else lurking behind the pain and shock. Couldn't put his finger on it but it was disturbing. Like facing a caged tiger, wondering when it had last eaten and how strong the bars were.

'Aye. I'm Alec Stewart,' said the man. 'I'm Ethel's brother-in-law. I found her.'

'When was that, can you give me a rough time for that?'

'This morning, 07.02.'

'That's very precise.'

'Old habits.'

Brown took in the inference of the twenty-four-hour clock. 'Were there any signs of forced entry or disturbance?'

'No. I have a key to the back door. Moved nothing, touched nothing.'

'Did you notice anything suspicious or see any strangers hanging about outside?'

'Just the dog.'

'Anything else?'

'Maybe Buster saw something. My brother Robert should be here but he's not.'

'Do you feel all right?'

Alec smiled wearily at the dog who had lifted his head at the sound of his name. 'Naw. I feel like shite, look worse probably, but I've felt that way for years, so I suppose you could say I'm all right.' He covered his face with both hands.

'I'll away and have a look upstairs.'

Alec mumbled from behind his hands. 'You do that son, detect away.'

Upstairs on the landing there was the scent of flowers, something sweet. Brown nodded to the young WPC sitting on a stool, eyes fixed on the half-closed door to his right. She leapt up as if on a spring and held out a pair of medical gloves to him. She was brand new, twenty or so, upset, anxious to do everything right. He'd felt like that once, when the Earth was young. He took the gloves and pulled them on slowly. Brown hadn't seen many dead people. He hoped McDowall would magically become organized and appear soon. He should be here, not at the station.

'I'm DC Brown, lassie. DS McDowall should be here soon. This your first death?'

The WPC gave him a wee sick smile. 'I'm just on the job a couple of weeks.'

Brown nodded. 'Well, until the main man appears we'll try and keep each other right.'

He paused at the bedroom door and took a deep breath. His hand touched the flowered plaque, *"Angela's Room"*, and pushed. The walls were a splash of overlapping posters. Fleetwood Mac, Abba, Rod Stewart, Elvis Presley, David Cassidy.

His first impression was Ethel was sleeping, a perception almost immediately shattered by the fly exploring her eyelid. She was a still life by some Dutch master. No disturbance, nothing out of place but the pills scattered on the carpet. It reminded Brown of his young sister's room. The woman on the bed was quite beautiful, must have been stunning when she was younger. She held that beauty even now. Brown got busy with the incident sheet on his clipboard, what the old hands called an idiot guide. He bagged the spilled pills, recording the scene on the Polaroid camera he'd found in the office desk, still in its box. He was unaware of time passing until voices floated up from outside.

A burst of misplaced laughter jarred him followed by steps in the hall. Brown heard McDowall's gravel voice and moved to the top of the stair to peer over the banister as the conversation wafted up to him.

'Well, Alec, are you home from the wars for good? Home is the Hunter, home from the Hill, back from the sojering long?'

'A while.'

'Didn't get a chance to speak to you the other day, obviously. Are you working?'

'Rootes at Linwood, but it's only three days now.'

McDowall scoffed. 'Not enough? I wish I was on a three-day week.'

'I'm chasing a security job in Barrhead.'

'Luck with that. This is an awful time for a reunion Alec. Everyone is sore hurt by this.'

McDowall stood like a rock over the other man, glanced around then dragged over the telephone seat and sat facing him. Nobody spoke. Alec held his hands clasped tight together on his knees and stared at the floor. McDowall pulled out two ciggies and, lighting both, passed one to Alec and they smoked silently for a minute.

'Cheers,' mumbled Alec.

'Ethel did it then, followed her weans?' McDowall asked.

'Aye. The last act but one you might say.'

'Last act but one?'

'Getting whoever did this. I take it you of all people, Angela's godfather, would be right on the case and even have the murdering sods in the poky already?'

McDowall nodded with more confidence than he felt. He decided there was enough bad news for today and gilded the lily. 'I got the file this morning, hot from the press, there's a squad on it as we speak. Sorry this has happened to your family, to good folk.'

Alec snorted. 'I'm sure the whole world is sorry. But Angela is still dead, and Ethel has snuffed herself. The last piece is still missing though. Do you know yet who did it?'

'Knowing is not proving, and my two main suspects have scarpered. Our enquiries are progressing and there's nothing to be done for now. Forensics are inconclusive, and nobody is talking coherently except one junkie we had a hold of. It's getting someone to finger them. Most of the witnesses were drugged out their brains, two are in the hospital and the rest would all testify that Elmer Fudd killed Angela. Noddy might well be an accomplice. I may call in the Lone Ranger.' Brown come down the stair and squeezed past McDowall.

'Here's my oppo DC Brown. He's got a university

education, lot's smarter than me.'

'Everyone is smarter than you.'

McDowall bent over him. 'Alec. I know the why of what's happened here but now the men outside need to come in and take Ethel away to find out the how. Do you know what she used?'

'Morphine tablets left over from her mother's prescriptions; I think. Drugs they'll say, runs in the family, same as Angela.'

McDowall sighed. 'When did you ever give a tuppeny toss what other people say? Best you go into the living room till all this ghoul stuff is by with.' Alec stood and nodded, McDowall closed the door behind him and looked at the floor. He peered up under his eyebrows at Brown. 'Well, Brown ma boy, let's have a look then, see what the damage is.'

They plodded up the stair onto the landing where McDowall forced a wee smile for the WPC who seemed on the edge of tears. 'Hi, Christine, what a hell of a way to start the day, hen. Been here long?'

'I was nightshift so stayed on.' She gave him a small, crumpled smile.

'Good girl.'

McDowall pushed the door open till it touched the wardrobe and stood looking. It was hard to detach himself from the pathos of it all and remain professional. 'Very considerate,' he told Brown. 'Left us no mess to clean up.' His gaze wandered across the toys, the records, tapes, posters, and the same school photograph of Angela as the one in the file. The frame had twisted slightly in Ethel's hand to spill some of the tablets onto the floor. The water in the glass was clear and dust free, a faint smudge of lipstick on the rim. Her eyes were not quite closed, and she seemed to be just awakening, surprised out of a heavy sleep. He knew she'd picked this room to die in deliberately. Somewhere warm and safe, holy ground. The only blemish on the perfection of it all was she had dribbled slightly. A uniform came to the bottom of the stair and called up.

'Medical is here, Frank, along with the photographer plus two boys from the morgue with the shell.'

'Okay. Do you have all you need from up here?' Brown nodded.

'Then I suppose we should let that prancing photographer in here. I'll go down and have another wee word with Alec.' McDowall pointed to the diary on the dressing table.

'We'll be having that I think.'

'Are you okay with this, being a close family friend?' Brown asked. 'You should get somebody else assigned to the investigation.' Brown stepped close and whispered. 'Frank, I don't think your pal knows about his brother Robert, nobody's told him.'

McDowall paused at the bedroom door, head down, shoulders slumped. 'Limping Christ,' he groaned. 'Me left with it again. Right, I'll tell him for others won't be as compassionate as us. Give Ethel all the dignity you can and don't let the bodysnatchers treat her like a meat parcel when they come up.' He took one last sweep around the room. 'This is a place filled with hurt, like nothing you've ever felt,

Jim boy. We'll nail those who did this if it's the last thing we do.' McDowall exchanged silent nods with the doctor as they passed on the stairs. The bodysnatchers waited in the front hallway, the shell propped up against the wall. McDowall shook his head.

'You two are as subtle as a boot in the goolies. I'm surprised you didn't bring the shovels with you and save time. Get that thing out of sight.'

When McDowall entered the living room Alec was by the window watching the subdued hubbub in the street. Against the wall behind the door was a cocktail cabinet, all glass and mahogany. McDowall opened it and pulled two crystal glasses from the rack and poured two malts, one larger than the other. He walked to the window and stood alongside Alec. After a moment weighing both glasses up, he gave the double measure to Alec, who took a good belt and closed his eyes. McDowall sipped and waited.

'I'm not surprised by this you know.' Alec spoke softly. 'Ethel really believed in the whole religion thing you know, redemption and the afterlife. That Angela wasn't gone but was still here, lingering up there in her room and about the house. She knew her wee lassie was dead like, but hadn't gone away, not yet. It was as if she was still here along with Kevin and her Mum, waiting for Ethel. I understand all that and what Ethel did. It wasn't an act of despair or grief, not for Ethel.'

'What was it then?' McDowall prompted.

'Belief! An act of faith. That Angela was waiting for her in some other place. Here in this room. Ethel just went where

Angela was, nothing to hold her here. Not now.'

Alec crossed the room for another whisky offering to pour for McDowall who shook his head covering the glass.

'Best not. I've a boss that thinks smoking and picking your nose is a filthy habit.'

Alec sat on the couch and stared into his glass, the bottle between his thighs. 'What's going on? You've not looked me in the face since you came downstairs. Where's Robert?'

McDowall cleared his throat. 'Nobody's told you?'

'Told me what?'

McDowall cringed inwardly. Christ on a bike, he thought, why did he always get stuck with the messenger of death job? 'I'm sorry Alec. Robert died last night. A stroke here at home then a massive heart attack. He died in the ambulance. Did Ethel not tell you?'

'Why should she? She hated me and obviously had other plans. Anyway, my phone's cut off for non-payment.' Alec took a good gulp at the whisky. Memories flooded into his head, his chest hurt and his eyes stung. Flashbacks of Robert helping him at school, fighting for him. Sharing peas and vinegar at the chippy, big plate and two forks. Diving into the canal to save him. His throat choked, and it was a while before he struggled back to the present. 'You can bet I wasn't on Ethel's, "to do", list. She hates me because of Kevin.'

'Never understood what Kevin's death to do with you?'

'Everything, according to Ethel. When he wanted to join the Marines, Robert and Ethel both asked me to change his mind and. I honestly did my best, told him some reality horror stories, but he was dead set on it. Maybe he read too many Victor and Commando comics growing up. Robert accepted Kevin's decision, but Ethel believed it was me who influenced him, that I'd encouraged him. He was killed in Ulster by a bomb, torn to bits, sealed coffin. She never spoke to me again.'

'That's heavy.'

'Aye, well worse things happen at sea.'

'How've you been then?' McDowall asked him. 'Must be a year since we last spoke.'

Alec slurped the whisky, spilled some and wiped his sleeve. 'I've been not bad.'

'Any news about your family, Alec? Any word about your wife and daughter? Angela used to ask about them often,' Alec stared into the whisky shaking his head.

'Don't know where they are or how they're doing. I got Christmas cards from Anne for a wee while which gave me hope they would come back. Written by Sheila obviously, but that faded away after a while. Then my letters came back stamped, "not at this address." They'd moved away from Boston; telephone number was changed. The US Postal Service is worse at disclosure than an Irish bank. No forwarding address they told me. I phoned them once and a very polite lady told me it was impossible to pass on any information without the permission of the addressee and I was not on the list. But this is not what we should be talking about. Let's stick to the present. Have you and Deputy Dawg made any progress with Angela? I want their names, Frank.'

McDowall checked the door was shut fully. 'We have two

main suspects, two brothers called McGrath. Do you know them at all?' Alec shook his head. McDowall regretted mentioning them by name immediately. 'That's confidential anyway and for now they are both on the run, missing. We had one gabby informer who absconded, but we'll have him back and grill him. There's also a lassie who was at the party with Angela, but she's gone walkabout.'

'Beth Sharkey?'

'Beth indeed.'

'When you get them back? Not very promising, is it?'

McDowall squirmed and finished his drink. He looked about him then set the empty glass on the rosewood table. No coaster. Ethel would have a fit. 'I should go back upstairs I'll come back and see you in a minute, let you know what's to happen and that. You can decide what you want to do about Robert. He's in the hospital morgue for now but the Co-op will collect him today.'

Alec said nothing, engrossed in the framed picture of a bus run to the beach at Saltcoats.

McDowall left him, closing the door softly.

In the hallway, Brown was watching the ghoul squad wrestle the shell round the bend in the stair, sweating faces contorted, dying to swear. They could all hear the body thumping about inside. The WPC stood on the landing above them, hands over her mouth. She'd learn soon enough there was no dignity in this, so it might as well be now. McDowall took Brown by the arm and steered him into the kitchen.

'Well, what do you have, what's the story?'

Brown scanned his notes. 'No apparent violence, death is estimated by the doctor at about 06.00 this morning. No suspicious circumstances. Almost certainly a suicide, he says.'

'We can all just bugger off home then, case solved? As far as I'm concerned Ethel and Robert were murdered as surely as Angela. So, no rest for us till everybody involved is in the clink. What we have here is Macbeth and King Lear all rolled in one.' He stuck his hands in his pockets jingling his change and they watched the black Sherpa van take Ethel off.

He muttered something Brown didn't catch.

'What was that, Frank?'

'I said, Mills of God...' McDowall lit up.

'Eh?'

'From the Bible Brown, about revenge. Says, *"the Mills of God grind slow but exceeding sure."* To be honest, I thought God would have gotten his finger out years ago and maybe ground a bit faster and sooner. I'll tell you this, if God worked for me, I would sack him for all this mess. Go start the car. I'll not be long and there are two files on the back seat of the car you need a read at. I'll bide here a wee bit and look around Angela's room again. I'll be out when I have a chat with Alec.'

'You okay, Frank?'

'Right as rain so I am, everything's just torrapeachie. Off you go for a read, there will be questions later.'

When McDowall got upstairs, he faltered at the bedroom door and stood there aimlessly, out of steam. He couldn't go in just pulled the door over slowly till it clicked shut. Enough for now. He went back downstairs into the living room. Alec stood by the window still holding the whisky bottle, its level somewhat diminished. He'd discarded the glass. Buster came up behind Alec and nudged his leg, looking up at him with watery eyes, slowly thumping his tail against the armchair.

'You're wondering what all this means, dug.' Buster slobbered over his sleeve licking off the whisky. 'Logically I should take you a one-way trip to the vet, but it's a toss-up which one of us he puts down. Maybe do us both cheap.'

'Are you taking the dog with you?' McDowall asked. Alec ruffled its ears. 'Can't do that. I stay in the high flats so it's a rigid no pets rule. Buster is done for unless somebody takes him.'

McDowall looked at the dog. The dog looked at him, whined, and tilted its head.

'I'll take him,' he blurted.

Alec gawked at him. 'I don't recall your Irene being a dog lover.'

'If I want a dog, I'll have a bloody dog. My uncle Tommy had our dog put down when I was ten, for convenience's sake. I loved that mongrel and I never forgot the look on its face out the car back window as he drove away. Haunts me still and this thing is looking at me the same way. I was powerless then but not now. So, just you shut up and give me the dog.'

'Irene will not like this.'

McDowall took the lead off the hat stand. 'There's a bonus.'

Alec produced Buster's bowl and dog food. The dog scampered out the door and waited on the path while they locked up. McDowall put Buster on the back seat where the dog slobbered down the back of Brown's coat. He and Alec exchanged smiles. Curtains twitched across the road. Nosy neighbours.

'Do you need a lift somewhere, Alec?'

'Naw! I'll walk a wee bit then I suppose I better at least try to go down see Lorraine. There will be lots to do. Never planned a triple funeral before. Any idea when we'll get Angela and her Mum and Dad back?'

'You know I can't say when. Robert is straightforward as the hospital issued a death certificate, but Ethel will be a post-mortem. Depends what that turns up. Be Wednesday at earliest.'

Alec snibbed the gate and stood gazing back at the house. Ethel was now going to be cut up the same as Angela. So much promise destroyed over the space of a short weekend. Crushing as his own pain was it didn't compare to what Robert had suffered in his mind and Ethel's soul couldn't bear. Both had escaped by different routes to the same destination. Wherever that was.

McDowall fidgeted with his hands in his coat pocket.

'I wish I could do or say something that mattered, Alec.'

Alec shrugged. 'All things pass Frank. Are you sure about Buster? You're not getting yourself into bother with Irene?'

'Naw! She'll love it, company about the house.'

Alec snorted. They shook hand.

'I'll be in touch over what we find,' McDowall told him. 'We'll have it all sorted out quickly. Come into the station and see me anytime.'

Alec gripped McDowall's hand tight, leant in close. 'I'll be looking as well so don't take a year to find the murdering bastard who took Angela.'

McDowall and Brown drove away leaving Alec standing in the drizzle. God, he wanted the last of that whisky bottle, but he resisted and strode off down the hill. Nothing in his head now but a huge funeral pyre of his whole family consumed forever. His old raw emotional wound of Anne and Sheila sprang into flame with growing pain and guilt.

Better for these McGrath scum if McDowall found them first.

Alone in his Spartan flat with his demons and nightmares, staring out at the rain, Alec sank back into the painful shredding memory when Sheila left him. He remembered the dreadful day he had marched all the way to Bearsden from Paisley to see her parents, desperate for any shred of an answer. Sheila's dad was stony faced, never allowed Alec past the porch out the rain. Her mother abused him over her husband's shoulder. Very restrained of course, muted because of the neighbours. No way were they going to tell him anything, doubtless sworn to secrecy.

'You have only yourself to blame,' she'd told him. 'All those times away at the drop of a hat with Sheila worried sick. No money, no life to speak of. And then the drinking. You're a monster. I told her to leave you.'

Her husband had intervened.

'You and your bloody Marines,' he'd growled. 'Why didn't you take the job offer in my business, be a real husband and father? Do you have any idea how distraught Sheila was when you re-enlisted for a third tour? Did you have a death wish? Did you need the adrenalin burst as badly as the drink? And one thing spiralling into another till it overwhelmed Sheila. My daughter was never cut out to be a Marine wife, you knew that. I said so at the time, but you blanked it out. I know you loved her and she you, but loneliness withered her.'

Alec had stood mute, unable to respond, for this had been his last port of call, hoping to find some explanation, some help. He remembered the crushing humiliation and pain of his tears mingling with the rain. Bled out of words at last, they had stood for a time silently, Alec mutely begging they would say where his wife and child were, while they just wished he would go away.

Her mother eventually had turned in tears and gone inside. Sheila's dad came out into the rain with an umbrella, took Alec's arm and guided him down the path.

The rest of his leave he'd passed crushingly alone and in a fog. Robert and Frank tried to help him, but he evaded all contact, refusing to answer the door to them and ripped the phone out.

He'd broken on a reef and sank into utter despair. He was on the bedroom floor in soiled shorts and a pool of vomit when two Ministry of Defence Plods and a Marine officer from welfare forced the door. One of the Plods lifted his head by the hair and compared his face with a photograph.

'Are you Sergeant Alexander Stewart, Royal Marines,

RM206862? You are honking, mate, a total crab.'

Alec only managed to croak and wave his arms about as they dragged him into the bathroom and dumped him under the shower. On the way to Faslane Base they'd stopped at Shandon Brae to let him throw up and smoked while he recovered from the dry heaves. One gave him a bottle of water and a Mars bar which he managed to keep down. They handed him over to the Duty Officer in the guardroom and the system enfolded him in its barbed wire embrace.

He'd felt safe.

Back at Golspie Road McDowall faced reality. It was one thing to promise Alec he'd find the McGraths, another in the execution. Everything hung on finding Beth Sharkey and Michael Brodie, both still in the wind. It would take hours of plodding through the files and lots of footwork to find either of them. Only then could he bleed them for the McGraths and then Hammond. McDowall banged the paperwork on their desk in front of Brown.

'I'll write up the fatality report and do the crime scene narrative.' McDowall began to realise how much he had taken on and was glad he had Jim Brown working the case with his experience and street cred. 'We know who the guilty are and I want to destroy any notions you might still have that the good guys are winning.'

'Were you always this cynical?'

'Ever since I woke and found my dad packing my Christmas pillowcase at the foot of the bed. Very traumatic.'

Brown opened the file at the school portrait of Angela. McDowall shrugged his coat onto the floor and sat, spoke from memory.

'Angela Stewart, twenty years of age, late daughter of Robert and Ethel, all of them deceased between Friday night and now.' He picked up the picture, traced her face with his fingertips. 'Angela wasn't as pretty as this when last I saw her and now, she's on a slab. She's had everything taken from her and we will get who was responsible.'

The phone rang. McDowall lifted the handset and dropped it back on the cradle. 'We should put all our cunning and ability into cases, but never ever our hearts and souls. If we do, all this crap and evil will corrode us. Never become the thing you hate. Break your heart so it will, it has mine.'

'And is your heart in this Frank?'

'Heart and fucking soul.'

Brown put the files in his briefcase, took out a box of pens and a packet of paper hankies and arranged them on his side of the desk. McDowall admired the briefcase.

'Going on holiday?'

'Present from the wife on my detective promotion.'

McDowall grinned and took a brown paper supermarket bag out the desk drawer. 'This is my briefcase, got it free with the messages.' He tapped the combination lock on the Brown's briefcase. 'Just as well it's lockable for this place is full of bastard thieves, and if you can remember the numbers by the end of the first week that'll be a bonus. When I've done the suicide paperwork, I'm off to have a chat with

McVicar. I'm meeting him in the Whip Me and Screw Me.'

'The what?'

'The pub on the corner.'

Brown smiled. *"The Whippity Scourie?"*

'My name is better.'

'What if Tannock is looking for you, it's only 5p.m., what will I tell him?'

'The truth, he'll no believe you and think you're taking the piss, it'll do wonders for your career.' He paused in the door. 'By the by, Tannock has told me we're off to Glasgow Wednesday morn so I'll give you the heads up on that tomorrow, eight sharp. Some free crime prevention advice, lock that box of pens away safe or you'll never see them again. This place is full of thieves. Be early tomorrow.'

'Hope Irene likes the dog. It'll be a nice surprise for her.'

'Hope you get the dog dribble off the back of your coat.'

Irene McDowall struggled out the taxi, surprised to see her husband's car in the drive. Wonders never cease, home on time for once. An avalanche of bags spilled from the back seat, one of them bursting and dumping packets of croissants, muesli, brown bread, venison sausages, and tins of Baxter's soup over the pavement. All from Marks & Spencer too. She scowled at the dented cans then the young driver.

'I can remember a time when the taxi driver would help a lady with her bags.'

The driver was unperturbed. 'Ah mind ma Granny telling

me that.'

Irene gathered up the bags and treated him to her best witch glare. She left the rear car door open to let in the drizzle and waddled to the gate, bumping it open. McDowall had been watching for her and opened the front door. He opened his mouth but she barked before he could speak.

'Don't just stand there, Francis. Come and help me get the stuff on the pavement. I don't suppose it crossed your mind to come and get me at the shops?' He ambled out into the puddles, the water soaking into his slippers. Irene looked pointedly at his feet and put on her crabbit face. 'If I'd intended your Christmas present to be worn in the garden, I would have bought you wellingtons.'

He smiled. 'Frog or elephant ones?'

Unamused she pushed past and sailed into the house. McDowall cradled the spilled shopping in both arms and juggled up the path. He might get a circus job when he retired. Irene was all business in the kitchen tins and packages disappearing into the MFI units. It seemed to him the cupboards must be devouring all this food as he was never home.

'Did you pick up Grant today?' Irene asked.

Here we go he thought, filling the kettle. 'Sadly, I couldn't. I had to hang back and discuss mighty and impotent stuff with God himself.'

Irene brushed him out of her path and he subsided into the kitchen chair trying to decide if he had sat down or been shoved. Not important, leave it.

'I know fine well you didn't pick Grant up. I told Moira you could. She had to get that nice neighbour of hers to do it.'

'I know you said I could, but just saying so will not make it happen.'

'You didn't phone. You really must try and put your family first, Francis. Would that not be nice for a change? Did the thought never cross your mind to phone and offer to get me at the Cooperative when I finished work?'

McDowall got up and tried to help her by placing the eggs in the fridge but she dragged the box away from him. 'You're no help at all, the eggs go in the chicken egg basket Moira got in Aberfoyle.'

Provoked by her attitude he failed to hold his tongue. 'Look here, Irene! Who do you think I work for, the Cleansing? Do you think I can just take off when I like? Excuse me, this interview is now suspended while I bugger off and get my grandson from nursery.'

'You should plan things better, you're just a dog chasing its own tail.'

'Will there ever come a day when I will do something right in your eyes? He stepped aside and cracked his head off the edge of the cabinet door. A tin of asparagus fell and rolled away across the floor. 'Bollocks! That fucking does it, Irene, enough is enough.'

Her jaw dropped, she stared at him, amazed. 'Don't you bring your gutter station manners into my house. What's got into you, Francis?'

Buster barked. The two of them looked at the back door

then each other.

'Go and deal with that,' she ordered him. 'It's that mongrel from forty-two in our garden again.' She resumed packing away the shopping, dismissing his petty rebellion.

McDowall gripped the worktop. 'No, it's not forty-two's mongrel actually.' He stepped to the door and let Buster in, panting and sliding over the tiles leaving a trail of muddy paw prints. Irene gave a tiny shriek and stared open mouthed, lost for words. McDowall picked a towel up and began to dry the dog.

'That's the first time in years I've been able to shut you up, Irene. This here is Buster. He is my dog and will be sleeping in the back hallway.'

Irene stared from him to the dog. 'Are you mad, Francis? Have you taken leave of your senses? Did we not decide on a no pets rule? What do you mean, your dog? Where did it come from?'

McDowall knelt and ruffled the dog's ears. 'We, decided on nothing, you just telt me as I remember. This was Ethel Stewart's dog until this morning, but I'm looking after it now. It's cried Buster, but I might call it Dug!'

Irene opened and closed her mouth three or four times. 'God Almighty,' she croaked. 'And why can't Ethel look after her own dog?' She waved a hand to ward off the dog. 'It's not staying here, take it back, get rid of it!'

McDowall grabbed his coat off the back of the kitchen chair, kicked a loose can of peas across the floor. 'Ethel can't take care of her dog anymore because she is the poor besom who topped herself this morning up the Castle. Oh, and her husband Robert is deid as well from a heart attack on top of a massive stroke. Do you mind their daughter, Angela? She'll not be at the choir or helping at the church fete anymore, for she's deid as well. That's if you could bother your arse asking me what I did today. I don't know what's upset you most, Irene. Is it the dog or Robert and Angela being dead, or just the sheer inconvenience of being down a soprano in the choir?' He put the lead on Buster. 'Or are you most peeved about not knowing all this from your gossipy friends? This is my dog, it stays.'

Dismayed, she flopped into a kitchen chair unable to retort until she could speak. 'I tell you this, Francis, you can decide between that beast and me. Just like you decided between your fancy woman across the back garden and me.'

'You can't pull that emotional knife you keep forever handy and stick me with when it suits. And don't give me any more ultimatums, Irene, you might regret the outcome. I was talking to Alec Stewart today who's had more trouble in his life than you have ever seen. Don't push it. I've had a disaster of a day, thanks for asking. The dog stays and you will just like it or lump it. And another thing, stop calling me Francis.' He slammed out the back door. Feckit.

Walk the dog.

Sweetie shop for caramel wafers.

Pub.

Not necessarily in that order.

*

CHAPTER 6

Brown spent another three hours at the desk but left when he realised he was no longer reading or absorbing anything and just staring numbly at the words. Death was a growth industry it seemed to him and it was time to go home. The desk phone rang as he got to the door, someone from a payphone, he heard the pips and the coins dropping, drew breath to reply but was interrupted.'

'It's me.'

'Hullo Frank, checking up on the slaves are you?'

'Checking you're not into my biscuits or using my teabags. Near done yet?'

'About half way. I need to ask you a question.' Silence; only the humming of the open line. 'Will Hammond be looking for out fugitives as well as us?'

A long pause until Brown asked, 'are you still there?'

'Hammond can't afford to let any of them testify so best we find them first.'

'And what if Alec Stewart finds them first?' McDowall hung up.

Brown drove home in a daze to his third floor flat on Main Road. He flung his coat at the hook, dumped his briefcase on the floor, grabbed a beer from the fridge and turned on the stereo. Carol had already left for her nightshift at Thornhill Hospital. She'd left a note saying they needed to get a dog so as someone ate his dinner, now cremating in the oven. He crossed to the record player and dropped the arm on the vinyl. Dvorjak swelled and filled the room. He kicked off his shoes and closed his eyes sinking back in the armchair. He couldn't relax, his brain was spinning as fast as the turntable. The briefcase fell over and spilled the files across the floor as if they were creeping across the carpet like a living thing. He gulped at the Bud, scooped up the files and dumped them on the dining table. He moved to the couch after a while and at some point, the cold official language overtook him and he fell asleep surrounded by the disembowelled folders.

He'd opened a tomb.

The buzzsaw ringing of the phone just after six sent Brown fumbling blindly over the back of the couch for the handset, flopping himself and the couch onto the floor in a shower of cushions and loose A4 paper. By the time he found the handset whoever it was had rung off. He went to shave, the face staring back at him had crusty dribble down one side. He groaned and plunged his face into the sink and tried to drown himself. If he had a gun like an American detective on television, he could have shot himself. The phone rang again but he ignored it and was packing the files back in his briefcase when McDowall was waking the whole close with battering at his door.

McDowall pushed past him. "What time do you call this? You look awful, did somebody poke you in the eyes with a stick?'

'I was up all night with research. I just need coffee.'

'Coffee?' McDowall scoffed. 'Real polis drink tea. Coffee then, while you peel the bog paper off your kisser. Open your eyes when you shave or get an electric one.'

'Was Irene okay about the dog, pleased?'

'You're pushing it now.'

'I'd have paid good money to see that.'

'When I left this morning, Buster was drooling the laundry basket.'

Brown followed him into the modern MFI kitchen and got the kettle on. They leant against the kitchen units while he teased the pink toilet roll from his chin and McDowall bit his nails.

'So, Jim, did you get much homework done?'

'Your admin is horrendous. Everything stuffed away anywhere. Near midnight before I got home. Its shambolic, the station bin area is more organised.'

'Shambolic, is it? A vast improvement for me, glad I made an effort. You and Joyce should form a gurning club. Give us ma coffee then.' McDowall slurped, made a face, turned and spat it down the sink. 'God Almighty! That's reeking, what the hell am I drinking?'

'Camp Coffee, its chicory, Carol and I like it.'

McDowall washed his mouth out with water. 'I'm poisoned so I am. Not another word out of you till I get a mug of tea. Who's the most important man we keep a close eye on in this case?'

'Alec Stewart.'

'Damn right, good boy.'

'Hammond isn't connected to Angela's death.'

'I don't care.'

Michael Brodie was as stupid as he was cocky. He made the bad mistake of staying in Paisley and collecting debts he was owed from users he supplied. Both were in Hammond's employ and in no time at all they had sold his whereabouts to Gillespie for a fifty pence bag.

'Brodie's surfaced.' Gillespie announced as he burst into Hammond's office.

'Crap does float then. Do we know where he is now?'

'You couldn't make it up, thick as mince so he is. He actually asked Tam at the cafe to get him a taxi to the Waterloo Street bus station. Off to the coast to see family, he said. I know his mother-in-law lives in Port Glasgow and he has a sister in Saltcoats. I'll be checking her out first anyway, then the mother-in-law.'

Hammond banged the desk with the flat of his hand.

'Yes! I want this prioritised, so forget the Liverpool trip until this Brodie thing is cleared away. Get a hold of those two dimwit McGrath brothers and have them help clear up the mess they've made. Take Gerry and Steff, we can count on them, but make sure the McGraths take part for I want them chained to us by this. I'll leave the mechanics of it to you. Anything else?'

'Nothing you'll like. I had our properties checked during the night and those that Brodie knew about are empty. Plundered.'

'Get Brodie killed.'

Gillespie nodded. 'Are they still to do the Central Station pickup? Our suppliers will not be best pleased if anything goes wrong. Trusting them two bampots gives me the heebie-jeebies.'

'Once they're in deep over Brodie we'll own them. Get at it. That Gordon will be in one of two places, either the bookies or the Stag Bar at the west end. Get the boys, press-gang the brothers and wrap the Brodie boy up by tonight.'

'Okay. I'm on it.'

'I want the McGraths feart, not done in. They're no use dead although that might change soon if they don't perform. I expect you to keep your two sidekicks in hand about the McGraths, but Brodie goes. Are you tooled up?' 'As ever.' Gillespie tapped his coat pocket.

Steff and Gerry were waiting for Gillespie at the Junction 27 Cafe in the lorry park at the back of Gilmour Street Station, sitting in a hot fug of smoke at the usual debris strewn table with cold tea and an overflowing ashtray. Both were in their late twenties. Steff had black flowing locks swept back in a DA. Gerry was bald, sensitive about it and covered it with a flat cap, but best not mention that in front of him. Neither drank heavily nor did drugs which made them almost saints among the rest of the foot soldiers. Best not to make jokes about that as well. This was their local, where they could always be found between jobs, smoking and drinking endless mugs of tea. Neil always knew he could contact them here or at the warehouse. Steff never said much except to nod in agreement with anything Gerry said. He wore a donkey jacket which never seemed to leave his back. Always carried a rolled newspaper with him, stuffed in his pocket. More than one sad bastard had regretted winding him, for inside the paper was a steel CO2 gas refill for an extinguisher. It always came as a bit of a shock when Steff dispensed a slap with his paper and said it was just giving folk the bad news.

'Huv ye heard the news?' Gerry would ask a slow payer.

'Naw? That's a pity. Steff, gie this bhoy the bad news.' Gerry always wore a double-breasted Burberry coat fully belted up, its capacious inside pockets accommodating a bottle of Irn-Bru and a machete in a leather sheath.

'What's on the day then?' Gerry asked when they were settled in the Sherpa van.

'We're off to Port Glasgow. We'll be picking up the McGrath brothers. Brodie has been flushed out and we are going to take our property from his thieving broken hands.'

'Nothing like starting the day with a good hiding.'

Gillespie grinned wolfishly. 'A hiding won't cut it now.'

'It's the full bhuna then?'

'Once we have what we want we'll be seeing a friend off to the coast.'

Eddie McGrath was in the Stag Bar finishing off his first pint of the day and decided he'd have another. His brother was outside in the lane, guarding the stash and doing some passing trade from both the corner pubs and the office block across from the Paisley High Court. Amazing the number of lawyers and such that smoked the weed. Feck Gordon, let him stew. The pub was a midden, smelly, badly lit. A place where sleeves stuck to years of filth on the tables, smeared with the remains of beer and pie breakfasts with pools of spilled drink on the bar and floor. The air was rank with a blend of stale beer, vomit, urine, and unemptied ashtrays hidden under small mountains of crushed fag ends. The unwashed clothes and bodies of the regulars was enough to gag a ferret. A bear would have been at home here. A swaying boozer lurched out the gent's toilet with his fly down, followed by a peroxide blonde woman who crashed into a table and a scuffle broke out.

Eddie lit up and leered at his reflection in the flyblown gantry mirror.

What a night with that Angela, what a rare goer she'd been, drugged up to the eyeballs, sweet as toffee. Only problem was she'd croaked it and the cops were sniffing around big time. Now that McDowall was on their case, they'd have to make sure Beth Sharkey didn't flap her trap about anything to do with Angela. Another session with her would be good as well.

He banged on the bar and another lager was put up.

Gordon should have stood up to that slick bastard Hammond when he'd taken Liverpool off them? It would be easy to kill the fucker, over in a second.

He went to the gents and on returning found an old

boozer drinking his pint. Eddie punched him on the side of his head tossed him to the deck and stomped him a couple of times. Stepping away laughing he became aware the other trogs were arming themselves and cutting off his escape. He gave the old fella a parting kick and legged it out the door down the block where Gordon was. Three dossers screeched after him as far as the door but like vampires stayed out of the light.

In the lane he ran straight into Gillespie who had Gordon by the throat. Gerry and Steff came from behind, grabbed a brother each and rammed their faces up against the roughcast. Gillespie tipped the metal bin over into the long grass with his foot and retrieved the plastic wash bag from underneath.

'That'll do nicely. Now listen up you two glaikit bastards, here's what's happening. Mr Hammond is not pleased that when you were giving him the Liverpool pitch you neglected to fully inform us of the major problem developing because of you two.'

'What problem, Mr Gillespie? Everything's fine.'

'Really? Best rethink that. Refresh what memory that hasn't been drug-rotted about how Friday night went at your den up the Feegie?'

'A party is all.'

'A party is all?' Gillespie punched him low down, Gordon fell to his knees and spewed. 'More like the animals escaped Calderpark Zoo.'

Eddie broke free and launched himself at Gillespie. Mistake! Gerry felled him with a smash to the throat with his rolled newspaper then slammed his boot on his neck pining him to the ground.

Gillespie continued. 'You see, Mr Hammond has been told, through his polis sources, that a lassie was done to death at this party and in a way that Mr Hammond finds, what were his words again? Oh aye, it was, "abhorrent, horrendous, reckless, and above all stupid." He was under the delusion that you two were meant to be guarding his hoard at the flat and is worried now that the doings there have focused McDowall's attention on all his affairs. Instead of doing the job you're paid for he finds that you have dogged off and got that useless tosser Brodie to do the night watchie for you, and it's all gone pear-shaped. To make things worse, Frank McDowall is on the case and is even now slavering at our heels like a bloodhound. As if that's not bad enough this Stewart lassie's uncle, a guy called Alec Stewart, is asking about you two all over the West End. Not good.'

Eddie spat. 'We're not afraid of some auld tosspot.'

Gillespie smiled at that. 'Is that right? I would be if he was looking for me. That aside, seems the money due us for supplying your wee soiree is now missing as well as any unsold product. Now, it might well be in some cops' locker, maybe actually in the evidence room at Golspie Road, but we hear that's not the case. Is it stashed in your mother's hoose, or maybe in your pockets at this very moment?' Gillespie raised his eyebrows, waited for a response. 'Naw? See, where it's no stashed is Mr Hammond's safe. A mystery. Where could it be? Starter for ten, no conferring.'

Gordon spoke up. 'Brodie said still in the flat, but it's still crawling with cops when we went back. We need to wait till the coast's clear.'

'Did he now? Suddenly you're full of informative ideas, but I hear different. I think he's scarpered with the dosh and drugs and you two have nae idea where he is. We've been to the flat, and what did we find there; Gerry?'

'A big hole smashed in the partition wall Neil, where Mr Hammond's cash was safely stashed. Nothing there now, just a big hole.'

'That's right my son. Just... a... big... hole, which is where you two'll wind up soon if I don't get answers. Money gone and not so much as an IOU left. You must be crapping yourselves, or if you had two brain cells you wid be. Brodie is your man and you two are liable for his sins.'

'Haud oan,' Gordon shouted. 'That's out of order, we took nowt.'

Steff punched him again. Gordon fell to his knees beside his brother. 'Jist shut yer hole.'

'Thank you, Steff. Where was I? Oh right, I mind now. You both vouched for Brodie and apart from the lassie being killed during your sordid wee games there are other problems. First is that there is now a great spotlight shining on any connection with Mr Hammond between your clusterfuck, the dead lassie, Brodie, and you two. Second problem is the runaways. Brodie and this whore you supply and pimp, Beth Sharkey, need to be dealt with. Mair bother. Lucky for you two Brodie has surfaced like a turd in Port Glasgow and we,' he made a circling motion with his finger. 'This happy wee gang, are going to deal with your mess for we're off on a wee bus run. You know, singsongs and rounders on the beach.'

'Back of the bus cannae sing, cannae throw yer granny and that. And the pokeyhats are on you two.'

Gordon struggled up. 'If we're going to help, we need something in return. We want the Liverpool thing back.' Gillespie shook his head, gestured to the boys who dragged them onto their knees. He then made clear he was done talking by pulling out the famous Persuader, checked the chamber, shoved the muzzle against Gordon's eye.

'This Mr Nice Guy thing disnae suit me. Are you getting in the van, or what? Van or shot, van or shot?' he chanted waving the muzzle in front of their faces. 'Make your mind up time.'

The muzzle looked like a railway tunnel with no light at the end to Gordon so the, 'or what', option did not appeal. Even Eddie had the brains to hold his tongue. They were marched to the van and Gerry opened the back doors. The McGraths froze when they took in the bag of tools piled in on the floor and recoiled. Gordon felt the Webley behind his ear and. Gillespie shoved them inside onto a mound of ropes sacks and rolls of plastic sheeting. 'Nervous boys? You should be.' The doors banged shut.

Alec had a doctor's appointment for three that afternoon after coming off his early shift. Everything was behind at the surgery of course, and picking up a copy of *National Geographic* he spent the waiting time staring at a picture of the rainforest. When his name was called, he missed it the first time, only responding when the receptionist raised her voice.

Doctor Mandelstam had retired and been replaced by

Doctor Turnbull; a young GP who always seemed slightly lost. Probably imagined himself in Harley Street, so Johnstone was no doubt a culture shock. Meant well, but had no idea about combat stress, always avoided eye contact. Alec took a chair and Turnbull reached for his prescription pad, already scribbling a repeat. Same old same old.

'Mr Stewart, how are you now, much improved, I hope?'

'How are you finding your new medication, the Elavil?'

'As useless as the last lot, you might as well prescribe whisky and be done with it. I'm still not sleeping, fragmented by the same dreams.'

'You're ex-military, have you thought of applying to Erskine Hospital, seek psychiatric help? I could refer you, but you need to ask for help. Do you want referred there as an outpatient?'

'I'd sooner fucking die.'

Turnbull sighed. 'Depression is common to men like yourself. Erskine would give you some purpose, help you to rebuild, allow the medication time to take effect. I'll prescribe a higher dosage for you.'

Turnbull was lost, his eyes downcast, the Biro clicking like a morse key. Frightened by what he might see. Alec knew he was well outside the boy's experience, and found himself outside in the waiting room with a prescription for more antidepressants and double the dosage for sleeping pills. Again! An addition was a referral letter for assessment at Dykebar Hospital. He left the surgery and sat on a wet bench in Craigdonald Park staring at the daffodils swaying in the wind. and totally drained of emotion. 'I wandered lonely as a cloud...' sprang into his head. He knew now that McDowall, for all his venom and good intention, would never find who'd debased and killed Angela, not in a month of Sundays. He was also constrained by the law he tried to serve and may as well handcuff himself. Alec would do some unfettered asking of his own about the party and who held it. He'd start right now with whoever owned or let the flat. It was high time he saw the place where Angela had been torn from this life.

McDowall might be constrained by the law.

Alec would make his own.

Standing rigid outside the Knox Road tenement Alec stared up at the top floor windows where Angela had died, gathering the courage to go in. He shoved aside the sheeting over the closemouth. By the time he reached the top landing, he felt as though he was wearing divers' boots and stood staring at the battered door, inert as Lot's wife. Four days ago, Angela had come here and never left. A length of two-by-two had been nailed up to secure the door. Alec checked over the banister, listening, but all was quiet. He took two steps back and kicked the door in, waited as the echoes died. Nobody came. He took a deep breath and strode into the hallway. To his left the bedroom door was open, He entered reluctantly, dreading his reaction. A huge freshly broken hole had been torn in the plasterboard wall.

The bed.

He could hardly bear to look at the bed. Soiled and stained, the reeking mattress askew. Where they had violated Angela with bestial disregard and where the summer promise of her life had ended in demon darkness. He couldn't stay here, not now, not ever. It was plain what he had to do now. Heartbroken and in turmoil he turned away dropping his medication and referral letter to the floor. He knew what he would do now.

What he was good at.

Michael Brodie's partner, Chantelle, was in the waiting room at Port Glasgow Bus Station with their two children. Over an hour they'd sat here and although the baby was asleep at last her hand still rocked the pushchair automatically. The ten-year-old pressed his face to the window and spoke his first words of the day, 'There's Da getting aff the bus.'

Chantelle spotted him easily in his charity shop mismatch outfit and bright red backpack as he crossed the concourse in that furtive shambling way he had. It hadn't always been like this. He'd worked in the shipyards till he'd fallen into the basin while stoned out his box. After that it was petty crime, drugs and drink. She'd hoped for better but then he'd robbed her mum, the final straw when he stole from her own purse and kept the benefit money. Not even enough left to feed the weans. His peely-wally face wore it's permanent scowl and she realised in a moment of clarity that he was a total loser, would always be a loser. She wanted more for her kids.

'Right,' he growled, 'up the road.'

'Have you got any money, for ma mum says she'll feed the weans but not you.'

'Fuck her. Ah've goat money.' He pulled out a crumpled wad of notes and shoved them at her. 'Tons more where that came from.' He showed her inside his backpack.

Chantelle stared in disbelief, then found her voice. 'Whose money is that? Stolen for sure.'

'It's fair wages. I took it from the stash at Knox Road and a couple of other places.'

'Ya total zoomer, Ah've got news for you. Dae ye know Hammond sent that big grizzly Gillespie efter ye? Its aw roon the toon. He was down at your sisters in Saltcoats. Slapped her a wee bit. Did ye know that? Are you in the shite?'

'What've ye done? Who's this deid lassie they're talking' aboot? Dae ye know what? Ah'm fed up dashin aboot the place. That fuckin monster Gillespie is looking for gear and money that's went missing. Is that what's in the bag?'

'Naw! It's stole frae the McGrath brothers.'

'Fucksake!' Chantelle erupted. 'That means its Hammond's money. You and they two glaikit bastards are well matched. You three were meant to be guarding it, you are one idiot bastard. What are you going to do now? You better have a plan, ya twat.'

'Best plan ever. Some guys on the Port still owe me good cash for gear and I'll be collecting it over the next couple of days. We'll stay at your maw's place, then middle of next week I'll phone ma dad and take the ferry over the water. We'll be fine in Donegal.'

'Donegal! On a fucking farm? It's a ruin, falling to bits, damp as a sponge. Ma weans urnae goin there. No way, Jose. What about ma bingo and the hairdressing? I'm no living on a decrepit farm in the middle of a stinkin' bog. All ma pals are here. Ma mum and dad are here. What are we doing without the Social, the benefit money? Are you going to pit me back oan the street or just shit money out yer arse now?'

Brodie lost patience, slapped her. 'Shut yer whinging. I cannae think straight with your racket. Stay here if you like and wait till Neil finds you. Keep yer gob shut and let's get up the road.'

Chantelle cowered away, her face red and angry. 'Ah wiz goin out with the lassies tonight.'

'Dae Ah give a toss? 'You're goin' naewhere till I get all the money I'm due and the ferry tickets fur Ireland. It's the chippy and a bottle of White Lightning. Shuttit and shift yer arse.'

*

CHAPTER 7

Gillespie had an inkling where Brodie was, for the sister in Saltcoats had no good words for her brother and, after a wee slap or two, informed that the wee shite was hiding out with that cow of his. For all she cared Brodie could take a one-way sewage cruise on the sludge boat *M.V. Dalmarnock*. He'd probably run home to his mother-in-law. After press-ganging the McGraths, the crew headed for Chantelle's mother in sunny Port Glasgow.

The shabby blocks of tenements where she stayed on the hills above Port Glasgow was known as, *The Gibby*. A ghetto of boarded up windows, covered in reinforced plastic sheeting known as, "council curtains." Supposedly vandal proof but every kid in the scheme could open them to ransack and burn. The closes and the souls of those held there were full of crap and rubbish.

A block away there was a potholed car park beside a row of small shops which gave them a view up the street. Four of the shopfronts were steel-sheeted leaving only a fortified Asian grocer, a smelly charity shop, and a chippy. They would sit here until it was dark then go visit Brodie. Let the wee nyaff relax and think he was safe. Gillespie sat in the front with Gerry and Steff, the McGraths hunched on a box in the back. Gillespie could see in the mirror Gordon was apprehensive about the plastic and tools.

'Nervous, are we boys? Worried all that gear might be for you two?'

Gordon looked feart but calm to Gillespie, but Eddie the headbanger brother had a permanent snarl about him. He could be a whirling dervish that one.

'Relax.' He told them. 'If it was your time, we'd be scraping bits of you from the underside of the van by now. Tragic accident like.'

The light faded early and they got out in turns to pee in the bushes next the swing park. By 6p.m. it was dark, dim park lighting came on and the chippy began a steady trade. 'Hoo!' said Gerry. 'Clock this.'

Two figures staggered out the wrecked toilet bock. Neither was Brodie. They swayed against each other as if their feet were nailed to a deck. One produced a can of lager and tried to open it. His partner grew impatient and snatched it away, sending it flying along the footpath and bursting open in a foaming cascade. Both the drunks rolled over the metal fence and began to fight. One fell out of sight behind a bush and the other braced his hands on the top of the fence and began to stomp up and down on his mate's head.

Gillespie ordered. 'Go sort out they two blootered bampots.'

Gerry had only cracked the door when Brodie appeared from the swing park path, stopping when he saw the two drunks fighting.

Gillespie doused the courtesy light and barked. 'Stay!'

Brodie's baseball cap was pulled down to his ears, hoodie

up, and despite twitching looks behind him failed to spot the van. Brodie watched the fight for a bit, but when the victor reeled away with the can he strolled up to the fence, vaulted over and raked through the losers' pockets. Nothing there, so he gave him a farewell boot and went on towards the chip shop.

Gillespie snorted. 'You'd think he'd the brains to stay indoors? It's as well he's glaikit, makes it easier for us for we don't have to storm into the house like gangsters. We'll wait till he's left the chippy and then grab him. Gerry, take Eddie and go wait the other side of the swings by the toilets. Take that sandbag for his heid. You other two.' He pointed at Steff and Gordon. 'When they have him on the deck open the side door and I'll drive across the grass and we'll sling him in the back. Keep him quiet.'

Gillespie started the van, Gerry and Eddie ran over to the toilets and hid behind the bushes. Brodie came out with a newspaper parcel in both arms., scanning up and down the street before making for the park. As he came alongside the toilet block Eddie pounced and smashed him to the ground. The van revved over the kerb and drove quickly across the grass to the thrashing bodies. Brodie tried to fight back, but it was just pathetic panic stuff, girly slapping and squealing. Steff stepped out the side door and cracked him over the head with his newspaper club. They scooped him into the Sherpa and slammed the side door. Gillespie turned the van, stopped on the footpath.

'What's the problem now?' Gordon demanded.

Gillespie pointed. 'Bring the chips, I'm fucking starving.'

Steff drove the van up past Tate & Lyle's sugar refinery and out the Loch Thom Road to the visitor centre car park. Brodie had regained his wits by then and freaked out, screaming, scrabbling and kicking at the back doors. Gillespie shifted into the back and squatted on a box.

Brodie kept shrilling. 'Leave me alone! It's no ma fault, the money's still in the hoose.'

Gerry whipped the sandbag from Brodie's head.

'Would that be the money you took from Knox Road and the other two flats?' Gillespie asked. 'Only asking nicely the once.'

'Under the mattress in the baby's pram. Don't hurt me, please don't hurt me.'

'Now that saves a lot of bother.' He patted the side of Brodie's face. 'Who's a good boy then? Tell me everything you told McDowall. Don't lie, leave nothing out, we've got all night. If I'm convinced you might even get a chip. Begin!'

Brodie babbled all he had told McDowall, falling silent for short periods to think, and make sure he missed nothing out. It seemed they might have to shoot Brodie to shut him up and Gillespie boxed him across the head twice to silence him. 'Enough! Stoap yer bloody raving. Tell me where that whore of yours is disappeared to. Her that brought this Angela lassie.'

'I don't know. When the crazy stuff started in the bedroom I ran with the gear and the night's takings. I was just keeping it safe, I was bringing it back, honest. Not keeping it.'

'Pish!' Steff thumped him.

'Right!' said Gerry and gave him a dunt in the throat with his newspaper. Eddie sniggered. Gordon tried to stay out their way, be the invisible man.

Gillespie went on. 'Let's get it right here. Beth brought this Angela lassie to your pigsty, then she was drugged by these two,' he pointed to the McGraths, 'and gangbanged to death. Is that about the gist of it?'

'Aye, but I never touched the lassie. I shot the craw.'

Gillespie glared at the McGraths. 'He's your man. Does Brodie speak with forked tongue?'

'He's just a fibbing wee shit.' Eddie shouted. Gordon realised Gillespie was thinking about seriously hurting them if he suspected for an instant they had been involved in taking the goods and held his tongue.

'Where did this Beth bird go?' Gillespie asked.

'We went back to her place up the Castle. See, me and Eddie thought we best dump the deid lassie's car away from the flat, so we got the keys oot her handbag and took it. On the main road, we saw Beth in a phone box and picked her up.'

'Who was she phoning?'

'A taxi, but she was having to wait an hour so we got her in the car.'

'A taxi. How do you know that?'

'She telt us.'

'She telt you? Och, brilliant detective work. What a couple of brammers you are. Did you consider this taxi might be van sized, with a go faster stripe and blue disco light? Where is she now?'

'At her flat when we left her in the morning.'

'So, she's disappeared for now, but we will find her. It's best you two gormless gits do as you're telt from here on in. Let's get on with the job in hand. Time to visit Brodie's family, his wife and weans will be wanting their chips. Nobody better be shitting me, especially you two!' He pointed at the McGraths. 'Tie this wee chancer up with that tow-rope and get that bag back ower his heid. Gerry and Steff, you'll come in with me. Move!'

Brodie began to moan, banging his head off the side panel in time with his keening.

Gerry drove back to *The Gibby*, slowing down to check the crudely daubed numbers on the closemouth walls, stopping at number twelve. Gillespie glanced around. Most of the street lighting was out, the streets deserted. Litter hung like discarded Christmas decorations to the bushes and garden railings, plastic bags cracked in the wind, broken glass glittered like a disco ball.

Gillespie sighed. 'What a pit, like the Bogside after a night's rioting. Turn down the back lane on the left and we'll stop beside the bin shelter. Kill the lights.' The time for talking was done. Gillespie checked the lane and satisfied himself they could drive straight out the other end. 'Okay! Gerry, Steff, let's go. As for you two rapist bastards.' He glared at the McGraths. 'I've got the van keys. If you're thinking of taking a hike, don't. If I come back and find you two away with or without Brodie,

I'll run you down. And that's no a turn of phrase.'

Gillespie and his two boys disappeared into the unlit close. Litter snatched at their feet; a couple of cans kicked in the dark clattering away off the walls.

Steff swore. 'Ma Maw wid be scandalised. Dae these mingers never sweep the close?'

Gerry paused and struck a match. 'It's a bulldozer they need. Here, bottom left.'

The match singed Gerry's fingers and he dropped it into a darkness broken only by a faint orange glow from a solitary street light. Gillespie rattled the letterbox and a light came on inside shining out the fanlight above the door. They heard Chantelle shouting at Brodie.

'About time you were back, they chips better no be cauld. You better have pickles.'

The door opened in a splash of light. Gillespie stepped into the hall and punched Chantelle on her temple, dumping her on her back, out for the count.

'Sorry, nae pickles.' He stepped over her.

Her mother ran into the hall, poker in hand. She knew immediately who they were, stood silent and still, shielding the boy close behind her. The baby began to screech.

'Pram? The money?' Gillespie demanded.

She pointed into the first bedroom. Steff went in and overturned the pram raking through the blankets ripping the mattress out. He came out with bricks of notes packed inside a scabby holdall, and some gear stuffed into a plastic shopping bag. Gillespie hefted the holdall in his hand, knew right away this was nowhere near the amount taken from between the partition walls of the flats.

'Where's the rest of it?' Chantelle's mother dropped the poker. Gillespie sensed she was holding back, stepped close and grabbed the boy by the throat. 'Do not eff me about.'

'In a backpack under the sink, leave the boy.' Steff fetched it. Gillespie shoved the boy away and seized the mother by the chin.

'We were never here. There was no money. She,' he nodded behind him, 'fell over blootered and knocked herself out. Agreed?'

She nodded. 'Michael?' she asked.

Gillespie smiled. 'The bold Michael is none of your concern anymore. Did he really think he could pochle the likes of me? If you know what's good for you and your scabie brood, he was never here either. Like the polis say, he'll be assisting with our enquiries.'

When they returned to the van Gillespie was gratified to find the McGraths had decided bolting would not improve their situation in any way. Eddie had thumped Brodie a couple of times to shut up his whining, giving him a burst lip, which leaked out onto the sack over his head. Brodie had also peed himself, the urine stream ran along a gutter in the metal floor and dripped under the door, the air pungent with the smell. When the doors banged open Brodie panicked, his head jerking back and forth like a Meerkat, trying to anticipate where pain might come from now.

The money and gear were stuffed into the tool compartment under the passenger seat.

In the back, Gordon shuffled forward on his knees as they pulled away, leant on the back of the driver's seat.

'I'm thinking we'll get the train back, no haud you guys back any. You've got lots on.'

'Really? You two thinking is like crap running uphill. You can still share Brodie's hole you know. What do you think of that?'

*

CHAPTER 8

Between Port Glasgow and Kilbirnie the land is scattered with smallholdings and farms, linked together by single track roads and potholed farm or Forestry tracks. Not a busy place in the dark and there are spots shielded by high hedges where a man can carry out his business undisturbed. A windless night, a dim moon struggled to pierce the veil of low cloud lying in the hollows. Steff knew exactly where he was going for his cousin managed Kinnock Mains Farm just off the Dalry to Largs Road, so knew the ground. As he approached the farm gate, he turned the lights off and took a Water Board Road running north towards Pendeavon Reservoir. A mile short of the dam he followed a narrow dirt track where the high hedges rattled like witches' brooms along the panels. The van rolled crazily from side to side then the offside mirror broke with a bang. Brodie squealed.

'All very Tam O Shanter,' Gillespie thought.

The track faded out as the van rocked and rolled like a carnival ride. Brodie stirred himself and screamed.

'Where are we? What's happening? Christ's sake, I've got weans.' His voice rose higher still. 'Please let me go. Fucksake! Answer me! Please, DON'T KILL ME!' His voice rose into a shriek then broke into sobbing.

Eddie punched him. 'Shut yer gob, ya wee weasel. Don't worry about yer missus by the way, I'll be seeing tae her bigtime and the weans can be my slaves.'

Gordon spoke not a word and tried to keep well out the way. This trip was going like a runaway train and Casey Jones was not at the throttle. His only idea now was to survive the coming train wreck and last through the night.

Steff pulled into a gateway and stopped where a rough footpath snaked down to a bog where the cows gathered out the hard weather, shielded by a drystane dyke and a tight stand of hawthorn trees. Steff turned off the sidelights plunging them into darkness.

Gillespie paused halfway out the door. 'Please tell me somebody brought torches.' Silence. 'Arses! Get the headlights back on then.'

They pulled the sobbing and kicking Brodie out of the van down the field and dumped him by the bog, his muffled pleading unheeded. The engine noise had flung flocks of crows cawing into the night sky their wings rattling the bare branches like dry bones. The headlights threw their shadows long across the bog, dancing like black writhing tentacles, the trees stark and gaunt in the sudden blaze of false daylight. Two sheep watched; their demon eyes glowing. The place stank of cowshit and things long dead and rotting. Hysterical now, Brodie leapt up and ran but in the black dark under the hood he went full tilt into a tree and fell over stunned.

Gillespie pulled the tool bag out and tipped the contents on the grass. A pickaxe, spades, two saws, a crowbar, and a tool roll of butcher's knives and choppers. Gerry pulled Brodie up to his knees, ripped away the sack and held him by the hair. His face was streaked by sweat, tears, blood and mucus. He had chewed his bottom lip bloody.

'How is this thing going down then?' Steff asked. 'I think the new boys should do the business.' He laughed. 'They can show us what Brodie is made of.'

Gordon stepped back against the van, hands held out in front palms out. 'Whoa! Hold on a minute. Nobody said anything about doing anybody. I thought he wis gettin' a hiding.'

Eddie was right up for it, grabbed up the crowbar. 'I'll dae it. Never killed anything before apart frae dugs and such but never a real person.'

Brodie dry retched and fouled himself.

'Feksake, Michael! Have some pride. What a reek.' Steff kicked Brodie over on his side. Gillespie pulled the Webley out his pocket, checked the chambers. He pulled Gordon away from the van and shoved him in front of Brodie.

'Did I give you a choice? Pick up that knife or I swear to God and the Devil both that you and Brodie will be sharing the same hole this night.'

Gerry and Steff tore Brodie's jacket down to his bound elbows and ripped his shirt open. Gordon was trapped, caught in razor wire with no escape. He picked up the knife as if he were another person, that all this was nothing to do with him. Hands slick and trembling he stood in front of Brodie who flung himself against his legs, begging.

'Gordon! Don't do it, don't do it. We go way back.' Gillespie lifted the Webley and pointed it at Gordon's guts.

Brodie trembled and made animal noises his breathing hard and fast in great tearing hyperventilating gasps and shrieking terror in his eyes. His whole face crumbled like a trampled cake. Gillespie prodded the side of Gordon's head with the barrel of the Webley.

'It's an auld gun so this is, but it's served me well since Korea. Never misfired yet, but we can test that now if you like.' He cocked the hammer.

Gerry wound a rope across Brodie's mouth pulling it back hard choking off his screams. Brodie gnawed at the rope, blood running down his chin, his wrists raw and bleeding from his struggles to free himself. Gordon stared in horror at Brodie's wildly heaving chest and diaphragm and thought how blood looked like engine oil in the dark. The pistol muzzle ground into his ear. He closed his eyes and stabbed at Brodie's chest.

The blow had no strength behind it, the knife skidded off the sternum leaving a deep open gash up over his shoulder and took off a bit of his ear. Brodie fell onto his side wriggling and shrieking.

Gillespie shook his head. 'You're one useless bastard, what a fucking Jessie.'

Gerry seized Brodie by the hair, grabbed the knife from Gordon's hand and plunged it repeatedly in and out Brodie's midriff up under the ribs. Eddie brought the crowbar down on the top of Brodie's head felling him. His legs still jerked and kicked. Eddie pulled the crowbar free in a spray of gore then did an Apache war dance around the twitching body.

'Did you see that? Did you see his heid pop??'

Gillespie put away his Webley. 'We don't have all night, so chop-chop.'

They stripped Brodie, bagging his clothes for burning, their mouths covered from the steaming stench of dismemberment. Steff took four attempts to remove the head with the edge of a spade. Feet and hands came off quicker. They separated his joints at elbows, knees, and hips.

Among the bloodlust Gordon grabbed the bottle of Buckie doing the rounds and tried to keep up appearances. The body parts were shovelled into the peat bog. Using fence posts, they rammed the pieces down and covered the pit with slabs of peat. They turned the van around and drove back down to the Largs Road. Neil let the McGraths off in Paisley with a final warning.

'Breath a whisper about this and you'll get a one-way ticket back up there. Now fuck off.'

*

CHAPTER 9

For McDowall, the dog thing did not go well at all and Tuesday night he attempted sleep on a blow-up torture bed in the spare room, rolling onto the floor at regular intervals. He'd trailed the long phone lead up the stairway and barely got settled down before it rang. It was McVicar; apologising for missing their meet at the Western Infirmary Pathology lab but would be at the Procurator Fiscal's office in the morning.

McDowall snarled, 'You keep worse hours than Dracula.'

McVicar had already hung up. Wide awake now and with slim chance of any more sleep he crept downstairs and slipped out.

Exhausted with weeping, Irene had retreated to what she now called, "her room", and forted herself up. She heard him creeping about and came onto the landing in curlers and dressing gown. From the landing window she watched McDowall disappear along the path into the Bluebell Woods at the end of the street. She'd always realised most of his doings would remain a secret to her. Where on earth was a grown man going, wandering up the braes at this time of night?

McDowall was at the kitchen table with cereal and toast when an early morning phone call from the Deputy Fiscal Findo Gask summoned him to a meeting with McVicar. He'd just finished his tea when the doorbell chimed, and it was

Brown, fresh as a daisy. What it was to be young.

'What time do you call this?' McDowall growled at him.

'You said to be early. You look awful, are you okay?'

'Crabbit as ever. Leave me alone, back's broken, up half the night. I'm dying.'

'McVicar left a message at the desk. Apologises for missing you at the Western Infirmary yesterday and can we get him at the Procurator Fiscal's office this morning. Him with the queer name?'

'You mean Findo? McVicar phoned me last night as well, must be getting senile. The whole world is determined to wake me up.'

'You're in a state, what happened to your face?'

'Nothing. Walked into a big bush.'

Findo Gask had come from Perth originally. In his late thirties, single, lots of prosecutor experience from the Edinburgh, Perth, and Glasgow High Courts. Lived in the office his secretary said. McDowall was one of those who thought the only thing good that came out of these places was the road to Glasgow. Initially that had warped his thinking about Gask, but it did appear after a while that the boy knew his trade, for he'd helped McDowall put away more than a few villains over the years. As McDowall and Brown entered the lobby they met McVicar. He took McDowall's arm and led him to the side of a marbled pillar.

'I can't wait, Frank. I can tell you the forensic evidence is inconclusive.'

'Inconclusive! Utter pish! You know as well as me it was they two lowlife McGrath bastards instigated this. Can we charge the four druggies we found in the bedroom?'

'Not in my remit who gets charged. I've left a report upstairs with Gask and one for you in real English, an idiot guide. So far the Fiscal's Office supports the tragic accident theory and the raping and murder is a total loss.'

McDowall knew deep down he had expected this, knew in his gut that the whole thing was a chocolate teapot but was finding it hard to admit the reality in this. He'd known the evidence wasn't good but not for a second had he thought the McGraths would walk away scot-free.

'Did you hear that?' he asked Brown, who nodded. 'It's a liberty. We'll see the Gask boy about this.'

Up the stairs they went, entering the outer office but McDowall didn't pause as he passed the secretary.

'Morning, Kathleen,' he greeted her and kept going. 'Just going in to find Findo.'

Gask was at his cluttered desk behind ramparts of files and peered at them over his spectacles. 'Frank, I heard you on the stair like a Naval boarding party.'

McDowall grinned. 'I like to warn folk I'm on my way, like an away team bus trip. Any chance of a brew?'

Findo waved the papers in his hand at Brown. 'Good to see you, DC Brown. Still stuck with Frank? I can get my secretary to refer you to the Samaritans if you like.'

McDowall plopped into a chair, leant forward, and plunged right in. 'I met McVicar in the lobby, so what's all this kack he tells me about evidence being inconclusive?'

'It's very simple. The Fiscal won't proceed on the evidence available. Not enough for a jury. Best that we hold what cards we have for a better result later. The press may be in a frenzy but we're not going to be stampeded into a flawed prosecution which will fold at the first hearing. While you may suspect the McGrath brothers of having assaulted Angela Stewart and contributed to her death, nobody there can say they saw them do so. Probability is not evidence and forensics are weak. The trial judge would throw us out into the street with what we've got. We can go for manslaughter if we can prove they supplied the drugs.'

'I don't want the small fry, I can lift them any day of the week. I want the top of the dung heap and I'll do what needs doing to get them.' McDowall thumped the arms of the chair. 'This sucks so it does. God forbid the Fiscal be made to look a fool, he sure disnae need any help for that. I've got two witnesses who can put both the McGraths in the same place as the victim. One Michael Brodie and a lassie called Beth Sharkey.'

Findo grimaced. 'There are no statutes covering weird and evil people unless they break the law. Half the officers at your station, and yourself, would qualify. Neither of these witnesses are to be found.' Gask sighed. 'Brodie?'

McDowall squirmed. 'Absconded from Johnstone Police Station.'

'Uhuh. Beth Sharkey?'

'Vanished like a panto wizard in a puff of smoke.'

'Statements from neither I take it?'

'I'll have my hands on them shortly.'

'What crime do you intend to charge them with?'

'Drug trafficking, possession of same, just for starters.'

'They'll make a deal, plead guilty to possession. Brodie provided the drugs sold to him by the McGraths. It's stretching the elastic a bit., but I could push for culpable homicide.'

McDowall growled in frustration. 'I don't care if the charge is shooting Bambi's mother.'

Gask leaned back clasping his hands behind his head.

'What else have you got?'

'Murder! Angela Stewart is dead in case you've forgotten. As are her mum and dad.'

Gask sighed. 'I know very well a young girl is dead, I have the disturbing evidence before me. I am also aware of the ever-widening disaster that overtook her family. Ask yourself some hard questions. Can we prove murder?'

McDowall squirmed. 'We can't even place the McGraths in the same flat on the night never mind the same room as Angela.'

'Exactly. Will I tell you what half a dozen defence briefs I can name will do with this?'

McDowall ground out his cigarette, mangling it in anger. 'Get me a warrant to take them off the street and into my clutches. Put me in the same room as Brodie and Sharkey I promise results, we'll be home and dry.'

'No Frank, we'll not be home and dry. We'll be in the

deepest legal disaster imaginable.' Gask held up a hand to stop McDowall butting in. 'Wait! The defence will say a young naive girl was lured to a drink and drug dive where she fell into the hands of beasts. She then partook of the drugs available, which rendered her thankfully insensible to what followed. It will be swept aside as a tragic experimentation with drugs resulting in a fatal outcome.' He flicked the post mortem report open. 'Asphyxiation, inhalation of vomit and other body fluids into the lungs. Her respiratory system seriously depressed, followed by heart failure. The jury will be told that an inexperienced young girl dabbled in drugs for the first time and paid a terrible price.'

McDowall exploded, leapt up. 'Pish! Total pish! What about the sexual activity, was that not rape by any standard of proof? This is so much shite.'

'Sit down you big gorm.'

'We have witnesses.'

'Hopeless! I have statements from drug jakeys on whose word I wouldn't send a dog to Milton Dog Home. This Beth Sharkey whom you say was the voice on the 999 tape, sounds hysterical and her identity has not been established as the caller. Assumption, and what is assumption Frank?'

'The mother of all cock-up.'

'Both your witnesses are proving harder to find than Amelia Earhart.'

'That wee tadger Brodie told me what happened.'

'Illegible notes of yours, scribbled in the bar after the event, are unsubstantiated and unsigned. From the druggies that could speak or sign anything, there's sparse sense to be found. These people could have been on Mars that night, some thought they were. Any competent defence lawyer could have their evidence quashed in ten minutes. Hell! I could do it in five. Not one of them seemed aware of where they were, what year it was never mind the day, and knew nothing of Angela. Nobody could ID her picture. Nobody saw anything, nobody remembers anything. Their gibberish statements are useless.'

Gask slammed the file down and pushed it away across the desk. 'We have nothing to convict here as regards the death, nothing we can win.'

'Sometimes fighting has nothing to do with winning. A jury might believe us when they see the sleazebag McGraths in the dock.'

'Ah, yes. The great imponderable of what a jury might or might not do. We're going with six charges of possession.'

McDowall snorted. 'You're right, most juries can't decide what biscuits they want with their tea.' Silence fell for a while, broken softly by McDowall. 'Did McVicar say about numbers?'

'Don't do this, Frank.' Gask shook his head and looked out the window.

McDowall put his forehead on the desk. After two weeks of not smoking, Gask opened his desk drawer, took out a whisky bottle, glasses, and fags. Brown declined both the alcohol and the fag and stared at the folder. Gask and McDowall lit up in a hush punctuated only by the sonorous ticking of the pendulum clock and the rustle of the biscuit wrapping. Findo rolled the packet over to McDowall who leant forward and caught it as it plunged off the edge.

McDowall and Brown broke the bad news to Alec Stewart as he started his shift in the security gatehouse at ScotCon, a large construction firm at Barrhead. He was caustic.

'That's your best efforts then, all over, tragic accident, what a shame never mind. Swept away like it never happened? All just buried with my family.'

'I know it's shitty but unless Beth Sharkey or Brodie turn up, our case is stalled for now. I'll continue to monitor things and hopefully there will be progress later, but for now we've nothing on anybody. The Fiscal's office will not take this on at present.'

Alec nodded. 'I've been asking around the town and the same names come up. Two brothers? Right scumbags called the McGraths? Ringing any bells? I know them from the football. A few years back they ran supporter buses to away games and a betting pool which they used to buy drugs. The polis wirnae interested then because they had their cut. Was it them, the brothers?'

McDowall laid his hand on Alec's arm. 'You know I can't tell you anything.'

Alec had observed both policemen's body language when he'd mentioned the names. Brown sat back and looked embarrassed, McDowall pursed his lips and folded his arms. Dead giveaway. Alec rose and put on his uniform tunic. 'Thanks for dropping in but I'm late for shift. I'll see you later no doubt.'

He left them shamed.

McDowall sighed. 'He took that well, considering.'

'You think?'

'If Alec Stewart cries havoc and let's slip, we'll regret it one way or the other. From now on we give him no more information about the McGrath brothers.'

On the way back to Golspie Road both held their own council. McDowall knew Alec would never threaten what he wouldn't do. Subconsciously he knew why he'd mentioned the McGrath brothers.

So did Brown he imagined.

Beth Sharkey didn't hang around at Knox Road when the McGraths were done with her. She was tortured the following morning by flickering flashback realisations of what Angela had suffered, every image searing her mind.

Angela had picked Beth up at the bandstand in Johnstone and had been okay with Beth asking her to pass by a friend's flat to pick up some money. Truth was, Beth was hurting badly and had desperately needed a fix. She had only meant to be five minutes. It didn't happen that way. Angela insisted on going up with her, probably to monitor her but dressed it up as hoping to meet some of Beth's friends. Beth had no friends, only zombies in the same weird gargoyle world as herself. There was no talking Angela out of it and guarded, as she thought, by her Christian values, followed Beth into what was to become the pit of Hell.

The McGraths had immediately swarmed around the two of them, but Angela put the brothers down, repulsed by the behaviour going on around her she quickly realised this was no place for her and said she would wait in the hall and could Beth be quick. Beth took a hit in the bedroom and another fix for later went into her handbag. Gordon insisted Beth take a drink to Angela and after a wee bit of pushing she took her a Coke that Eddie poured. Events overtook Beth and the next thing she knew was that the brothers were guiding Angela between them into the bedroom. The rest of the time Beth spent there was a riot of images, shattering music, and a massive feeling of floating detachment.

Later, she went into the bedroom to find Angela naked across the bed. Both McGrath brothers were using her for sex. Others had cheered and clapped, waiting their turn. Beth had lost track of time, floating away into a rippling kaleidoscopic world. As she'd gradually came down, she became aware that every guy there seemed to be rotating into the bedroom in gangs of three or four. She vaguely remembered Eddie groping her in the hallway and saying they were skedaddling.

At some point Beth had returned to the bedroom in a daze. She had sex with two more men against the wall from where she could see into the bedroom. Angela was comatose, naked across the stained bed, unresponsive to what was being done to her. Everything tumbled around Beth's head in a flickering horror movie. Angela choking, convulsing and gasping for air even as the abuse continued. Then she'd vomited and stopped breathing.

Beth had panicked and stumbled into the street for air. She slumped against the phone box at the corner and on an impulse sought help. Angela had been good to her and now she needed rescued. Beth dialled 999 and asked for an ambulance giving the address, her speech slurred and broken adding it was a drugs party and to bring the Police as well. She hung up and stepped onto the pavement just as the McGraths pulled up in Angela's car. She froze.

'Who're you phoning?' Gordon asked.

Beth thought quickly. 'A taxi, but they say it's an hour.'

Eddie jumped out and flung the seat forward. 'Get in.'

Beth climbed in and Eddie sat beside her in the back then unzipped, grabbed her head and shoved it into his lap for the duration of the journey.

Beth heard the McGraths leave in the morning remaining terrified and cowering in the toilet until she was sure they weren't coming back. She slumped between the bowl and the wall slowly recovering from the blows Eddie had given her and came to the realisation that, when the police talked to Angela's parents, then the minister, and the Social Work, they would soon know all about her and where she lived. They could be here at any minute. In a panic she forced herself up on wobbling legs and in a dazed stupor washed her lower body with a grubby towel. She began to throw essentials into a holdall. She would be stupid to wait here, it was time to bolt. If the McGraths discovered she'd called 999 then she was dead.

Her half-sister had a flat in Anderston where she could hide for a while before deciding what to do. She didn't have much cash, but could go back on the game for a while, feel out her old haunts off the Glasgow Green and London Road. When things calmed down, she would run down south, get lost in a big city. She left by the back close into the service lane down to Beith Road and boarded the Glasgow bus. She had to get as far away from the McGraths as she could. Running for her life and from her life.

When McDowall and Brown arrived at Golspie Road, Joyce waved them over to the front desk. 'How did it go at the Fiscal's then? Are you getting a warrant?'

'Not this side of hell.' growled McDowall. 'Furthest they'll go was to alert the beat plods. It looks as if the whole thing's going to be a washout. Lack of evidence, no reliable witnesses. Findo says the defence team could just plead not guilty, sit down and still win.'

'Jeez, how did what's his name, the uncle, take that?'

'Pleased as Punch, watch this space. Is there any good news for us?'

Joyce leafed through her clipboard. 'Not even close. It's all bad. Do you want the bad news or the horrible news?'

McDowall shoved his hands deep in his coat pockets, dragged at the fag hanging from his bottom lip and blew smoke up towards the ceiling.

'I vill ask zee questions, vot about the car?'

'Found burned out on waste ground at the back of Coats Mill, nothing there.'

'What about our witnesses? Start with the bold Brodie?'

'Dropped off the edge of the world. We found his wife and weans at her mothers in Port Glasgow. All they did was greet all the time we were there. Searched the place, of course, but he's well gone and they're saying nowt.'

'Gillespie's got to them. Brodie has other family, a sister in Saltcoats, check that out. What about the other one, the elusive Beth Sharkey?'

'Got her address from Social, two uniforms went up. The place is empty and the door had been kicked in, the flat was wide to the world. The neighbours have stripped it bare of anything not nailed down. They also denied they'd seen her all weekend. She's well away, probably back flogging her body again up the city. Vice in Glasgow are looking for her in the Blythewood Square area and around the Green but working girls are tight as the Mafia and never use their own name. Pictures of her and Brodie have been circulated to each shift, we have to wait and see.'

'Brilliant! Just torapeachy. Our one and only star witness and blabbermouth is flung out the station like a used chip paper by no less than our own Inspector, and we don't seem able to chase up the bold Beth. A slip of a druggie lassie, still half spaced out her box has evaded us. More to come no doubt. Brown, let's get back to our office, review the evidence and await developments. That Joyce, is detective speak for not having a clue where to look or what's next.'

'One more fly in the ointment by the by,' Joyce said.

'Whit now?'

'Tannock is away for two days, some conference at the Police College in Dorking, but wants updates from you.'

'He can go coco. Interesting he's off his mark when the Glasgow thing is going down. Does he know something I don't? Never mind, best with him out the way I suppose. I feel unleashed. Right, Brown, office.'

McDowall dumped his coat on the office floor. 'The door is closed!' he shouted into the corridor. 'Right, young Brown, tomorrow is our away day to the big bad city. Let's get an early night for once.'

'I like Glasgow,' Brown ventured. 'Went to Uni there.'

'Aw aye! I'd keep quiet about that around the station. Liking Glasgow is deviant stuff here in the sticks, where men are men and dogs are feart. Why don't you get us a cuppa then, milk two sugars, and I'll tell you what's happening tomorrow. A dookie biscuit would be good, fair bring you up in my estimation.'

Brown got the tea but no biscuits and found a space on the littered desk for the mugs.

'Look, if you want me to review things, I think I'm up to speed with McVicar's report and the statements.'

McDowall shook his head and splashed tea over a file.

'Godstruth! Enough for now, my brain's melting. I want to chat about tomorrow, some ground rules. Firstly, we're not in charge, just along for the hurl and maybe to carry the can. The operation is run by City of Glasgow Police who think we're from Brigadoon. Even worse, the British Transport Police will be included because the drop is at Glasgow Central Station. The best way to screw everything is to have more than one police force liaising. One force equals disaster. Two forces, a dogfight. Three forces, an Old Firm rammy. If it goes legless somebody will be left without a chair when the music stops. Won't be us. We're meeting with a guy called Devaney, an Inspector in British Transport Police in Glasgow Central. He couldn't plan an orgy in a brothel. Tannock is safely away on his course leaving his master plan and any fallout to us minions.'

'Do you not know this Devaney at all?'

McDowall grimaced. 'Yep! He used to be at Paisley but got promoted and transferred himself to BTP. He disnae like me so I'm not expecting much co-operation. Any-way-how, finish your tea and get away home to your wife. Pick me up in the morning.'

Brown wondered just how short the list of people Frank liked was. 'The wife will be wondering what's going on if I come home the same day I went out. Are you staying on here?'

'Let's see.' McDowall leant back hands behind his head. Irene just spent a full day with Buster. So, it's either go home, go to the pub, or kill masel'. What do you think?'

Brown thought the best outcome might be for McDowall to kill himself.

'My guess is the pub, but I'm away home. I want to see Carol before her nightshift. Apart from days off we're leaving notes on the kitchen table.'

McDowall supped his tea down an inch and added a wee chaser of whisky from the desk drawer. Brown shook his head, made to speak, grunted and crammed files into his briefcase. 'Haud your wheesht. Leave it be.'

McDowall caught his own distorted reflection in the

wrinkly glass of the office partition and saw a wee short fat guy with a guilty look staring back. Was it not the definition of an alcoholic he wondered, that it's not how much you drink but that you *needed* that one drink? He toasted his reflective alter ego and decided to have a dram later and think about it.

Brown paused at the doorway. 'Right that's me away.'

'Remember son, the time to worry is when the fridge notes stop appearing. Flowers are always a good idea, even if she's still mad they'll do for your grave.'

Findo Gask was already at the bar of the Whippity. McDowall struggled through the off-duty police officers and firemen, climbed up onto a stool and raised his hand to the barman. A whisky appeared. Findo toasted their reflections in the gantry mirror.

'Do we have a drink problem, Frank?'

McDowall sipped. 'Naw. Lift glass pour in, swallow. Let me give you a demo. Pity we only have one gub.'

Findo snorted. 'At night I can't stop my brain racing like a hamster wheel. I tell myself the drink smugs me and I can sleep for a few hours.'

'I don't bother with excuses any more. Changing the subject, I've always wondered about your name. Is it Swedish or something?'

Findo laughed. 'No. My mum and dad were hippies before the term was coined, travelling people really. Tinkers. They went about Scotland and Ireland in an old Scammel army ambulance truck, finding casual work where they could. I was born in a lay-by off the A9 Perth Road one wild night, a bit earlier than planned. As if Gask as a surname wasn't bad enough there was a signpost pointing the way to a village called Findo Gask. My parents literally took that as a sign.'

'You were lucky, it could have been the road to Amarillo.'

They both started to sing quietly. *"Is This the way to Findo Gask"*, their shoulders heaving with suppressed laughter.

Findo asked if McDowall's parents were still alive.

McDowall got another round in. 'My mum is dead, tuberculosis.'

'And your dad?'

'Never my dad and a father barely. He did the deed and buggered off, never saw a penny from him. Mum was a single mother when that kind of thing shamed a whole family and got you shunned, and her family were all Wee Frees. Mum refused to go on what was cried, "a holiday", to have me and hand me over to the nuns or Barnardo's. I vaguely remember my granny when I was little helping with her widows' mite until she died. Mum passed on soon after worn out and alone. I was twelve. I remember mostly listening to her weeping and coughing every night. That and sitting on the landing listening to the sound of the brass bed when there was not a shilling for the rent man. My so-called father is alive but I hope he dies badly, and soon. One day I'll repay him for all the hurt he gave my mother. Enough about that bastard.'

Findo took the hint, opened a bag of crisps and changed tack. 'Your pal Alec Stewart and his dog were in earlier. Looked just like you, frazzled.'

McDowall paused mid swallow and quickly glanced around. 'Still here is he?'

'No. Got slung out because of the dog. You look guilty, what have you been up to?'

'Best not burden your conscience with knowing.' McDowall relaxed. 'I spoke to Alec Stewart today. Told him the case was closed.'

Findo snorted. 'How did that go?'

'Calm as a cucumber he was, very stoic.'

Findo waved to the barman and ordered two large Talisker.

McDowall watched the ice melt in his tumbler and tried to still his anger, his raging frustration fuelled by images of past wrongs but mostly Angela. A lifelong litany of failure in most things stretched behind him like a rusty chain. His reflection in the gantry mirror peered back at him, the real McDowall, hiding behind the bottles. Wondering how far he was now willing to go. Somebody should have a plan.

Alec Stewart no doubt had a plan.

McDowall's reflection had a plan.

Why not him?

*

CHAPTER 10

Irene had lain in bed that morning listening to her husband and Brown talking in the kitchen. Francis had let that dirty dog out the back before he went but now it was in the back lobby and she shoved the pillow over her ears to mute the barking and scratching at the kitchen door. As soon as she heard the front door shut and the car pull away, she had stolen downstairs and nervously peeked into the kitchen.

Buster sat with his head to one side, regarding his handiwork. It had scratched the paint off the bottom of the door in its efforts to get out the kitchen into the living room. She hated dogs, with their casting hairs and smells and messy habits. She was nauseated by the smell from the dog's wet coat. Where were those incense sticks she got at Christmas? She turned and reached up to a top cupboard. Behind her the dog sprang up from the old duffle coat and trotted across to wipe its damp hair across the backs of her legs. Irene screamed, dropping the incense sticks, and leapt behind a kitchen chair to fend off the dog. The beast snuffled the incense sticks before, satisfied they were not for eating, plodding back to its bed, snuffling across her once spotless floor tiles on the way. Irene controlled her breathing with an effort.

How could he do this to her? Francis knew she loathed dogs, animals of any kind in fact. Filthy beasts. She worked her way past it to the back door and flung it open, prodding the dog with the mop. She tried to retrieve what had been the clean laundry as it was trailed past her, but Buster began to tug playfully, and she recoiled against the wall, gave up trying to free her Irish linen tablecloth from his jaws. She helped it down the step with a push from the mop and stepped into the back garden.

'Morning, Irene.' It was her neighbour, May Clarke. 'Is everything all right?'

Irene smiled fixedly. 'Yes, thank you May.'

'Is that a dog you have now?' May asked.

Irene gritted her teeth. 'No! I don't have a dog.'

'Aah! I must have been mistaken then. Just a stray.'

Realising how ridiculous she must look in her dressing gown and slippers clutching a mop and a torn tablecloth like the Turin Shroud, Irene turned to go back inside. The door swung shut behind her and the double throw security Chubb lock dropped into place with a thud. She let the mop fall, folded her arms, and gripped her elbows till they hurt. She closed her eyes. This! This was all his fault. May came over to the hedge, smiling sweetly.

'Oh, what a shame, you're not having a good day. Never mind, you can call your daughter from my phone and bide at my place till she comes with a key. We can have a good gab.' Irene ground her teeth. All morning with May, wonderful. She whispered. 'By God, you'll pay for this Francis McDowall. You and that mutt both.'

McDowall wasn't home till nearly midnight. The lights were

all out, the sleeping bag laid out on the couch like a caterpillar with Buster on top of it fast asleep, tongue lolling.

He tiptoed to the loo then stood silent outside the bedroom door for a while, listening. There was a sliver of light under the door but as he raised his hand to tap it went out. There might as well have been barbed wire and minefields. All that was missing was a sign on the door, *"Achtung Minen."* He retreated downstairs where Buster remained master of the couch. He noticed the dog's collar had an enamel address tag shaped like a pink heart. Leaning closer he saw it was engraved. *'Love. Angela.'* He retreated to the armchair and passed the night in self torture, afraid to sleep.

In Anderson, Beth's sister shook her awake in the morning, dragging her from oblivion into a cold damp world. Condensation was heavy on the windows and it was not yet light. Her nephew, Daren, stood leering down at her, his wee beady eyes stripping her. That boy gave her the creeps even though he was only thirteen. Fat sweaty wee pervert bastard always had his hand down his pants.

'Get up!' Marina said. 'If you're staying here, you better get some money earned.'

'God's sake gie me peace. Ma heid is full of glass. You got a drink in this hoose?'

Daren lifted a bottle of vodka from among the rubbish on the floor by the couch and strolled over. Beth sat up groaning and gulped deeply from the neck of the bottle. She gasped and the foghorn in her head quietened. She became aware the blanket had dropped and the wee perv was staring down her T shirt. She raised the bottle again and the boy reached out and squeezed her breast. She pushed him away.

'Get aff me, ya sicko. What the feck's the matter with you?'

Marina came back through from the kitchen. 'Get your hands aff ma boy.'

'Well tell the perv to keep his hands to himself or I'll rip his tadger off. Perv!'

Marina thumped the boy across the ear and shoved him towards the door.

'I'm taking him to school then I've got a punter coming here at half nine for the full service, so you can shift yer arse out of here. You'd best think on going on the street again. The bills don't pay thersel and there's nae freebies here. Ah'm no shagging my arse off tae keep you, so you better start thinking aboot sucking on something other than that voddie bottle. Ah don't know what you're running from but it's probably something that will do me and the boy nae good. You can pay your way or take yer fanny somewhere else. Is this something tae dae with that pimp Brodie, or they two other prats you whore for, the brothers fucking McGrath?'

'Ah had tae get away in a hurry, frae the brothers, best you don't know. Ah plan to get some money and head down south. I'll sign on the buroo in Partick as Elizabeth Sharkey for now. I can tell them I was job hunting in Leeds and got robbed on the train, lost all ma money, my National Insurance and dole card. I might get an emergency loan then I'll get ma shit together and go out before you're back. Guthrie owes me money as well but I've seen neither hide nor hair of him. Speakin' of shit, do you have any gear in the house?'

Marina opened the front door and pushed her boy out onto the landing, crossed into the kitchen and pulled a margarine tub from the fridge. 'There's some scag here. I expect it back when you do a trick or two.'

Marina fished out a small bag and brought it over. Beth reached out but her sister held out the other hand palm up.

'Money! This isnae the Sally Ann, so cross ma palm wi the crinkly stuff.'

Beth fumbled through her bag finally producing a fiver.

'It's all Ah've goat.'

Marina took the money and then tossed the bag.

'When you get yersel away out best try for punters doon the bottom of Finnieston Street and along the Clydeside. When it's dark you can try Glesga Green or Anderston bus station. The far end of the Gallowgate is no bad after dark and so is Dundas Street where the London bus goes from. Don't be fussy and don't come back till ye can pay fur yer keep.'

She banged the door behind her making no mention of leaving a key. Beth was abandoned even by her sister now.

Touching herself gingerly she wondered if there was ice in the fridge. She would stick to blowjobs for a while if she could. She agonised about what had happened to Angela, but she had called the ambulance. That must count? Her life was shambolic but at least she still had it, unlike Angela.

The three months Beth had been befriended by Angela

was the only time in her life she had felt better about herself. Felt hope. She had only fallen back into the habit a couple of times, just grazing from time to time to stop the pain. Well, more like ten times. When she was nearly dried our she felt things were not all shite and there was a chance after all to shake off all the bad stuff. But she had thrown away the best chance she had ever had.

She'd been introduced to Angela at the kirk hall during a boring church disco. Girls down one side of the floor boys down another, the hall seething with unexploded boiling hormones, while the ladies of the church group patrolled against close contact. Beth had pigeonholed Angela as a do-gooder just looking for her latest Girl's Guide badge at first. Despite Beth being a bitch Angela tolerated Beth's foul tongue and gross habits, and slowly began to get responses beyond grunts and shrugged shoulders. Things improved enough for Beth to be included in Stewart family days out, but Ethel flat refused to have her in the house. Angela's dad had always been a gentleman to her and used his car to flit her few sticks and baubles into her council flat. He'd also slipped her money from time to time and took the two girls to The Little Chef for treats. Beth was crushed, she'd betrayed everything.

All caring had died in her and now even the sex was nothing, meaningless. Wasn't that supposed to be an act of love? It was a degraded thing for her now, to be numbly endured till the huffing and puffing were done and the money earned to buy more of the heroin. She would exist now in this dark world, back chasing the dragon till it caught her. The split burned her fingers and she struggled up unsteadily.

Stripped bare now of all emotion, unable to weep for herself or even a little for Angela, she lost all hope.

This was it then for her. She had been a fool to think she could evade the life dictated by her craving, that it wouldn't return in all its fury and reclaim her.

She rummaged in her bag and laid out her working girl kit on the bed. The leather pencil dress with the long zip down the front, her patterned stockings and calf length boots with heels. She washed and dressed quickly, applied basic makeup, and slipped into a short jacket. The bedroom mirror told her she still had something to sell that men wanted. She did look good. When she met her eyes in the mirror however they told another hellish story, there was no more spark there than in two black puddles holding yesterday's mud and rain. Eyes were the windows to the soul Angela had said, if so Beth was damned. She slung her handbag across her shoulder and took a handful of condoms from the kitchen drawer.

On impulse, she also took a small kitchen knife and slipped it inside her boot. She'd better hurry, she would try Anderson for punters then walk up the Gallowgate, might get some trade on the Glasgow Green. Maybe get some midday punters at their lunch on the benches. Four or five tricks at a fiver each should do for now. The McGraths would be looking for her but she had to hang around until Brodie paid her what she was owed.

She could trust nobody now.

McDowall strode up platform twelve at Glasgow Central platform trailed by Brown, turned sharp right away from the

Transport Police Station, and crossed the concourse past the big WW1 shell, heading for the Union Street entrance. Brown caught up with him at the top of the Glasgow Central steps where he'd stopped to buy a Daily Record.

'Do you think it'll be one of Hammonds lot that turns up?' Brown asked.

'I'm hoping so, I need a lever to get at him. It won't be him or Gillespie, they'll send somebody disposable like Gillespie's two zoomers. My money's on our elusive witness Brodie or the McGrath brothers.' He glanced around the concourse. 'I'm dry as a witches tit, I need a drink.'

'I thought we were meeting that British Transport Police Inspector?'

'Not right off. I need a wee jolt before I meet with Paul Devaney.'

He grabbed Brown's sleeve and crossed to the kerb, head turning back and forth and suddenly took a gap and dragged him out into in the Union Street traffic. Horns tooted tyres squealed.

A taxi driver leaned out his window and shouted. 'Hey, you two wankers, watch where you're going. Are you foreigners or what, spacemen maybe?'

'Close,' McDowall replied. 'Paisley.'

They crossed over Gordon Street and entered the Horseshoe Bar. He stopped just inside the door, eyes adjusting to the light. This was a man's pub, not like these modern disco pubs and wine bars with their juke boxes and bandits beeping and clattering. The Horseshoe was a place you could gab across the table and watch the fitba on the telly. Already the bar was crowded by smoke blurred punters serenaded by the clink of glasses and laughter. Waiters weaved back and forth among the hubbub dishing out drink and food. Stovies, mince and tatties, haggis and neeps. McDowall stopped just inside the door absorbing the smells and chatter. Brown bumped into him.

McDowall grinned, breathed in the blend of spilled drink and pies and full ashtrays. 'One of the benefits of Glasgow after eleven is civilised drinking. The forefront of culture, where you can get a man's breakfast, a pie and a pint.' He strode to the bar and ordered two large Glenmorangie and two bridies.

Brown pulled a face. 'Frank, is it no maybe a bit early?'

McDowall slapped a fiver on the bar, punched him playfully on the shoulder. 'Pish and nonsense, this will put hairs on your chest. Relax, it's my round. Believe me, we'll both need a drink to survive this day with Paul Devaney.'

'I thought you two had been partners for five years before he transferred. I've heard canteen rumours. Did you fall out?'

'Big time, sunshine.' McDowall splashed a little water into his glass and took a very healthy pull. Brown raised his eyebrows, drowned his own measure in water, took a deep breath and sipped, screwing up his face. McDowall laughed.

'In the name of the wee man will you stop playing with that and take a good swallow. Think of it as detective training.'

Brown reluctantly did. His eyes watered, his throat took fire, his sinus exploded.

'There,' smirked McDowall. 'Hardly hurt at all.'

'We better not be long.' Brown pointed to the gantry clock.

'Take it easy, boy. You'll be giving yourself a heart attack if you keep worrying about things. Get that down your neck and we'll have another.'

The very idea appalled Brown, appearing in front of this Devaney smelling of drink was not a good idea. He thought they best get out of here and more to the point get McDowall away before he got into a session.

When he'd made detective a year past this was not how he'd imagined it to be and not what his motivation had prepared him for. Uncertain what he'd expected at first but here he was, plunged into a world he'd only viewed from the outside. As a uniformed constable looking in, he'd seen a group where everyone drank, smoked, and subverted most procedures in pursuit of a quick result. From what he'd learned it seemed detecting for them consisted of creating what they thought had happened then uncover and reveal only the evidence that would prove their scenario, ignoring anything that was inconvenient.

Brown had never met cops before who were comfortable with being judge, jury and executioner. McDowall seemed well at ease with being all three with no defined borders.

Brown knew many a bright career had fallen into the abyss for failing to support any status quo systems and habitual disregard for procedures exercised by local CID. McDowall was undoubtedly the local CID Mafioso, and Brown was now convinced that his reaction to the system failing or blocking him would be to find some way to circumvent it. If Findo Gask chose not to prosecute then he feared McDowall would almost certainly do as he wished and what was required. How far would his boss go down that road, and how far would Brown follow McDowall remained a major question.

He changed the subject.

'This Devaney then, what's the story between you two?'

'It's personal I said, and a long time ago.'

'I just want to know if it's going to be a problem?'

'Are you messing with ma heid, Jim? A problem shared is a problem halved, do you think? Well, it's not, it becomes a more complex problem and its useless interference. This is the second time you've asked me, leave it alone.'

Brown backed off. 'I don't want to open old wounds. It's supposed to make you feel better, talking about it.'

'Shite and bollocks! All it does is depress and confuse two folks instead of one.' McDowall drained his glass and finished what was left of the other glass as well. 'Right then, we're ready as we will ever be, so let's ride out to battle the baddies like Lobey Dosser. My hero so he is. The Prince of Partick.'

'Who's Lobey Dosser?'

Frank was incredulous, struck dumb, for a second. 'You don't know who Lobey Dosser is? The Glesga Cowboy on his hirpling horse?'

Brown was embarrassed, out his depth. 'Of course I know. It's on the telly.'

'My bahookie. It's a cartoon in the papers.'

'I knew that.'

McDowall punched him playfully on the shoulder. 'Naw ye didnae. The Dosser knows how to deal with baddies. And then some. Let's go.'

As they left one door into Drury Street, Gordon McGrath came in the other, ordered a pint, four bags of cheese and onion crisps then perched himself on McDowall's warm stool.

Inspector Paul Devaney was very aware of the time and the absence of the two Paisley officers. He glared at the clock in his office again then his watch, but it told the same story. It was eleven thirty. He was not surprised; he had only heard two days prior which CID officers were coming. The memo lay on his desk still, and at first he'd thought someone in the West was having a laugh. Of all people, they'd sent Frank McDowall. Still stuck at DS so at least Devaney outranked him. Typical of him to be adrift, not caring and running to his own maverick timetable. Devaney had resolved to keep his temper while the backstabbing bastard was in his office. He would never forget what that cheating devious shite had done and brought ruin to both families. Frank and Irene, Paul and Claire, best friends.

Then McDowall had shagged his wife.

Devaney dismissed their denials and lies. God alone knew how long it had been going on but he'd been uneasy how close his Claire and Frank were becoming for some time before both families took caravan holidays together, but he told himself he was paranoid, it was all innocent. During that holiday Devaney was aware of an undercurrent, the two of them creating situations where they could be alone. Wee walks and beach combing, harmless fun, and always taking the kids as chaperons. But something was just not kosher, and Devaney tried to raise it subtly with Irene, who laughed and said she trusted Francis. Did he not trust his wife? Turned out Irene had been in denial, hoping it would all just fizzle out. But it didn't, and Devaney had supressed the suspicion eating into his bones and his gut.

It had all erupted at a party in the Devaney house in front of the whole shift. He had been chatting in the living room and seen their reflection in the conservatory window. Claire and McDowall were by the buffet, standing close, silent, her head down almost on his shoulder. Then she reached out and softly brushed her fingers across the hairs on his forearm.

Devaney had stormed in and decked McDowall in a shower of paper plates and buffet titbits. Uproar screaming and denials, both wives in tears, McDowall telling him through a burst lip nothing was going on, it was the drink, trying to brass it out. Impossible now to keep it secret with all the gossiping piranhas gawping on, may as well have been a full-page advert in the *Evening Times*.

At work, word spread like wildfire, the sniggers and winks grew into mockery and outright laughter for Devaney while McDowall was treated like Jack the Lad. What had made it worse for Devaney was their connection was emotional. Even if he believed nothing physical happened between them the tableau in the conservatory had been the last piece of the jigsaw. Devaney gave Claire an ultimatum which cowed her, sold the house and applied for the BTP job. That safely under his belt he'd resigned and moved to Garnethill.

Even now he seethed with the caustic humiliation, reignited by the picture on his desk of Claire and the children. And now the smug bastard was about to waltz into his office. In the main office the two Glasgow CID officers were making a nuisance of themselves chatting up the female typists. Their names were Coyle and Boyle which sounded like a comedy duo. One looked like a Kojak clone even down to the hat, the other wore a loud checked coat and Rupert the Bear flared trousers. Kojak had a fag instead of a lollipop and wobble walked on platform shoes. Out of patience, Devaney opened the door and waved them in. He had delayed long enough.

They had just settled around his desk when Devaney's internal phone buzzed and as he reached for it he could see the receptionist waving at him. Two men were by the front desk. One was Frank McDowall. Short and grey-haired, scruffy, his tie loose, looking like he'd picked his outfit out of a charity shop. The usual bag of rags in his bunnet and grubby Gannex. The younger man in his thirties he didn't know. Smartly dressed by a Marks & Spencer catalogue, carrying a briefcase. Devaney hung up and watched them weave across the office, eyes staring at his backstabbing, cheating, lying, one-time best friend. He couldn't believe that McDowall had the gall, the sheer balls, to come through here and tear open all the old scabs and sores. Devaney seethed as McDowall entered the office lazily waving his warrant card and grinning hugely all the time.

'Greetings, earthlings, we come in peace. Lock up your daughters and bring out your whisky. I'm DS Frank McDowall, and this is DC Jim Brown. Started without us, have you?'

Devaney glared at him. 'The late Frank McDowall. I see nothing has changed with you.'

Brown nodded and waved a hand to the room in general then picked a point on the wall and stared at it in embarrassment. McDowall seemed unfazed by their reception. Dominating the space, McDowall merely widened his grin and shrugged out of his coat crossing the room before flinging it down behind the chair in a heap, then sat down and pulled out his ciggies.

'Well, let's press on. We're right sorry to be late.'

'Apology accepted,' Devaney growled. 'Let's move on. These two officers are from Glasgow CID. Detective Sergeant Boyle and his junior, Detective Constable Coyle.'

Nods all round, on their feet for quick handshakes, then they all grabbed a chair. McDowall stared at the ceiling rose and blew smoke, waiting till Devaney shuffled some papers and drew breath to make introductions.

McDowall cleared his throat. 'I'll bring a note from my mammy to the headmaster next time.'

Brown closed his eyes and groaned inwardly, watched McDowall brush ash off his worn corduroy trouser leg and grin at Devaney, seemingly enjoying poking a sleeping bear.

Devaney leant back in his chair, one hand gripping the edge of the desk, the other turning a pencil end over end. 'You haven't changed a bit, have you, Frank? Still the cheeky bastard, butting head-first into everything.'

McDowall drummed his fingers on the desk. 'How's Claire keeping these days?'

Devaney remained tight-lipped gripping both arms of his chair. 'I can have you replaced with one phone call, so don't push it. I know Tannock would get rid of you in a heartbeat, so just sit quietly, get briefed then get out my sight.'

McDowall moved his chair away from the desk. 'You're right, we don't have time for this crap, all in the past.'

'Not for me.'

An awkward silence followed, filled by shuffling and sidelong glances until Brown cleared his throat loudly. Devaney took a deep breath.

'Okay. Let's deal with the job in hand and get out of each other's face. The situation so far; a package placed in a locker was discovered by BTP when two neds tried to break it open. The bag was searched, the drugs put back and then the case was passed to City of Glasgow Police.' He passed out A4 photographs.

'Two days ago this man, now identified as one Anton Tenescu approached the locker, took the bag out, opened it then replaced the package in the locker. He was taken into custody.' He tossed over a mugshot. 'Suddenly Mr Tenescu is very popular. Everybody wants to talk to him. Customs, yourselves, people from Special Branch. He's apparently a well-known courier of almost anything and has been deported from various countries on about five occasions. Police forces in England and Interpol have expressed interest in him. He had on him three different passports, same man, various identities, all Eastern European.'

McDowall asked, 'What's this Tenescu saying?'

'Nothing. And he won't, because Tenescu has Diplomatic

Status. He's attached to the Bulgarian Embassy as part of their exports mission and that's been confirmed. He'll be released to the Consul and then reported to the Foreign Office for travelling out with London without seeking prior permission.'

'So, this guy has just walks and we are helpless?'

'We attempted to hold him to frustrate any attempt to warn anybody else. That proved impossible diplomatically, so all we can do is watch the locker and hope somebody will come to collect.' Devaney produced a map of the concourse. 'The newsagent kiosk directly across from the locker area is being refurbished and we are taking advantage of that. You four'll replace the workers today. There's a one-way glass window facing onto the locker in question. There is a camera set up behind the destination boards and we are recording onto a VCR. A still and video camera is already set up inside the kiosk.'

He turned to McDowall. 'A British Rail van's been organised and it will sit out of sight till the drugs are picked up, then you will use that to follow whoever does the pickup. Intention is to follow the bag through to Paisley. So, basically we now wait and see what happens.'

'That's the master-plan then?' McDowall scoffed. 'We just sit on our hands until something happens? Surely the moment this foreign guy was released the game was a bogey?'

Boyle butted in. 'We delayed the decision to release Tenescu until midnight under the guise of security confirmation. He told us diddly squat what, so it's all guesswork. It all depends how quickly this Tenescu guy raises the alarm once we're forced to release him. If nobody shows my boss will hand over to the Regional Crime Squad, open the locker and follow on from there.'

McDowall shook his head. 'So, we're at the mercy of the baddies?'

Boyle shrugged. 'Only up to a point. On a practical level, we'll be wearing painter's overalls and carrying their gear on a trolley. If you want tea and butties for the get them now.'

Devaney got up and moved away from them to the window and looked down across the concourse. He was raging still, amazed at how quickly his anger had ignited, engulfing him in pain like a flamethrower. Two years and the sight of the bastard still made him sick inside. He understood very well how ordinary people killed. He watched McDowall's reflection on the inside of the glass and became aware he was staring at the framed photograph of his wife Claire and the two children on top of the desk. He crossed the room took the frame down and put it away in the drawer. He wouldn't have that bastard looking at his wife and children.

McDowall had destroyed his marriage.

McDowall could smell her hair, feel her fingers caress his face as if it were yesterday. The way she threw her head back tossing her hair. He heard her laugh. It staggered him that even now she could hurt him. He felt as if he had been kicked, could hardly breath. It was a relief in a way that Devaney had taken the picture down, all best forgotten, he couldn't go back to where Claire had sent him. At the time McDowall had thought her a coward, Afraid of what had grown between them. How could she love him but go back to Devaney? Later he'd understood it was for the same reasons he found it impossible to leave Irene. He drifted, zoning them out, barely listening to the rest of the briefing, lost in remembering. Her name the only thing in his head, over and over like an insane mantra. He didn't hear a word of the briefing until he realised someone had asked him a question. Then he became immersed in the nagging need to get on with the real investigation. Find those who'd killed Angela.

He could admit to no one that he'd start awake in the night and see Angela standing by the bed, accusing him. Only for an instant, then gone. He was certain Alec Stewart saw ghosts, not only battlefield apparitions but the wraiths of his family. How is a man not crushed by that? He knew that madness driving Alec now and he'd never rest until he took everything from them. McDowall's whole existence was peppered with constant guilt at his failure to apprehend the McGrath brothers. It was high time he harnessed his own hate. Then everyone was standing and the office door opening. He hoped Brown had been paying attention.

'I think we've covered everything.' Devaney said. 'Two of my men will show you the way and organise overalls.' Two of Devaney's men in British Rail boiler suits were waiting at the office door and showed them downstairs to a locker room where a platform trolley waited, heavy with dust sheets and tins of paint. McDowall broke away and went into the Gents toilet. He filled the basin and immersed his face, blowing bubbles, straightened up and stared at himself in the mirror. Drips fell from his chin onto his shirt, his tie dangled in the sink. He thought that meeting could have gone better, mostly his fault it didn't.

For an instant he glimpsed Angela peering over his shoulder and spun round.

Better if he'd told Tannock he just wouldn't and the reason why. He'd supposed he could face it out by being professionally detached, but that had gone South thanks to his smart mouth. His self-control had vanished like snow off a dyke. The toilet door banged against the wall. Brown came up behind him glaring at his reflection in the streaked mirror.

'Who stole your scone?' McDowall growled.

Brown held up both hands and backed away against the sinks. 'Stole my scone? Explain what went on back there, and who's this Claire woman?'

McDowall pulled the roller towel to a less dirty bit and dried his face and hands. Flecks of fabric stuck to his chin and he brushed them off into the sink.

Brown folded his arms and leaned against a cubicle door. 'I know I'm just the new guy on the team Frank, but we've known each other for years so do you think you can tell me what in the name of fuck is happening. What's with Devaney and who's Claire?'

McDowall decided Brown was due some explanation, but not the whole story. 'Okay. Paul Devaney and I were on the same recruit's course at Port Glasgow. We became close but went to separate stations as constables. He went up the ladder more than me and eventually made Inspector in Paisley. He was as keen as me back then to nail Arthur Hammond and I persuaded him into a big raid on the warehouse at Sneddon Street. That was a disaster and he was pilloried along with me and we fell out about it. He transferred to this job in Glasgow, blamed me for putting his career down the drain.'

'And Claire is his wife? Tell me you didn't shag her.'

'Still none of anybody's business.'

'Right Frank, could I just get through the rest of the day without my future in CID terminating in Tannock's office.'

The door banged open again smacking off more of the chipped tiles. Coyle and Boyle came in and tossed overalls onto the floor.

'Fuck me' Coyle began. 'That was a laugh a minute but it's time for the big boy's rules of engagement.' He pointed a finger at McDowall. 'Until I want your input, which'll be no time soon, stay quietly the fuck out of my way. I don't care what is with you and Devaney, or if you shagged every female member of his family plus the dog as you were leaving. Everything clear? No questions?' He cupped an ear. 'I need to hear it.'

Brown cleared his throat and nodded, wishing he could sink into the floor.

'Got it,' said McDowall. 'I do have a question though.' He kicked at the overalls. 'Have these things ever been washed?'

None of the scurrying commuters gave the four painters a passing glance as they pushed a trolley loaded with paint tins, stepladders and dust sheets. Brown felt like a prat. His overalls were tight and uncomfortable and he sent a mental memo to self not to attempt any crouching or sudden squat thrusts. Coyle and Boyle looked at ease in the part. McDowall now, well, he was a painter. Irn-Bru in one hand, Daily Record folded to the racing page, gravity-defying fag on his bottom lip.

A notice on the whitewashed window of the news kiosk apologised for any inconvenience and directed callers to the main shop in Gordon Street. Coyle unlocked the door and they began to shift the gear inside.

Up in the BTP office, Devaney stood behind the destination boards peering through the gaps down into the concourse. One of his constables lifted a handheld radio, checked the channel.

'What are you doing?'

The constable paused, surprised. 'I'll need a radio to monitor what's happening. I've to have the van sitting on the ramp once they got into position.'

'No need, I'll be running things from here so I'll keep the radio.' Devaney took it from the constable. 'Bring the van into the service yard and wait till I give you the nod.'

'Yes sir.'

'I'll handle it all from my office.'

Taking his mug and the radio through to his office he closed the door and the blinds. He sipped his coffee with two hands, gazing at the handheld radio in the centre of his desk. He reached out and switched channels on the radio.

The kiosk was divided into two small rooms, both about five-by-five yards. A counter ran underneath the mirrored glass window where a stills camera was set up. An interior door hung by one hinge with a broken toilet sign on it. The floor was gone in there, the joists bare. Judging by the smell, the lavvy was blocked as well, the reek mixing with plaster and paint smells. McDowall took out his hip flask and stuck it under his nose.

'It wid gag a horse in here.'

'Don't breathe, then,' Coyle advised. 'Are you going to give us a hand with this stuff?'

McDowall blew smoke, swept the rubbish from the only chair. 'If it's all one to you, boys, I'll do as I'm told.' He smiled grimly and sat. 'Observe.'

Eddie McGrath had decided to make life easy for himself. Instead of nicking a van as Gordon told him he'd slunk that morning into Hammond's garage next to the warehouse where he knew the Sherpa they'd used to transport Brodie to his death was kept. Nobody was about, and the keys were behind the visor as usual. It took no time at all to drive off and get on the road for the Clyde Tunnel. He smiled, imagining the look on their faces when somebody noticed the van gone.

Arriving in Glasgow he found a parking space in Waterloo Street opposite the Bus Station from where he could see the Hope Street entrance in his wing mirrors and settled down to wait. Let that smug git Gordon sweat a wee bit yet. He started on his first Mars Bar, feeling very chuffed with himself. Gillespie would assume somebody was using the van and when he found out that was not the case would want to deal with that in-house and he'd send the boys out to find both van and driver. Eddie was suspicious of Gordon meeting

Hammond alone about Liverpool. Something reeked. His brother could be double-crossing him, freezing him out for a better deal. He'd acted like a right Jessie while they chopped Brodie up, squealing like a girl. Not so much of a hard man now. Eddie figured Gillespie must have been impressed by his performance at the killing. Made his bones, as the Mafia said. As for big brother, he would bear the watching. The dark slug of suspicion festered in his head and began to grow.

Gordon McGrath left the Horseshoe Bar and came into Central Station under the wrought iron canopy from Gordon Street. The station was busy which suited him just fine. Gillespie had given firm orders about waiting until after three before making the pickup but for a mad minute Gordon toyed with the nervous impulse to go ahead and get the exchange done right now. Eddie was nowhere to be seen, so he got a Bovril and a sausage roll from the snack kiosk and moved towards the platform car park. He took a wide detour around the Police Office and walked down the exit ramp. Humiliation boiled and seethed in his gut over Hammond taking the Liverpool Docks deal away. When he got a minute he'd phone his uncle and have him reuse to deal with anybody but his nephew. That'd sort Hammond out.

He knew taking part in the Brodie murder had been the peak of their enslavement to Hammond. This was way beyond the lassie in the flat, this was murder. As surety for their total compliance Gillespie loomed in the background with threats of doom and violent punishment. Then he had a thought that would have been pure mad a week ago. He could have it all. Today. The money, the drugs, get free of

Hammond who thought his new suppliers were a big secret instead of being all over Paisley. He and Eddie were too far down the food chain to be noticed. They Bulgarians would hold Hammond responsible for the loss, and if he was lucky, just kill him. Gordon jumped up onto a street junction box and perched there waiting and wondering.

Ten minutes later a Sherpa van marked, 'Hammond Enterprise's' turned past him and parked outside the Waterloo Bar. Gordon leapt down terrified, shrinking back into the pub doorway trying to decide which way to run until Eddie leant out the window and waved.

Gordon ran across to the driver's door. 'How could you be so fucking stupid, have you gone totally Tonto? You scared the shit out of me. I told you to steal a van.'

'That's what I've done, stole it. You don't think I waltzed in and asked Big Gillespie if we could borrow it, did you? That would be mad right enough.'

'You're a fucking moron. Can you dig us any deeper in the shite? He waved any more discussion away. 'I'm not hanging around here till three now, waiting till Gillespie turns up looking for the Sherpa. You stay here but keep the engine running. I'll be back in five minutes.'

Boyle pushed his face against the kiosk window.

'Heads up boys, I think we have a player. Yon wee guy in the parka, his head going like a jewellery box ballerina. See him? He's just pulled his hood up'

Coyle began to take fast pictures but he was too late to get a face shot. Brown tried to raise more than static on the radio. McDowall flung the newspaper between the exposed joists and stood up.

'What're you all doing crouched down like German snipers, he can't see us.'

Parka man produced a key.

'We have a winner.' crowed Boyle.

McDowall pushed to the front and wiped a sleeve across the glass. Something about this guy was familiar but the hood gave no face view from here. They watched the locker opened and a holdall lifted out. McDowall made for the door.

'Right, lets grab the wee fucker.'

'Whoa up there big man, let's stick to the plan where we tail them and see where the goods go. Get Devaney on the radio.'

There was no joy with the walkie-talkies because Devaney had by now turned off the base station in his office. Dodging around Coyle, McDowall was first out the door, jumped up on a baggage trolley and spotted his quarry heading for the exit ramp. He roared at the others to head that way and set off in pursuit.

Gordon McGrath heard the shouting which was enough to spook him into a jog. Rattling like a broken pump, McDowall arrived at the car park barrier to find no van.

'Where the fuck's our bloody van?' he roared as the other three joined him. Boyle was still rabbiting into the radio with no effect, nobody was listening.

McDowall dodged down the ramp, weaving between taxis and baggage trains shouting over his shoulder. 'Find the van and follow on.'

He dashed into Hope Street but got no sight of McGrath so he climbed onto a wobbly bin and scanned all ways. Car horns drew his attention as a van pulled into traffic opposite the bus station. He fell rather than jumped down and ran out into traffic weaving through vehicles trying to keep the van in sight as it turned down Wellington Street towards the river. But not before he'd caught sight of the writing on the side panel He tripped and fell to his knees gasping, clinging to a lamp post. Spots tangoed in front of his eyes.

Coyle found the BR van in the yard and, horn blasting, drove through the red light and down the Exit ramp. Brown pointed to where he glimpsed McDowall a block away just rounding the corner. When they pulled up alongside him he was on his knees, gasping.

'Gods' truth,' he croaked. 'The Three Stooges are here. Any sign of them?'

'Well gone,' said Boyle, 'never even got the plates.'

Coyle put a lit fag in McDowall's mouth. 'Drag on that, do you the world of good. You do know you're facing the wrong way for Mecca.'

'Don't care who I'm praying to, it's working fine. God is very quick today. I know where they're going. That was Hammond's van. Get it phoned in.'

Devaney watched from the first-floor window as McDowall climbed from the rear of the van and glared up at him. Devaney smirked and lifted the telephone. He spoke to his wife, Claire, told her he was finishing early and to come collect him, right now. By the time McDowall crashed in he was forted behind his desk. Coyle and Boyle had left without a word or even a nod. McDowall slammed the door behind him. Devaney intended to savour every sweet moment.

'What a disaster, Frank, shame it went pear shaped but these things happen. Tannock will be disappointed no doubt, but it's sheer bad luck.'

McDowall kicked the filing cabinet. 'Bad luck, my arse.'

'This is your doing, you slimy fuckwit. Your revenge.'

'Revenge for what? Have you hurt me in some way?'

Brown tried to calm things down. 'Look, what's done is done. We need surely to decide where we go from here. Why don't I get us all a brew?'

'Why don't you do that.' McDowall snapped and walked to the window to calm himself. And there she was, in the car park. Claire. Looking up at the window. He thought he'd been hit with a train, put his hand on the window where her face was. She looked up and saw him, hugged herself tight across her breasts and stared at her feet, unable to look at him. Frank's heart ripped. Devaney smirked at his reflection in the window.

Brown was at the tea trolley when he heard the crash. McDowall appeared in a rush from the office, took his mug, drained it.

'What the total fuck's going on?' Brown asked.

'Right! Let's go. That's the hot debrief over.'

Brown could see Devaney through the office door,

struggling up with a burst lip. McDowall was away down the stair and Brown only caught up with him at the car park barrier. He was staring across at a slim blond woman standing by a car. The woman bowed her head, lifted both hands to her mouth. McDowall seemed aware of nothing but her, his vision tunnelled on her face. Brown yanked at his arm, but he was in a silent bubble, heedless of everything.

'Are you mad, Frank?' Brown hissed. 'Did you thump Devaney? I didn't sign up for this crap, Frank.'

McDowall just shoved his hands deep in his coat pockets, made a sucking noise. Brown persisted, gripping his arm.

'Did you tell him about the van, the lead on Hammond?'

'Naw. Not giving that knob diddly. We'll be handling that side of it from here on in.'

'Tannock will crucify you.'

'Sufficient unto the day son. I think we've overstayed out welcome.' He turned away, didn't look back. Brown watched the woman staring after him as he went.

Brown saw her face crumble.

Then he got it.

*

CHAPTER 11

The McGraths drove off the Kingston Bridge by the Cook Street ramp and took the Paisley Road through Govan. Gordon sat quietly with the holdall resting at his feet like a live bomb, not believing what he'd done, only now grasping the possibilities and the consequences.

Eddie broke the silence. 'Went okay then?'

'Aye, but there's a wee change of plan.'

'How so?'

'I decided we were due compensation for being robbed of Liverpool by that smarmy git Hammond. So, we're having the drugs.'

'Jeez! You ripped off Hammond?'

'I did. Feck him and his suppliers both, and that big shite, Gillespie. He'll be sorry he stuck that cannon of his in my face.'

Eddie slapped the steering wheel. 'Limping hell brother, you really have some set of balls. Here's you worried I took their van and then you go and blag everything. You do know this isnae the usual supplier, this lot are big bad Commies?'

'I don't give a toss who they are.'

'I heard the new source was Bulgaria, I think.'

'Peasants and goat shaggers. They'll be looking for

Hammond, not us.'

'What's the plan then?'

'We disappear for a day or two and lay low. We'll hole up at that derelict farm, Taylor's old place at The Steadings just off the Braes Road. The big barn there can hide the van. We get Ma to bring our money and stash from the house and we take off for Newcastle. From there we get our arses to London where there are opportunities for two guys with money and product. We'll top up our drugs and money by raiding all the planks we know about. We're playing with the big boys now brother. Sky's the limit. And we have fifty thousand in used notes. We are fucking rich.'

Eddie gawped at him. 'You took the Commie money as well? Solid hardcore, brother.'

McDowall spoke not a word till they arrived back at Golspie Road station. He and Brown sat silently in the car. McDowall was aware Brown was gagging to get away, to bury this day behind him and distance himself for the storm that would follow.

'The Stewart family funeral is tomorrow. I intend to go; we should both go since we've failed them. I'll get you at the cemetery, be there for nine.'

Brown nodded. McDowall jumped a taxi home, quietly let himself in, dropped his coat over the hall table, kicked off his shoes and tiptoed into the living room. He poured a whisky from the sideboard, loosened his tie and padded across to lean on the kitchen door frame. Two places were set at the small kitchen table. Napkins even and a candle. Irene didn't turn from the sink. He felt her silent reproach.

Her pain.

'So, you're back. How did Glasgow go?'

'Bit of a train wreck to be honest.'

'I see.' She lifted her apron and dabbed at her eyes with it. McDowall hung his head and hoped it was the onions. His guilt flailed at him.

She turned and blew her nose. 'Did you speak to Devaney?'

'Work stuff. I left it to the others mostly.'

She held his eyes with hers. 'Did you see her?'

There it was, the white-hot question she needed to ask, ripping like a blade across his conscience, stinging in its rebuke, gangrene of the memory. He didn't blame her for he had turned every endearment uttered by him to dust.

'No,' he lied.

She sighed. 'Sit down, I know you won't have eaten properly all day. I've made you gammon steak and mashed potatoes with beans. There's bread and butter with custard and jam roll for afters.'

McDowall felt a surge of compassion at her effort. He had hurt her so many times over the years and his guilt was as crushing as her pain and humiliation. She brought both plates over and sat across from him but still could not look at him, avoiding his eyes.

'There's more. Devaney sabotaged the whole thing to stuff me and I called him out on it. Things got a bit skelly and we fell out.'

Irene sipped at her water. 'And?'

'I dragged him over his desk and banjoed him. Twice.'

Irene stretched across the table, took his whisky, drank it straight over.

Thursday was a grey flinty day, everything funeral weather should be. The wind tumbled cloud and harr across a sky shredded by cold silver talons of light. The high stone wall marked the final boundary between life and death, the here, and hereafter. The slimy trees were bare and dripping, their branches creaking in the wind, black claws reaching for the living from that other place. McDowall found Alec Stewart at the back of the cemetery, his back to the wall. Alec offered a hip flask, McDowall took a sip to be sociable.

'Thanks for that, Alec, a wee starter for the day. You didn't go to the Kirk?'

'I'm not wanted. Shunned by the family, cast out into the darkness among the heathen. The roof would likely fall in anyway.'

'How is any of this your fault?'

'Black sheep. Easy target. Also, I'm told my big brother left me his house. Not gone down well with Lorraine or the Stewart clan in-laws at all.'

'Family. Worse than the Mafia sometimes.'

'Speaking of which, where's Irene?'

'At the Kirk. The choir is part of the cortege.' Jim Brown came up behind them but only nodded. Alec sensed a strain between them, raised his eyebrows at Frank who just shook his head wanting to leave it alone for now. Faintly they could hear a piper playing a lament, floating softly on the wind, the tap of a lonely snare drum keeping the pace. Mourners streamed up Abbey Road like a black snake. Guides in uniform, the church choir in white surplices, the WRVS in blue blazers. The pipes fell silent, only the drum now, tapping out a slow march, followed by the school pipe band with instruments slung. The three hearses wound their way over the crunching gravel.

Not a sound as the pallbearers bore the caskets to the open graves.

The Reverend Goodwillie praised the dear departed, calling them a light in the darkness, all very caring persons, loved and respected by all. A tight-knit Christian family who gave fully of the spirit within them, always ready to offer help. It was all true, Angela had been something special and McDowall felt his eyes stinging. Lorraine spotted Alec and sent a pallbearer across with a wee numbered card.

'Three.' murmured Alec and marched across to take his place on the slippery battens alongside Robert's coffin. As they lowered them one by one, the minister intoned.

"May the angels welcome you into Paradise, the martyrs rejoice."

Alec was grim as a headstone, thinking Viking funeral revenge, about those responsible having their throats slit and dumped into the graves. Weeping would not do it for him. The lone piper played *'Flowers of The Forest.'* ripping out their hearts until the crowd melted away.

Alec returned to where McDowall stood by the wall till

only they remained under the tree, serenaded by the whirling craws disturbed by the pipes, wings clattering like a bag of bones. They passed the flask back and forth listening to the gravediggers thump the mud into the graves.

'Have to ask you, Frank, any progress? Or does everyone want it just tidied away?'

'Looking at it coldly, you'll see there's little to link anybody to anything.'

'Coldly you say. I can manage that. I can do Baltic.'

'Listen Alec, somewhere down the road they'll make a mistake. Bragging to the wrong person, telling the tale in the wrong place. Nothing is surer than we'll nail them for something.'

'For something Frank, is that what Angela and her Mum and Dad are now? You're godchild, my flesh and blood. Just something? The law doesn't get them and that's okay, is it?'

'I know what you are Alec, what you're capable of. Tell me you won't do anything stupid.'

'Define stupid for me. You know me, firm belief in the rule of law.'

'Pity we both can't take the same road in this.'

'Some roads are best travelled alone.'

McDowall changed tack, aware Alec's idea of justice was putting two in the head. 'I take it you are not welcome at the purvey?'

'I wouldn't mingle with that lot anyway. Vultures.'

McDowall rattled the change in his pocket. 'I fancy a pie

and a pint. My treat. You?'

'Aye. Just give me a quiet minute alone.'

He walked across to the graves, remembered he'd not been here since young Kevin was put in the ground with bugles, guard of honour, and three volleys. Ethel had refused the War Graves Commission headstone. He lifted two sods of mud, squeezing them hard in each hand till the water squirted from them like blood. The hollow thud as they landed on each lid was like a full stop, an end of all things.

The Wallace Bar was quiet, not a lot of lunchtime trade. They sat under the high window with two pints and grey mince pies on paper plates. McDowall sipped his beer, wiped his lips with the back of his hand.

'What's the plan now, Alec?'

'I'm moving into Robert's house now that the family has blagged what they fancy. I can take Buster off your hands now.'

McDowall didn't argue, secretly relieved and ready to trade the dog for brownie points with Irene. They finished their pints in silence, each sunk in the morass of their own thoughts. They left the pies as a fly feast and sauntered up the road in silence. As he fiddled with his keys and unlocked the door McDowall asked, 'Will you come in for a brew?'

Alec shrugged. 'Naw thanks, I'll leave it for now. I don't like much to be indoors now.'

Alec waited outside with the garden gnomes while Buster was fetched along with a bag of doggie accessories. The mutt bounded out jumping around his legs.

'At least he's happy to see me. My best pals are a cop and a dog, the dynamic duo. I'll away down to the Legion Club and have a pint.'

McDowall watched them go, thinking Alec looked like a wee lost boy. Irene was still at the funeral purvey in the church hall, so, in an attempt to erase the dog McDowall took an aerosol to the house until he coughed, covering any lingering dog smell with lavender.

Greta McGrath always worked the Thursday all day and was behind the bar at the British Legion dealing with the lunchtime rush of four punters. A small granite faced woman wearing a stained green Bri-Nylon overall, a fashion icon to synthetic fibres crowned by big black dyed hair and rollers.

'A face like a box of broken sticks,' her boss had once commented.

She barely came up to the same level as the beer pumps and stood on a box to reach the till. She'd just slammed the drawer shut and sneaked a gulp at a pilfered whisky when Malkie Douglas waved at her from the end of the bar. Greta picked up the truncheon from under the counter.

'You're barred, ya wee knob. Get yersel oot of here smartish.'

'Haud oan a minute Mrs.' Malkie leant on the bar and whispered to her. 'Ah've goat a message from yer boys.'

'Why would they send the likes you with any message? Ye don't know what day of the week it is. Give us the message if ye mind it and bugger off.'

'You've tae go intae their rooms and turn their beds upside doon. They said ye wid know whit tae dae then and bring them whit's there.'

'Bring them whit and where? Tell them tae dae their ain running aboot.'

'They're lying low for now up at The Steadings. They say it's where ye used to take some of yer punters in their cars.'

'Ah've goat the message, get oan yer bike and scram.'

'Dae Ah no get a reward?'

Greta leant across the bar and rapped her knuckles on his forehead. 'Whit part of barred is no getting in there? Hallo, message delivered, fuck off. Next time you take a shite in a pub, ya clatty bastard, lift the lid first. Take a hike.'

Nobody noticed the man in a black tie leave with his dog and follow Malkie out. Greta made an excuse to her boss about her boys being in bother and she had to go to bail them out. He found that easy to believe but warned her she would be docked an hour.

'That right?' she said. 'Ah'll be sure tae let ma boys know that when Ah see them.'

'You can tell them as well that one of our regulars has been asking after them. Alec Stewart? Was in early with his dog. Sat in the corner quietly nursing a pint. Did you know that fucking gangster Gillespie was in this morning wanting to know where your boys were? I don't want any bother brought here Greta.'

'Then mind your own fucking business.'

She flung on her coat and took a taxi home. Not only this

Stewart guy was looking for her sons. Gillespie and his two glove puppets had been in earlier, sniffing What had they done now? When she pushed her boys' room door open it was like a bulldozer clearing the floor. A wave of cans and carry-out containers whose rotting remains layered the feral stink of sweat and soiled underwear. She picked her way over to the twin beds her feet sliding on glossy scud books and a couple of used condoms.

She flipped over Gordon's bed. Mystery solved. There were five brown plastic bundles a foot square taped to the springs. It was the same under Eddie's bed. Tearing the corner of one, then a second, she found tightly wrapped banknotes in some, drugs in others, all sorted into polythene bags.

She knew her boys had been stealing from Hammond for years, but a dribble skimmed off the top she'd thought. A shortfall this big was going to get noticed. It was going to get them killed.

How did those eejits expect her to move all this up the Steadings?

Fat Bob the taxi driver had groaned lifting Greta's case into the boot and struggled even more to get it out when he parked on the single-track road at the bottom of the Steadings track. He slammed the lid and stood gasping, looking around him.

'Are ye sure ye want dropped away oot here? There's bugger all here but sheep shaggers and dug walkers.'

'It's fine,' said Greta, drawing her kaftan tightly around her skinny frame. Ma boys are picking me up. How much?'

'A fiver.'

'Robbing bastard, ye should wear a mask.'

The driver snatched the money from her fingers. 'It's a fiver 'cos Ah've nae doubt got a hernia frae lugging your case in and oot that boot. Is it bricks or bodies you have in there? Did ye forget yer shovel, ye auld witch? It's you that needs the mask by the by.' He looked at the fiver. 'Whit? Nae tip?'

'Aye! Its high time ye changed yer knickers. If it was you that was in ma bags Ah wid need a forklift.'

She hobbled to the edge of the road dragging the case and fell when her polyester bell-bottoms caught in her heels and tripped her. Cursing fluently she sat atop the case and lit up.

The old house at Steading 5 was derelict now. A corrugated sheet roof still covered half the barn, the breezeblock walls largely intact. Most of the cottage roof had collapsed inside and the plywood shuttering on the doors and windows were soaked and warped or peeled away from the frame where folk had shimmied inside.

The last tenant, Old Turner, had died five years since and the buildings taken by the banks and left to rack and ruin. Not a slate remained, just rotting roof boards. Nettles and weeds had reclaimed the ground inside the house walls. Everything not screwed down had been stolen. The debris of drunken parties was strewn all over the yard. Cans, bottles, carry-out containers, two sodden stained mattresses arranged on the only part of the barn with a floor. In the yard a rusted water windmill creaked and groaned atop a sealed off well. The trees had grown tall, moving and groaning in the wind but screening the ruins from the road. Soon they would fall and embrace the ruins. This had been a place for the McGrath brothers to hide stolen cars and their first base when they began dealing in drugs drink and sex. It took both of the brothers to force the sliding door wide enough to drive the Sherpa in, but it jammed when they tried to close it and they left it slightly open. They walked down the track in the gloaming to meet their mother.

Greta was sitting on the case chain smoking when Gordon appeared out the dark and barked at her.

'Are you fucking mental? Ye might as well put up a big neon sign.'

'Me fucking mental? Ah'm no the barmy tosser that's been cheating Hammond. You and that other yin are being hunted big time. And not just by Gillespie.'

'Who? Foreign guys?'

'Naw, some old guy with a dog, Stewart or something. Drinks in the Legion.' Greta stumbled as she rose and Gordon steadied her. 'What's the story with this lassie deid at your flat in Knox Road. Tell me you and Eddie wirnae involved in that, it's the talk of the Steamie.'

'We were away when all that happened, it was that gang of jakeys that Brodie lets hing aboot there. McDowall's trying to pin it on us.'

'I knew my boys wouldn't do anything like that.'

Gordon was glad of the dark. 'Never mind all that, how are you getting down the road?'

'Bill the Bonker from the Legion will be here in ten

minutes tae pick me up. What are you going to do now? Are you two on the run?'

'Never you mind. We'll stay hid till tomorrow. I've got a plan to get away across tae the continent. Holland maybe.'

'Yer big plans are turning to dross. Big Gillespie was in the Legion this morning first thing with them two hand puppets of his. Word is out that naebody is to help you and anybody that disnae shop the pair of ye is deid for sure.' Gordon dropped to his knees, unzipped the case and the smell of chips and vinegar wafted out.

'I stopped at Sandro's on the way and there's a couple of cans as well.'

'Grand stuff. Haud oan a minute, there's only nine packets of money here.'

Greta bent down beside his head. 'If you two are buggering off, then Ah'm gointae need something to tide me by in my old age.'

Eddie shoved her tumbling backwards into the ditch where she flailed like an old sheep on its back. 'Ya grasping auld shite. Maybe we should leave yer thieving carcass in the fields wi the rest of the auld coos.'

Gordon pushed him away. 'Leave her alone. One packet won't break the bank.'

Greta rolled away from the nettles and retreated cursing down the hill to where Bill the Bonker was flashing his car headlights, afraid to come closer. The brothers grabbed the case and returned to the barn where they opened the packages, making two stacks, one drugs and one money. They ate the chips as they contemplated exactly what they'd done. This was how Gordon intended to lift himself from the gutter.

'Right,' said Eddie, 'let's be splitting it up this up right here right now, equal shares, down the middle, fifty-fifty.'

That took Gordon by surprise. 'What? Why split it at all now? You'll just fritter it away on drugs and whores. This money wid last you a lifetime of drugs and whores if that's whit ye want.'

'Ah'm fed up getting scraps, palmed off with just enough to get stoned and pished. Handed out like pocket money.'

Gordon smiled, placated him. 'Of course you're getting fair shares, brother. What we'll do is move half of the drugs to your end of the case, then half the money to my end. See? Now we each have a space, all torapeachy. Okay now, happy?'

'Fair do's. And I can do what Ah like wi ma share?'

'Definitely, wee brother, anything you say.'

Eddie pulled the case over to his side and rested an arm on it. 'Dae ye think she'll manage with us gone?'

'Ye think? Forgot already have ye that she's kept a fair share of the money? As long as there are mugs tae shag her she'll be fine.' Gordon checked the time. 'I'm knackered so I'm grabbing a wee kip in the van. You keep a lookout for now, then me. It's just after four and getting dull already, so when it's full dark wake me and we're for the off. You can sleep all the way to Newcastle.'

'Are we no changing motors? The polis are maybe looking for this thing.'

'Dae ye really think Gillespie reported the van nicked?'

Gordon climbed into the front and lay along the bench seat, Eddie pulled up a crate and settled down to watch the farmyard through the gap, resting his back against the wall and keeping the case within arm's reach.

Neither of them had known anything of their father except blows. Greta had turned to the whoring on the side to pay for school bus-runs and to keep them in shoes. She'd had a worse life than her sons he knew, one dead end job after another and paying the bills with sex. Thieving seemed only right, to take what they were denied all their lives. Now he stood a chance at escaping the sewer.

In the distance, he could see a snow-topped Ben Lomond across the Clyde. He checked Gordon wasn't watching, pulled a half bottle of cheap Lanliq wine from inside his jacket and took a long chug.

*

CHAPTER 12

Alec followed Malkie from the Legion Club down to the footpath on the bank of Black Cart Water and ambushed him. He'd always found a mix of violence and a fistful of drug money persuasive. Within minutes of thumping him once before shoving a fiver into his jacket, Alec knew where the McGraths were. Leaving Malkie crumpled on the path he then followed his usual dog walk route past Highcraig Quarry before contouring East and splashing across the Brandy Burn, the water nudging the tops of his wellies, the dog trailing after him its belly submerged. He had to flop up the bank. Buster gave a forlorn bark and Alec knelt and reached down and pulled him out of the water by his collar. Alec's right leg fell back in and chilled water filled his welly. He lay on the bank gasping while Buster looked at him accusingly as he shook the water from his coat.

'I know, I know, we came too far,' Alec said as he sat on a rock to empty his welly.

He rested on the bank and smoked, watched the dusk morph to night, readying himself. He had no real plan except to confront the McGraths. What happened after that would be reactive not deliberate. Today had been rough. His family and its future swept away by scum, an end of all things at the graveside.

Hard self confessions crowded in. His wife and child had

not been taken but fled, from him. He had driven them away, a drunk and a wife beater. That could go on his gravestone. He had always thought the worst thing that could happen to him was to die alone and without the love of his daughter. It seemed now that was exactly what he had achieved. All of it gone, and all down to him, a long list of bad choices writ large. Tonight would see the end of his search for the McGrath brothers.

It was now nearly full dark. As a child he had feared it but now it concealed him from all his mistakes. His friend, his blanket. From here he could see all the way across to the snow-streaked rampart of mountains at the head of the loch. He could see Ben Lomond and The Cobbler catching the last rays of sun on their topping of snow. These were the very first hills he had climbed as a boy from the Boy Scout outdoor centre at Auchengillan so long ago. He felt the chill now and rose whistling for the dog, taking the old farm track that contoured down the shoulder past Steading 5. He stopped on the rise and lay in the grass scanning the derelict farm buildings for activity until the Western horizon turn from crimson to black.

Many of Alec's boyhood memories lingered in this place. He heard the groaning rattle of the windmill blades straining against its chain tether close to the well. By the well he paused at the concrete wall and lifted one side of the mesh, peering down to the black water mirror reflecting the moon. On a summer afternoon long ago when they were boys together, a skinny Frank McDowall had nearly died in that well. Horsing around like Errol Flynn in Captain Blood fencing off pirates he'd tumbled in. One minute he'd been there then gone, the only sound his falling and the splash echoing up the shaft. He didn't cry out. Alec was first there. McDowall's white face stared up at him as Frank clung white knuckled to an old metal step in the wall. Neil Gillespie had been one of the other two boys there.

Alec had taken charge, a rope was found, and he'd been lowered into the depths head first and Neil had hauled them both out. Long time ago and those four boys all gone different ways now. He'd acted without thinking, and ever since it seemed. His whole life unplanned and rudderless as a barque before the storm.

Buster had halted by the barn wall and peed, then growled and gave short barks, pointing to the barn, ears flat tail up. Tyre tracks in the mud stopped at the sliding door. Malkie's mumblings were confirmed. Alec crouched quickly covering the dog's muzzle, listening intently. A vehicle door slammed. He rose slapping the side of his thigh as he passed the dog, but Buster ignored the heel command and raced ahead into the barn.

'Shit!' His adrenaline pumped and he pressed against the outside wall keeping to the shadows. He heard voices inside, then Buster yelping in pain. Alec moved along to the gap in the door, walking on the outside of his feet softly, heel down first, making no sound. From there he peered into the gloomy barn, watching and listening.

'Fucks sake, Eddie, leave the bloody dog be.'

'Who the fuck is you shushing? It's just a scabby dug.'

'It's maybe not up here on its own.'

Alec's breathing bumped up, Malkie had told him the

truth, the McGraths were here right enough. He heard heavy footsteps inside and something metal crashed against the door, bouncing and clattering. He searched the ground for a weapon and picked up all he could find, a slimy piece of two-by-two timber. Inside Buster snarled again. Alec swung himself around the door and went right, careful to stay close to the wall wielding the timber in both hands like a samurai sword. One shadowy figure held Buster down with his foot, the other leaned against a Sherpa van.

Alec knew who they were.

The McGraths, who'd destroyed Angela.

All his rage and training went coldly berserker, all the arid years of anguish and pain focused on the immediacy of this moment. He let the red mist sweep over him and followed his instincts now his whole mind and body ready in those seconds. The van headlights blazed on robbing Alec of his night vision. He raised his hand to shade his eyes. Buster twisted free from Gordon and clamped his teeth on Eddie's ankle who kicked the dog off. Alec stood trapped in the fierce light, transfixed centre stage.

It was a sign from the Devil, his trigger.

He backed against the wall, aware of Eddie moving left to widen the field and block the exit. Alec had no intention of running. The need to begin regardless of cost was overwhelming. Aware Eddie was blinded as him in the glare Alec took the initiative, leapt forward and whacked him rapidly twice across his raised forearms with the timber. Eddie grabbed hold of it and tore it away from him cackling as he raised it over his head. Alec took the opportunity to step swiftly inside his swing arc, gripped the front of his coat and headbutted him letting him fall back snorting blood. Buster joined in by gnawing at Eddie's arm.

'Fucksake!' Gordon shouted. 'Can you not clatter an old man? Do I have to do everything myself?'

Alec maintained his momentum, stamping down on Eddie's sternum using his body as leverage to get height and weight over Gordon. Although Alec believed in his mind he was still a young Marine galloping over Dartmoor, he was out of condition. His leap fell short and he folded to his knees like Superman exposed to Kryptonite. Gordon punched him twice in the stomach while Eddie flung one arm round his neck and began to kidney punch him. Alec got his legs up and kicked Gordon away. They both mobbed him and as he fell, a boot coming in like a piston smashing into his head. Alec fell backwards against the side of the van like a puppet with the strings cut. As he scrabbled into the gap between the van and the wall they followed up kicking. Alec curled up and nursed the pain, using it to fuel his resolve.

Thinking him finished the McGraths closed in. Eddie stomped him.

'What's your problem anyway, grandad?'

Gordon put a hand on Eddie's shoulder and peered from behind him.

'Hold a minute. Don't you know who this is?'

'Couldn't care fucking less. I'm doing him and his dug.'

'This is the guy that's been going around the west end asking about us and Brodie. This is the uncle, the big war hero

Gillespie said was asking about us all over the West End.'

Eddie sneered. 'We're shitting oor breeks. Where are your medals now John Wayne?' He leaned down and punched Alec's face. 'See what you've done to my nose Action Man?'

'Before I kill you I'm going to eat your dog.'

Alec saw them through a crimson veil, knew if he didn't get up these two were going to stomp him until he was a beanbag. Rolling onto his hands and knees his whole body shrieked pain at him, confirming he was still alive.

He had a splinter flashback of watching helpless as a mob in Oman trampled a woman to death and knew how swiftly it was done. Their shrill cries of *'qutil asaahira.'* and her bones snapping still splintered his nightmares.

Eddie bashed his head into the wall. Alec's vision blurred, his movements becoming erratic and weak. He had to get up. He heard the voice of his combat instructor screaming at him.

'It's all in your head, son. Get fucking up. Your body says no but as long as you move your mind your arse will follow it. If you lie here, you'll die.'

Alec felt the sole of a boot on the side of his face, grinding down, tearing his skin. Eddie yelled in Alec's face.

'Want to know what she was choking on when she died? Alec's whole focus now was to stand and fight. Attempting to lever himself up, Alec slashed his palm on broken glass, the pain focusing all his effort. He felt for the neck of the broken bottle. Using the van door handle he dragged himself up onto his knees, his forehead pressed against the van door.

'There's life in the auld bastard yet, Eddie.'

'No for long.'

Alec felt two hands on his throat, the thumbs compressing his larynx forcing his tongue up into his mouth. In a red blur he grabbed the wing mirror with his left hand and pulled himself up onto his knees driving the jagged bottle in his right up into Eddies crotch. Felt it go in deep and hard, relishing the animal scream. Alec pushed himself upright, roaring in bloodlust, tearing and twisting the broken bottle out of Eddie, who fell backwards screeching, his hands pressed vainly into the massive femoral wound, the blood flooding into his clothes. Gordon tried to catch his brother as he fell back on him but slipped under the sudden weight and hammered his head against the metal of the van. Alec reached over Eddie's shoulder forcing Gordon's head back and rammed the bottle into his neck.

Both brothers convulsed under him, gurgling, screaming crimson bubbles. Alec rolled backwards into the corner with the bottle held out in front, but the brothers were finished.

Alec thought his heart would burst, had trouble focusing. Black spots danced in his vision like mosquitoes. His trembling arm fell to his side. The stench of the blood brought flashback images of other places, other kills. His pulse was roaring in his ears his lungs pumping like bellows as he ate the very air in huge frantic gulps. Buster trotted over beside him teeth bared and growling at his tormentors.

Eddie stopped thrashing first. Gordon blew bubbles of blood past the hands pressed to his massive throat wound for a wee bit longer. Sitting against the wall Alec stroked Buster's head and watched them die.

Summoned to Tannock's office earlier that evening McDowall thought it best to break habit and knock on the door instead of charging in. He checked his reflection in the landing window. While obvious he'd made some effort by wetting his hair down, he still looked like a bag of frogs. Tannock, of course, knew it was him at the door and it was a full minute before he was bidden to enter the Holy of Holies. McDowall grabbed the back of the naughty chair and made to sit, but Tannock shook his head at him.

'Please remain standing, Detective Sergeant. This is a chat regarding your conduct in Glasgow. I trust you don't intend to be dragging any more senior officers across desks?' McDowall knew a hatchet job when he saw it, so he clasped his hands behind his back and stared at the portrait of the Queen on the wall above Tannock's head. Least said soonest mended he thought, let's see what he's got to say. Tannock let the silence drag, taking in the stained cardigan with buttons missing, shirt untucked on one side and the scratched and bruised face.

'What on earth happened to your face?'

'Late night walk up the Bluebell Woods. Tripped in the dark and snacked my coupon on various trees on my way down the slope to the burn.'

Tannock sighed. 'You've been a sore trial to me since I arrived here, but you seem to have surpassed yourself today.' Tannock held up a waving hand 'Do not speak. It's best you say nothing. The Regional Crime Squad operation at Glasgow Central is history. We've been embarrassed by you and made fools of. The drugs are gone, the money is gone, the perpetrators have evaded pursuit.' He pointed a rigid finger. 'While the McGraths were getting away, you're dragging Devaney across his desk and assaulting him, in front of two detectives from City of Glasgow Police.'

'Allegations, but no statements,' said McDowall. 'Is that Devaney's version? He tripped and smacked his coupon on the desk on the way over. Maybe it was him was drunk? DC Brown was not present at the time, he was getting us a brew. Neither were the two Glesga Dicks. As for the office staff seeing, the blinds were down.'

'Yes. DC Brown has already stated where he was and saw nothing. He's protecting you. Does that make you feel good, persuading another officer to lie from misplaced loyalty?'

McDowall stared at the wall. 'Loyalty is never misplaced.'

Tannock ignored him. 'The only redeeming result of the whole day is that nobody has made a written complaint, all the witnesses struck blind it seems. There is a further allegation that you were drunk.'

'Drunk? No way was I drunk.'

'Several people from the office staff to the Glasgow detectives say they smelled drink from you. That you were under the influence.'

'Absolute bollocks, sir. Devaney's pressured his staff. I'd been to the pub the night before so that must be it.'

'Then the only mitigation I can offer the Chief Constable is that one of my detectives was perhaps under the influence when he allegedly assaulted a senior officer. This is no defence, Sergeant McDowall, nor an excuse. It is the reason for your hooligan behaviour. Admit you have a drink problem and that today this interfered with your judgement in this disgraceful situation. Will you at least give that?'

McDowall stared out the window and held his tongue. He prayed for this day to end, allowing his mind to wander to Angela, hoping Tannock would be done with him soon. For now, he zoned the droning out and lost himself in a hazy plan of sorts.

Alec had sunk into shock and his brain took shelter in passing out, only waking when Buster began licking the blood from his face. Staring at the corpses, he felt neither remorse nor satisfaction. He had quenched a primeval thirst for revenge, to rob them of everything they had taken from him. The world was well shot of them both. He removed his reeking coat and flung it in the back of the van on top of a plastic sheet held down by a large holdall. He hauled the bag out and unzipped it, struck dumb by its contents. Bundles of brown wrapped blocks about a foot square and bricks of banknotes in heavy duty polythene. He had never seen so much money in his life. He re-zipped the bag and looked from it to the two bodies weltering in their blood up the side of the van.

No way was this the McGrath's stash. These two were nothing but messenger boys, not to be trusted to empty a payphone. This was serious money for heavy people. Who were they transporting it for, and to where? This had to be a meet he realised, and there could be others here shortly, a lot more impressive than these two. They would be looking for this holdall. Galvanised by passing headlights on the road he ignored his racked body and rose slowly and painfully.

'All in the mind, son, all in the mind.' The ghost of Corporal Craig whispered as Alec clung to the van door whimpering.

He put the holdall outside the barn then took the plastic sheet from the van and spread it next to the bodies but there was little room for manoeuvre, so he let off the handbrake and rolled the van forward. He slid the bodies onto the plastic one by one and dragged them to the van where he had propped a sheet of corrugated steel at an angle. He manhandled Eddie onto it, lifted it level and slid the corpse into the van tipping him off. His brother joined him in quick order.

A search of the barn produced solidified paint tins, some thinners, a small drum of two- stroke oil and two forty-five-gallon drums of waste oil. Alec covered the bodies with rotten timber, waste paper, a mattress, and the mower fuel. A rusted pick punctured the van's petrol tank, then the drums so the waste oil ran down the slope around the van. There were enough scraps to make a petrol-soaked torch from a piece of timber and a sack. Retreating to the door he touched a lighter to the sacking which flared immediately, showering his hand in sparks, and burning hessian.

Tossed underhand it made a lazy fiery arc through the side door of the van. A fireball forced him to retreat as a hungry fire raced across the ground to feed on this sacrificial pyre. Dark rolling smoke convected down and vented from every roof opening boiling to escape, drawing a strong draft past his head. He knew it was time to be away from this place, but he had to see, to witness and relish their destruction.

He watched until his face was dry and hot, before backing away slowly gripped by the images as the flames licked and danced around the bodies, bursting their skins and consuming Angela's killers. Alec wished they had been alive, and that Angela could have heard their screaming.

Like Angela's, unanswered.

He forced his battered body into motion, grabbing the holdall and fell across the fence to the path downhill. Buster came panting behind him. He had plunged into the Brandy Burn and was splashing its cool water on his injured face when he heard the roar behind him. Turning, he saw the glow in the sky as the roof timbers fell in throwing a vast cloud of Hell-tinted black smoke against the stars, twisting like vented devils.

Tannock pursed his lips and closed the folder in front of him. McDowall still frustrated him by his no comment attitude.

'Fine! You're entitled to hold your own council until a formal hearing. You're not suspended for now but you are switched to desk duties for the foreseeable future. You'll not leave the station while on duty without my express permission. You are relieved of all serious crime investigations as of now. I intend to bury you in dross Detective Sergeant, until you resign or learn to control your temper.'

There was a knock at the door and Brown came in.

'What part of do not disturb was misunderstood?' Tannock snapped, 'Is there nobody in this station who can obey my simple instructions?'

'Sorry, sir.' Brown handed him a radio flimsy. 'That's from car Fox2. They're reporting a major blaze up the Auchenlodment Road and are following two fire engines to the scene. They can see the flames from the Kings Road Fire Station.'

Tannock peered at the message over his Gepetto glasses.

'Where is this Steading place?'

Brown stepped to the wall map and pointed. 'Up the top of Auchenlodment Road, about a mile south of the Fire station.'

Tannock nodded, passed the note to McDowall with a smirk. 'Perfect timing for you, Detective Sergeant. This is the sort of thing you will be dealing with in the future so best get into your stride as soon as. Take DC Brown with you.'

McDowall went, Brown made to follow but Tannock called after him. 'DC Brown, a moment if you will.'

On the way to Steading 5 Brown decided to clear the air between him and McDowall. 'What's with your face, has Irene been punching you? I might get some of that as well?'

McDowall waved a hand dismissively. 'I fell in the garden, hit my face.'

'Uhuh. I need to get something off my chest, so don't interrupt me till I'm done. Today's been a bloody shambles. You involved me in your private vendetta that could see you charged and my career brought up short.'

'That why he wanted you to hold back?'

'Don't fucking interrupt! Tannock's already asked me for a statement and tried to bribe me with a promotion. I told him I was at the tea trolley and saw nothing.'

'And that's the truth.'

Brown clenched the steering wheel and missed a gear. 'Have you got nothing to say?'

'I have actually. Pick any forward gear and turn on the lights before we get booked.'

They finished the trip in silence and parked behind a fire appliance sitting in the roadway its pump roaring, basking the trees in flickering blue with its disco beacons. They were met by two grinning black faced young constables.

McDowall laughed. 'You look like the Black and White Minstrels. Did you get to play with the big boy's toys? Are you only in the polis because the Fire Brigade widnae take you?'

'Apart from the sky-high flames how did you know where to go, do you know this place?' Brown asked McDowall.

'A crowd of us played up here when we were boys. There's a well in the farmyard that I fell into doing a balancing act, nearly drowned.'

'How did you get out of that?'

McDowall grunted. 'Alec Stewart rescued me.' He didn't mention his other rescuer had been Gillespie.

The blaze held everyone spellbound, the dark slashed by whirling blue beacons, the appliance headlights projecting the flickering shadows of men and machines against the smoke. Sub Officer Crombie was coming down the track and suggested they wait by the road for now.

'Just a wee derelict barn fire then, we can get off home?' McDowall asked.

Crombie took off his helmet and wiped his black face with a filthy neckerchief.

'There may well be fertilisers and such which would make it a chemical incident should they get wet. My boys can get in soon and check it out. There's also what looks like a van inside the barn. A Sherpa van I think. And unless my nose tells lies, there's fatalities involved.'

'A Sherpa?' McDowall was alert to the idea this might be Hammonds' van. He sniffed, caught that smell on the wind. Knew it from cases where the scene was torched to destroy evidence.

'A courting couple, you think?'

Crombie shrugged. McDowall handed out some chewing gum. 'No early night for us then. How long to cool down and let our boys in?'

'An hour or so if the building is safe, what with the heat taking nearly all the mortar from between the stones both gable ends are wobbly. I've sent for Building Control, who might want to knock it down, but a good shove would probably do it.'

'No way. This is a crime scene now so once you're done I'll be having it.'

A Fire Brigade staff car had arrived with a senior officer

who spoke to Crombie but left him with it. More importantly a van arrived from the Fire Station with bacon rolls and a tea urn. Leaving two firemen on a jet at the barn the crews took themselves down to the road where they sat with their feet in the ditch feeding their black greasy faces on strong sweet tea and the bacon butties. They invited McDowall and Brown to join them and they all sat in silence munching a roll and supping a polystyrene cup each. A half hour passed, the Brigade van went off to refill the tea urn and McVicar turned up to join them.

'Well, it's yerself.' said McDowall. 'Doctor Death himself.'

'You can talk. More bodies, Frank? You could be considered a suspect serial killer with your deadly harvest increasing. What do we have?'

'Two toasties in a van up at the barn Crombie says. Wanna go up?'

'Why not? Lead on McDuff.'

McVicar changed into overalls and wellies and they all went up the track with Crombie. The Fire Brigade had strung bulkhead lighting cable from a clattering generator and the yard was well lit. There was the coppery reek of a barbecue gone wrong, a blend of hot warped metal, rubber, wood, clothing, and meat. Crombie cleared his men from inside and hawked a great glob of phlegm against the wall. He and McDowall used a crowbar to force open the rear doors of the van. Brown held back. The bodies were intertwined with each other and whatever rubbish had been piled across them had in some parts shielded them from the worst of the fire. McVicar reached in with his rubber gloved hand and lifted a smoking timber. A black and red hand sprang free and fell out as if grabbing at them, reaching for the living.

'Fuck's sake!' Brown leapt back. 'I cannae go this.' He turned on his heel and left the barn.

Crombie grinned. 'New is he? He'll need to get used to this kind of thing.'

McDowall smiled. 'Not good with squelchy dead folk, sheltered upbringing.'

'Now then Sub Officer,' McVicar asked, 'can some of your crew assist me to remove this debris layer by layer, so we can see who or what we have here?'

'Nae problem for us. Just hope they stay in one piece.'

*

CHAPTER 13

Graeme Hammond was early into his office Friday morning, and five minutes after seven called the loading bay to discover the McGraths had not appeared. 'Is the van there, check inside for a blue holdall.'

'Actually, boss, the van's no back either. Nobody knows where it is.'

'Those bastards! How could they fuck this up?' He slammed the phone down and strode out onto the walkway, shouting down into the darkened warehouse.

'Neil! Steff! Gerry! Get your arses up here.'

Gerry stepped out from underneath the mezzanine.

'Here, boss. Steff and me are here.'

'Where's Gillespie?'

'He's nicked home. He helps his mum with getting up and that. He's gone to see to her. Back within the hour he says.'

'What is he now, a fucking night nurse?' He tossed down the Daimler keys. 'Go get him and tell him I don't pay him to help the Social Work, he's meant to be here when I need him.'

'Will do.' Gerry lifted his eyebrows to Steff who shook his head. No way would he be passing on that suicide message to Neil Gillespie. When he peered through the kitchen window Gillespie was washing his mums' dishes at the sink when the buzzer sounded. He was expecting nobody so picked up the poker on the way to the window where he twitched the curtain aside. Gerry grimaced a smile and waved. Gillespie opened the window and waved him over.

'What the fuck do you want, a room?'

Gerry danced from foot to foot. 'Hammond said I was to tell you that the van's missing and they two bampots urnae back from Central Station. He thinks they took it.'

Gillespie grunted. 'Typical McGrath shit. I telt him they two couldn't pish without splashing their boots. What else?'

'Hammond wants you back right away. Said you worked for him not the District Nurse. Right now he said.'

'Did he now? Well, I'll be back when I've seen to my mother, you wait there.'

He finished the dishes and saw to his mother. As he bed bathed and got her into fresh clothes his long dead father stared at him from his picture frame on the bedside cabinet. A hard man, a fair man, honed by harsh times. Gillespie remembered his long gurgling death after years of work at Turners Asbestos, every breath a nail in his coffin. He brushed her hair and kissed her, set the record player softly repeating Vera Lynn's wartime favourites.

It was high time he took charge of young Hammond.

Hammond had resumed his heavy drinking, realising that the expansion of his empire was not going smoothly. He'd chaired a meeting at the Masonic Halls where his father's old cronies had obstructed him at every turn. The matter of the old guard would only be resolved by death it seemed. No open rift yet but a definite reluctance to change anything or bestow the succession firmly on the young Hammond. He had greased a lot of expensive palms this year between Paisley and Pemik in eastern Bulgaria, not a cheap thing. It had seemed promising at first, easy-peasy Japaneasy. He had wanted to move away from the old ways of his father and expand the business to full potential. Because of the McGraths all that was now endangered.

Graeme had always crouched in Arthur's shadow until his old man was diagnosed with lung cancer, far too late for any treatment that would do any good. Palliative care was what they called it and not much time left to the auld git. The cancer spread to his other organs and a fall and stroke in the warehouse had left him dribbling and helpless. Sadly his speech remained unaffected. They employed a nurse but six months of home care had left Graeme disgusted with the pungent smells of urine and nappies which permeated the house. Graeme's wife Emily had insisted Arthur be consigned to an expensive private nursing home where both hoped he would do the decent thing and die soon. That hadn't happened, for Arthur's generation died hard. Graeme had toyed with ordering Neil to smother Arthur in the night but was unsure if he would be obeyed on that score.

On one visit he'd stood over his father in the darkened hospice room with a pillow in his hands, listening to him snorting and bubbling. Thinking himself alone he leant close, justifying it in his head by asking why it was a dog could be put down but not a man. A chair had scraped in the darkness behind him and startled he spun round. Gillespie had been sat in the shadows next to the wardrobe, his huge shovel hands opening and closing like traps. Neither spoke. He took two slow steps towards Graeme, breaking the spell.

He'd dropped the pillow, backing towards the door then turned and left without a word. Gillespie never mentioned it but didn't let him visit alone again.

The time between visits to the home grew further apart, it being far too stark a reminder of mortality for Graeme and killing any empathy left in him. He'd consulted his lawyers, Haggerty & Lomas, resorted to the Law and took over both the legitimate concerns and the smuggling completely. The other members of the board and the shareholders had acquiesced silently, their only interest the monthly cheque and distance from the source of this wealth.

Determined to build his own reputation, Graeme had decided to continue his father's newborn arrangement with the Bulgarians. A man called Anton Tenescu had introduced himself to Graeme at an antiques fayre in Edinburgh as his father's contact and invited him to a meeting. He went on holiday to Turkey, was smuggled across the border in a diplomatic car and driven to Tenescu's dacha on the coast of the Black Sea at Varna.

On a sun terrace overlooking the beach waiters circulated with trays of champagne in hand and pistols in their belts. The other visitors dripped gold chains and Rolex watches, some wore Italian suits. Most had been involved with Arthur Hammond since the end of the war. Those in uniform with medals dating back to the Great Patriotic War were State Police or secret service. The Director of the State Railways was there representing transport and shipping interests. Two days passed drinking lots of Rakia, vodka, caviar, and girls. At the end of the week Graeme had a massive hangover, a dose of the trots and a deal signed in blood and vodka. He'd returned home with gifts for his wife, Emily. A string of local pearls and a diaspore crystal blazing yellow and set in a ring of two coiled trees. He'd also taken home a dose of the clap which strained domestic bliss for a time for which his gifts were insufficient. Emily had departed to the villa in Nerja for six months and had been extracting blood from him since her return.

The wicket-gate banged in the warehouse and he retreated behind his desk with the decanter until a grim-faced Gillespie crashed in with Steff and Gerry. 'You're here then?' he barked at Gillespie, almost instantly realising what a mistake that was. Gerry and Steff retreated onto the landing.

Gillespie stared back deadpan. A small smile, raised eyebrow. 'Is there a problem?'

Hammond sat back down and fell silent. Gillespie helped himself to whisky. 'Well, young Graeme, it seems there's no shortage of problems this morning. I hear from Steff that the McGrath duo are nowhere to be found, nor is our van. I could have walked back from Glasgow quicker than them.'

'Where are they?' Demanded Graeme.

'Drunk somewhere, no doubt, or overdosed on the drugs. Dead would be the best result for them.' He took out a pack of Players full strength. 'Let's run through what we do know, calmly. Discover how deep this pool of shite is we're stood in.'

Hammond would not be stilled and interrupted.

'They steal my fucking van from under your noses and go to Glasgow. At some point along the yellow brick road they hump me and disappear.' Hammond slammed the table with his fist and threw the empty glass against the wall, shattering into splinters. 'They stole! From me! Drag them from whatever hole they're hiding in. I want them looking like they done ten rounds with Muhammad Ali.'

Gillespie nodded. 'Well, I never liked the idea of using they two,' he growled, 'but we need sense rather than dynamite. The McGraths don't have the brains God gave a brick, so they won't stray far from their usual haunts for too long without us hearing about it. There's a bigger problem than those two muppets. What is going to happen when the boys from Bulgaria realise they are not getting paid?'

Hammond waved his hand dismissively. 'I'll deal with them when they arrive.'

'It's a sure thing Mr Anton Tenescu will soon be down from Glasgow like a peep of gas and asking some searching questions.'

'You two comedians!' Hammond shouted Steff and Gerry back in. 'Stop standing about like Francie and Josie. Get out and bring the rest of the boys into the warehouse.'

Gillespie restrained himself with an effort, folding his hands tightly in front of him. 'What we don't need is the Commies gunning for us. For now, we accept the loss of the drugs, pay the Bulgarians twice for a repeat prescription.'

'Good, that's good. We'll say nada about the theft of our property, just there was a glitch, but people have been punished. Use the money in the wall from the stash at the

Feegie Park flat. We can draw on some other wall safes as well.'

'Aye well,' replied Gillespie, 'there's some bad news on that front as well. This morning Steff and Gerry checked around a few Johnstone and Paisley flats where we have money stored between the partition walls. At the flat where the Angela lassie died there's nothing but a big hole and an empty space where the money used to be.'

'How many stashes did they two know about?'

'Eight or nine. It's the same story at two other hidey holes. The addict sentries put up zero fight and didn't report this. Me and the boys have chastised them. That leaves us what's in the remaining stashes and your big safe here.'

Hammond leapt up in a rage, sweeping the tub of pens onto the Persian rug. 'They're not getting away with making a fool out of me. I want you three to take your arses out there and find them. I want them tortured and fucking killed as a warning.'

Gillespie nodded grimly, rose to his full height, forcing Hammond to look up at him. 'I'll start tonight with the card schools and the back rooms of the Stables Bar, then move on to the drug howfs along the Cartside. Fear and violence will loosen tongues.'

With them gone Graeme took himself into the private toilet and flung water on his face. He stared at the water gurgling away, gripping the taps to still his trembling, part rage, part fear. His father had always dealt with the Bulgarian suppliers, some sort of blood bond from the war. He'd overheard enough over time to know they were not the usual dealers and this Tenescu represented a boss who was a pal of his father's from the partisan war. Even Hammond senior had feared him a little. As Hammond stood at the window watching his men leave he remembered the name now and shivered as if someone had walked over his grave as he whispered it.

'Willy Drahujck.'

Next morning Joyce Fairbairn stuck her head into McDowall's office to find himself and Brown eating bacon rolls at the strewn desk. Both turned smoke-reddened, watery eyes on her and smelt like chimney sweeps. Joyce shook her head.

'Have you two not even gave your faces a lick and a promise? You're like a couple of Gorbals weans. Never mind. A motorist at the desk has just reported something right up your street, Frank. There's a dog running down the Largs Road with a hand in its mouth,' She read from her note pad. 'The Water Bailiff at Muirshiel, a Mr. Forbes, phoned it in as well, as have motorists.'

'A hand?'

'So he says. It's his dog and it's penned in his bin area.'

'Not something you get every day.'

'A dog with a hand is worth two in the bush, or something like that,' joked Brown. 'Left or right hand?'

'Sounds a very Masonic murder,' grinned McDowall.

Willy Campbell from the Dog Section was already in the Castle Semple car park when McDowall and Brown arrived thirty minutes later.

'Morning, Willy. What've we got here then?' asked McDowall.

'Dog finds hand,' said Willy, 'Dog wants to keep hand. We're negotiating.'

'How's that going then?'

'It's a big dug. We seem to have reached an impasse.'

'What's an impasse then?'

'I don't know, I'm not a dictionary. I'm past watching this much longer. The dog's refused every trade, even part of my Lorne sausage.' He pulled his baton and strode towards the dog.

Mrs Forbes came out her kitchen and crossed over to them. 'Godstruth. What are you like? Oot ma road.' She strode forward clicking the fingers of her right hand and crumbling a fruit scone with her left, allowing the crumbs to leave a trail. The dog galloped out past her and followed the sweet hot crumbs into the house hoovering up the scraps then dashed back for more. She grabbed its collar and trailed it to the dog run. She slid the bolt home on the gate, turned and scorned them. 'How many grown men does it take to get a hand aff a dug?'

McDowall nodded sagely. 'Shame Willy, and you ready to brain that poor animal. Hardly subtle, was it? Honestly, you'll have to take up baking. I was expecting some shepherd lore.'

'I live in Port Glasgow, Frank, not Port Ellen. 'Twas a sad

day I left the croft.'

Willy used a small coal shovel to scoop up the hand and bunged it into an evidence bag, handing it to McDowall who gripped it in a handshake.

'It's a right hand so we can safely say this guy's wanking days are over.' He nodded at the police dog. 'Can your Satan follow this back to where the other mutt found it? Hopefully the rest of this guy might be there.' He laughed.

'Then we can solve this puzzle.'

'No bother. We'll just give him a whiff of it.'

Satan jumped from the van and Brown went the other side of the bonnet, scared the dog was going to hump his leg again. Willy opened the bag and covered the dog's nose with the hand, allowing him to catch the scent. Satan tilted his head to one side to look at McDowall and salivating.

'He doesn't seem much interested, does he?'

'If you would take your smelly smoky bacon self away a bit ma dug might well get a whiff of something other than the McGrath brothers.'

Stung, McDowall joined Brown. Satan took one whiff and began to strain at the long leash, pulling Willy along the uphill track running north between high hedges and hawthorn towards the higher reservoir which lay just under Irish Law. McDowall passed the hand to Brown.

'We'll follow up in the van in a while. Meantime have someone get this to McVicar and we'll see what the hand will have to say.' He strolled across to where the Water Bailiff's wife leaned across her gate. 'Can I ask you a question, Mrs

Forbes?'

'Sure, Mr McDowall, ask away.'

McDowall smiled at her. 'Does your kettle work?'

She obliged with tea and fruit scones. McDowall picnicked on the bench, soaking up what sun there was, while Brown fretted to get on. Eventually McDowall rose, shouted cheerio into the house and strolled to the Dog Section van. Brown jumped into the driver's seat and started the engine.

McDowall grinned, 'Is there something between you and Satan I should know about? You can tell me in complete confidence, otherwise I'll be obliged to make something up.'

Brown ignored him and drove off up the rough tractor track after Willy and Satan. They soon came up to where dog and handler were lying in the grass. Willy came to the van, Satan stuck his head inside the driver's window and panted at Brown.

McDowall chuckled. 'You've got that dug ruined, Jim. What do we have then, Willy?'

'Fifty yards up on the right there's a clump of hawthorn in a dip sheltered by the angle in the drystane dyke, also a stinking peat bog, a mix of peat and cowshit. Obviously where the beasts shelter from the rain and wait for their feed for the ground's badly cut up. That's what probably churned up the site and exposed the original hand. That smell is in the air, Frank. Satan's unearthed an arm, just from elbow to wrist but missing a hand. And everything else.'

'You sure?'

'Well, it wisnae waving at me, but Ah'm no blind ye know.'

'If that radio in your van works we'd better get things on the road. Summon the circus.'

Brown was like a dog with a bone and set to work. Setting up inner and outer cordons, making sure they didn't fall foul of all these new-fangled protocols and checklists. Buzzing here there and everywhere, master of the clipboard. McDowall sat with Willy on the grass, watching McVicar do his magic tricks and hopefully deliver the killers into his clutches. The hand had a pinkie missing.

'So,' said Willy. 'If fingerprints confirm the hand once belonged to Brodie then it's a good bet the rest of him is stuffed down into the bog.'

'It's his wanking hand. Maybe his Ma killed him for playing with himself.'

'You have a low mind, Frank, I never abused myself when I was young.'

'That's because you're a Wee Free. You lot don't have sex standing up because you're feart it will lead to dancing. Let's go down and see what they've found.'

Forensics had dug a small trench across the bog and drained off some water, but the level soon came back up. A foot in a cheap trainer sat to one side, secured in a clear bag. The blowflies and a myriad of insects were already buzzed around in clouds, waiting to feast. Forensic provided nasal masks and a large jar of Vick. Even with his nose bunged up, McDowall could taste the sweet stench of corrupting flesh coating the roof of his mouth.

Brown updated him. 'I've organised shovels and buckets and the constables say Tannock is thinking about sending someone to take over.'

'Then we'd best get the rest of Brodie found before that happens. What else?'

'The Fire Brigade is sending us low level pumps and lighting, but the nearest is Clydebank. I've ordered catering and the tent.'

'All we need now is some beer, folding chairs, and for the rain to hold off.'

McDowall's good mood was deflated when he saw Tannock's staff car turning up the reservoir track and park on the soft verge. As ever, there was good news and not so good news. Tannock emphasised that Angela Stewart's demise was now officially an accidental death, and the case was closed. McDowall was to surrender all he had on that to records. However, Tannock had received orders from headquarters that McDowall was to stay on both the Brodie dismemberment and the McGrath burnings, establish any connection between Brodie, the McGraths, and Hammond. He also brought news of positive identification on the McGraths. Wpc. Joyce Fairbairn could assist on condition it didn't take her away from station duties. Apart from that McDowall was to have any resources he needed.

Tannock looked around, jiggling his car keys, evading McDowall's smug triumphant grimace and asked, 'Can I get my car turned up here? Is this a cul-de-sac?'

'Nope, it's a deid end.'

By the time Graeme Hammond had finished moaning and

blaming everybody but himself, the search for the McGraths was exhausted. Nobody knew anything. Gillespie called a halt and told them all to be back at it first thing. Some petty cash was handed out and half a dozen men began to trawl the Paisley boozers. It was near midnight before Gillespie got back to his Mum's.

All the lights in the house were blazing and the medication he had left on her bedside cabinet lay untaken. Bell, the warden was getting a slap. Her breathing was noisy tonight, rasping like a punctured bagpipe, even though she was propped high on her pillows. Her mouth hung slack and she was dribbling a fair bit into the oxygen mask. Gillespie knelt by the bed and wiped her chin. He switched off the bedside lamp leaving the door ajar so the hall light shone in. His Mum had grown afraid of the dark as she got sicker, like a child, as if it was death's lobby, her only comfort to have all the lights blazing. Gillespie himself had never been scared of the dark, and knew death was not afraid of the light.

He draped his coat across the kitchen chair, opened the fridge and found the makings of a sandwich. White thick bread with butter, ham, cheddar cheese, onion, beetroot, and a fair dollop of brown sauce. He poured lager from a can with the lovely Penny in scanty swimwear on the side and sat at the table where he could see the bedroom door and hear his Mum struggling to fill her lungs. This was a new sheltered housing project all one bedroom on one level. Gillespie did not officially stay here but the Warden had needed only one look to know who he was and said nothing. He slept on the couch, his mother's guardian and watchman. He despised Graeme Hammond's treatment of his own father, buying his care. For his care was given freely for thirty of his forty-two years, as a son should. Big difference. Sandwich finished, he spread pages from an old Evening Citizen on the dining table.

He eased the Webley from the reinforced leather holster stitched inside his coat pocket and placed it on the newspaper with a soft thud. He stared at it, listening to the loud ticking of the old mantel clock and his mum's snoring. He would go in and turn her soon, check her oxygen. He unloaded the six 38 calibre rounds examining each one for flaws, then broke the gun down, field stripping the cylinder and trigger mechanism.

He pulled the barrel through with the wire brush and oiled each part before reassembling and reloading. It was a nightly ritual.

The revolver had been part of him since Korea. Procuring it had marked a personal acceptance of who he really was, what he was good at. He was good at killing. None of his victims were of more value than a dead dog to him. It was his scorpion nature. The Webley kit had once been the property of a Lieutenant David Strachan, now part of the Flanders mud. The same weapon had been the sidearm of a young officer in WW2 and again in Korea where Gillespie had taken it from the twitching hand of its owner.

He'd been working in Fairfield's Yard when called up for National Service in nineteen fifty. Although he'd intended to emigrate to Canada on the £10 scheme he instead went to Crieff and *The Kings Own Scottish Borderers*. After basic training they left Liverpool on the *Empire Orwell*, via Cape Town where the brainy ones deserted. Gillespie did not. On landing at Pusan they were trucked north through a country in chaos, to the Naktong River.

Gillespies' first kill was a fat Chinese soldier on a donkey shot with a Bren gun from 500 yards on his first sentry stag. He felt like God Almighty with total power over those who lived, those who died. Nothing in his life since had come close to how he'd felt at that moment. While his mates looked on in either awe, horror, or respect, he whistled *Mack the Knife* and reloaded. All he said was, 'One.'

Habitually he took no prisoners and when ordered to take three back, claimed they tried to jump him. He became a stretcher bearer because of his size and left in charge of the hopelessly wounded, abandoned in a bunker just behind the line. There they were overdosed on morphine till it ran out. The two real medics tasked to stay disappeared in a puff of smoke, leaving Gillespie with seventeen moaning casualties and his dick in his hand. Stupid to remain he told himself. These poor sods were fucked either way for they would be bayoneted or have their brains bashed in with rifle butts.

Out in the trench he found a loaded burpgun and returned inside. Folding a blanket he went to the first helpless man, very gently placed the blanket over his face, touched it with the muzzle and fired one round into his head. He was at ten when a cry of horror came from behind him. An officer stood just inside the entry fumbling at the flap of his pistol holster.

'Are you mad? Stand still. Stay here, I'm fetching the RSM.'

He'd turned his back to leave and Gillespie fired a quick burst into his back, the rounds exploding in red mist and gore from his chest. After finishing off the remaining wounded he took the Webley and joined the exodus flooding south. At Pusan he boarded a hospital ship bound for Japan by simply taking the end of a stretcher and walking on board unchallenged due to his Red Cross armband. By the time the Army caught up with him in Japan he only had a month left. He declined their suggestion he re-enlist and went home to his mother. He'd taken a job with Arthur Hammond and found a unique outlet for his skills.

He checked his mum's oxygen cylinder, lay down and fell asleep like a child.

After a boiling bath to ease his bruising and clean his scabbing face Stewart supped a can of Tennents and stared at the money bricks piled across the kitchen table. Each contained five thousand pounds and the brown slabs were worth more than he knew. Stewart's first instinct was to wait till his next lone nightshift at ScotCon and consign the drugs to the furnace. On reflection they might be a valuable bargaining chip. He steadied the can with both trembling hands, the reaction to the killings hitting him now in jagged images. He wondered if he would ever sleep safe and dreamless again.

He forced himself to move and fetched his old Marine duffle bag from the hall cupboard and tipped it out onto the floor. There was that battlefield blend of hessian, rust, brass, mouldy socks, cordite, and gun oil, the perfume triggering old memories. He dug through old webbing pouches crammed with four by four, gun oil, an empty rifle magazine, mess tins, mouldy biscuits. Some clothing crammed into the large pack, mostly lightweight greens, DPM combats and woollens which he put in the washing machine. He searched further and found the detritus of another life. Dog tags, paybook, discharge documents, his green commando beret with the bronze cap badge.

And then what he was looking for.

The Sykes Fairbairn fighting knife slid easily from the oiled scabbard. Seven inches of deadly black matt finished steel blade. The Rolls Royce of killing tools, designed only for that purpose, useless for anything else. He knew for instance it could not open a coconut. As a recruit he had sliced his left hand to the bone attempting that. He had learned that the Hollywood notion of Commandos creeping up on sentries, grabbing them around the face and stabbing them in the side was total bollocks. A stabbed man could beat you to death or at the very least scream like a banshee. He remembered the instructors' mantra.

"Left arm around the jaw. Gouge the eyes, heave back till the head is on your shoulder, then drive the blade under the chin right up to the hilt. Try and not stab your own hand." He sheathed the weapon, sliding it down the inside of his boot and secured it with the elasticated straps. He would not be caught defenceless again. The drug packages went into the garden hut for now behind half a dozen concrete slabs. He broke open one money bundle, peeled off a handful, the rest went into his kitbag and behind the inspection panel under the stairs. Alec bagged every stitch he had on for burning. His clothes would go into the garden incinerator later along with the holdall from the van. Exhausted, he slid into his sleeping bag on the couch and fled into dark flame shot dreams.

Beth had no luck with punters around Anderston Bus Station because no more than three minutes after she went up a lane to pee two other girls cornered her in a doorway.

'Who the fuck'r you?' A big heavy girl in a tight sweater and mini pushed her up against the wall. 'Unless you are one of Pete's girls, then fuck off out of it. This is our territory. Speak up, ya cow. Are you deef and dumb, foreign or stupit?'

Beth shrugged them off and took two steps back, sank to her haunches dropping her hand onto the knife in her boot. 'Nobody's ma pimp, I work freelance.'

Two rough characters in flared denims and short leather jackets had come into the lane hobbling on platform shoes. One grabbed leopard skin jacket and shoved her towards the street. 'Get yer fanny back to work and gie yer gub a rest. Who the fuck is this?'

'A poacher.' The other lassie told him. 'Mooching aboot efter oor tricks.' The bigger guy forced Beth into a recessed fire exit.

'Listen up. Ah'm thinking this isnae yer first hurl up the city, so you know you don't just breeze in and start to fuck around with our trade. I'm Pete and I run all the girls on this block. From Waterloo Street down to the Clydeside at Finnieston and back up to Central Station. Don't get smart with me, if you want to work this area then Ah'm yer pimp. Gettit?'

Beth nodded.

'Good girl. Let's see what you can do.' He pulled his flies open and began to fondle himself. Beth dropped her big bag in defeat and knelt on it, pulled a johnny from her pocket.

Pete laughed. 'Don't think you'll be needing that, hen. Wee bit of extra for the boss is in order.' He grabbed her head and forced her mouth onto him. 'Watch the lane, Phil.' He told the other one. 'You can have seconds.'

Beth closed her eyes as one followed the other. At least she had a pitch now plus protection of sorts and knew why the other girls had been chewing gum. Pete told her the prices and to get down the riverside and work between Finnieston and the Green. If anybody challenged her she was to use his name. She could charge what she liked but Pete and Phil would take half and if she held back she would not be the first to take a midnight swim down the Broomielaw.

The dog with the hand tale was all over town by midday. Gillespie was in his usual booth at Junction 27 when Gerry and Steff brought him the updated news. He closed his book, a Western, and walked to the payphone, called Hammond, who went crazy. Gillespie held the phone away from his ear then hung it up.

'Headless chicken dance from that one', he told the boys. 'Right. First things first. We find the van, find the McGraths, retrieve our property, erase them and the van both. Questions? No? Good. Let's start our enquiries, I think we'll visit with that hag mother of theirs. Legion Club first and see if she's working the bar there. If not, she'll be getting pounded somewhere or at her midden hoose.'

Greta was not behind the bar, but the manager knew where she was and shortly after that the three of them walked right into Greta's living room to find her in a cloud of fag smoke with two cronies playing cards. The table was littered with ashtrays, vodka glasses, and what seemed to be extremely well-ironed banknotes. Nobody moved, nobody spoke.

Gillespie surveyed the scene and nodded. 'Well, is this not nice, what do we have here then? Macbeth's three witches, each wan uglier than the other. Should you lot no be stirring a pot?' He pointed at the visitors. 'You two know who I am?' They nodded. 'Good then, threats are no needed, fuck off.' The other two Gorgon haired pensioners left in a stramash of flying coats and handbags. Gillespie sent Gerry and Steff to search the house, tipped the card table crashing across the room and sat facing Greta.

'Whit dae ye want?' she snarled. 'Ah know nothing. They two monkeys of yours better not be making a mess in ma hoose, wrecking ma things.'

Crashing sounds came from upstairs as the boys trashed their way from room to room.

Gillespie snorted. 'You're living in a sewer, they couldnae make more mess if they shat on your stairs. Haud yer wheesht now and tell me about your boys.'

'Ah've no seen them for two days,' Greta squirmed. 'You should know where they are, were they not doing a job for Hammond?'

'That's right enough, they were in Glasgow but they seem to have forgot the road home. Maybe they should have left a trail of Smarties like Hansel and Gretel.' He picked up a pristine tenner. 'Or maybe, a trail of nice crispy banknotes. Always meant to ask, Greta, are your boys twins?'

'Naw. Are ye blind?'

'I wondered because I was amazed that somebody could fuck you twice.' Gillespie lifted notes from the floor. 'Not for two days, you say? Thing is Greta, here's the problem. Your boys are adrift with valuable goods belonging to Mr Hammond, also a considerable amount of money taken from us. Are you following me?'

She nodded, dragged at her fag, and nervously stubbed it out.

'You can see we're keen to find them, very worried about them so we are.'

'Ah don't know nothing about all that.'

'Strange. See, these notes you and your mates are playing with are nice, brand new and mostly twenties. Whereas.' He lifted her purse and took out some screwed-up notes. 'Your normal money looks as if it's been gnawed by a dug. You can see what I mean. If you and your other two grannies had been playing for twenty pence a card that would not have raised my suspicions. But twenty-pound notes?' The noise upstairs stopped and he heard the boys coming down. Gerry locked the front door while Steff flung a slab of hash onto the couch and handed Neil a wad of banknotes.

'Under the mattress.'

'Again! What is it with mattresses in your family?' He wiggled the money in Greta's face. 'Were you going into the loan shark business? Don't even bother thinking up any mair porkies to tell me. Last chance ya hackit auld boot, denials are fucking useless. One last time, where are they?' She didn't answer. Gillespie stood.

'Bring her through.'

The boys grabbed an arm each and marched her into the kitchen, feet off the ground. Gillespie grimaced and swept his arm across the top of the cooker. Pots and pans clattered into the floor. The boys slammed her hand onto the hotplate.

'Not that plate, that's the fast ring. I want this slow so use the wee ring. Now Greta, everybody squeals eventually. Give us a hint where your two windae lickers are hiding, and where the rest of our gear and money has gone?'

'Ah widnae tell ye if Ah knew, which Ah don't. So, fuck off ya dipshit.'

Sighing theatrically Gillespie switched on the ring.

'Maybe when you smell your hand burning we might get some sense out of you.'

Greta never made a sound and after a few seconds Neil was impressed. 'Ready to spill your old whore guts yet?'

'Ah kin dae this all day, you bastard.'

'I believe you could.' He felt for heat over the ring but it was stone cold, so he flicked the cooker main switch off and on a couple of times, nothing. 'What the fuck's going on here. Is your cooker working?'

Greta laughed. 'Cooker works fine but there's nothing in the meter, electric is cut aff.'

Steff smashed her face down on the cooker, splattering blood across it as Greta lost a fang.

'This auld witch has some set of balls.'

Gerry opened the drawer and found a pair of scissors. Not nail scissors but the dress-making kind his Mum used to cut patterns with on the floor. The sort of scissors you could have sheared sheep with. Gerry stuffed a greasy dishcloth in her mouth. It took two knuckles thumping into the sink before she cracked. They left her slumped in the kitchen with a towel over her hand, screaming curses after them.

'Tough old bird,' Gillespie observed. 'All the same that war generation, stubborn as fuck.'

Now they knew all about Steading 5, what exactly Greta had taken up to her two boys and when. She had spilled their plan to disappear south to Liverpool, which Neil thought they might manage if somebody pushed them onto the right bus. The bit about Holland he dismissed. They two had once got lost going to Ayr. Were they still at the Steadings or already running?

Back in the car Gerry dived into the rear footwell and emerged waving a newspaper.

'I knew it. I saw something in the local paper this morning about the Steadings, a fire with two guys roasted.' Neil snatched the paper. *"Two dead in barn fire."* screamed the headline. A photograph taken at a distance showed the building collapsed. Neil could see the roof of a van, the outline of a Sherpa. The place was stiff with polis so no chance of getting up there.

'Back to the warehouse and find out from our man in the polis if these two deep fried kebabs are the moron McGraths and if the money and drugs are up in smoke or not. Drive!'

The Fire Brigade had arrived at the Brodie murder site off the Largs Road and set up a submersible pump, dropping the level of the water and straining it through a fine mesh filter from which the smaller bits were retrieved. It was dusk before they were done. Brown took charge of the bits, listing them on his clipboard. Head, one; Arms, two; upper and lower; Hand, one, left; Torso one, bisected under ribcage, two parts; Thighs, two. Lower legs, two. Feet, two, one in a Nike Waffle trainer; Plastic box, one, containing various organs and parts.

'My God,' joked McDowall, 'it's like a human jigsaw.'

McVicar washed his hands in a bucket of disinfectant. 'I cannot find the genitals.'

McDowall shrugged, 'Well, he's not exactly going to be doing much shagging, is he?'

'Nonetheless, it's untidy. Missing parts are not good.'

'Maybe the mutt had a wee snack before he went home with his carry-out. Will I question him, one bark for yes, two barks for no? Or will we just analyse his next shite?'

'We should question Brodie's family again,' Brown suggested. 'They must know something.'

'Of course they know something, they've been got at. You can follow up on that, and make sure before clocking off tonight that my admin, which is your admin, is up to date. Got to keep Tannock happy,' McDowall cackled. 'He'll be spitting blood he sent me on two cases he thought were dross and that both have turned out to be murders. Get it right up him.'

On the way back down the track McDowall voiced a thought that it must have been a very interesting run up the hills from the Port in the back of that van. Who now would profit from Brodie's eternal silence? Not only those who butchered him but those who were responsible for Angela. Answers could fit on a postage stamp.

*

CHAPTER 14

Next morning at Golspie Road, McDowall made no effort to avoid Tannock but sought him out.

'Morning, sir,' he beamed. 'A bit of progress to report this morning. The two bodies taken from the van at the Steading are now firmly identified as the McGrath brothers, and the van is registered to no less than Hammond's Company Director, that big murdering bastard Neil Gillespie. This is all connected via the McGraths and Brodie to the death of that wee lassie Angela Stewart.'

'How is it all connected then?' asked Tannock. What real evidence do you have?'

McDowall sat on the window sill and joined the dots for his boss. 'Look, Angela Stewart dies at the McGraths' flat while a drugs fest orgy hosted by the unlamented Brodie is in full swing. Brodie falls to bits, panics, and disappears with cash and some product only to turn up disassembled in a hillside bog. Now, Brodie said the McGraths were responsible for Angela's death the very first night we had him in here. It was Hammond who sent the brothers to Glasgow to pick up the drug shipment that was in the locker. I saw Gordon McGrath there, not fifty feet from me. They give us the slip due to a lash up and later turn up barbecued at the Steadings in a van registered to Hammond's business. The connection to Hammond is obvious, so I want to have him in here and roasted a wee bit himself.'

Tannock leaned back and sighed. 'Graeme Hammond will not be approached by you without my express authorisation. We are still smarting from your last attempt to apprehend him and the legal mess you initiated. Prior to this morning, I had fully intended to suspend you because of the allegations made regarding your conduct in Glasgow, but I made the mistake of seeking advice from Superintendent Reid. You know him?'

'Was his best man.'

'Within the hour I receive a phone call from the Deputy Chief suggesting that as no official report has been made, it would be regarded as a favour to him if you remained in charge of these investigations and the Glasgow debacle allowed to wither from lack of interest.'

McDowall kept a straight face but was chortling inside. 'Sometimes sir, it seems being in the right golf club is just not enough.'

'I wouldn't be too quick to crow, Detective Sergeant. There is a condition. I raised certain concerns regarding your drinking problem and told the Deputy it was a contributory factor to your bizarre behaviour in Glasgow. That you had perhaps been drinking on duty and smelt of alcohol when you reported to Inspector Devaney.'

'I never drink on duty,' he lied.

'Nonetheless, allegations have been made.'

'Aye, and I know who the alligators are.'

Tannock passed over an envelope. 'This is a letter

informing you that a condition of you remaining on active duty is that you seek help by attending weekly meetings of Alcoholics Anonymous. I believe it's held in the Salvation Army Hall somewhere off Clyde Street in Glasgow every Friday. Effective as of now.'

McDowall read the letter, crumpled it up and tossed it back on the desk. Tannock smirked as he smoothed out the crumpled sheet.

'This is official, Detective Sergeant, from the top, and considering your accumulated black marks probably best you accept this. Starting this Friday, you will attend twelve weekly meetings.'

McDowall left before the red mist descended. Downstairs he showed Brown the letter.

'No more than expected,' said Brown, 'you were lucky to get off so lightly.'

McDowall snatched it back. 'Tannock's just a wee jumped-up pencil neck. First meeting is tomorrow night. It says here I can bring a friend.'

'You don't have any friends.'

McDowall smiled at him.

Brown sat back, grimaced. 'Why are you looking at me? Are you asking?'

'I am. We could go to the pub and just say we went.'

'I just need to make sure it's not a date.'

The big sliding door of Hammond's warehouse was wide

open when McDowall and Brown arrived in the afternoon. They were halfway down the aisle before Steff and Gerry blocked their passage. McDowall stopped, his hands deep in his coat pockets.

'Tell your boss I'm here tae see him.'

'About what? Dae ye huv an appointment?' Gerry nudged Steff and they both sniggered.

McDowall indulged them. 'Listen twat, wearing a donkey jacket just means you have a donkey brain. As for yer mucker here in his Salvation Army rejects, he looks like Frank Spencer, or a flasher we're looking for. Did you rob a grave to dig out they checked flairs and winkle-pickers? Get out ma road before I boot yer balls into the roof of your mouth.'

Gillespie heard the raised voices and strode onto the office balcony. 'Steff! Gerry! That's enough, mind your manners. Mr McDowall, why don't you come on up?'

The policemen pushed past the monkeys and went to see the organ grinder. Hammond was in an armchair behind the desk. He waved them to chairs in front of the desk but McDowall chose a big couch against the far wall from where he could see the room. Brown stayed by the door watching the two gorillas loitering on the balcony while Gillespie dragged a chair across and sat cowboy style facing him.

'So, Mr McDowall, how can we help you the day?'

'No doubt you'll have heard about the fatalities at a fire up the Steadings?'

'Terrible stuff. Do you have names yet?'

'Gordon and Eddie McGrath. Brothers. I believe they

worked for you.'

'They did not. I know of them of course, wee chancers hanging on the edge. Now and again we threw them a bone, a wee bit of casual work. Bottom feeders.'

'You wouldn't know then what they were doing in Glasgow yesterday?' Blank faces. 'In Glasgow Central station to be exact, in a van registered to this company? Later found burned out at the murder scene with the McGrath's done to a turn inside? A right wee Baby Belling that turned out to be. In fact, your name, Neil Gillespie, is down as the registered keeper on the documents. Now I'm curious as to why a van is stolen, taken without the consent of the owner, that would be you, and at no point does the owner, that's you again, inform the police of this crime? It's not like losing a bunnet or a brolly, is it? Did you not want the van back?'

Gillespie grinned. 'Truly tragic about the McGraths, in fact we were up to see their mother, extended our sympathies, but there's no connection with our organisation except as casual employees. As company secretary, of course my name is on the logbook but I didn't know the van was stolen. It's used as needed by our employees, the keys always in the ignition. I just presumed Steff or Gerry were using it. The McGrath brothers obviously knew where the keys were and took it for some purpose. Can't trust anybody nowadays. I can't be expected to know where our fleet is at any given time.'

McDowall snorted. 'Fleet? Is that what you're calling one Sherpa van and a clapped-out Bedford TK? I think if someone took the company bicycle you would know where it was.'

'We are glad you found the van. If you give me a crime number I'll get onto our insurers. Is that all Detective Sergeant? Anything else we can help you with today?' McDowall made a show of writing in his notebook. 'That's all for now. There are a couple of other things I need to ask. Michael Brodie is all over the papers, page two no less, Angela Stewart on page four. He's also all over the fields come to that, and he did work for you. He guarded one of your vacant properties. Do you know anything about what happened to him?'

'Only what I read in the papers. Very sad, terrible end. Must have crossed somebody with no scruples at all. Vicious.'

'Ahuh. When did you last see him?'

'Never met him, so couldn't say.'

McDowall changed tack. 'Here's another name you might know then, starter for ten. A wee lassie named Beth Sharkey, sometimes calls herself Clarke. She was a prossie for the McGraths who's disappeared since the death of Angela Stewart. Heard anything about that either?'

'Angela Stewart, of course, who hasn't? That tragic wee girl, terrible. Only what the papers say. As for Beth Bigboobs, apart from Brodie being her pimp I can't help you there. She's maybe returned to old haunts, old habits.'

McDowall stood to leave, tapped Gillespie's chest with his pencil. 'See you, you should be a detective. We'll be back.'

Gillespie saw them out and returned upstairs. Hammond was freaking out.

'That bastard knows something,' he raged. 'Not satisfied

with hounding my father now he's got it in for me. All these questions about Brodie and now he wants a hold of this Beth Sharkey whore. Fuck knows what the McGraths tell her when they were out their skulls? What did they not tell her? Use your contacts in Glasgow Vice. We can't take the risk she knows what the McGraths knew. Get to her before McDowall. Why did he not mention the drugs or the money? I don't want any more surprise visits from him without my solicitor here.'

Gillespie tried to calm Hammond. 'McDowall's just guddling for fish. As for this Beth bird, I really don't think she's a problem. Her brain is wasted and she's no doubt gone back to her sleazy underworld existence.'

'I don't care what you think. What I care about is our new partners thinking I can't keep order. I want all leaks, real or imagined sorted, so you tidy up the dross.'

Anton Tenescu had returned to the cramped office located above the bakers' shop in Tradeston. The baker was a man called Penko Dimov who was in his fifties and from the same home town as Anton. Penko's wife and two teenage daughters lived and worked at the villa in Aryia, hostages to his good behaviour. He'd been pro-Nazi during the war and a member of *Brannick*, the *Einzatsgruppen,* a secret which he wished kept from the State Police.

He knew of the flour drums in the back store which carried a large red circle. He had guessed what they contained long ago, another link to the chain that shackled his existence. These gangsters, these *Izmet,* could never let him go now. If they discovered how much he knew or had guessed, they would kill his wife and girls.

Upstairs, Tenescu poured a vodka and decided what his best course would be. He must challenge these idiots who had so mismanaged something so simple. Order drugs, pay for drugs, have said drugs delivered promptly to test this more direct route, lose drugs and money. Let them be consumed by fear and dread for tonight, for in the morning he would surprise them in their lair and hear some no doubt useless explanation.

Returning downstairs Tenescu checked the seals on the marked drums of icing sugar and passed a letter from home to Penko, full no doubt of family and goats and the kids doing well at college. Penko's illiterate wife was not reading or writing these letters and the blurred pictures from time to time were not his children. Anton possessed the certain knowledge that Mrs Dimov and her daughters had been dead these three years past. A fatal bus crash and fire. The letters were all written by the schoolmaster, a means to keep the threat to his family alive and Penko slavishly servile till they were done with him. Tenescu left the shop and walked north across the Clyde to the Blythswood Hotel, where he was registered as Anton Ivov, a chemical engineer from Varna with a passport, and visa to prove it, in the hotel safe. Nobody cared to ask anyway. In his room, he opened a journal at a bookmark and began to write the catastrophic events of the day as he understood them. In due course, this would be examined by his uncle, when he returned home. Soon he hoped, for a man could not get a decent *Skara* grill here in this awful country.

Beth had settled numbly into the self-degradation of whoring, but there were extras the girls were expected to help with. Payment always in advance and if the trick had wads of money the signal was given to one of the pimps. When a man is focused on a certain thing his eyes are closed or at the very least he is paying little attention to his surroundings. Then Pete and Phil would rush him, for it's hard to fight or run hobbled with your trousers down and your tadger hanging out. That was worth another fiver to Beth. Taking wallets from hip pockets was also fair game for the girls.

There were designated spots down the dock wasteland at the bottom of Finnieston where drivers could be taken for car business. Solitary places, where pimps could lie in wait and drag punters from the car. Sometimes they took the car as well. Her pimps fed her alcohol and anything else she wanted, and she fell again into that zombie voodoo place. Sometimes she was lucky and got hotel meets which were more civilised than a kneetrembler in a doorway up a city centre lane. She barely had enough to pay rent to that cat of a half-sister and feed herself. The Sally Ann canteen wagon fed the girls twice a week with hot soup and sandwiches. Their unfeigned goodness reminded her of Angela and all the many other things she had betrayed and lost.

Things went Tonto one night when a guy in a Jaguar offered fifty to come back to his place in Kelvingrove. Jeez! That was posh. She put her hand on the car roof and waved. Phil appeared from nowhere as if by magic.

'What's happening here, mate?' Toothy grin.

'I don't want any trouble here. I'll just be off.'

'Haud oan, no panic, friend, we're all adults here. We have to watch our girls, can't just let them go away with anybody at all.' Reaching into the car Phil turned the engine off and took the keys. Fearful now the man froze, hands on the wheel. 'Okay then,' said Phil. 'I've got your registration number so you make sure Beth is back on her corner in two hours. Enjoy your rumpy pumpy, away you go then.'

As the car pulled away he waved Pete across with the car.

'I've waited years tae say this, follow that car.'

Traffic was light and Beth kept the punter's attention away from the mirrors by slowly fondling him as they went. In ten minutes, they were at the punter's front door in Kelvingrove Street. Phil and Pete pulled in down the street a bit. Beth got the fifty before she would get out the car and stuffed the notes in her bag. While the punter hung up their coats in the hall, Beth closed the door on a piece of card, holding the Yale open. Straight into a bedroom on the left they went. The house was a palace, a four-poster bed for God's sake, silk sheets.

Kenneth, well that's what he said he was called, stripped off and told her to undress and get into bed. When she slid in beside him he was more than ready with a condom already in place. She was soon staring at the ceiling and he was powering away between her legs. It was just as he grunted and cried out in pleasure when her two pimps crashed into the bedroom.

Pete whacked him on the back of the head with a lead cosh, putting him out like a light. They dragged him out the bed by the ankles onto the floor where Phil kicked him repeatedly in the head. At first it sounded like a coconut being bashed, a kind of solid sound, but he only stopped when it sounded mushy. Pete kicked the naked man in the balls. Beth hid her face.

'You, get up, get dressed, get oot.' He handed her a bit of paper with a phone number on it. 'Call this guy from a payphone, tell him to bring his van here and gie him the address. You did good, keep the fifty for yersel.' He slapped her to get her moving. 'Shift yer arse, what are you waiting oan, the second coming? Hahaha.'

Beth made the call from the nearest pub, ordered a triple vodka, paid with Kenneth's smooth banknotes. Was he dead? This was like Angela all over again, Beth wished for an end. Phil and Pete found two suitcases above the wardrobe and began to fill them with choice items. They didn't know much about antiques but did know expensive gear when they saw it. Jewellery, watches, suits, shoes, anything that glittered or was heavy went in one of the cases. Their victim had not moved all this time. Pete crouched down and shook him.

'Is he deid dae, ye think?'

Phil shrugged. 'That'll teach him to no get into cars wi strangers. Let's go.'

They crept out and loaded their loot into the boot. A good haul for minimum effort and bother. The cases could stay safe enough in the Partick lockup till tomorrow. He knew an antique dealer in Paisley who would take everything off his hands.

Brushed off by Gillespie, McDowall retreated to a pub,

Junction 27, to squeeze his informants, who seemed to have been struck by group amnesia or had bunked off on sighting him. Brown got the round in and planted a pint of lemonade with a straw in front of him.

'What's that?' McDowall demanded.

Brown smirked. 'The last straw maybe?'

'Smart ass.'

'What now?' Brown asked.

'Obvious, Watson. We're going to finish our drinks then visit Stalin's Granny, see if she knows anything.'

The McGrath house was locked up tighter than a drum when they arrived. McDowall climbed onto the coal bunker and peered through the kitchen window. Greta was slumped at the kitchen table with a bloodstained towel covering her hand. McDowall banged the window three or four times but got only the finger in response.

'Well, Jim, it seems our assistance is required, blood and signs of vast mayhem are visible. You're fit and well made so let's have this door forced sharpish. Show me what you're made of.'

Brown pulled a length of scaffolding pipe from the scrap heap in the garden and smashed in the lower door panel. The noise alerted the neighbours who threatened to call the police. McDowall shouted they were the polis and to go fuck themselves. Brown crawled through the opening, cringing at the grease and other slimy spillages on his hands from the linoleum. He unlocked the door and McDowall strode into the kitchen, stood over Greta and prodded her with a finger.

She roused slightly and peered at them through swollen eyes.

'McDowall. What the fuck do you want? Ma boys are dead, is that no enough for you? Is that not how the polis wanted them? You never even came and telt me.'

'I was busy washing my hair. Broon breid is what they are right enough and not before time.' McDowall surveyed the increased shambles. 'Jeez, Greta. Have you been tidying up?'

Brown crossed to the sink to wash his hands but recoiled. 'What is that?'

McDowall peered in. 'Seems like one, naw two fingers, in bits. Yours are they, Greta? This will seriously cramp you dipping the till at The Legion Club. You know Jim it seems Greta is in dire need of an ambulance. Find a neighbour with a working phone and get one here.'

Greta moaned, put her head down on the table.

Brown gave her the eye. 'Will you be okay here on your own, with her like she is?'

'Well, she's not the height of tuppence, I don't think she's goin tae attack me one-handed and I'm definitely not going to shag her, so that's all your angles covered. Go.' Brown left and McDowall pulled over a chair to sit facing her.

'Greta, you want to know what I think? I suspect you've had visitors who asked questions about your boys you couldn't answer. Now I think you should tell me who they were and what they asked while they were cropping your fingers off.'

'I had an accident gardening, cut masel with them big scissors there.'

McDowall guffawed. 'Gardening! Has Percy Thrower made The Legion Club his boozer then? Now if you had a flamethrower on your back I might believe that. Was it Gillespie and his two hounds who came howling? You can tell me in confidence you know.'

'Go fuck yersel.'

'I thought you were made of meaner stuff. Don't you want to visit vengeance on those who cremated your boys? Are you sure it wasn't Gillespie done the business on your boys?'

'I'll take my own revenge on whoever did it. I don't need you or your kind for that.'

'I've got the advantage of more resources than you. I saw your boys in Glasgow yesterday, did I not say? I also saw what was done to them up the Steading. Not pretty. It would have been a better result if I had arrested them. So why don't you tell me who came here calling, what they asked and what you told them?'

'Fuck off!'

McDowall took her hand in both of his and squeezed.

When the ambulance arrived, McDowall and Brown helped her into it and drive away.

'Did you get anything at all out her we can use?' Brown asked.

'A fair bit. I gave her a hand to see things clearly. Seems her finger pruners were Hammond's crew right enough. That's a dead end for no way will she finger them, excuse the pun. Says she took drugs and money up to her boys at the Steadings and they were fine then, waiting for full dark before shooting off south. Thing is, Jim boy, what did we not find at the Steading?'

'Neither drugs nor money.'

'Correct! Regrettably my first theory that Gillespie and minions had done the deed and taken back their goods now lies in ruins, if Greta is telling the truth, Gillespie asking her where her boys and their goods were that means he didnae know they were already a mixed grill. So, Hammond did not kill the McGraths, nor has the money or the drugs.'

'They've no idea where it is or who robbed them. Who did take it then?'

'Someone else was there who did the killing and took their drugs and money. Now who jumps to mind right away? This Eastern European mob? Possible, but it's a long reach and not a whisper of them except this Tenescu guy. Ask yourself who wanted the McGraths dead more than any other living person? Who has the skills and massive motivation to carry that out given the chance? A man who is by nature a risk taker and has the capability, and is no novice at the bloodletting?'

'Alec Stewart. Would he be that daft?'

'Daft? Never that. For Alec, killing them would be easy, a deeper pleasure than you know. Is he mad enough to have taken that risk? I've had a brammer of an idea. Let's go ask him.'

There was no reply to McDowall's hammering at Alec's front door, apart from Buster's barking, but the back door was wide open and in the living room they found Alec face down on the couch, out for the count. Alec's right hand was swathed in a tea towel secured by masking tape. Brown shook him hard but got no response.

'Is he ill, drunk, or both?'

McDowall prodded two empty whisky bottles on the floor with his foot.

'Drunk as a skunk is my guess. Looks like somebody slapped him about the face with a shovel, Let's get him up and find out what he's been up to last night.'

They rolled him onto the floor where he fell on his back waving his arms weakly in hangover semaphore, screwing up his eyes and muttering in *Parliano Glesga*. His eyes squinted open, focused, and he groaned before slurring,

'Frank McDowall. Jesus wept. What the fuck do you want? What time is it?'

'Nearly twelve so it is. You've missed the best of the day, as your dad used to say.' Grabbing an arm each they lifted him into the armchair.

'Make coffee,' McDowall told Brown and plopped himself onto the settee. 'See if there are any chocolate digestive in the press. Tunnock's teacakes would be even better.' He lit a fag and gave it to Alec, waiting for him to become capable of clear speech. Eventually Alec sat up and squinted at him from blowtorched eyes.

'What's up then? Has Irene flung you out? Why else are you in my house at this ungodly hour?'

McDowall made his wee sucking noise through his teeth.

Brown brought in a huge mug of coffee which Alec held under his nose in both hands, forgetting the cigarette in his mouth and dipping its glowing end in the coffee. McDowall leant down to see his face and made sure he was at least semiconscious.

'It's been a very eventful couple of days, Alec, so let's make a list of things I'm confused about. We've found Michael Brodie, or what's left of him, stuffed into a bog not far off the Largs Road.'

'In a state, was he?'

'In bits, like the filling for one of McGregor the butchers steak pies.'

'You came here to talk about steak pies?'

'Just in the passing. While I don't think you know anything about Brodie, I'd like a chat about a wee fire up at Steading 5. You know where that is?'

Alec slurped his coffee. 'You know I do. To be honest, I'm not really following this.'

'Let's simplify it for you then. Where were you last evening between the hours of two and seven? I don't want to know you walked the dog scratched your arse then took a dump, stick to the highpoints but it's kind of important that you have a strong alibi.'

'That's easy, I was here getting drunk as you can plainly see.' He pointed at the two empty whisky bottles.

'Two whole bottles? You should be in the hospital. It's as well you drowned that fag or your breath would catch fire. Were you alone?'

'I had the whole family over to celebrate me getting the house. What do you think? Buster was here, ask him if you like.'

'All on your lonesome then, not out at all for any reason?'

'I stayed home and got plastered. It's the only way I can sleep now. Why don't you stop dancing round the last chair and cut to the chase?'

'The McGrath brothers are dead. Very messily slaughtered by an unknown hand.'

Nobody said anything for the next minute. Brown poised his pencil over his notebook. Alec fumbled one of the bottles from the floor and drained the last mouthful. He offered the plate of biscuits to McDowall.

'Don't take a chocolate one, they're for visitors, not for the likes of you. How did the McGraths die then? Not easily in their beds I hope, not quickly?'

'You'll be pleased to know they probably died in fair agony, and then somebody burnt them to cinders, no doubt in preparation for Hell, if you believe that sort of thing.'

'I do believe in Hell actually; I've been there, so Devil scud it into them. I'm sorry somebody beat me to the punch. You have no idea how many times I planned their end over the last while. They had lots of enemies you know.'

'No kidding?'

'So how did it happen?' Alec knew he had to be cautious, let McDowall lead.

McDowall finished his tea cake and watched Alec closely. 'That's confidential for now. No real details yet although the papers have lots of made-up stuff. The McGraths were the two roasted bodies found in the barn up at The Steadings. You mind Steading 5, don't you, Alec? Taylor's old place till the cancer rotted him. We played there when we were young.' Stewart nodded. This was dangerous. McDowall had nothing concrete but he was suspicious and probably just following the string to see where it led. Best not be gobbie, he warned himself.

'Post mortems are today so we'll know more by tonight or tomorrow at the latest.' McDowall held Alec's eyes watched his body language but there was no clue there, nothing. McDowall reminded himself that Alec had written the book on interrogation.

'So, you never crossed the door last night?'

'Nope. Am I a suspect, Frank?'

'Kidding me? You've got a triple motive.'

'I walked the dog back here after the funeral, shut the curtains and sat in the dark. I plead guilty to killing two bottles of whisky.'

Alec took himself into the kitchen and put the kettle on for more coffee, followed by McDowall who folded his arms and leant over the sink. It stank more of whisky here than anywhere else.

'What's with the bandage, nothing trivial, I trust?'

'I fell on some glass.'

'Uhuh! Is that burns on your fingers? Was it hot glass?'

Stewart laughed. 'Never try to make toasted cheese when your pished.'

'Don't get me wrong, Alec. I've no complaint that the McGraths have been torn screaming out this vale of tears. Their own mother is more upset at losing two fingers than her two sons, but the Law takes a dim view of people killing each other for revenge. While there was still hanging, revenge was the law's job. Me? If the gangs stick to murdering each other I'm willing to let them get on with it. Look, forget about another brew I'll give it a miss this time. Me and Brown need to crash on, baddies to catch and that. Thanks for the biscuits.' He put the last teacake in his pocket. 'I'll see you some night in the bar no doubt. Let's go, Jim, nothing for us here.'

Stewart watched them drive off then rested his forehead against the door trying to land his flying brain. What had all that been about? Just a logical step to find out if he had an alibi for the timeframe. Just ticking boxes and rummaging or did McDowall have some serious evidence? Suspicion was enough that the drugs and money needed shifted sharpish. The money he could bury or hide somewhere, the drugs he had no idea. Various solutions in rapid order. Burn them, flush them away, keep them as a bargaining chip? He felt energised, focused, detached, like the first time he'd seen the elephant although it was important not to be panicked into movement, it would be the pits if he did that and nailed himself. Let things settle for now, wait and see. He had a sudden brainstorm warning.

'Christ on a bike!' he muttered to the door.

He'd left something. With his fingerprints all over it. He had to go back and check. Still might be lying under the van. Or McDowall had it and was toying with him.

The ginger bottle knife.

Back in the car, Brown quizzed McDowall. 'We got out of there awful quick, you near took wings. Do you believe him?'

'About what?'

'Being home drinking all the time? No confirmation of his alibi.'

'I rarely believe anybody about anything these days. The bold Alec will be off to nightshift at six tonight, so I want you to come back later and check with the neighbours either side. Don't ask specifically about Alec, just ask if they saw anything untoward in the street and if everything was as usual. Dog walkers and stuff like that, if you follow.'

'Is he our prime suspect now?'

'He's got motive, capability, and the skills set, but so do other people we know. Hammond's crew for instance. The Bulgarians are an unknown for now. I don't see how Alec could have found out where the McGraths were and carried it off in such a short window. They stole from Hammond and tried to run so we'll be revisiting that. For now everyone is suspect. Hammond, the Bulgarians, and oor Alec.'

McDowall kept from Brown that the wellies in the corner at the back door had mud on them, and when he'd quickly stooped and crushed some between his fingers it was moist inside. More puzzling was he couldn't say why he'd held that back.

The McGraths corpses found their way to the morgue where McVicar set to work. What had once been flesh was burnt black with burst open wounds and bone glinting through in places, especially the skulls which had been unprotected. After general observations, he and his assistant had begun by searching pockets which yielded heat damaged driving licenses and Social Security cards, house keys, money, the everyday clutter everybody carried. Packed tight in a wallet they had survived legibly. The clothes had to be cut away in layers, clinging and sucking as they tore free, releasing smells of Sunday roasts, bonfires, oil, till both bodies lay naked and exposed, black and red.

It was well into the afternoon before McVicar was supping a mug of tea as he stood over his handiwork. Cause of death in both cases were deep incisive wounds severing major arteries in the neck resulting in massive blood loss and shock. Whoever inflicted the fatal wounds had known what they were about.

Eddie McGrath had sustained massive lacerations to the lower body. The scrotum was almost severed and ragged deep wounds in the thigh, caused by a jagged weapon twisted in the wound, had torn open the femoral artery. The victim had used his lower clothing in a desperate attempt to staunch the blood flow. Although the groin wound would have been rapidly fatal, what had caused death in both cases was the severing of all the mayor blood vessels in the neck, possibly by the same weapon. Both victim's trachea were severed deeply with scratches on the vertebrae. There were small shards of glass within the wounds.

Gordon was less damaged by fire and heat as his brother had been placed on top of him. His fatal wounds were almost identical to his brothers except for the groin damage. More force had been applied in this case, almost severing the head. Inspector Tannock was informed and organised a close search of the barn and immediate area once the Fire Brigade judged it safe to do so. This had produced a box filled with every rusting farm implement thought to fit the bill.

McDowall handed Irene the letter from Welfare about the AA meetings when he got home. She said nothing much beyond he should go, and it was time he took his drinking in hand. She sounded tired but gave him a touch on the shoulder as she left for choir practice.

The gesture shamed him.

Brown came to pick him up just after 6p.m. and they arrived at the Broomielaw ten minutes before the meeting at seven.

McDowall voiced his opinion. 'This is just so much bollocks. I mean, everybody in the station drinks. There's been binges where guys were recovering in the cells. Missing for days.'

'Aye, but they drink with spaces in between, Frank. You drink like breathing, it's your first recourse when the shite is in the fan. Who drinks whisky because they're thirsty?'

'Me. I think better when pisht.'

'Like I drive better when pisht. Anyway, you were lucky Tannock took this road.'

'Did you have any input in this, maybe your attempt to save me from a fate worse than death?'

'I suggested you were in bother with the drink when he

interviewed me. As a friend it was the only other option open to me. It was that or the insane path, which might have been more believable. It was all confidential.'

'Confidential? In the polis station? You know fine you could whisper a secret to a jobby and by the time you'd flushed it off to the coast and washed your hands everybody would know what you'd whispered.'

'Stop moaning. Remember that suspended to Tannock means by the balls, thumbs or neck. Let's get going, enough ducking and weaving.'

The Clyde Street Citadel seemed to be well locked up but down the lane a door hung open with about a dozen people waiting outside. A disjointed lot, staring at their feet or the walls, unfocused most of them and avoiding any eye contact. Five were women, a couple of teenagers, some forty-somethings, and two auld street geezers who smelt of wet pavement and urine. Two office clerks in suits, one in a British Rail donkey jacket and the rest looking as if they'd been dragged through a hedge backwards. Obviously rough sleepers.

Two of the wild haired women, in dirty denims and layers of gigantic shapeless pullovers, were standing close to each other guarding a rubbish filled shopping trolley ignoring everyone else and passing a swiftly disappearing rollup back and forth. It smelt like pot. McDowall drew breath to suggest he and Brown took themselves away along to The Clutha Bar but just then the inner doors banged open and two Salvationists in uniform smiled at them all. A shapely thirty-something woman and an older guy, both cheery beyond reason and greeting everybody in the love and comfort of Our Lord Jesus Christ. The lassie had one of those wee Victorian bonnets on her head tied by a black bow. McDowall surrendered and was waved into the hall along with his new besties.

The hall doubled as a storeroom for banners, brass instruments, hymnals and bibles strewn about the pews along the walls. The odd pool of water overflowing from buckets stained the bare wooden floor, some rusty damp streaks ran from the steel window frames and the breath fogged on the air. Enough to drive a man to drink. It was good the large wrought iron radiators were decorative masterpieces for they were non-functional. On the upside, there was a cauldron of steaming Bovril and hot pies.

Out of sheer habit McDowall dug in his coat pocket for his hipflask. Brown hissed and shook his head. A circle of mismatched plastic chairs formed a half moon and they were invited to take a seat within the magic circle.

'Join hands now. Let us bow our heads in prayer,' intoned the older guy. McDowall was taking nobodies hand till he saw some sort of medcert. The man smiled at him and continued.

'The blessings of Almighty God be upon you. Let us beg His forgiveness for our sins and His aid and help in our daily struggles against the temptations of the Devil. Amen.' The lassie handed out paper cups of Bovril then prayer books. She maintained her fixed smile throughout, nodding to each one of them as she passed around. McDowall used his prayer book to prop up his wobbly chair and supped at the Bovril. It was weak and gruesome with lumps and no salt, congealing fast. The pies were grey and tasteless and he wondered if that's where the incurable drunks wound up.

Cheery guy opened the ball, he and his acolyte beaming across at him and Brown.

'Well. I see we have some new faces in our wee group tonight so let's all give them a warm welcome.' He initiated clapping around the circle.

McDowall whispered to Brown. 'Warm welcome? Is he going to light a candle or two so we could all huddle round it for a heat?'

Applause over, the rest of the group stood one by one, gave a first name, and said how many days they had been sober. One guy claimed a total of ten days' sobriety, but from the staggers of him it was probably no more than ten minutes. Brown realised the ritual of introductions were coming around to him. It would be daft to sit here and say he just came with a friend. Nobody would believe that anyway. He stood up and followed the format he'd just witnessed.

'My name is Jim. I'm an alcoholic.' Clapping. 'And I've been sober for a month.' More smiles and nodding. Everyone now looked at McDowall who stood up and managed to kick over the Bovril cup.

'Awe crap, sorry about that, and apologies about my language, lassie. I really don't have any drink problem. I just came to support Jim here. So, I'll leave you all to it and get him when he's done. I'll be in the Clutha.'

Total silence, Brown staring at him open mouthed and struck dumb, McDowall turned on his heel and left. It was warmer outside. He was in the Clutha Bar on his first glass when he spotted Brown in the gantry mirror and steeled himself for a massive bollocking, but Brown said nothing, ordered a pint and took a table in the corner. After a few minutes McDowall joined him and they sat in silence. Brown avoiding looking at him and McDowall realised he had to break the ice.

'What are you in the huff for? For God's sake, will you say something.'

'Don't you speak to me yet. What a wean you are sometimes, it's well by time you grew up. Everything's a damn joke to you. Do you think for a minute Tannock is kidding on about suspending you? He intends more than that if he can manage it. You need to get real; do you have any idea what Tannock will set in motion when he finds out about this latest escapade? He'll go full throttle for dismissal.'

'How will he find out, only you know?'

Brown shook his head. 'You know, for a detective you are a witless wanker sometimes. Inspector Gadget is what you are. Did you not pause to think the Sally Ann will say you left your first session when they report on your progress? And where does this leave me, am I just to dig a big hole about the other five meetings that are booked for us? We've been pals a long time, Frank, but I tell you now that no way Jose am I doing that, not even for you.'

'That lot were all a crowd of smelly losers and dossers, that's not me.'

'Maybe not yet, Frank, but you are sure getting there.' Brown finished his pint. 'Right, let's shift, some of us have wives and homes to go to.'

'I thought we might as well have another, seeing as we're

here.' McDowall went to the bar and tapped his glass to summon the barman. Brown followed him and covered the glass with his hand glaring at him in the gantry mirror.

'If you don't get into the motor right now, I'm going to your door and shop you to Irene. Worse than that I'll then shop you to Moira. Same threat if you walk out of any more meetings.'

He sent the glass skidding down the bar. 'How do you like them apples?'

*

CHAPTER 15

The following morning Gillespie gathered all his men again at the warehouse and received their overnight reports. No trace of anything, nobody was talking. Zero results from threats, beatings or having fixes withheld. He had them wait and went upstairs to report to Hammond, who was seething at the lack of progress.

'The McGraths are dead by an unknown hand, for it wasn't us, and our goods are gone, for its plain McDowall doesn't have them,' Hammond snarled. 'Somebody butchered they two useless dicks and that same somebody took our gear. Whoever they are they represent a danger to us. Find them out before they decide to slaughter more of us. I'm beginning to think this is some takeover move by the Bulgarians.'

Gillespie had also wondered if it might be so, but if that were true Hammond and himself would be dead already. Steff stuck his head around the open door.

'Boss, Neil, morning. That guy from Finnieston, him that runs the whores, is here with a couple of suitcases to fence stuff.'

'Sneaky Pete?' asked Gillespie.

'Aye, the very same. He's got some nice stuff from a posh pad in Kelvinside. That aside, he's telling me he has a new tart working for him.'

'Is he offering freebies? I wouldn't touch his tarts with yours.'

'He says her name is Beth Sharkey.'

'Get him up here,' Hammond barked.

When Sneaky was allowed to leave, Hammond gave Gillespie new priorities.

'I don't care if you think this Beth whore is not worth all the hassle of digging her up, but Brodie pimped for her and kept her supplied with punters and fixes. She knows all about me and I'll bet she knows even more about the McGraths, everything over the last five years. It's a yellow brick road straight to me. Get her seen to.'

Gillespie disagreed. 'I think we're opening a can of worms here. We should let things cool down for a while.'

Hammond banged his desk. 'Is there nobody just going to do what I say? I'm fed up with you and the rest of them offering opinions. My father would not be getting this argument from you. Just get her found and dealt with.' Gillespie controlled himself, remained stony-faced. Arthur Hammond had known what he was doing, the son hadn't a clue. He let Hammond calm down before answering.

'Greta McGrath says she took them up a suitcase of money and drugs far more than was to go in the locker at Glasgow Central, so we have to presume it was her two boys cleaned out a few of the hidey-holes in our properties. We've been back to the McGrath flat and stripped it. We recovered some money but no drugs, there's nothing there. Could be she hid the goods for her boys or sold them on, but even missing two fingers she is still keeping schtum. Sneaky Pete tells us this Beth Sharkey is bunking with her half-sister in Anderston. We're up there tonight.'

'I'll feel better when all this is bye with. We can't have McDowall sniffing all over our business, not when the Bulgarians are about to happen.'

'McDowall is at a disadvantage in that the police have to be seen to obey the rules. Us now, we don't have any rules, we can make it up as we go.'

Gillespie decided the smaller the crew, the better. Just himself Gerry and Steff. They rooted out Sneaky Pete in Partick at his usual haunt, The Rosevale Bar, and invited him to help them. Not very keen on that he said he was busy, but they just grabbed him and bundled him out to the kerb. Once he was safely in the back of the car Neil pulled out the Webley and checked it.

'Whoa big man, nae need for that.' Sneaky told him. Gerry licked his lips. 'Can I hold it a minute?

'Naw. You can't hold your own dick without pishing on your shoes' He tapped Sneaky on the back of the head with the barrel. 'You! Tell him where he's going.'

Duly encouraged, Sneaky Pete assured them he could help get Beth to somewhere they could have a good talk. He suggested his ice cream van garage on Helen Street in Govan, near Ibrox. Gillespie kept Sneaky supplied with poppers and such to sell from the vans. It would be quiet and empty until the morning. They would be undisturbed and soon discover everything Beth knew.

When they got to the flat in Anderson nobody was in, or at least they weren't for answering the door and their pounding was ignored. Not a problem. Gerry shouted 'Bailiffs!' and began to boot the door in. A neighbour stuck his head out a door two along and demanded to know who the fuck they were. Steff walked along towards him shouting.

'We're the Three Wise Men looking for Jesus. Get yer fat arse back inside before Ah give you the chib.'

That was that sorted. Nobody was at home so they ransacked the place. Furniture smashed, settees and mattresses slit open, spilling out their guts. Gerry noticed a freshly painted wall and that was burst open. Nothing, a dry waterhole. Gillespie was displeased and grabbed Pete by the throat.

'No drugs, no money, no Beth.' and dragged him outside to balance him over the third-floor veranda rail. 'Are you having a laugh? Have you made the mistake of telling me porky pies, promising what you can't deliver? If you don't come up with the whereabouts of this Sharkey slag I think I might use you tae dent a car. Are you yanking my chain? Neil shook him like a rat. 'Where the fuck is she?'

'Haud oan, haud oan, we're all muckers here. Okay, I was stalling a wee bit but haud yer horses, we can make a wee deal here. You must ken that she's an investment and a good earner. I stand to lose out of this if you damage her, so compensation is due I think. If you guys mess her up badly then no punter will pay to shag her. How much is it worth to say where she is the night?'

Gillespie ran out of patience as he realised this nyaff thought he was taking part in a negotiation.

Out came the Webley.

Pete paled and his jaw dropped open, so Gillespie took the opportunity to shove the barrel in his mouth.

'Let's talk about if it's worth extending your creepy wee life a couple of minutes more. Tell me where she is now, or I won't even count.' Pete gabbled something indistinct, it was hard to talk with four inches of steel in his mouth. The gun was pulled out his mouth but rested it on the end of his nose where he could see down the barrel. 'Say again,' Gillespie prompted.

'She's up Finnieston Docks the night, working ship's crews along Dumbarton Road as far as Partick. She's probably in the Anchorage Bar.' Pete stuck a finger in his mouth, spat some blood at his feet and splattered Neil's shoes. 'Awe, that's no right, you broke ma tooth, Ah'll need the dentists.'

'That's the least of yer worries.' Neil told him and nodded to the boys. 'Hoist him.'

They grabbed an ankle each lifting fast and heaved Pete over the concrete banister, watching as he crumped onto a car roof then bounced onto the bonnet, sliding off to lie groaning in the street. Steff cackled. 'Better than the ten-pin bowling, that is.'

A cold drizzle had just begun when Beth got lucky and picked up a sailor in the Anchorage Bar. He was up for a gobble then a kneetrembler in the lane at the back of the derelict units on Minerva Street. They agreed on a fiver for the works and made their way down a pend behind a small builder's yard, having to squeeze past a skip to a dead end. Beth used this lane lots for walking tricks, she had some cardboard and an old carpet here and had rigged a sheet of scrap polythene for shelter of sorts. The guy began to grope her, but she shoved him away.

'Back off, bigboy, slow it down. This isnae a test drive, its cash in hand before anything goes in anywhere. Nae free hurlers.' She put her hand out and wiggled the fingers. 'Cross ma palm with silver.' She checked the note in the street light, stuffed it in her bag. 'Right then, get it oot.'

She moved onto the nearly dry carpet and dropped her big sack bag down. She wasn't taking any chances, and nobody could steal anything if she used it to kneel on then as a cushion for her bum. Her punter was ready, put one hand on the edge of the skip and the other on the back of her head and shoved himself into her mouth. Beth closed her eyes and let him get on with it. Soon she had him hard and had to put one hand on him to stop his thrusts choking her. Her other hand searched around for his wallet in the hip pocket of the trousers at his ankles.

'Right!' he grunted. 'I'm ready for a ride now.' He knelt between her legs and Beth slipped her pants down to her ankles and lay back opening a condom. Before she had the johnny on he had gone limp.

She tittered. 'Lot of use that's going to be. Was that just a beer and hope hard-on?'

'Ya cheeky wee stinking whore. It's your fault. I want my money back, robbing bitch.'

Beth pulled the short-bladed kitchen knife out her boot,

jabbing at his arse twice. He jumped up roaring, fell backwards, his trousers round his ankles hobbling him. He grabbed her by the coat as she tried to bolt, yanked her back and smacked her head off the edge of the skip. Beth lashed out with the knife again, catching him across the ear. Next thing somebody had grabbed the guy by both arms and flung him away to the other side of the lane.

'Well, hullo, Betty Big Boobs,' said Gerry, 'How's it gaun then? Nice wee pad you have here, done it up nice so you have. We're sorry tae barge in but we need a word.'

'She cut me, she fucking cut me,' screamed the sailor, staunching the blood.

Gillespie grabbed his collar and looked. 'It's nothing but a scratch. You're lucky she never had yer willy off. Maybe you should look on us three as a moral intervention and fuck off now.'

The sailor stumbled away shouting from the end of the lane. 'Bastards! I know what's going on here. That bitch set me up for you three fuckers. I'll be getting the polis to you.'

Gillespie ignored him and cupped Beth's chin in his hand. 'I don't think he'll call the polis, do you Beth? Pathetic so he is, but not as pathetic as you are, hen. You were easy to find, before you ask. Your pimp, Sneaky Pete, was very helpful but had to drop out the search due to health issues.' The boys laughed. Gillespie dragged her to her feet. 'All we had to do was sit in the car watching the Anchorage, and sure enough out you came with Popeye the sailor.'

He reached out and removed a pubic hair from her lip with his gloved hand then grabbed her chin and hoisted her on tiptoe.

'This is as good as it's ever going to get for you, standing out the rain here in a minging lane with a horrible taste in your mouth, your knickers at your ankles and the wind blowing up yer jacksie. Myself on the other hand, I just want home to my mum. She's not keeping well and I like to be there to make sure she gets her Horlicks with a wee sensation in it, takes her pills and such. So, I'm going to ask you some questions about the McGrath brothers. Mind them? Good news first off, they're fucking dead. Bad news is they took some serious information with them as to the whereabouts of Mr Hammond's property, stolen by them. Since we can't ask them what we are needing to know we'll be asking you.'

'I don't know anything. Not about anybody or any drugs or any of the goings on.'

He moved his hand sharply a few inches and skelped the back of her head off the skip.

'Best you be silent till I ask you to speak. My mammy needs me early the night so I don't want to be long at this. I want quick answers to quick questions. You really think we're glaikit as you are? That you can tell us you hung about with them two McGraths since you left school and don't know anything? Don't speak, a wee nod if you understand.'

Beth nodded. She began to moan. 'Please, oh please, don't hurt me.'

If Gillespie hadn't been holding her she would have fallen.

Her body trembled and her bladder betrayed her, hot and burning, soaking into her shoes and the panties around her ankles. A despairing prayer screamed inside her head, to God, her long gone mother, to Angela, to anybody who might save her.

Gillespie turned her head to one side and whispered in her ear.

'Question one. Starter for ten, no conferring…'

Shortly after midnight two constables from Partick Police Station passed the end of the lane. One shone his torch but saw nothing. His partner fidgeted and danced grabbing at himself through his Gannex coat.

'Jeez I'm bursting, Tommy. I need to pish so I'm away up the lane. I got pills from the doctor but they're useless.'

'Another slash! It's not a doctor you need, it's a plumber.'

His mate disappeared into the dark already struggling with his fly buttons. By the skip he at last fumbled himself free and let it go in a steaming arc. The plastic sheet covering the skip flapped in the wind and he noticed there was a shelter of sorts between the gap and the wall. Something rustled and he thought it was a dosser. His torch beam washed over a pair of feet in heels and he jumped back squealing. Tommy ran to help and saw the lassie lying there badly beaten, her head a mass of clotted blood and hair. A rat scuttled away from the light.

'Right you, holster your pencil and radio this in.'

First thing the next morning McDowall got a call from Glasgow CID. It was from an old pal of his, Ronnie Leckenby, who began with, 'Do you want the good news or the bad news?'

'You never call with good news.'

'That Beth Sharkey you're looking for has turned up in Finnieston.'

'A break at last. Is she saying anything?'

'Not so much. She's deid. Some punter beat her brains in off the side of a skip. The body will be getting moved shortly so get up before noon if you're coming. Minerva Street.'

McDowall called Brown who made it round to the station car park in twenty minutes. They climbed into the Hillman Imp squad car.

'This thing is an embarrassment,' said McDowall. 'The Rootes wreck.'

'All there was. You do know I'm actually on rota leave today?'

'Stop girning. Welcome to the real world. Minerva Street. Just drive.'

The lane was roped off, Police everywhere knocking doors, up and down the closes and into any of the wee workshops that were open. Ronnie Leckenby shook hands with McDowall.

'Hope you've had the full breakfast; Beth Sharkey is no pretty picture.'

He lifted the rope and they trudged up the muddy lane. Not a lot of room at the end so they stood waiting for McVicar and his acolyte to finish. Ronnie passed the fags and they smoked silently till McVicar came out. He was carrying a large lady's handbag.

'Frank, good morning. Are you not a bit out of your way up the big bad city?'

'Nice bag, Doc. It goes with your Rupert the Bear troosers. Is that in place of not having a kilt on? If you can confirm this is Beth Sharkey for me it would be a step forward.'

McVicar handed him the bag.

'Usual stuff one would expect. There's a Social Security card and a letter for an appointment next Tuesday for interview, so it would appear it is she. Positive identification will be confirmed in our report' He peeled off his gloves. 'Poor girl, what a horrendous place to die. In this seedy place, fouled and with no dignity.'

McDowall nodded. 'Angela died in a worse place. Sharkey has the benefit of being the most unconcerned person here.' He slid past Ronnie and peered into the gap, shaking his head. Brown came and stood beside him, mouth and nose covered by a tied handkerchief, like a bandit. McDowall drank it all in, the tastes, the smells, the pathetic awful waste. Ronnie cleared his throat and read from his notebook.

'Found by two beat constables at 02.02. Way I see it, it was probably a trick. The shelter suggests she used this place a fair bit, but it seems somebody didn't feel he had his money's worth. From the blood and brains on the edge of the skip she's been dunted repeatedly aff it, but what did for her was getting her skull smashed off the big lifting lug which put her out like a light.'

'Was she robbed?'

'Only of her life, guy probably panicked and took off when he realised he'd killed her. Look, Frank, if you have another theory I'd like to hear it. What more do you know?'

'People were looking for her other than us. It's possible they found her.'

Ronnie looked unconvinced, eager for the simple solution to close the case. 'Okay.' He made a face and a scribble with his pencil. 'Illuminating as always, Frank. Send me what you have. In the meantime, we're going to carry on house to house and ask around the bars in Finnieston Street and Dumbarton Road.' A constable shouted Ronnie away.

'You think Hammond's lot are involved in this?' Brown butted into McDowall's' thoughts. 'They wanted to find Beth as bad as us because she was the only one left who maybe knew where the drugs and money were and exactly what happened to Angela.'

'Anything is possible when you don't have a scoobie what's going on Jim. Are all the killings down to Hammond, or is it all down to different folk blundering about in the dark? Well, let's think on it but for now back to Johnstone and update Tannock with the joyous news we have found one of our witnesses. When he's cock-a-hoop over that I'll mention she's brown breid. Best you go and fill in Ronnie, give him everything.'

'All of it?'

'Yep. I'll be in the car.'

The shell arrived from the morgue and they waited until it was gone. While Brown scribbled McDowall mulled over events and his options, making a checklist of the deceased.

Angela and her parents, all dead along with Brodie and now Beth Sharkey dead, the McGraths slaughtered. It seemed Hammond was connected to all this blood, in a frantic effort to silence any loose ends. Seven deaths, four murders. They were going to need more officers.

And not forgetting Alec Stewart with the huge motive and a marshmallow alibi backed up by Buster the dog. His gut just did not believe Alec was home drunk that night. Neither himself or Hammond's crew had any idea the brothers had been hiding at Steading 5. How could Alec have tracked and killed them?

It just wasn't possible. But he had no other answer.

Hammond was in his office finishing off a full Scottish breakfast sent over from the Tasty Cafe when Gillespie came in and laid a business card and a medal complete with ribbon on his desk.

'There's some foreign guy down the stairs,' said Gillespie. 'He gave me this.'

Hammond took the medal. His father had one the same in the drawer of his desk, the partisan medal of the Great Patriotic War. This was someone from East of the wall.

'I've been expecting this. The big guns are here it seems. I'll see this Tenescu guy on his own. I know him from when I went to his villa.'

Anton Tenescu entered the office as if he owned it, ignored the outstretched hand. Graeme offered to take his hat and coat but the offer was declined. Tenescu sat on the

Chesterfield with his back against the wall, easing the crease in his trousers.

'I had come here to see your father and to discuss the future development of his business,' he said, his English perfect. 'But I understand that your father has suffered due to illness and is no longer capable of conducting his affairs. My sympathies. It is with yourself as his successor then I must speak on a delicate matter. It would seem both our latest shipment and the payment for it has vanished. I had come to pay my respects but find I am the one being disrespected.'

'This slight hiccup is being dealt with as we speak.'

Tenescu nodded without belief. 'The thieves are dead, I am given to understand?'

'They are.'

'But when you catch thieves and dispose of them it is surely the point to retrieve what was stolen? Tell me all is well, for whatever is lost is your problem. My principals in Varna are displeased and have asked me to communicate certain realities to yourself. Product has been delivered as you specified, in good faith. It has now been taken from your possession as has the money with which you were to make payment. Therefore, it would seem to us that you are in arrears in your payment for the goods. We can and will of course replace the product which has been stolen, for twice the agreed sum.'

Hammond spluttered. 'Double. Do you think we zip up the back? Why should I pay you twice? The stuff was stolen.'

'Stolen from you, Mr. Hammond, not from us. We are unpaid for the original order which we delivered and now you wish another shipment at the same price. We must be paid for both.' He stood and took his time donning his hat. 'My instructions in this are very rigid. I am to hold back the new delivery until full payment is made in advance. You will be pleased to hear that we have stocks on hand to resupply very quickly.' He placed a business card on the desk. 'When you wish to proceed, I can be contacted at the number on my card.'

He bowed slightly and left, closing the door gently after him. Hammond restrained himself for all of ten seconds before picking up a crystal ashtray and smashing it off the back of the door. Gillespie appeared, hand inside his coat gripping the butt of the Webley.

'That Bulgarian nonce threatened me. Me! In my own fucking office. What fucking now? Any bright ideas on getting out of this?'

'Simple,' said Gillespie. 'We follow him.'

'What for? He's not got our money.'

'But he does have a stash of drugs as back-up, he said so. If he thinks the city's full of thieves let's prove it to him. My guess is it's stored where he's based. I'll get one of the boys to follow him.'

Gerry had no trouble tailing Tenescu. Onto the train at Gilmour Street to Glasgow Central, then followed him south over the King George V bridge to a small bakery under the arches in Centre Street. After a few minutes, he walked past the front window and saw Tenescu climb the stairs to the first floor. He waited, but Tenescu did not reappear. He strolled to the Laurieston Bar on the corner with Oxford Street, called the warehouse from the payphone and waited till Gillespie and Steff arrived. By then he was a couple of pints ahead of them. He told them where Tenescu was.

Gillespie was sceptical. 'A bakery? What the fuck would he want with a baker?'

'I hung about for a while but he's still there.'

Gillespie checked the Webley under the table. 'No use hanging around then. Time to visit this uppity bastard. Impress on him who is top dog here in Scotland.'

They cruised past the arches and parked down the road near the corner where they could see the front door of the bakery. Roller shutters were down over the front window, but the door was clear, showing a light. Neil decided to wait ten minutes or so and see if Tenescu moved elsewhere, if not they would crash in.

Penko the baker had cleaned the bakery with frantic zeal till it shone like a showhouse. He had been on edge all day, filled with anticipation. It was the first week of the month. That meant a letter from his wife, Ana. She could not write of course but had a letter written every month by the children's schoolteacher. He hungered for news of his darling girls, Yana, who was eight years, and Rosa who was twelve. He hoped his wife managed to save the money he sent home, for soon they would have to think about a dowry for the elder girl. The entry bell tinkled as the front door opened and closed and he left his little room at the back of the shop to wait in the corridor. Although his English was limited, Penko liked to use it when he could as he knew it pleased Tenescu.

He bowed in a respectful greeting.

'Good evening, *Gospodine*, I hope you had a fruitful day.'

Tenescu grunted. He despised this peasant who was beneath him yet seemed to think they could converse, perhaps even be friends. He laughed aloud at the thought and Penko mistook that for progress.

'Is there a letter from home sir, some news perhaps?'

'I will go to my office and see. Perhaps your good wife has persuaded the teacher to write for her again.' He turned on the stair and leered maliciously down at the baker. 'Now I wonder how your wife and daughters pay the schoolmaster for his writing? Have you never over the years wondered what he is perhaps getting in exchange?'

Penko struggled to keep the subservient smile on his face yet inside he seethed, his rage supressed, his fists clenched tight. How dare this creature dishonour his wife and girls? He knew nothing of the love between a husband and wife, the blood bond to be had with a child. In his own land he would be entitled to kill this creature for the insult to his family and honour, but not now, not here in this place. Penko hung his head in shame as Tenescu laughed at his humiliation and called back down to have tea brought him. Raging, Penko went to the samovar in the small kitchen and prepared the brew.

When it was ready, just so, china cup and sugar bowl, cream, he spat in it before climbed the stairs. Tenescu was in the toilet so he put the tray on the large desk and waited. As he glanced around the office, where he was allowed only occasionally as it was always locked when his master was away, he noticed the secure drawer was lying open. He peered inside and saw a packet of letters tied with brown string, the envelopes the same brown drab as all the hand-written letters from Ana had come in. Puzzled, but starving for news, he ignored the danger of being caught and took them, leafing through in seconds. He was confused, how could there be suddenly six letters? Only one letter per month had been allowed him, both to receive and send.

The envelopes were stamped and postmarked, but this was February and the postmarks were months ahead, all the way to July. How could this be? The toilet flushed, he crushed the letters to his heart, unwilling to return them to the drawer. He heard the tap running in the toilet. Crushing the packet into the drawer he fled downstairs, brain reeling, fleeing from this knowledge to the warm space beside the oven where he hid and wept, refusing to accept the reality of his discovery, the awful imaginings it brought to his soul. He had been betrayed. Penko heard Tenescu descending the stair calling out for him.

'Where are you, lazy cretin? Get the cash books for me and today's takings, I have a lady to meet in town. *Tuk Burzo.*' Tenescu clapped his hands impatiently. Penko wiped his face on his apron to hide the streaks his tears had made in the flour on his cheeks and came out, his eyes red angry wounds in the white mask of his face.

'What are you doing skulking back there?' Tenescu demanded to know. 'I asked you to give me the books for today.'

Penko set his servile face and placed the ledger in front of his master and opened it at the required page, stepping back respectfully. Tenescu checked the figures while Penko stared at the back of his neck and clenched his fists to control his trembling. At last he spoke softly.

'Was there any post today, *Gospodin*, word perhaps from my Ana and the girls?'

Tenescu continued reading the ledger pages slowly.

'I'll tell you when there is word. There is no news at present, but the posts are slow. Why don't you spend the evening writing a long chatty letter to your family? Say you might see them soon.'

'And shall I, master?'

Tenescu licked finger and thumb, began to count the money.

'Shall you what, Penko?'

'Shall I see my wife and children soon.'

Something in his tone alerted Tenescu who turned to reprimand his impertinence, but he was too late by far, for the massive marble rolling pin was on its way down.

Penko had killed animals on the farm and was skilled in stunning them before bleeding. His first blow took Tenescu across the face shattering the nose, on the return sweep he struck his neck behind the ear. Tenescu went down like a slaughtered goat. Penko bound him at wrist and ankles with baling string. He went to the door and checked the street was quiet then turned off the front shop lights. Leaving Tenescu unconscious he raced up the stairs and tore the letters from the desk drawer carrying them back down and pulling his master into a sitting position, flinging water into his face. Tenescu began to moan, spitting blood as he came to.

'Are you mad?' he snorted, choking on his own blood. 'Release me immediately. Do you forget who I am, cretin?'

Penko remained cold, very aware he'd taken a step he could not retrace.

'*Godspodin*, calm yourself. I know well who you are and what your uncle is. Myself being just a stupid peasant, I would like you to explain this to me.' He held up his letters. 'How is it that these letters of love and hope to my family,' he clenched his fists over his heart, 'written with my heart's blood, are still in your keeping and not home with my wife and children? Has there been, as you say, a postal strike?'

Penko slapped Tenescu across his smashed face with the packet, staining them with blood and snot, and punched him about the eyes five or six blows. He lifted the other packet in front of Tenescu's swelling eyes, almost closed now.

'And here. Here we have letters supposedly written by a schoolmaster in Varnya for my wife to send to me, each bearing a date stamp exactly one month apart. As I am just a poor peasant in your service I ask you to explain this miracle to me.'

He punctuated each word with a blow across the face. 'My letters are unsent, yet my wife it seems speaks to the schoolmaster and he replies to me, how is this possible?'

Tenescu spat blood onto the floor and gasped in pain. 'You stupid *selyanin*, peasant dog. My uncle will have your life for this. Your wife and children are dead, you fool, for more than two years now and soon you shall join them.'

Penko sank back on his haunches, overcome by anguish. How could this be, what monsters would do this thing? He grabbed Tenescu's broken nose and demanded the truth. Tenescu told him through his blubbering of the bus crash and his beautiful Ana, his sweet girls Yana and Rosa, trapped crushed and burned to death, and these demons kept it from him to ensure his slavery.

Penko raised the rolling pin high above his head.

Tenescu screamed.

Penko screeched the names of his lost ones with each splintering blow. One for Ana, another for Yana, the final crushing impact for his youngest, Rosa. Spent, he reeled back, blood splattered against the wall. Gradually the madness left him along with his raging cries and sobbing he sank to his knees. Slowly he became aware he was not alone.

In his red fury he had not heard the entry bell tingling. Penko turned his head and saw three men in the front shop, shadows against the dying sun streaming through the doorway, all unknown to him. The big one at the front cocked his head to one side and grinned.

Gillespie had grown impatient and entered the shop silently with Gerry and Steff. Eventually the little guy with the massive rolling pin had run out of steam and sank to his knees. His head swivelled slowly and stared at them with that thousand-yard stare that men have after killing. Gillespie nodded and smile at him.

'Is this a bad moment sunshine? No chance of a last-minute birthday cake I suppose?'

Penko dropped the rolling pin on the bench. Gillespie strolled deeper into the shop taking stock of the wild-eyed man spattered with blood, Tenescu with his shattered head, the flies already exploring, and the letters on the floor soaked in blood and brains. He prodded the corpse with his boot.

'This a bit awkward. Tenescu won't be telling us much now. Maybe this wee fella can tell us something. Doesn't seem to be a pal of the deceased.' He pointed upstairs. 'Okay, let's move this wee chat up the stair. Lock the front door boys and put the shop lights out.'

Upstairs in the office they flung Penko into Tenescu's still warm chair and Gillespie perched himself on the desk looking down at him.

'Let's me and you have a wee chat now. Do you speak any English?' he asked slowly. No answer. 'What's your name?' he shouted, firm in the belief that if you spoke slowly and loudly enough everyone understood English. The baker started to gabble with the odd word of English flung in. Apart from fuck, bastard, and Glasgow, they were still baffled when he stopped his rant, but they got all the emotions from tears to rage.

Gillespie put his hand across his mouth to quiet him. 'Stoap! Shush. Let's keep this simple.' He pointed to his own chest and enunciated his words. 'My name is Neil. Neil.' Then pointed at the man. 'What... is... your... name?' Understanding dawned.

'*Aah. Noshten Pazach. Pekar,*' he blurted.

Gillespie smiled and nodded, none the wiser that the wee guy had said he was the night watchman and baker. 'Okay, Noshten, whatever. We need to ask you some things.' They began a stuttering mime back and forth. Gillespie pointed at Tenescu thumbs down, the baker nodding vigorously, grinning then nodding or shaking his head, or both. The boys made more tea, but the baker chose to drink from the neck of the vodka bottle. Things progressed like treacle going uphill with most mime misunderstood or leading to dead ends.

'This is like charades in Dykebar Hospital.' Gillespie flung his hands up in exasperation.

Gerry had a brainwave, pulled a sample bag out his pocket, and mimed poking the contents up his nose. It was as if a light went on in the man's head and he laughed aloud. Gillespie recognised the comprehension on the baker's face. That here was a chance to trade, to come out of this mess perhaps alive and ahead of the game and he smiled encouragingly.

'Yis. You all, kom plise.'

Penko took Gillespie's coat sleeve, leading him back downstairs to a row of metal Dexion shelving in the backshop where five-gallon drums nestled. He waved toward them in triumph.

'Here. Here u zee. You vant, yis?'

Gerry whispered, 'Is this guy the full shilling? It's not a Domestic Science lesson we're after. Does he think this is a City Bakeries takeover? Its fecking icing sugar and flour back here.'

The baker gabbled away, smiling and nodding and indicating the drums on the middle shelf, his finger stabbing at a red sticker on each, becoming more agitated the less they heeded him.

Gillespie held up his hand. 'Shut the fuck up!' and they all fell silent. He moved forward and tapped a finger on the red circle on one of the five drums all marked the same. He raised his eyebrows.

Penko raised his arms in triumph. 'Yis, Yis. Dugs, plenty dugs.'

They pulled a drum out and unclipped the top to peel back the metal lid. Gillespie produced a penknife, took a pinch of the powder on the blade and held it out to Steff who took a snort. Nothing at first then he jolted, stood tall, his eyeballs popped, his eyebrows shot up and his jaw dropped, leaving him gasping for breath.

'Fuck me with a feather, that's a megawatt jolt boss, so that is. This is better than anything we've had so far.'

Gillespie nodded. 'Aye. They must have been cutting it here with the flour, or Vim for all we know. Maybe we should take the bakery over after all. We'll not hang about here with Mr Stinker getting smellier by the minute. Get that drum resealed and into the boot with any other drums with a red circle on them.' While the boys did that he pulled out a hipflask and offered it to the Bulgarian, who drank and thanked him. *'Blogodarya Gospodin.'*

Gillespie was amused. 'Neither of us have a Scoobie what we're saying here, but I can see you're a man that probably wants nothing more than the quiet life, make some cash and get your arse back home to your wife and goats, maybe shag both for all I know. Right?'

He lit two fags and gave the baker one. Penko nodded repeatedly in puzzled agreement, friendly but wary and keeping the rolling pin within reach.

'Listen up pal, my problem is what to do with you. The tidy part of me says I should probably have the boys drown you in the sink, or put one in your ear, then burn the place down at our arse. But another part of me says just leave you here to go or stay as you like. Smashing your boss's head in did give us a wee problem as we wid have liked a chat with him first, but all's well that ends well. We got the goods and you are now free as a bird.' Gillespie stood, the baker did as well but he moved back a little against the wall, nervous still.

'Okay, *Noshten* or whatever your name is. I suggest you leg it before your boss there begins to smell and the Council sends some nosey parker to check the drains.'

He patted the side of the man's head in farewell. As he turned away the baker took a hold of his sleeve again and gesturing towards the floor hatch asked, *'I parite?'* He rubbed forefinger and thumb together. *'I parite?'*

'Sorry pal, nae idea what you're saying. Parite? Just you keep the parite and enjoy every mouthful. Take care.'

Penko watched them leave in amazement, relieved to be drawing breath still. He stood stock still and waited till the street was empty then dug out another bottle of the good vodka and opened the trapdoor into the basement. He dragged Tenescu's body to the hatch and dumped him down in a flail of arms and legs, his head thumping like a melon leaving a trail of blood and brains. One of his eyes had popped out on the floor. Penko squashed it under his boot and descended into the cellar to sit in the dark, drinking slowly, mourning his family. He also wondered why those crazy Scotsmen didn't want the two suitcases stuffed with money he was sitting on.

*

CHAPTER 16

Being a detective, the suitcase in the hall was the first big clue to McDowall. Irene waiting in her best coat and hat avoiding his eyes was the second. She was subdued, on the verge of tears. His daughter Moira was not shy however and had a tongue like a stiletto.

'Mum is coming to stay with me for a while. She just can't bear it here anymore, putting up with your drunken behaviour and the way you treat her.'

McDowall ignored her and stepped close to Irene. 'Is this true, Irene, you're for the off?'

Moira butted in between them. 'Mum doesn't need to explain anything to you, she'll come back when you mend your ways and appreciate her more. She's left you a letter on the sideboard, she's at the end of her tether.'

McDowall stepped forward. 'Shut your poisoned gob, Moira. It's done more damage than all the legions of Adolf Hitler. Don't interfere any more in this. Your mother and I can work things out without your blackhearted noisy advice that nobody asked for. Look to your own family, hen. For now, bugger off out my house and wait in the car.'

Cowed for now, Moira picked up the suitcase and stepped outside but waited on the path.

Irene was weeping quietly. 'I'm going, Francis, because I

can't be here anymore with you. You inhabit a different world from me. My world is full of nice things. The Kirk, the choir full of my friends, home, love and family. Your world is full of despair and thieving and killing. You mix with the scum and bring it home here, to us. You've become those you hunt, you have the stench of death about you, Francis. It's carried everywhere inside you. My world is full of angels and light, yours full of darkness and demons. You've become a man tainted and possessed. Infected. I need away from your warped world. Nothing has been right for me since you killed the fairy tale when that witch Claire stole you away. I don't think you will ever really come back to me. Let me go.'

McDowall hung his head staring at her shoes, could think of nothing to say, just nodded. He stepped to the side and Irene went out the door pulling it shut behind her the Yale snicking into place like a full stop locking him away from them. A deep raw silence filled the house. He felt like weeping but he couldn't, wouldn't. He found himself trailing around the house aimlessly, picking things up, putting them back or taking them to another room. He made a brew and sat by the phone waiting for it to ring. It didn't and later he had a whisky which turned into a session. Numbed and empty he stared at the pristine envelope on the sideboard propped against their wedding picture. He wouldn't be opening that anytime soon. Far too much truth in there.

He found himself doing stupid wee tasks, dusted then hoovered the whole house, something never attempted by him. He collected every scrap of rubbish and took it out to the bins. In the garden he stood looking over the house roofs in the direction of Moira's house.

His neighbour's back door opened, and May Clarke came out with a binbag in one hand and that wee kid-on yapping dog of hers on her arm. Christ! Was there to be no end to the tortures this night might bring. Nonetheless he was polite. The ferret dog began to yap.

'Evening, May, how are you?'

'I'm fine, thank you. Was that Irene I was seeing earlier, away with her daughter?'

McDowall sighed. This woman should spy for the KGB.

'Aye, she's away out with Moira, they're going away for a few days, a girly thing.' He thought to himself, 'if she mentions the suitcase I'm goin tae shove that dug down her throat and pull it out her jacksie.'

'Where's the dug ye used tae have, Mr McDowall? I haven't seen him for a day or two. Such a quiet thing, never knew he was about. Och he's no deid, is he?'

'No, May, not deid, he just looked that way. We don't have him anymore. He's away back to his last owner, kind of.'

'Oh. I thought I saw you and the dog up the Bluebell Wood the other night. I mind 'cos it was the night of that awful fire where they two poor boys were burnt.' McDowall had zoned her out and she prattled on. 'Are you working on that case, Mr McDowall? A terrible thing right enough. I don't know what Johnstone is coming to. Murderin' folk all over the place, it's all you see in the papers these days. Were they gangsters? That's what they say at the pensioners afternoon tea.'

McDowall stared up the garden. 'Sorry, say again.'

'The night of the murders up the Steadings. I was walking

Skye and am sure your dog was on the track, but it wis getting dark and I wisnae sure so I just came away. To be honest I felt uneasy. You know, it makes ma skin crawl tae think I wis anywhere near there. I was saying to my cousin Agnes that it might well have been the murderer I saw. Enough tae gie ye the heebie-jeebies.'

'Haud oan, May, back two spaces. You say it was Buster you saw?'

May hesitated. She had just been jabbering but now she was on the spot and wavered. 'Well, I was up till now. I suppose it could have been another dog but the one I saw had white socks like Buster. It's just what I read in the papers and the local wireless asking anybody who was up there that evening to come forward. Give a statement like. I was going to go down in the morning but I suppose talking to you is statement enough, is it not? Chatting to you saves me all the bother, what with my dodgy knees and heart.'

'Aye. Right enough, don't you bother.' McDowall didn't even notice May go in, but he closed his own door feeling as if a bus had hit him. He walked slowly into the living room to the sideboard. Alec had Buster by Thursday night. The man with the biggest motive ever to snuff the McGraths. McDowall didn't bother with a glass just lifted the bottle and drank from the neck. Gasping he stared at his reflection in the mirror letting the Meccano bits slide into place. All he could manage was, 'Fuck me, Alec. Fuck me rigid.'

Gillespie returned to Paisley in triumph with one hundred and twenty-five kilos of product retrieved and the Tenescu problem sorted. Hammond was less eager to break out the champagne thinking Tenescu's demise would not be well received no matter how softly the tale was told.

'What are you worrying about? It's sorted.' Gillespie poured two whiskies giving one to Hammond. 'This wee baker fella, Noshten Noshup or whatever, is taking the fall. We'll say he killed his boss, which is the truth by the way. Tell them the baker obviously took off with everything he could carry, problem solved. We say the cupboard was bare when we arrived.'

Hammond was unconvinced. 'Risky. I need to know how best to put this over to those Commie bastards. If they even get a whiff of us being involved, they'll come for blood.'

'Best consult your dad and run this by him while there's time. He knows how they think. Was it not him made all the connections during the war fighting in the Bulgarian mountains for a year with the partisans?'

'I can't stand any more war stories like how him and Audie Murphy won the war on their own. That care home's a money pit.' He checked the time and struggled into his coat. 'We can manage tonight if we hurry, get there before eight when they drug all the coffin dodgers.'

Gillespie masked his seething contempt for the son, comparing his own care for his mother with young Hammonds callous attitude. And now he wouldn't even reconcile and let the old man die in whatever peace he could find. Total waste of space so he was. It might be a good thing if the bloody Bulgarians took over, and done away with Arthur's boy in the process.

Once it was dark Stewart moved the money out from under the stairs and packed it into thick green plastic garden bags. Ethel's sister Lorraine had taken what sentimental keepsakes she wanted and made a start on bagging clothes, so he was careful to place his bags the other side of the hallway. He remembered there were more garden bags in the hut and, taking the padlock key, lifted the two money bags and went out, intending to put them behind the spare slabs in the shed. It was full dark, and he stumbled against the bins, knocking one over. Swearing creatively, he dropped the two bags and bent to retrieve the spilled rubbish. He crammed it into the bin and was stamping down with one leg in the bin, when a match rasped and flared behind him.

'Jesus Fucking Christ!' He fell backwards onto the wet grass, one leg still in the bin.

McDowall stepped out of the shadows by the downpipe into the light from the kitchen window and blew the match out.

'No, not Jesus. Just your friendly neighbourhood polis. Here you are on your arse with one foot in a bin, is this a commando thing?' McDowall held out a hand. 'Let me help you up, ya big fearty.'

Stewart wiped himself down, there was a cold wet patch on his bum. 'You near gave me a heart attack. What the fuck are you doing hanging about my back door in the pitch dark? Are you back at the Peeping Tom and flashing again? Is that no how Peter Manuel started out?'

'Funny, very funny.' McDowall stooped and picked up a

binbag. 'Hefty. What's in here, Brodie's missing bits?' He laughed, lifted the lid on the metal bin and dropped it in.

'Eh! What? Oh aye.' Stewart forced a laugh thinking fast. 'Lorraine was up and bagged most of the clothes so I'm dumping the junk stuff.' McDowall waved his hand for the other bag. Stewart handed it over and watched it dumped on top of the other one. He cleared his throat and spoke with an effort. 'Frank, what are you doing lurking in the dark here? Are you moonlighting nightshifts with the Cleansing Department part time or just going really weird?'

'Weird? No more than usual, but good of you to ask. Define weird if you're a polis. The fact is, this isn't a social call at all. I was just chit-chatting with my neighbour earlier the night and she gave me some disturbing tittle-tattle right out the blue, concerning you no less. Why don't we pop inside and you can give me some of Robert's fine malt unless it's all scudded?' McDowall banged the bin lid down and ushered Stewart inside as if the place was his.

The house was in darkness at the front except for the orange streetlight shining in the big window. McDowall bumped into the armchair and plopped down.

'What's this, Poverty Hall, not paid the lecky bill?'

Stewart poured into the good crystal glasses and handed McDowall a fair two fingers of the amber nectar which he put under his nose and breathed in deeply.

'Talisker?'

'Laphroaig.' Stewart lifted his glass and toasted. 'Robert, Ethel, and Angela. Fairest of the fair.' McDowall echoed the toast and they drained their glasses. Stewart refilled and then sat on the low windowsill, silhouetted against the street lights, and faced McDowall across the room. Their glowing ciggies danger lights pulsing and fading in the dark silence.

'Do you sit about in the dark often?' McDowall asked after a while. 'I do.'

'The dark's an old friend I'm not afraid of. I don't need light for thinking, nor for finding the bottle or my gub.'

'I know what you mean.'

He told Stewart about the Sally Ann Alcoholics Anonymous meeting and they laughed. Conversation fell away and the night lay between them like a curtain, neither of them really wanting to pull it aside and start down a road they couldn't retreat from. McDowall was loath to begin for fear of getting answers he didn't want that would compel him to a course he didn't want to steer.

Stewart felt as if he'd entered a narrow wadi in the Yemen or a damp Ulster lane and just knew there was an ambush or a bomb there. He remained silent, waiting to see where he was led. Problem was, McDowall was doing the same thing. Stewart's fag had burnt down and singed his nicotine-stained fingers. He stubbed it out by dropping it into a cold cuppa on the floor and spoke.

'How's Irene these days? I saw her at the funeral but didn't get to speak to her. Is she in her bed like a normal person, unlike yourself?'

'Irene's staying with Moira for a while. For the best.'

'Sorry to hear that. Been there myself, got the T-shirt.'

'Uhhuh. Well, this is all very cosy sitting here all pally

Stewart, but the thing is, I've not dragged my sorry arse up here in the middle of the night to help you finish the Laphroaig or greet on my buddy's shoulder.'

Their voices disturbed Buster who came in growling then panting in pleasure and came to McDowall, who ruffled his ears. Buster responded by placing his head on his knee and slavering on his thigh. Alec crossed the room and parked himself on the coffee table in front of McDowall.

'Why don't we stop the music and the dancing around each other? We have too many skint knees, malt and hangovers under the bridge for that. What have you come to ask me?'

McDowall leant forward until they were only a foot apart and they held each other's eyes.

'One more time. Just for me. Did you or did you not tell me and Jim Brown that you were home all night on Thursday, got pished and fell asleep on the couch?'

'I know it's not much of an alibi when my drinking friend was a derelict dug, Buster the Boozer hound, but that's what happened.'

'And you told us you had nothing to do with murdering the scumbag McGraths?'

Alec thought, '*not murdered, executed.*' He cleared his throat. 'I had nothing to do with the murders up the Steading but with my whole being I wish I had. I wanted to slit their gizzards and leave their carcasses disembowelled on the graves of my family. Had it been me, that's where you would have found them.'

McDowall nodded, his face blank his brain in turmoil. He didn't believe Alec. 'See it from where I'm standing. I have this nosy neighbour through the wall who's one of those gossiping busybody folks you're barely aware of half the time, but they notice everything, hear everything. I suspect she could be Stalin's Aunty. Tonight I bumped into her at the bins. She asked after Buster.'

'So?'

'She's got a dog, well more like a toy thing that should be on wheels, a wee rat yapping jackshit mutt. Anyway, she walks it every night and always the same route. She goes up Auchenlodment Road to the Bluebell Wood near the old quarry. That's by the Steading.'

'Aye, we played up there as boys.'

McDowall wiped his finger around his empty glass and licked it, stared into the glass. 'She seemed to think I still had Buster. Is that no funny? Said that when she passed she saw him on the track just short of the road. Now the confusion for me is, Alec, if you were here pished on the couch, what was Buster doing up the Steading?'

Alec made to refill McDowall's glass but he waved the bottle away. 'You know who I mean?'

'I know exactly who you mean, it's the May Clarke who does the flowers for the Kirk and volunteers at the Oxfam Shop. She's been blind since she taught at Wallace Primary. Does she not have specs as thick as ginger bottles? She couldn't find her own tits in the dark with both hands. Did you know her nickname is Mrs Magoo? It could have been any dog or even one of the black sheep off the hill. It could have been Champion the Wonder Horse, but it wasn't Buster.'

'You can vouch for the dog, Alec but it's not his alibi that's wobbly. Thing is, he can't confirm any part of yours. Talk to me.'

'I know you're here because nobody wanted them dead more than me, plus anybody else that had to do with Angela. I regret I didn't murder them, but it wisnae me.'

Alec then realised that if this was unofficial or McDowall would have that Brown with him or at least a uniform with a notebook out. All this was just a chat then. Just fishing, casting the net, see what turned up. Alec settled down, calmer now but just as careful. 'What else?' he asked.

McDowall rose and took his glass into the kitchen, washed it and laid it on the draining board, turned and leant back against the worktop, arms folded. Alec watched him from the living room. 'See, Alec, it's always been the wee things that do the job for me, the simple stuff. The big things tend to jump right up and bite your bum.'

'Tell me what these wee things are.'

'You have motive in triplicate and unquestioned talents for mayhem. You have a dodgy dog alibi is all. You can see why I might be curious as to what you have to say?'

'Not what she said, in fact. Never at any time did she say I was there for I was here. She thinks she saw a dog that might be Buster. You know as well as me that she needs to ask folk at the bus stop which bus is coming, and that's in daylight. I was here all night, with Buster, pished. We were both pished in fact.'

McDowall changed tack. 'While you were making a brew for Jim Brown and me the other night I checked your wellies at the back door.'

'So, as well as hanging about back gardens you now have a rubber thing going?'

'There was dried mud on the uppers and the soles were wet. So was inside.'

Alec chuckled. 'Jeez, Frank, you've become a right Indian scout, the big white hunter. I went out to the bin with the rubbish with them on about ten minutes before you two arrived.'

McDowall nodded and put his glass away. He was aware Alec Stewart knew all there was to know about interrogation from his time in Ulster. This was a dead end for now. He crossed the room to the bookcase and picked up the black and white photograph of Alec, his wife and wee girl at the seaside. 'Where's this?'

Alec took it off him and set it back on the mantle.

'Scarborough. A thousand years past. It's the only picture left of us all together. When she left, I thought she'd taken all the photographs with her, but it turned out she burnt them in the barbecue.'

'She? Can you still not say her name?'

'No! I can't. I won't. She took too much from me. She destroyed me when I needed her most and left me broken.'

'I know what it is to be broken.' McDowall turned to face him, placed a hand on his shoulder then leaned in close and whispered into the dark. 'I know you did it. I only have the feeling in my gut. I don't know how you found them and nobody deserved killing more. I'd love Buster just to bark out you took him a walk up the Braes and murdered the McGraths. I know it in my bones. Everything I ever knew or learned about you is screaming it at me. Tell me true, Scout's honour.'

Alec scoffed. 'Honour, if it ever existed, died on a hundred battlefields long ago. I didn't murder them but if I knew who did, I wouldn't tell you, Frank. How the blazes, nae pun intended, would I have known where they were? Even the polis with half the force looking for them couldn't find them so how was I supposed to?'

'You had every reason, the deep compelling need to do it, and you definitely have the capability. I remember the first time you came home on leave; you were wearing a green T-shirt. Do you remember what was printed on it?'

'I do actually. It said, "Join the Marines. Travel to far distant lands. Meet exotic people. KILL THEM!" It was all youthful bravado, I was eighteen, Frank, stupid.'

'Not bravado now though, is it? We both know you've killed men before, by every means possible in every corner of the world. How many is it now? Twenty, thirty maybe? Do you even remember?'

'Never counted. Some did, it seemed to me a sick thing to do, but I'll tell you something. All of them were better men than the two McGraths. You're on private ground now. Don't push it!'

'Have you come across a Michael Brodie in your travels?'

'The guy chopped up and left in a bog? Just what I read

about the hand thing in the papers. Never met him. Am I getting blamed for that as well or does the water bailiff's dog need an alibi?'

'No. I know who did that as well.'

'What happens now?'

Not wanting to cross any more lines McDowall sighed.

'I go home to my bed and hopefully sleep a little. You can do as you like.' He ruffled Buster's ears on the way to the door, stood a second in the doorway and made that wee sucking noise with his teeth. 'As the Sheriff says in the cowboy pictures, don't leave town.'

He closed and locked the door behind McDowall, went into the kitchen and threw up in the sink.

Gillespie had eventually got across to Graeme Hammond the serious situation they were in with the death of Anton Tenescu. The Bulgarians would undoubtedly come soon, seeking answers to their boss's vanished nephew and the man with the best advice was Arthur Hammond.

At Dunrobin Care Home, Staff Nurse Brenda Rafferty was not amused to have them ringing the bell that late at night and gave them short shrift when she answered.

'Weeks you don't come then suddenly you think you can roll up here in the middle of the night upsetting my routines when we're short staffed and trying to get folk into bed. You'll wait till that's done.'

Gillespie apologised for the hour but Hammond, graceless as ever, snarled back at her.

'I'm here to see my father. I pay a king's ransom to keep him here. I never expected he would last this long. Don't you know who I am?'

Unintimidated she crossed her arms and stepped up to Hammond. 'Don't you take that tone with me you wee bauchle! I ken just fine who you are, my mother boxed your ears more than once when you were young. I also know what you are. You have no say here on my watch, so you'll just wait till I have a minute.' She marched them into the office and closed the door leaving Hammond to stew there for ten long silent minutes before she returned with a folder which she flung on the desk.

'Since you've turned up at last I'm giving you an update on your father.'

She told them Arthur was sedated most of the time, his awareness levels fluctuating as his pain management dosage increases. If he deteriorated further she would be considering transferring him to the Beatson Institute, if a bed became available. Graeme appeared uninterested but she pressed on.

'Mr Hammond's respiratory function is seriously imparted by the cancer and there is a significant amount of fluid building up in his lungs despite a drain inserted this afternoon. His morphine dosage is as much as we feel he can take and he wanders in and out of reality, sometimes speaking to people in his head in what sounds like Russian. This deterioration will accelerate into the final stage of his condition. Sometimes he has very lucid moments and recognises members of staff and visitors. Well, some visitors, for your family have been scarcer than diamonds among the coal around here. He's semi-conscious so you have fifteen minutes. Don't stay longer.'

They made their way to the room where Gillespie stood by the bed and taking Arthur's hand in his paw and spoke softly.

'Mr Arthur sir, can you hear me? It's Neil Gillespie. We sorely need your advice. Graeme's here as well.'

Arthur struggled to take a few deep ragged noisy breaths. 'That... useless... cunt,' he gasped. 'What's he... fucked up... now?'

Every tortured word bubbled the yellow fluid in the drain bag, like a kid blowing down a straw into his ginger. Gillespie knelt by the bed so his face was level with the auld man's ear and whispered all that had happened concerning the McGraths and Tenescu. Arthur listened silently with closed eyes. When the tale was told he waved Graeme over, grabbing his coat sleeve when he was within reach with sudden ferocity and strength, dragging him closer. The effort produced a spasm of choking and he snorted phlegm tinted with blood into his mask. Nauseated, Graeme cringed and pulled away slipping out his coat to get free. He waved a hand to have Gillespie deal with this, who picked up a towel and cleaned the mask out.

Graeme grabbed his coat from the bed. 'I've had enough of this nurse crap, it's giving me the boak. I'm off.'

Arthur regained his breath and drew two huge rasping gulps of air his lungs crackling like twigs in a fire. He recovered and snarled at his son with undiminished venom.

'I'm still... head of this family, so... sit on your fucking arse right now... or I'll have Neil make you.' The drain bag percolated crazily. Gillespie pulled the chair nearer the bed and sat Graeme down, towering over him like a double wardrobe. Arthur sucked at the oxygen for a full minute before he settled and could gasp on.

'I should have used a condom the night I seeded you. Tenescu is the nephew of the main man in Bulgaria, you arse. It disnae matter a jot it was the baker that killed him. He was in our charge, our responsibility, and we'll be held to account.' He attempted to sit, his breath rasping painfully. Gillespie helped adjust the pillows, his breathing eased and Arthur continued. 'His family won't let this pass lightly. You have no idea what's going to happen. The Bulgarians are not the Wombles you seem to think they are and when they come it'll be worse than an Old Firm rammy.' He wheezed to a halt like an old blown steam engine, reached out and gripped Gillespie's hand with surprising strength.

'Do you understand?'

'I understand, Mr Arthur,' he replied. 'With Tenescu dead our main means of contact are gone, so I'll get word to them about his killing. We should emphasise we have secured his goods and have them in safekeeping. We could take them and blame the baker, but we won't, they will be returned. It's very important we show good faith here.'

Arthur nodded. 'Where's… the…body?'

'Still at the bakery. We left it with this wee baker guy who said his name was Noshten Pazach or something like that. I thought if they found him there they'd know we had nothing to do with it.'

'Send that name with the information. If we are to salvage anything from this, including our skins, we have to be careful.' He fumbled the mask down, barking and gurgling at Graeme. 'You will do exactly what Neil says. Get men back to the bakery and hope Tenescu's body is still there and not in the dock basin. Get it taken somewhere refrigerated for now. Source a coffin of some sort, then at least we can tell them we have given his body due respect.'

'And the wee baker guy?' Neil asked. 'He has no English and no family here.'

'Do what you should have done at the time. Silence him.'

Seething with anger Graeme tried to speak, to assert himself. Gillespie raised a hand to cut him off, taking command now.

'I'll get that done. We still have that phone number for some guy in the Bulgarian Embassy. I'll get things rolling.' Arthur gasped and choked his back arching with the struggle to cough and breath. There was more blood inside the mask. Gillespie pulled the call cord and they were ejected by the Staff Nurse. Exhausted, Arthur took refuge in oblivion, returning into the coven of his nightmares.

There were no pipers for Beth Sharkey. No weeping family or loved ones, no good ladies from the WRVS, no church choirs. Only the stark reality of Glasgow's Eastern Necropolis and a deep muddy trench by the west wall. The Salvation Army had opened a layer for her in a common grave among the other paupers and those with nobody to mourn their passing or care for them. Beth would be 6G layer four. She arrived unheralded by candles incense and pomp, nor book and bell. Nobody there asked for whom the bell tolled just so long as it wasn't for them. Not even the dignity of a hearse was hers, for she came by the black van from the Glasgow Mortuary driven by George the mortuary assistant.

He had prepared the body, bathed her, put on her shroud, brushed her hair across the massive head injury, gave her a wee bit of makeup. He had tried to write a wee deid ditty for her, but sadness overtook him and he found no words. Before he screwed her down he'd kissed her like she was his wee girl, like her Daddy should have.

The Social had tracked down her sister Marina, but she had just squinted around the door, shrugged her shoulders and after inquiring was there any money, closed it in their faces. Beth's two case workers were crying. The girl from the Sally Ann carried a heather posy. A uniformed constable accompanied Detective Sergeant Reid from City of Glasgow Police. Beth's murder was still unsolved, and George supposed it a penance they were here, as well as to see who turned up. It was known for the murderer to attend their victim's internment. The only other mourners were the gravediggers in that muddy uniform of bunnets and boiler suits, wellies, and mud-smeared donkey jackets. Two were the worse for drink, their faces purpled and livid. They slid the coffin from the back of the van, laid it across timber spars and carried her briskly across to her last pitch. The Sally Ann guy read from the Bible, the bit about Jesus saving Mary Magdalene, but nobody had saved Beth.

A hymn followed, *"The Lord's My Shepherd,"* sung by the Salvationists mostly, the rest of them mumbling and shuffling. George couldn't help wondering if Jesus had been on a tea break while somebody was pounding this wee lassie's head off a skip. The heather posy was laid on the coffin lid and then everybody took a cord and lowered Beth into the cold dark earth. In a final farce the coffin floated, bobbing in about a foot of water like a badly built canoe.

The gravediggers made the stock black jokes about burial at sea and began to shovel the mud into the grave, thwacking on the wood, rocking Beth as if she were struggling to break out until the weight sank her. Heartsick, George turned away. Reid and the constable asked him for a lift back to the Tollbooth. Back in the van they sat in silence staring out at the fallen gravestones and collapsed graves. Reid voiced his opinion that he would hang those who toppled memorials in the graveyard. George produced three cans of lager. They slurped the lukewarm froth.

George sighed. 'Any nearer finding who did the lassie in?' he asked Reid.

'No, we are not. And before you ask, the chances are fucking zero.'

'It's a pure bastard shame, so it is.'

Alec Stewart was in Johnstone's Abbey Road cemetery with Buster, who curled up on Angela's grave and whined. From where Alec sat on the bench he could see his own parents grave beside the caretakers house.

'Hullo Robert, come to let you know what's happened. Angela, it seems a crime to have your beauty rot away in the ground. Ethel, I don't suppose you're pleased to see me at all because of young Kevin, but I think you will be glad with my news. The animals who did this to us are dead. I killed them with my own hands. I wanted to bring them here and slit their throats over your graves, but that's frowned on now.' He chuckled grimly. 'It was all chance, luck, but either God or the Devil, I don't care which one, put them in my path and enough to say I took everything from them. You should know they died badly, screaming in their own shit and full of terror as I intended because of what they did to us. You remember Frank McDowall? Well, he's on the case and that might be a problem. He knows I did it, got no proof at all, but he knows in his gut I did it.

On the upside, I've come into someone else's money and think I'll get away for a while, let the blood dry and the smoke clear. I'm sick of sharing a bed with death, so this is probably goodbye for now. Thanks for being my big brother, and for being there when Sheila left me taking my wee girl. You took care of me when I was broken.

Angela, thanks for being my wee girl as much as you could be and for all the hugs and kisses you gave your sad old uncle. As for you Ethel, well, I hope you can forgive me now that you know the truth, that I didn't want Kevin to enlist, tried to change his mind and when he was killed I wept for him like a son. Kevin, my boy, *"Semper Fi"* as the Yanks say. I'm not sure what I believe anymore but it comforts me to imagine you're all together. If Ethel's right I'll join you all one day, but not yet I hope, not yet.'

He took four rocks out his pocket, selected from the rockery in the garden at home, and sat two on top of each headstone. 'I'll try and get back here before I go, Robert, and plant some of the roses you loved from the garden. Cheerio. Say hullo to Mum and Dad.'

By the time he'd ambled back home it was dusk. He put two bridies in the oven, thought about a whisky but resisted and fed Buster. Alec had never been a man to panic but even he recognised it was maybe wise to get some distance between him and the law. He was spooked more than he cared to admit by McDowall's visit, thinking it was perhaps subtle advice to do a runner. On the plus side, knowing was not proof and May Clarke was not reliable, blind as a bat and a kind of plasticine woman with the impressions of the last person she had talked to. However, he did need to move the money and drugs.

When McDowall had picked up the bags and flung them in the bin, Alec near had a heart attack. The two bags now sat on the couch either side of him while he considered what to do. At last he decided. He split one of the money packs and took five thousand pounds from it, which he stuffed into his old Bergen. He went out and got the heavy pinch bar in the hut used to bash holes in the garden and wrapped it in a sandbag to muffle the sound. With that he levered the three feet by two concrete cover from off the drain trap at the head of the garden. He dropped everything else into the pit, double-bagged like a good carryout, levered the slab back and from five feet you wouldn't even know the trap was there.

After camouflaging the lid with dried leaves, he went back inside and packed a collection of random hill clothes into the Bergen on top of the money.

It was high time he took to the hills.

Fought on his own ground.

When the Hammond crew returned to Tradeston the roller shutters were pulled down over the window and front door of the bakery. Gillespie rattled the padlock.

'Let's try the back. Hammer and jemmy.'

They found a loose lavvy window through which Gerry, being the skinniest, was fed, and he unbolted the fire exit to allow them to file in. The place was hot as hell, all the heaters on and the oven had fired up on a timer. Neil strolled into the front shop, taking off his coat as he went, while the boys searched the ground floor. He took the Webley from the holster, checked it, and leaned on the counter top. There were cakes and doughnuts in the display case. Steff picked up a bridie and sniffed at it, it seemed okay so he began eating. Within minutes the boys came back down the rickety stairs from the small office in the loft.

'Nobody here,' said Gerry. 'The office is trashed, the safe is lying open.'

Gillespie grunted. 'There's a surprise. Wee Noshten was smarter than he looked then, maybe letting him go was a mistake and I'm beginning to wonder how much English he understood. Okay. Find a bin or something and put all the office papers you can find in it.' He pointed to the blood trail on the floor leading to a closed hatch in the floor. 'It would seem the late unlamented Mr. Tenescu is still here, unless the wee guy baked him in the bridies.'

They exchanged looks, pulled faces, the bridies went in the bin. The hatch in the floor was not closed fully as if left in a hurry, and when Gerry grabbed the handle and hauled it up a cloud of flies rose buzzing in their faces. They all stepped back pulling jackets up over their mouths, retreating into the front shop waving their arms wildly till the flies swarmed at the ceiling around the fluorescent lights. The big blue neon bug killer began to stutter and crack like a machine gun. Eyes watering from the stench they peered down into the bowels of the shop. The light from above showed Tenescu's legs up to the knee, the rest in darkness.

'He's got nae shoes. Where's his shoes?' Steff gagged.

Gerry slapped Steff across the back of the head. 'What's with the shoes? It's not as if he's planning to walk somewhere.'

'He's deid, he disnae need shoes.'

Gillespie waved the Webley towards the hatch. 'Shut yer gobs, the pair of you. A couple of loons so you are. Let's go down and get this done.'

They wrapped aprons over their faces. Steff yanked a light cord on the way down causing another insect explosion, flies big as bats.

Tenescu, in life a bit of a dandy fella, was not so pretty now. His smashed head was stuck to the concrete floor in a pool of sticky congealed gore in which insects feasted. His shirt was up under his armpits and his tailored trousers opened and pulled down to mid-thigh. There was more gore here, lots of crawling things buzzing and seething around the massive wound left by somebody removing his tackle. Gillespie guessed Tenescu had really pissed off the wee baker guy. Foreigners; savage tribal lot.

Gerry flailed his arms at the flies, stared a minute, then made a wee screechy panicky noise and bolted up the stairs.

'I'm fucking out of here.'

Steff stepped up close careful not to tread on anything squidgy. 'Aw, that's just no right man. Why wid ye want tae dae that? I could see the point if ye wanted tae torture him, but when he's deid? Just well outside the norm, man.'

Gillespie nudged the body with his foot, the flies rose again. 'Get the rolls of plastic from the boot of the car and bring that boaking Jessie back down with you.'

'Are we lifting him then, it'll be right messy?'

'He's hardly going up the stair himself and walking to the car, is he?'

They rolled the corpse in heavy plastic and sealed it tightly with masking tape.

'Right, that'll do it. Just so long as nothing smelly leaks over us. Get that rope and you two haul it up the stair.'

Steff brought the car down the lane to the back door. From there they struggled the squidgy parcel into the boot. Tenescu was taller than they thought and they had to batter his knees down and fold him up like a clasp knife to crush him in. Steff reminded Gillespie they really needed to get a new van for this kind of thing. It took two attempts to shut the boot and get it to catch.

Steff started the engine and asked, 'Okaydokey then, where to?'

Gerry leant forward from the back. 'I was thinking we could have Sneaky Pete store the stiff for us, at his ice cream van place. Lots of freezers there surely.'

Gillespie twisted in the seat and scowled at him. 'Are you gormless? Wid that be the Sneaky Pete we dropped two floors ower a veranda onto a car? I think you could say he has fallen oot with us, literally. I wid imagine he's in the Alexandra Infirmary about now. Take us back to the lockup we rent in Floors Street. There's a big chest freezer there.'

The storage yard was deserted when they arrived, the high boundary walls concealing them, but once inside the unit a major problem presented itself. The freezer was an upright and when the padlock was taken off they found it already had a load of dodgy butcher's meat in it. Gillespie stuck his hands in his coat pockets, fuming and shaking his head.

'What the fucking hell is this, and where the fuck is the big chest freezer that was in here? That wid be the big empty chest freezer.'

Gerry looked embarrassed, fidgeted.

'Well, my mum was wanting a chest type so me and Steff swapped it over for her and brought this one here. It holds the same amount. We could lay it on its back maybe. Plus, it's got a padlock. The meats from a couple of deer we ran down on the Braes Road.'

Gillespie exploded. 'Ya dozy prick. It's half the size. Houdini couldnae get a body in there, so how are we fitting Tenescu in that?'

'Chop him up. Like Brodie.'

Gillespie gritted his teeth in exasperation. 'And what do you think the Bulgarian reaction to that will be? Here's your nephew, handed over like an MFI flat pack furniture body, some assembly required? Do you imagine they will be very unchuffed? Could you two fuckwits manage to overpower the deid guy in the boot and get him in here without dropping him?'

They managed that, pecking and panting, the corpse sliding in their hands and multi-coloured body fluids swishing around inside the clear plastic shroud. They emptied the freezer and removed the shelves, unceremoniously crammed Anton Tenescu inside crouched with knees bent and head bowed. Gerry got a bass broom and shoved the body tightly into place, standing back to admire his handiwork.

'See! I told you he wid fit. All we have to do now is pack all this venison back in and that'll wedge him in place like a rock.'

Steff clicked the wee button that turned the outside light on and off a couple of times. 'You could actually have a wee read in here if you wanted.'

Gillespie closed his eyes. He was working with a guy who didn't know the light went off when the door shut. Body problem resolved for the moment they padlocked the freezer and left. Gerry threw the outside bolts and locked them. The two numpties dropped him off at his Mum's place and, once she was attended to, he lay soaking in a bath with a glass of whisky and a fag. The Webley rested on the toilet lid under a towel. Young Hammond hadn't a clue what was coming down, but Gillespie's instincts told him the Bulgarians would take this badly.

He was going to need more ammunition.

Brown, as ever, was early and waiting by the front desk with the morning papers when McDowall arrived at the police station. There was bad news and good news.

'The Sally Ann has phoned Tannock and clyped on you,' Brown whispered.

'About what?'

'Jeez, Frank. The wee matter of walking out your first alkie session and going for a dram, leaving me holding the can. Tannock is in his office with the Deputy Chief. Says you are not to leave the station till he speaks to you and you've to surrender all your files to me and Joyce this morning.'

'Any good news?'

'For you, naw! For me, yes! I've been re-promoted to temporary acting Detective Sergeant to fill in for you.'

'Where's Joyce?'

'In your office, now our office, gathering the files on all your cases. The McGraths' burning, the Brodie jigsaw, and of course the Angela Stewart inquiry. You're not even been left the stolen motorbike case.'

'Ah weel, worse things happen at sea. I don't suppose a brew is on the horizon?'

'It's hemlock you need.'

McDowall nearly missed his office because it had a door. The Saltcoats surfboard had been rehung. He pushed it open and surprised Joyce loading files into cardboard boxes.

'Frank. Did you get the message, about Tannock?'

'I did. I did.' He stood opening and closing the door three or four times. 'Is that no typical? The thing lies in the corner for two whole years, the Works Department deaf to my pleadings. Then, the day I get it in the neck they rehang the thing. I should haul it back off for sheer bloody spite.'

'Never mind that. Rumour is that it's you that might be getting hung. Tannock had me in his office first thing this morning, he was waiting in ambush at the front desk for me. Asked if I could step in and carry on with Brown in charge. He also pressed me hard about anything I might have heard about Central Station, again. The word on that is all over the canteen. Did you really walk out an AA meeting? He's also furious you'd ignored him and the Proc Fiscal about closing the Stewart case.'

McDowall dropped his coat on the floor, plopped into his chair and grimaced. 'Well, I think we can safely close it now. What with the two prime suspects turning up well done at a barn dance barbecue. Justice has been indeed served, not by me unfortunately. I was really looking forward to that. The McGraths are now a murder inquiry themselves now. What a waste of time, as if anybody gives a tinkers' damn?'

'Alec Stewart, you think he did it?'

'I know he did it, my dove, but that's not proving it. To be honest, I'm glad to see the McGraths done away with, unlamented even by their gargoyle mother. I think whoever did it should get a medal. Do you think it might have been divine intervention?'

'Devilish intervention more like.'

'Maybe God got off his arse at last and smote them with fire and brimstone. I can't really get up much steam to find their killer or killers. But I do have one hope.'

'What's that?'

'They were alive when the van was torched.'

Inspector Tannock was well pleased by the turn of events. The Deputy Chief himself had come down from Port Glasgow first thing that morning and was sitting at Tannock's desk reading the file he'd had compiled so carefully. Ian Robins was of the old school, risen to Deputy Chief from the ranks. He had been on the same recruit course as McDowall and then partners on the beat.

The file was a litany of McDowall transgressions over the years. A catalogue of official complaints from various outside agencies over the years. Everything from insubordination to beating suspects. Many of his suspects had begun their interrogation by falling down the cell steps. Robins himself knew of many reports not logged and this was the tip of the iceberg. Also in the file on his personnel record card was an equal number of commendations, there always being two sides to a coin. A complex man.

Latest was a strongly worded letter from the Salvation Army about his sins as well as memos of complaint from a multitude of sources going back years and copies of the interviews with DC Brown and WPC Joyce Fairbairn. The Deputy noted both these statements were unsigned and knew why. Brown and Fairbairn would have been very unwilling to condemn a colleague or be complicit in his fall. The canteen courtroom would not wear that.

On the desk before him was a letter of suspension awaiting his signature and Robins could see no way how he could possibly do other than sign it. It was tragic but there seemed to be no other course but this. Tannock moved the letter closer and placed a fountain pen by the Deputy's hand. Robins closed the file over ignoring the pen.

'You've been very thorough, Inspector, very thorough indeed. I don't have the time to read this comprehensive collection of Frank McDowall's sins and I probably know lots that isn't in here.' He made a face, picked up the pen, scanning the death warrant. 'I see here this is for a three-month suspension on condition of the Detective Sergeant attending all the AA meetings.'

'It is, Sir. I thought six months more apt, but the Chief did not agree.'

'Aye well, the Chief is very aware of your efforts in this matter, Inspector.'

Robins thought it was time to put this wee jumped-up backstabbing bastard in his place and remind him who had most braid on their cap. He uncapped the pen, scored out the three months and wrote in six weeks, initialled and dated the change and scrawled what passed for his signature under his typed name. Tannock took it and carefully blew on the wet ink. His smirk faded when he saw the change.

'Mr Robins, sir! I must protest at this further dilution of McDowall's punishment. Men have been dismissed for less.'

'That'll be Detective Sergeant McDowall to you. I fire and hire here, protest noted.' His finger rapped on the file. 'This officer has caught and put away more criminals than you've had hot dinners.' He sighed. 'Right, let's have him up and get this done.'

McDowall was summoned, did the walk of shame past the desk and up the stair. When he knocked and went in Robins was sat at the desk with his hat on as formal as could be. 'Detective Sergeant McDowall, good morning. We all know why we're here so let's proceed. I understand you have waived the right to have a friend or a Police Federation Representative present to support you. Is that correct?'

'That's right enough. I don't need all that crap. You here's good enough for me.'

A smile touched Robins 'stern face', he waved McDowall to a seat. 'Let's get on then.' He pushed the letter across to Frank. 'Your copy. This is a formal notice that with immediate effect you are suspended on full pay enabling you to take advantage of the medical assistance offered to you in relation to your recognised alcohol problem. Understand this, if you fail to make even one of the AA meetings during that period you will be subject to further discipline procedures at either the Chief Constables' discretion or that of the Police and Fire Board. Is that clear?'

McDowall folded the letter neatly. 'Crystal.'

Tannock butted in. 'That's it? The suspension diluted and no disciplinary action worth a damn? This is ridiculous.' He pointed a wobbling finger at McDowall. 'This officer should be dismissed; his locker emptied and be escorted off the station.'

Robins took his hat off, exhaled wearily. 'This matter is

now closed, and don't question my authority or judgment.'

Tannock fell silent while Robins undid his tunic and kicked his shoes off. 'Right Inspector, Detective Sergeant McDowall and I will be using your office for some personal one-on-one counselling. Thank you.'

Tannock left, flung out his own office.

Robins opened and closed the desk drawers. 'Does this guy keep any drink in here?'

'I think there's some brandy in the cabinet there, he keeps it for the Chief Constable, Police Board Members and such like.'

Robins dug the bottle out along with two glasses and poured himself a good measure of brandy. McDowall reached out for the bottle but Robins pulled it back and pointedly filled the other glass with water from a jug on the desk. McDowall stared at it.

'Water? Am I to drink that? Have you seen what it does to the soles of your shoes?'

'I'm making a point, Frank, and I hope you're getting it loud and clear, that it's not lost on you. This,' he poked a finger down on the desk, 'is the very last time I can save you. Big changes are coming with Regionalisation, and you need to get a grip if you ever want to see your pension. Go to the Sally Ann meetings, get yourself dried out. When you come back, I expect you to be sober and functioning something like a real person. Shave every day from now on, and for God's sake change that shirt. I've not seen a grubbier tide mark since we were at school the gither.' Robins swallowed his brandy, buttoned his tunic, crammed his cap on, and paused at the door.

'One last thing for now, Frank.'

'God save us, what?'

'First test of your resolve here. Don't even think about a drink or taking that bottle of Salvador away with you. Put it back in the cabinet. Here endeth the lesson. Love to Irene.' McDowall didn't drink the water, but then, he didn't drink the brandy either. As McDowall went down the stair Tannock passed him in supressed volcanic silence on the way up. At the front desk, he passed the letter across to Brown, who read it and passed it back.

'No more than expected, no more than you deserve in the circumstances. None the less, you're one jammy bastard.' Brown nodded over his shoulder into the lobby. 'You've a visitor.'

It was Alec Stewart, dressed for the outdoors, a rucksack the size of a filing cabinet on the floor, Buster lounging at his feet. McDowall slid through the inner doors and sat on the bench beside him. Buster sprang up and licked both their faces.

McDowall wished he were half as happy.

'So, how are you? What's happening?' Alec asked.

McDowall lit up. 'You've some fucking cheek. I wrote an update for my boss this morning insinuating the McGraths had lots of enemies who wanted them dead and that you had an alibi. I even added a bit that you had a witness, just didn't mention it was Buster. On the downside, I've been suspended for various reasons you won't care about and I remain convinced my best mate's been slaughtering his enemies. I'm going to be like those old lawmen in the cowboy books and hang a notice on my door. "Gone Fishing."'

'I didn't murder them.'

'You keep saying. Just semantics. You know something? This is the first time in all my years of service I've supressed information. There's no written statement from May Clarke saying she saw you, well Buster, up the Steadings that night.'

McDowall lit up. 'Anyway, what do you want?'

Alec hung his head. 'Once, when I was young, I wanted many things but that's all gone now and most of it my fault, or so people tell me. I think they might be right. But I just wanted you to know, unless you want to throw me in the pokey, that I'm getting out of here for a while. Am off to the hills.'

'I got your phone message but still you came here.'

'Some things need done face to face.'

'You're one ballsy bastard. I suppose you're wanting me to take Buster while you, "love to go awandering, along the mountain tracks"?'

'Buster's going with me, we'll do a bit of the West Highland Way.'

'A change of destination. Are you removing the only witness? It'll kill him, he'll never make it. If he does he'll have legs like a dachshund.'

'Maybe neither of us will make it back.'

'That would tidy things up. How long you planning?'

Alec shrugged. 'A bit of string?' He held out his hand.

McDowall made a face and hesitated before grasping it in both of his, pulling Alec close and whispering, 'You're not going to make a habit of this, are you?'

'A habit of what?'

Alec shouldered the Bergen and opened the outer door. Turning away towards his office McDowall called back over his shoulder.

'Give my love to Broadway.'

No sign of Joyce in the office so McDowall got busy collecting his personal stuff, which wasn't much. He pulled his good plastic bag from behind the filing cabinet and began to fill it. Old case files from what might be termed successes against the lawless hordes, some old black and white pictures of his recruit course and one of him receiving the first of four commendations. Some western novels, or "cowshie" books as his Mum had called them. Three plaques from the Boy Scouts and such. Not much here to stamp him into history. He packed everything into a cardboard box. He also stole some of Brown's pens. Joyce returned looking her syren best, tempting as sticky toffee pudding. She brought a mug of tea and a packet of Tunnock's Tea Cakes. Ambrosia! That lassie knew how to see a man off. She also perched on the edge of the desk in that pose that left him breathless with unattainable fantasies.

'I'm just back from my rota days Frank, so only heard this morning about all your adventures.'

McDowall smiled. 'What adventures might that be?'

'Dodging the Sally Ann meeting and thumping an Inspector. What a wonder you are. Don't worry, it's only six weeks, you'll outlast Tannock the Tyrant.'

'I'm only suspended you know. Thanks for the teacakes, did you think maybe I was to be shot in the car park.' He shoved a whole teacake into his gob while unwrapping another.

Joyce thought he looked like a wee boy raiding the biscuits. She left him to it but was back in ten minutes, leaning around the door, making a wee hesitant face.

'What's up, do you want the teacakes back?' He popped the last one into his mouth.

'Nothing that bad. You have another visitor.'

'Who's the popular guy the day then? Wait and I'll ask myself if I'm free. Who is it this time, the padre or the Salvation Army come to place me in custody? Tell me it's not the welfare officer, I couldnae stand him right now.' He picked up his box of junk and knock-knacks. 'Tell them I've left, gone, not here, whatever.'

Joyce gave a wry wee smile, stepped aside opening the new door fully. And there she was.

Claire.

Her hair damp down the back of her raincoat, eyes wide and fearful behind her drizzle splattered glasses.

McDowall stood stock still, the box held in front of him like a shield, his emotions in meltdown, incapable of any meaningful reaction. All he could see was her. Joyce waved her in and pointedly evading eye contact closed the door. Claire stood facing him about a yard away looking round his office, a small puddle forming as the water dripped from her raincoat onto the scuffed parquet floor. McDowall couldn't have moved to save his life. She gave a small flickering smile her eyes nervous.

'Hullo, Frank.'

He cleared his throat. 'Claire.' Whispered almost.

'I got away for the day to visit friends in Glasgow, or so I said, but I really came to see you, needed to ask you things. I wanted to surprise you.'

'Mission accomplished there then. I'm shocked, surprised and dismayed all at the one time. Discombobulated. I honestly don't know what to say.' He shook his head. 'Why are you here?'

She stepped closer placing her slender fingers on the desk. 'When I saw you at Glasgow Central everything came back, all the feelings I'd suppressed and what I'd given up. I need to know if you felt the same?'

'No. I minded all the hurt and pain you caused me and we both caused everyone else. It was selfish, a schoolboy crush wrote huge, all emotion and love.'

'I came because I've thought of nothing else since Glasgow but what might have been with us, the life we might have had.'

He shut his eyes. 'It's done, Claire. We were living in a Doris Day movie, a Hollywood fantasy, not real, romantic escapism. Creating our life would have destroyed so many others.'

'I can't sleep since Glasgow, can't eat. I think about you all the time now. Do you think of me even a little?' She took a small step closer, stretched out her hand towards his arm. He drew back crushing the box into a tight barrier. He couldn't meet her gaze.

'I tore out all that I felt and killed it to survive. What I felt for you was embedded so deep it tore my guts out to remove it. When I remembered you, it was only with guilt and hurt. I told you to save yourself and throw me to the wolves if you had to, put all the blame on me. You did that in spades Claire. Not only did you throw me to the wolves but you held their coats and pointed out where I was. You convinced Irene and my family and colleagues that it was all in my head, that I was ill, delusional. You destroyed me. All my friends and family treated me as if I was insane. Do you know Freud said the best way to drive somebody mad was to treat them as if they were? When I lost the plot with sadness I despaired and had to save myself by going to counselling with Irene, my every emotion stripped bare for comment by strangers. I lost my mind, so that you could point and say how right you were, that I was mad. Later, when I recovered the rags of myself, I thought of you not at all.'

She gave a low whimper, closed her eyes. McDowall watched the tears fill up her lenses before spilling down her cheeks. She trembled and put a hand on the box. 'Tell me you don't care for me anymore and I'll go. Never bother you again.'

McDowall dropped his eyes. Despite the many times he'd thought of this burning moment he had still been unprepared for the unemotional tidal wave and felt nothing one way or the other.

'I haven't loved you, or anything else, in a long sad time.'

'You hate me now.'

'Worse than that, I feel dulled, indifferent.'

Slowly her head fell, her hand to her mouth. Claire turned away, hesitating at the door, her hand slowly turning the Handle, extending every second.

He couldn't watch and studied the floor, hanging onto the box like grim death until he heard the door click behind her. Her perfume mingled with the rain hung in the room, the withered blooms of what might have been. He sagged and fumbled the box onto the desk, his breath coming in ragged gulps till he was eating the very air. He went to the window where he watched her cross the road to the car park in front of the shops. He felt numb, no emotion except a dull tearing ache. Joyce came in and stood behind him. 'Are you okay?'

'As ever,' he croaked.

Claire paused at her car, turned and stared at him across the short distance, then climbed into the car and started the engine. Joyce spoke softly over his shoulder.

'Go after her, Frank.'

'I can't.'

'Why?'

'It's a lifetime too late. She hurt me very badly and I don't trust her anymore.'

'There's still time if you hurry.'

'There's never enough time. Anyway, I still have hopes for you and me.'

'You're such an arse.'

'I know.' He gave her a wee sad smile.

She saw his wet eyes, laid her head on his shoulder for a moment. 'I'll get you another cuppa and a real big chocolate biscuit, a Wagon Wheel maybe?'

He nodded and wiped his sleeve across the steamed-up window but Claire was gone. Everything he'd felt he'd ripped out of himself. She left only an empty space with the rain dancing in the puddles.

When McDowall struggled out the car in his driveway with his box Jim Brown and Joyce were waiting on his doorstep.

'What's all this then? Have you two been sent with the loaded pistol, or is the death pill?'

He unlocked the front door and they followed him in. Brown picked a shopping bag off the kitchen worktop.

'No pistol for you, far too easy so that is. Anyway, if we left you with a loaded pistol, you would either clean or steal it.'

He walked to the sideboard and flung all its drawers and doors open. Brown and Joyce began to remove all the bottles and cans of drink, swiftly filling the bag.

'See this?' Brown told him, 'This is what real friends do. They drag you down the right road, the hard road. I phoned the Sally Ann and they said to remove any immediate temptation.'

Joyce gave him a hug then held out her hand palm up, flapping her fingers.

'Hipflask, Frank.'

McDowall stalled. 'It's empty.' They both laughed at him.

'Not since Adam said, "let's eat the last apple," has it ever been empty,' Brown said.

Joyce punched him playfully on the arm. 'As a supposed Dick Tracy kind of guy I'm amazed you haven't worked out why Irene's decamped to your daughter's house. Left you and your huge drink stash.'

McDowall surrendered the flask scowling. 'What now?'

'Relax your torn face,' Brown held up a newspaper parcel reeking of vinegar. 'We've brought pie suppers and Irn-Bru. A feast for kings.'

Graeme Hammond was home in the villa at Castlehill lounging in a black Chesterfield armchair, drinking malt and smoking a cigar. His wife Emily had cooked but he'd had no real appetite and now she was slightly smugged on vodka and not a little miffed at the wasted meal. She broke the cold silence.

'Did you see your father today?'

'I did. He's still taking his own sweet time to die. If Neil hadn't been there, I might have smothered him or turned off the oxygen. I'm told his decline is steady and he will go sometime tonight hopefully. They say he's too weak for transfer to the Beatson Institute, so finally the old coffin dodger will give up the fight and die. It's a matter of hours. I live in hope, he dies with none.'

'Will that release the rest of his funds to us, the Jersey accounts and his holdings in that godforsaken Balkan place?

What's it called?'

'Bulgaria, like the Womble. The directors don't know about half his holdings, so it will all come to us except what's company property. The lawyers are on it right now.'

Graeme was always cagey round her when Bulgaria came up in any conversation. She had not forgotten his return from there when he brought her a dose of the clap. He decided to confide in her and cleared his throat noisily, a sure sign he wanted to discuss something serious.

'Something important and perhaps dangerous to the business has happened, to do with the Bulgarian setup.'

She said nothing, waited.

Encouraged, Graeme pressed on. 'Our contact in Scotland, that Anton Tenescu guy we had over for dinner and drinks a few times? He's had an accident. What you might call work related.'

'A serious accident?'

'Terminal. One of his workers beat his brains out with a rolling pin.'

Emily stayed silent, drank more vodka, thinking it best not to mention that she and Tenescu had a quickie that first evening, in the garage on the back seat of the Daimler. He had visited her often after that, for afternoons of what they joked were, "mutual trade benefits." She topped up her vodka.

'Are the police involved?'

'So far they don't know about Tenescu. Nobody benefits from police crawling all over it, digging up all sorts of stuff. Those eejits I employ came away and left his body in the bakery along with the guy who caved his head in. They did bring away all the cash, all the product and the books. Any witnesses should have been dealt with. I'm not pleased with Gillespie who walked in on the killing then decided to let the baker away free as a bird. I wonder if he's getting soft.'

She raised her eyebrows at him. 'Did we not agree you would never tell me anything I could be questioned about?' She never wanted to hear any of these details but was happy with the indolent life his business provided.

Graeme went on. 'Thing is, although we didn't kill Tenescu, these people regard him as being a guest under our care, my care in fact. I ask you, what is that? Am I responsible for him like he was some idiot child? Anyway, I sent the morons back to bring the body somewhere more fitting, show a bit of respect. As of now it's…'

'Stop! I don't care how you clear this up and don't want to know. Are you, we, our children, safe? What if these people don't believe Tenescu was killed by the baker, think you did it and are going to replace them? Will they not surely come here, to Scotland?'

'Someone will definitely come to collect the body I take it, and their assets, which I'll hold intact till they show up. If it's all there they can't accuse us of anything. Probably only send one or two guys, nothing heavy. Why would we have killed Tenescu? He was our conduit with them. What do you think?'

'I think you're an idiot.'

He strode out in a temper and locked the door of his study behind him. He wondered how long it would be before somebody came in response to the phone call to that emergency number. He had no idea who'd answered or even where he'd phoned. Very detached response really, for they had heard his stuttering explanation of the disasters that had befallen both Tenescu and their shipment in silence. Then hung up. Sinister people, and from a cruel society where treachery was endemic.

When the pie suppers were finished Joyce called a taxi and McDowall saw her to the door, helping her into her coat. He rested his hands on her shoulders, face close to her hair, breathing her in. Took his courage in both hands.

'I don't want you to go,' he whispered.

She put her hands over his and gently lifted them away taking them down to her side where she held them a second. 'Don't, Frank. Please don't be kind to me.'

McDowall watched her walk down the path, waited till the taxi went. She didn't look back. When he returned to the living room Brown gave him a knowing look.

'I was hoping she might stay longer.'

'Uhuh.' Brown smiled wryly. 'Do I have to mention all the stuff about jiggery-pokery with workmates and friends and the calamity that always ensues? Anyway, that lassie would be the death of you. Right! Get your coat on, we're off to the pub.'

'Pub! Are you havering? If I show up at work or any welfare meetings with even a whiff of the drink it's goodnight sweetheart for me. I'm even getting my coat cleaned.'

'I'm going to teach you to resist the demon drink. You'll love it.'

CHAPTER 17

The Whippity Scourie was quiet, so there was only the barman to raise his eyebrows and express amazement when Brown ordered one lager and a fizzy orange.

'Are you kidding me on?' he laughed. 'Dae ye want wan or two straws with that, maybe a wee brolly stuck in an olive?'

McDowall shrugged out his coat and hung it over the bar rail. 'Listen up, you cheeky bastard. Is your drink license no up for a renewal hearing soon?'

Not another word from the barman. Brown ordered crisps and nuts and they moved away to an alcove. McDowall shifted the empties together and waved to Elaine the barmaid to come collect them. He'd gotten her the job and she gave him some wee tips now and then.

'Hi, Mr McDowall. Sorry about the mess, haud oan just a wee minute and I'll have all that away. Been run off my feet so I have. Have you heard about that auld bastard Arthur Hammond?'

McDowall took hold of her hand and sat her down beside him. 'What news wid that be, my lovely? Has he eventually done the decent thing and gone to his just desserts?'

'No yet, but word is he'll no be lasting much longer. Ma auntie works in the care home where he is as a cleaner and she says he's even too ill to be moved. Fell into a coma about teatime she says and its hours till he's deid she says. He was an awful bad man, there'll be none mourning him. My auntie says it'll be a moped following the hearse with the mourners.'

McDowall slipped her a pound note. 'You're a good lassie, Elaine. Run along now.'

Brown raised his pint. 'Well, that's something to celebrate. Let's hope he's in Hell an hour before a lawyer gets him off.'

McDowall sipped his orange juice. 'So, the death watch is begun for him. I wonder if he's afraid. My mum was. She hung onto my arm struggling for every tortured breath she took.'

He remembered the oxygen tent, the hissing ventilator and the last feeble squeeze of her withered hand. But mostly her eyes, the fear of leaving him alone as her eyelids fluttering that one last time and the rattle as she went. He grabbed Brown's arm.

'I need a favour. I need you to run me down to the care home and see that evil shite cast off this mortal coil.'

Brown shook him off. 'Whit? No way. That's just sick. Why would you want to do that? We're finally, the whole of the West of Scotland in fact, free of that man and his evil empire. It's like the heid of the Paisley SPECTRE has died, and you want to spit on his corpse? Let it go, Frank.'

'Can't. I need to see him and hope he can hear me. We can be there in ten minutes. It's the last thing I'll ever ask you to do for me.'

'I doubt that very much.' Brown sighed, guzzled half his pint, lifted the car keys off the table and stood. 'Okay, okay.

But no way am I coming in with you.'

They drove to Adams House in silence. Brown parked the car but McDowall made no move to get out. After a minute Brown spoke over the roaring demister and the wipers flapping.

'Full circle Frank, almost. This reminds me of sitting outside Robert Stewart's house the morning after Angela died. You just didnae want to get out the car and go tell them their wee lassie was killed.'

'Seems ages ago. Lots happened since then. So many lives lost or brought to ruin, all triggered by that one thing. Some deserved to die, some didn't.' Brown turned the engine off.

'Why are you here, Frank? Why the need to watch this auld monster gasp his last? Are you going to smother him?'

'Maybe. I've been chasing Arthur Hammond since I was a beat constable. Some said obsessed. Did you know my mum rented one of his single-end fleapits in Canal Street? She got tuberculosis there. Just accept I'm doing this and let it go at that. Please.'

'You used the magic word, amazing. I'll wait.'

'If you don't mind, that will be great.'

McDowall heaved himself out the car, went to the door and rang the bell. Eventually one of the harassed night staff came to the door and shouted through asking who he was here to see and did he not know visiting was done.

'I'm here to see Arthur Hammond.'

'Mr Hammond is close to death, it's family only now.'

'Well, his family are scarce as priests at an Orange Walk, so he'd better not be hauding his breath for any of those grasping vultures. I'm here, and that's the best he's getting.'

'Who are you?'

McDowall flashed his warrant card against the glass of the main door. 'Detective Sergeant McDowall.'

She let him through the inner door. 'He's in Room 22, along the corridor to the left. He's drugged to the eyeballs so you'll get no sense out of him.'

He took himself along the dimly lit passage. There was a stillness about the place, as if the building held its breath with the other residents, waiting. The door was lying open and a staff member on deathwatch was at by the bed reading *The People's Friend* by a dim night light. Only the sound of a pirouetting fan and the low thump of the oxygen ventilator whooshing up and down broke the silence. The girl stood when he came in and asked if he was family.

'I'm the polis, which is all the family he's got now. You been here long, lassie? You look wabbit, go and take a break.'

'I could use a smoke and I'm bursting.' She left.

McDowall shed his coat and cardigan, for the tiny room was stifling, and then opened the window. From the look of Arthur Hammond, it was hardly likely he'd catch a chill and die. He was plainly too far down the Hades Road to come back. The ferryman was waiting for him, he had that pale green tinge on his face, his time was coming.

The ventilator sat on a bedside cabinet, an enamelled

white thing with black hoses attached to the oxygen cylinder, hissing and clunking as the pump handle cycled up and down. He began to count its asthmatic beat and stared at the socket where it was plugged in, toying with the idea of switching it off. But he knew he wouldn't do that, make it easy.

He needed to watch Arthur Hammond struggle in fear for every breath he took. He'd pursued this man for years, consumed by a mission to put him away and end the havoc he'd inflicted on hundreds, no thousands of lives across the West of Scotland. Drugs, smuggling, prostitution, money lending, violence, murders, a helter-skelter of evil. Well, the bold Arthur had come to the bottom of the slide now.

McDowall was disappointed, he had wanted Hammond to be conscious so he could flay him with the darkness of approaching Hell, but here now was just a weak wreck of a creature struggling for air. McDowall was numbed, robbed in some way, found himself with nothing to say, his mind birling with clashing emotions. They said that hearing was the last of the senses to go, so he shuffled the chair closer to whisper in Arthur's ear.

Time was short.

'It's me, Frank McDowall. You remember me? I know you do. When my mum fell pregnant you put her out in the street. Did you think you would never die or face any accounting? Yet here you are now on the verge of the pit, and all your money, all your treasure, can't buy you one more second of life or one more breath. No family, no friend here to hold your hand. They'll all be too busy raking your bank accounts or jostling for control of your empire and assets. Not one single person here to see you into oblivion. Ebenezer Scrooge is who you are. They will be laughing at you in every bar in Paisley tomorrow.' Arthur's eyelids flickered.

McDowall went on.

'Are you afraid? I hope so. You're alone, abandoned, but then I suppose dying's the only thing we all do alone. You did nothing good in this world except leave it, and not soon enough for me. I hope there is a God. It would be a sore pity if you just fell into the dark without retribution.'

Arthur drew a huge rattling breath and his eyes popped open.

McDowall sprang back, startled.

There was blood and phlegm now, bubbling from under the mask, the drain bag seething like lava. McDowall pulled the mask away and the blood pulsed down Arthur's chin onto the bed forming red rings in the folds of his neck. He looked as if his throat was cut. The spasm seemed to clear his airway. McDowall reached instinctively for the call button but then stopped, folded his hands in his lap. Watched.

Arthur rolled his eyes and recognised him, attempted to reach for his hand. McDowall snatched it out of reach.

'Y... you!' Arthur gasped in a long exhalation.

'Surprised it's me? I wanted to see you die, make sure you were gone.' McDowall lifted the mask, tipped the contents onto the bedspread and made to replace it, but Arthur recovered enough to take two grating deep breaths. One to carry each word.

'I'm... afraid.' He rattled.

McDowall was remorseless. 'Good. I see the terror you

gave so many others in your eyes now. These are the last breaths you will ever take. You've shared a bed with Death all your life and your dying is the only good legacy you leave behind.'

Arthur moaned, grabbed McDowall's shirt with sudden strength pulling him closer, whispered in his ear and fell back. McDowall waited a full minute then pushed the call button. The staff came running but it was all over. Nothing this side of Hell could help Arthur Hammond now. Standing back against the wall McDowall stared at the dead face, wild and twisted with terror, eyes bulging, skin already turning green. What he'd thought would be a triumph was stale.

He took his coat and left, unnoticed.

Brown was in reception pretending he wasn't reading *Woman's Own.*

'It's done.' McDowall told him. 'Let's go.'

'Any last words?'

'Not that made sense, said Willy Drahujck was coming.'

*

CHAPTER 18

Penko the baker had bought a passport and Able Seaman papers easily enough in a Liverpool pub near Garston Container Depot. Then he signed on as Third Cook on the Motor Vessel *Empire Wallace*, berthed at Liverpool and bound for Boston. His bags were safely stowed in a sealed container for a reasonable price. His passage would be one-way and take fourteen days at crawling pace. The offloaded container would be collected by a countryman in Boston and for more money his valuables would be returned. He would then surprise his second cousin Boris, who ran a doughnut stall in Detroit. He would surprise Boris even more when he opened the suitcases.

Alec Stewart hitched a lift on a fish lorry headed north for Mallaig from Glasgow Fishmarket to pick up the early morning catch. The driver was not chatty, which was fine with Alec, and they were soon on Loch Lomond side, the moon low and darting across the water like a silver dagger. It was understood he would pay for the driver's' drink on the way and breakfast at the Seaman's Mission in Mallaig. Buster fell asleep on the parcel shelf. Alec knew a man who ran a survival school west of Loch Nevis on the edge of Knoydart, who was rumoured to have a bunker with things nobody was supposed to own. Brian Duffy, from the old days in Armagh and Oman, known to his mates as Zorba the Greek because he broke a lot of plates. Duffy would help him as a matter of course and Alec could fade away for a while into the vastness of Knoydart, living wild and moving every few days from bothy to bothy. He woke just past Tyndrum with Buster licking his face and Alec realised that this was now the only family he had left.

That was fine.

The dog, he trusted.

Brown lay sleepless, watching Carol, listening to that wee stuttering snore of hers. She was off for two days and they were away to Largs tomorrow. For now, it was enough to watch and hold her. Perhaps he should have told Frank that Tannock had had him up the big office and offered him a course at Hendon, something to do with what they were calling, "Community Policing." Tannock droned on about how this would be the coming thing when the new Strathclyde Police were formed and a clever young man like himself would do well to get in early on the ground floor. Brown had listened politely and nodded but felt this was a bribe offered for his signature on a statement he hadn't written.

He'd escaped at last by taking the folders and course notes away with him but was really thinking Tannock could stuff the course up his arse. Maybe one day he would say so. That would be the day he became a real detective. Or would that be the day he became Frank McDowall? He laughed quietly, Carol stirred but did not waken. He would drop in on Frank a couple of times a week during his suspension, take him some orange juice or ginger maybe a pie supper. Keep him posted. Keep an eye on him as well. Frank McDowall came across as stolid but Brown knew how hard this had hit him. He'd stick it out until Frank came back and hauled him out his chair. That should be a fun day, something to look forward to. He snuggled in, fell asleep smiling.

McDowall was nowhere near snuggled into anyone. He'd walked aimlessly up past what was now Alec's place, wishing he'd dropped everything and gone north with him. A mad brainless impulse to grasp the chance to be boys again together, repair those teenage strands, but the place was in hushed darkness. He checked round the back peering in at the windows.

A neighbour came out to challenge him and told him what he already knew. Alec was gone with the dog and a rucksack hours ago. McDowall nodded his thanks, his emotions chaotic as the links of his life dissolved. In growing despair he walked aimlessly across the Bluebell wood path past Steading 5 and down to his own house. Strange that he thought of it as his house, and not Irene's. A personal marker post passed he wondered, a chasm opened?

He hoped not.

Like Alec's place his house was in darkness, cold and barren.

He left the lights off, comfortable with the silent shadows.

Irene's old Singer sewing machine sat behind the living room door. He unclipped the wooden case and lifted the cover off, retrieving his emergency bottle. There was an old shortbread tin in the sideboard drawer with a view of Ben Lomond on the lid and faded gilt round the edges. He took it out and popped the lid open spilling old black-and-white pictures across the dining room table.

Grannies and uncles, soldiers, saints and sinners. All dead. Gone now save for that moment frozen in the camera lens, resurrected in the eye of the beholder. Cracked pictures of street bus runs to Saltcoats and Stevenson, school class photographs. That was him on the first day at Wallace Primary on the Main Road, at the end of the row in the too small jacket, sleeves halfway to his elbows, nose running. There was Alec at the back making a face, in a blazer and school tie probably borrowed from Robert. Must have been one of the few days he wasn't dogging it. Another one of him and Alec in shorts and braces standing knee deep in the sea at Saltcoats their arms around each other's shoulders. All toothy and in blissful ignorance of the floaters with bog roll sails all around them.

One picture torn in half, of his Mum holding him as a baby but with a man's arm around her shoulders. She had never said who the man was.

Mum had struggled against every prejudice to bring him up as best she could, with not two pennies to rub together. And that in a time when single mothers were outcasts and sinners, hard for them to get any kind of job and prey to every sleazy landlord. And if she was short of the rent, she would have to make it up somehow.

He was suddenly a wee boy again listening to the clattering brass bed. She had died of tuberculosis and a broken heart in Killearn Hospital when he was fifteen, contracted while renting one of Hammond's damp slums. He raked through the flotsam of his life and found his favourite picture of her, black and white with a fretted border and a wee blue ribbon for hanging it on a hook.

They were inside Nardinis at Largs sharing a Knickerbocker Glory, a vastly expensive treat usually beyond their means. One of the waitresses had taken the picture for them on the old Box Brownie. There he was, her young prince, with his best white shirt open-necked peering past the huge glass waving the two long sharing spoons in glee. Mum in her big hat and a nice summer dress, looking happy.

'Mum,' he whispered aloud as the tears ambushed him, unbidden. The pain was physical, ground glass in his eyes, a welding torch in his heart. He began to weep silently in the dark like an abandoned orphan child. Softly at first, then aloud, shoulders quaking, chest bursting, the photo in one hand and the bottle of Vat 69 in the other.

What had his Mum ever seen in Arthur Hammond?

*

ABOUT THE AUTHOR

Retribution Road is John's debut crime thriller. He is an ex-Marine and a retired thirty-year Firefighter. It's from these periods of his life he has taken characters and dialogue.

Married to Linda, he has three children and a dog.

Also a published author of poetry and short stories, his work has been featured in various anthologies.

Awarded third prize for his story, The Bothy King, in the *Scottish Mountaineer* Magazine, and has pitched his novel at Tidelines Book Festival.

Recently, his poem, 'Absalom', has been shortlisted by Hammond House Publishing and will appear in their 2021 anthology.

The Scottish Arts Council anthology, *Life on The Margins*, also features his short story, White Christmas.

Second in the McDowall trilogy, *Desolation Road*, is at fifty-five thousand words, the third is in notebook form.

John's collection of short stories and poetry, entitled, *Diamonds in The Coal*, is available as an e-book, from Amazon.

Printed in Great Britain
by Amazon